D0943709

Praise for Katherine John's Crime titles:-

So intriguing . . . cleverly woven together and tensely written – **Sunday Times**

John expertly weaves together information about the medical, psychological and procedural strands of this taut story of revenge and retribution - **Publishers Weekly**

Excellent chilling drama – **Manchester Evening News**

The impending doom starts on the second page and grows in chilling intensity all the way – **Liverpool Daily Post**

A chilling case, a fascinating mix of characters, plenty of twists and turns, a compulsive story - **South Wales Evening Post**

Rapidly building a reputation as a thriller writer - **Wales on Sunday**

BY ANY NAME
First published by Hodder Headline 1995
This edition revised and updated by the author

published by Accent Press 2006

ISBN 1905170254

Printed and bound in the UK
By Clays PLC, St Ives

Cover design by Emma Barnes
Image by Getty Images

ACKNOWLEDGEMENTS

I would like to thank my husband John Watkins who was brought up in Brecon and walked the Beacons many times, his brother Leslie Watkins a one time member Brecon Mountain Rescue team, and my mother and father-in-law Mary and Arthur Watkins for their many kindnesses and allowing me to use their homes as background for this book.
Last but certainly not least I wish to thank all the members of the armed forces for their hospitality and giving me so much of their time. I respect their request for anonymity.

And while acknowledging all the assistance I have received in the researching of this book, I would like to point out that any errors are entirely mine

Katherine John December 2005

Dedication

To Peter Lavery

In gratitude

What's in a name? That which we call a rose by any name would smell as sweet

William Shakespeare: Romeo and Juliet
Act II, Scene II

BY ANY NAME

Katherine John

PROLOGUE

Rain teemed down, needle sharp stalactites that glittered, silver threads in the beams of headlights, transforming the tarmac of the suburban street into a sheet of gleaming jet. The anonymous dark blue saloon car slowed to a halt at the kerb, the occupants waited and watched. A shadowy figure vaulted a low gate set at the entrance to a playing field. The car window slid down and the muzzle of a gun emerged from the shrouded interior. The soft plop of a silencer-muted shot echoed through the quiet street. The figure fell headlong on to the sodden, spongy grass.

Heart thundering violently against his ribcage, the hunted man explored his reflexes, tensing the muscles in his legs and arms. He felt no pain; he wasn't injured. Somewhere close by he could hear the roar of traffic. He had to move, keep going until he reached people. His only salvation lay in a public place.

The car door opened. He continued to lie still. Footsteps resounded above the splash of rain, squelching when the gunman moved from the hard surface of the road on to the grass. He opened one eye and saw a shoe; a highly polished black shoe laced with raindrops that sparkled in the reflected light of a street lamp.

Digging his toes into the ground he launched into a rugby tackle. Locking his fingers around the gunman's ankles he floored him. The hunter's skull crunched ominously against a fencepost, but the prey lingered only as long as it took him to kick the gun from his assailant's hand.

Zigzagging, he ignored the pain in his heaving chest and pounded towards the traffic. Ribbons of street lights shone down, bathing a roundabout in a soft, golden glow. The whine of engines closed in on him as drivers hit accelerators to give their vehicles the boost needed to negotiate the sharp incline of a slip road. Amber numerals flashed "50", but the drivers that shot past him either didn't see, or chose to disregard the directive. Misty, water-filled darkness obscured the road ahead, yet the traffic sped on in unremitting torrents raising a filthy, oily spray that soaked him and clouded windscreens, increasing the risk of accident.

Another shot whistled past his ear. He leapt in front of a car. The squeal of brakes and the crash of metal fracturing against metal resounded behind him but he didn't slow his pace. Driven by an instinct for survival that had chosen the motorway above the bullet, he dodged between vehicles that hurtled blindly onwards. He breathed easier when he reached the central reservation. Drawing cold, exhaust-laden fumes into his lungs he clambered over the barrier and changed course, running backwards to face the oncoming traffic.

To his right he caught a glimpse of smoking wreckage, heard the raucous strain of sirens, but he kept his head down and pounded ever onwards, his head jerking, his bare feet slapping the freezing skim of rainwater that iced the road. Surrounded by noise, dazzled by tides of headlights, he had no idea where he was going, only that he had to keep going. Wheels turned, spray spurted. The cacophony of horns escalated.

It would have been easy to succumb to the inevitable, to curl into a ball and wait for nothingness. But just when he thought he could stand no more, the gleaming headlights and blasting sound passed by, only to be replaced by another pair of threatening yellow eyes… and another… and another…

He continued to dodge between lanes, avoiding vans, trucks, cars, all the while keeping to the centre; fearful lest his assailants had gained the motorway. Running – running – his heart hammering so fiercely he wondered why it hadn't burst. His lungs burned, hot, searing, as he fought to siphon air into his beleaguered body. Blood surged through his veins, the drumbeat of pulses beating time with his footfalls as he swerved from lane to lane in an effort to escape the blasts of noise and blinding lights, but still they kept coming.

Weaving – roaring – blasting – until a single soft sound alerted every fibre of his being. His eyes strained. He searched wildly for safety. There was none. He ducked as another crack echoed towards him…

'If the reports are right, he should be here.'

'I can't see a bloody thing in this.' The police driver wiped the condensation from the inside of the windscreen with his sleeve.

'There he is!' the constable cried.

'The silly bugger's running towards us.' The driver switched on his siren.

'Just our luck, another bloody nutter. Ambulance?' the constable asked.

'Make it two. At least one car has crashed into the barrier ahead.'

The constable picked up the radio telephone. 'Car crashed – location?' He checked for landmarks as his colleague steered at hair-raising speed towards the inside lane, aiming for where the hard shoulder would have been, if there had been one. 'Ambulances… '

'Ask for one with special restraints for that bloody clown,' the driver interrupted.

The constable turned his head. 'Back-up's in place behind us.'

'Here we go.' Brakes smoking, siren blaring the driver swung the car sharply sideways in an attempt to corner the running man who was sandwiched between the inside and middle lane. Blue lights flashing, two police cars charged down the outside lane towards them but a car and a lorry blocked their path.

'You think the silly sods would slow down and pull back when they see police cars, damn them.'

While his partner concentrated on driving, the constable, who knew better than to analyze the risks his colleague was taking with their lives, took a closer look at their target. He was bare-foot, dressed only in jeans, his dark hair slicked close to his head by the downpour.

'Got the bastard!'

Their seat belts pinged, pinning them to their seats as the car screeched to a halt, bumper touching the barrier, cutting off the runner's exit from the inside lane.

Cornered between the parapet and the police cars, the man stood bowed, his chest heaving, his palms gripping his knees.

'Will you look at him!' The driver's cry echoed above the roar of the traffic.

'Is that what I think it is?' the constable looked to his companion.

The driver's voice dropped to a whisper. 'Fucking hell.'

The man climbed the parapet. Before the officers had time to move, he'd disappeared over the side.

'Alert all cars in the vicinity, make sure those ambulances are on their way.' The driver wrenched open his door, and joined the crew of the second police car.

'It's all right, sir.' A rookie constable looked over the edge. 'One of our cars was heading for the next slip road, they've got him.'

The driver looked down. The drop was over thirty feet but the man was on his feet, handcuffed to the door of a police car. He saw the officers pulling on rubber gloves.

'Blood?' he mouthed above the sound of the traffic, wind and rain.

'Looks like he took a bath in it,' came the answering cry.

CHAPTER ONE

The blue light was flashing on the ambulance but, forewarned by control, the paramedics had decided against using the siren because initial reports suggested the patient was in a volatile, traumatised state. They saw him when they approached the motorway, standing stiffly to attention, his wrist handcuffed to the door of a police car. The half a dozen or so officers on the scene were standing at a distance, away from the dark slicks of blood and gore smeared over his jeans and bare chest.

The ambulance drew to a halt. One paramedic jumped out of the cab and went to the back. His partner joined the group of police officers.

'What's the score?'

'He was running down the motorway. We gave chase; he jumped thirty foot, but doesn't appear to be any the worse the wear for his fall.'

'Superman, or high as a kite?' the paramedic asked.

'You tell us. There are glass splinters in the blood on him, but he's not complaining. In fact he's not saying anything.' The constable flicked a dismissive glance in the man's direction.

The paramedic ran a professional eye over the patient who continued to stand immobile and upright as if he were on a parade ground.

'Good luck with him.'

'Thank you.' The paramedic zipped himself into the protective suit his partner handed him, slipped on a pair of rubber gloves, and walked over to the prisoner. 'Do you have a name, mate?' he enquired casually, to no effect. 'Your name, mate?' he repeated.

'Wherever he is, he's not with us,' an officer asserted.

The paramedic looked to his partner, who was hauling a sheaf of plastic bags out of the back of the ambulance. Taking one, he approached the bloodstained man. 'We're going to bag your hands, arms and chest. Just a precaution until we can clean you up. If we hurt you, shout. All right, mate?'

The patient turned his head, but his eyes remained unfocused.

'You're bagging the glass?' an officer asked.

'It's best removed with a suction hose in casualty. We'll make sure the plastic sheeting hangs loose. You're not going to fight us are you, mate?' he asked warily, slipping the first bag over one bloody hand and tying it with tape.

The man gave no sign that he'd understood a word.

'I'll do his legs.' The paramedic's partner set to work. 'Nasty injury there.' He bagged the patient's swollen ankle.

'He jumped from the motorway,' an officer reminded him.

'He's in shock. Sooner we get him to casualty, happier I'll be.'

'He looks like the joints my missus wraps for the freezer,' a constable joked when the paramedics finished.

'Give us a hand to get him into the back of the ambulance,' the senior paramedic asked

Despite the paramedics' success the officer approached the patient cautiously. 'You taking him to the General?'

'Where else?'

'We'll see you there.'

The only free parking space outside casualty was marked SENIOR CONSULTANT but that didn't deter Dr Elizabeth Santer from driving her battered, neglected Ford into it. She locked the door, switched on the alarm and entered the building.

'Thanks for coming out.' The duty houseman, Alan Cooper, greeted her when she walked into the foyer.

'I wasn't doing anything special.' She resisted the temptation to add; "I no longer have anything special to do."

'He's in five. A police forensic team came in. They scraped and bagged samples of the blood and tissue plastered all over him. Very little was his own. He was covered in glass, but after we suctioned it off we found only superficial cuts. The only other external injury is a sprained ankle, which has been X-rayed and strapped.'

'Name?'

'We have none. He hasn't said a word. He's exhibiting all the usual signs of shock; lowered temperature, cold, clammy skin… '

'He was found running barefoot and half-naked down a motorway?'

'Yes.'

'It's freezing out there.' Elizabeth shivered. It wasn't much warmer in casualty. 'Anything else I should know?'

'We gave him a full physical. There's healed scar tissue from five old injuries.' He glanced at the report in his hand. 'Three exhibit the characteristics of healed bullet wounds; one in his right shoulder, one in his lower-right leg, and one in his upper-left arm. The other two, both on his chest could be knife wounds.'

'You've X-rayed the bullet wounds?'

'Yes and there's characteristic signs of bone thickening. The police are working on his identity. We're admitting him, at least for tonight.'

'You've advised the ward?'

'Yes and because of the blood and tissue, the police are mounting a guard until they've made further enquiries.'

'Tell the sister to prepare the private room next to her office. If we have to endure a police presence on the ward, Dave will want it somewhere that will generate minimum disruption.'

She pushed open the double doors that led through to the treatment cubicles. Two policemen were standing guard outside five. Elizabeth nodded to them before entering. She couldn't fault Cooper's caution. The nurses who were swabbing the patient's chest were both renowned throughout the hospital for their karate expertise.

'Good evening, or should I say good morning, Dr Santer?' one said when he saw her.

She acknowledged both nurses before turning to the patient. 'Hello, I'm Dr Santer, the psychiatric registrar.' Flicking through the notes Alan Cooper had handed her, she walked to over to the trolley the man was lying on. 'And you are?'

The man stared at her. His eyes were cerulean blue, startling in their intensity and depth of colour, and very different from the pale-washed blue, so common to Anglo-Saxons. His hair was a rich blue-black, his skin tanned Mediterranean olive. His feet overhung the end of the trolley, and Elizabeth judged his height as several inches over six feet. His chest was finely muscled but not in a body-building fanatical sense. There wasn't an ounce of excess weight on him.

She examined the bowls the nurses had been using. Alan Cooper had mentioned blood and tissue – he hadn't warned her it was brain tissue.

'If you won't tell us your name we'll put out an appeal,' Elizabeth prompted.

The man gazed at her for what seemed like an eternity to the nurses. But accustomed to dealing with the clinically depressed, Elizabeth was inured to periods of silence.

Eventually he made a brief unintelligible sound.

'Yes?' Elizabeth encouraged.

'I – I – don't – know,' he blurted.

She laid her hands on his head.

'There's no cranial injury.' Alan Cooper had followed her into the cubicle.

‘There’s no evidence of external trauma,’ Elizabeth concurred. ‘Does your head hurt?’ she asked the patient.

‘I – don’t – think – so.’ He spoke in quick staccato, accent-less tones as though he were mimicking an electronic voice.

‘Reflexes?’ Elizabeth inquired of Cooper.

‘Normal.’

‘How did you get here?’ She looked directly into the patient’s eyes. She knew the answer to her question from Cooper’s notes, but wanted to hear it from the man.

‘Ambulance.’

‘And before that?’

His face contorted with the effort of remembering.

‘What were you doing before you were in the ambulance?’ she repeated.

‘Running.’

‘Why?’

‘Bullets.’

‘Someone was trying to shoot you?’

He screwed his eyes shut.

‘Well, you’re safe with us now,’ she reassured. ‘I’ll give you something to help you sleep. We’ll continue this conversation in the morning.’ She scribbled a note at the bottom of the patient’s report before passing it to the senior of the two nurses. ‘Chloral hydrate to be administered on the ward. I’ll check him again when he’s settled in.’

‘You’re not going back home?’ Cooper asked.

She glanced at her watch. ‘There’s no point. I’ll be on duty again in another four hours.’

'I feel guilty for dragging you out.'

'Don't.' She motioned her head towards the door. 'You did the right thing,' she murmured when they were in the privacy of the office.

'You think he's suffering from amnesia?' Cooper asked.

'You don't have to be Sherlock Holmes to deduce he's suffered some kind of trauma. And trauma-induced amnesia is more common than most doctors realise.'

'He mentioned bullets. Could he be hallucinating?'

'Did the police say anything about any shooting?'

'No.'

'Then he could be delusional. I'll try to get more out of him in the morning. Has there been a public appeal?'

'The police took photographs and mentioned a press conference.'

'Let's hope someone comes forward to claim him.'

'The police are also searching the area for bodies.'

'Given the amount of blood and tissue I saw, I'm not surprised.'

'Funny to think he could be a murderer,' Cooper mused. 'Apart from the scars he looks normal enough.'

Elizabeth smiled. 'What do you think a murderer should look like?'

A nurse knocked and opened the door. 'One John West and two police guards gone up to the psychiatric ward.'

'John West?' Elizabeth looked at her in surprise.

'He was picked up on the westbound carriageway of the M4 heading out of London, it seemed appropriate.'

'And John?'

'John West has got to be better than John Doe, for a live man, hasn't it, Dr Santer?'

Elizabeth woke in the doctors' rest-room on the top floor of the hospital just before seven o'clock. Stiff and aching, she swung her legs down from the coffee table she'd used as a footstool, rose from her chair and went over to the vending machine. She'd tried all the combinations the machine had to offer and, no matter which she settled on, the coffee invariably emerged grey, insipid and tasteless but the tea was even worse. Succumbing to temptation she abandoned her diet in favour of hot chocolate. Clutching the plastic beaker, she switched on the television.

A clock filled the screen, its hands pointing to the hour. After a few seconds of cacophonous noise and dizzy computer hieroglyphics, a man who looked brighter and more alert than any being had a right to at that time of the morning, shuffled a sheaf of papers on the desk in front of him.

Arranging his features into a sombre expression that portended tragedy, he gazed directly into the camera and delivered the first item; a plane crash in Scotland. No survivors were expected to be found among the eight-man crew and ninety-eight passengers.

Long shots of a dark, wind-swept, snowy landscape strewn with wreckage, speckled with floodlights and the diminutive figures of rescue teams were replaced by a close-up of a blanket-swathed corpse on a stretcher. A sonorous voice droned in the background, detailing the time that the plane had gone down. A close-up of a news reporter followed. Blinking beneath artificial lights, shivering behind his microphone, he bellowed in an attempt to make himself heard above the howling wind.

'Yes, Peter, this is a terrible and shocking tragedy. Everyone here has been moved by the professionalism and dedication of the rescue teams, who have worked throughout the night to recover bodies from the wreckage, and who continue to search in – as you can see – these impossible weather conditions… '

The sound cut abruptly. The picture died.

'Weather permitting, we'll return to Mark live at the scene later. But for now we'll go over to Westminster and the Minister of Defence. Minister, would you agree this is a tragedy of mammoth proportions for the government?'

'Not only for the government, Peter, but for the country and the armed forces. I know I speak for the Prime Minister and every member of the cabinet when I offer my deepest sympathy and condolences to all the bereaved families. We must remember the victims of this crash were not only the leaders of our security forces, but family men who will be sorely missed on a personal as well as professional level.'

The camera cut back to the studio. 'Minister, could you tell us if there will be an inquiry as to why so many high-ranking officers from the security forces were travelling on the same aircraft?'

'I can't comment on that question at this stage, Peter.'

'Has there been any confirmation of an explosion on board the aircraft before it went down?'

'It's too early to discuss possible causes… ' the minister continued to skilfully avoid giving a direct answer to the interviewer's questions. '… it will take us some time to collate evidence as to possible causes of the crash… we are not aware of any recent threats from any known terrorist group… no, as yet no group has claimed responsibility… tragic as the situation is, it will not, and cannot be allowed to affect the international peace talks… '

Elizabeth sipped her chocolate and wondered why the media bothered to arrange interviews with politicians who were incapable of answering a direct question.

The bulletin moved on to the next item; a general shot of an anonymous conference room was followed by speculation on the agenda of the various super-powers, and the possibility – or not – of a global scaling down of nuclear arms. The effect the air-crash and subsequent loss of senior security personnel might have on the conference was discussed against a still of an anonymous foyer that the delegates would presumably enter, the red carpet they would walk down, and photographs of various high ranking personnel…

'Bloody well get on with it,' Elizabeth urged impatiently.

'Bloody well get on with what?' Dave Watson, the hospital's psychiatric consultant, and her immediate superior, walked in and made a bee-line for the coffee machine.

'Get on with putting out our mystery man's photograph.'

'The amnesiac you admitted last night?'

'You're an early bird.'

'I just finished reading the notes you put on my desk.'

'Couldn't sleep?'

'The twins have been awake all bloody night. I escaped at six. I never thought I'd regard this place as a sanctuary but after home, it's blissfully peaceful.'

'Poor Anna,' Elizabeth commented. 'Where's she's escaping to?'

'Bed, any minute now. I phoned the agency and asked them to send round a nurse.'

'A kind and considerate father.'

'Self-interest. Anna's hell to live with when she goes without her beauty sleep. So, how is our new patient?'

'Out for count the last time I looked at him.'

'I see you resorted to the innovative and advanced remedy of knock out drops.'

'Ssh!'

A police mug shot of John West filled the screen.

'… Hospital staff have named the man "John West" because he was apprehended on the west-bound carriageway of the M4. The police are appealing to anyone who recognizes him to come forward. If you have information, the number to ring is… '

'No mention of the blood and tissue splattered over him.' Elizabeth switched off the TV.

'No sign of injury other than his ankle?' Dave checked.

'None.'

'Well, that should stop him from dashing up any other motorways for a couple of days.'

'He wouldn't get far if he tried. There are two policemen stationed outside his room.'

'Public appeal should bring in something.' Dave made a wry face as he sipped his coffee. He abandoned it on the nearest table. 'Time I visited the patient to see if his memory has improved with the sunrise.'

'What sun?' Elizabeth tossed her own plastic cup into the bin.

'It's there. Somewhere above that grey sky and falling rain.'

'I hate early morning optimists.' She followed him out of the room and into the lift.

The hospital had been built in that great era of jerry-building, the 1960s. The planners, seeing no further than the outline of the box-like structure and the trees they'd sketched around it – that had never been planted – had located the psychiatric ward on the seventh floor. Three suicides in the first month after the ward opened had prompted the Health Authority to revise the original plans, but only to the extent of adding window-catches and locks that prevented the steel casements from being opened more than three inches, a modification that turned the ward into an oven in summer. However, the ill-fitting window frames ensured a plentiful supply of draughts in winter, and those, coupled with a lack of insulation on the flat roof, made it the coldest ward, no matter how high the thermostat. There was only one place colder in the hospital; the eighth and topmost floor that housed the canteen, staff rest-rooms and some of the administration offices.

The ward sister, who greeted Dave and Elizabeth after they entered using their pass keys, was wearing a thick cardigan and woollen tights in stark contrast to her thin nylon uniform.

'Is the new patient awake?' Elizabeth asked.

'Awake, breakfasted, showered, dressed – and uncommunicative.'

'Dressed?' Dave questioned.

'We found him a track-suit. The police have his jeans. He wasn't even wearing a pair of joky boxers to make us laugh,' the sister added. 'The officers told me there was nothing in the pockets.'

'He couldn't have travelled any distance wearing only jeans in this weather. The police should have a name for us soon.' Dave looked to Elizabeth. 'Shall we go visit?' He led the way. On either side of the corridor were glass panels that enabled the staff to check on the patients in the four-bedded wards. At the far end, nearest the ward office, two policemen were sitting outside a closed door nursing mugs of tea. Dave walked past them and entered the cubicle they were guarding. It held a single bed. Another door next to the window opened into a tiny triangular shower room.

The photograph on the broadcast had prepared Dave for the man, but not for the power that emanated from the figure that rose from the bed when they walked in. He wasn't uncommonly tall. Six foot two or three at most, but the muscles that rippled beneath the thin nylon track-suit, suggested coiled strength and his lean, raw-boned features, lent him the look of someone Dave wouldn't want to tangle with, for all his own fitness training.

'Please, sit down. That ankle of yours must be giving you trouble.'

'Not much.'

Elizabeth noted that the patient's voice had lost its electronic edge but was bland, neutral.

'Do you know where you are?' Dave asked.

'In hospital – or so a nurse informed me.'

Dave sat on the only chair in the room. It was bolted to the floor. 'What can you remember about yesterday?'

The patient frowned. 'I recall being brought here in an ambulance. Being checked by a doctor in casualty. Talking to you.' He focused on Elizabeth. 'I remember arriving in this ward.' He continued to stare at Elizabeth. 'And being sedated.'

'You were exhausted, you needed sleep.' She wished she hadn't sounded quite so defensive.

'Your name?' Dave prompted.

The man shook his head.

'Your work?

West's frown deepened with concentration.

'Think houses, villages, streets. Can you remember where you live?' Dave tried one prompt after another.

He tossed off the names of well-known places in the locality; shops, pubs, restaurants, estates, all to no avail. When their patient showed signs of agitation and left the bed to limp to the window, he rose to his feet.

'What causes loss of memory?' West asked.

'In short, trauma,' Dave answered. 'But try not to worry, in my experience it rarely lasts more than a day or two and we're only just beginning treatment. Meanwhile we have to call you something. The staff have christened you "John West".'

'I suppose it's as good as any name.'

Elizabeth opened the door; the sister was outside with the police officers. 'You have visitors, Mr Watson.'

Elizabeth smiled reassuringly at "John" before leaving. 'I know it's alarming, but as Mr Watson said, try not to worry. In a day or two everything should be back to normal.'

'Will **normal** be better than this?' he questioned acidly.

'Hopefully.' She closed the door and made a mental note not to toss off any more platitudes with those sceptical eyes analyzing her every word.

To Dave and Elizabeth's surprise, it wasn't only the police who were waiting for them in the conference room.

The hospital administrator, Julian Trist, effected the introductions.

'Inspector Barnes and Sergeant Pickett from the local police. Lieutenant-Colonel Heddingham and

Major Simmonds from the Ministry of Defence, Major Simmonds is an army psychiatrist. Gentlemen, our psychiatric consultant Mr David Watson and his registrar, Dr Elizabeth Santer.' Julian pulled a chair out from under the table for Elizabeth. Dave sat next to her.

'Our patient has been identified?' Dave asked.

'We've had no response, as yet, to our appeal for information regarding our man's identity,' the inspector informed them briskly.

'Thank you for trying.' Elizabeth tried not to sound bitter as she recalled the case of a vagrant who'd been brought in with amnesia two days before his death from pneumonia. He'd been left in the mortuary for six months before his body had been taken for cremation, bearing the label "**IDENTITY UNKNOWN**".

'Our people worked through the night.' Sergeant Pickett flashed Elizabeth his most charming smile before opening the file in front of him. 'They compared the blood and tissue smeared over him with the sample of his own blood taken by the admitting doctor. There were three distinct groups; his own, which is O, two AB negative, and one of those had foetal characteristics which means it came from a very young child.'

Elizabeth had tried to avoid speculating how the blood had been smeared over "John West". She disliked the thought of a killer on her ward, much less a child-killer.

'Have you found any bodies?' Dave asked.

'Not yet, but we've mounted an all-out search in the vicinity where he was found, including a house to house. The medical notes suggest our man could be suffering from… ' the sergeant flipped through his notebook. 'Trauma-induced amnesia, which – correct me if I'm wrong – means that if his memory loss is real, it's been caused by something he'd rather forget.'

'A simplified description, but one I'd go along with,' Dave agreed.

'In addition the doctor found several scars on his body, three of which appear to be healed bullet wounds. Apart from those he appears to be in the best of health?'

'I'd say A1 fit. There's no sign of injury or ailments apart from superficial cuts and his ankle sprain,' Elizabeth concurred.

'These scars, coupled with his military bearing suggest the possibility of an armed-forces background,' the lieutenant-colonel barked.

Dave sat back in his chair and eyed the army officers.

'His background could be military,' the police inspector agreed. 'Or it could be terrorist. We're running his fingerprints through our computers now but if he is a terrorist on some kind of mission, suicide or otherwise, we're not expecting to find anything. The organisations that employ operatives to do their dirty work for them have too many volunteers to draw on, to risk using a known suspect.'

'If he is a member of the British armed forces, he'll be reported missing sooner or later and you'll have his description on file,' Elizabeth interrupted.

'We are combing our personnel records as we speak, Dr Santer. However, as the security situation in this country is particularly sensitive at present… '

'Particularly sensitive?' Dave lifted his eyebrows.

'I am referring to the peace conference. But after the events of the past few years our security forces are on constant alert for terrorists targeting civilian as well as military personnel,' Heddingham asserted.

'You really think he's a terrorist?' Elizabeth probed.

'It's an option we can't afford to disregard.'

'His English is impeccable.'

'As is the English of many Oxford-educated sons of wealthy Arabs who fund Islamic extremist parties,' Heddingham said testily. 'Some even have blue eyes and a suntan from frequent holidays in the Middle East. He may appear British, Dr Santer, but he may also believe that dying for his cause will guarantee him a place in heaven. And the London and Madrid bombings have proved that this new breed of terrorist doesn't give a damn who they take with them when they go.' Realizing he'd been lecturing, the lieutenant-colonel modified his hectoring tone. 'But, as yet we have nothing concrete. In the meantime, we are here at the request of the civilian authorities to see if we can shed some light on this man's identity. Any suggestions you have that could help us to achieve that end would be most welcome.'

'Dr Santer admitted him. I interviewed him for the first time this morning. What do you think, Elizabeth?' Dave asked.

'He's lucid and can hold a conversation. He appears to function normally until you ask him a personal question.'

'For example?' Major Simmonds enquired earnestly.

'His name, address or occupation,' Elizabeth answered.

'Do you think his amnesia is genuine?'

'I have no reason to think otherwise.'

'You have a record of your assessment?'

'Of course. But, as Mr Watson explained, he only saw him for the first time this morning. And as the patient's been on the ward for… ' she glanced at her watch, 'barely six hours, the record is not complete.'

'Has he seen television or read today's newspapers?'

'No.'

'Does he have access to radio or television?'

'He has neither in his room, and as there are two policemen stationed outside his door he's not had an opportunity to leave it.' Elizabeth resented the questioning that she felt bordered on interrogation.

'Have you tried hypnosis?' Simmonds peered over his spectacles at Dave.

'As Dr Santer said, he's only been with us for a few hours, and he spent most of that time sleeping.'

'You **do** use hypnosis in amnesia cases?' Major Simmonds asked.

'When I believe the patient's condition warrants it, yes,' Dave snapped, at what he took as implied criticism.

Oblivious to Dave's irritation, Simmonds persevered. 'To good effect?'

'On occasions.'

'I trust that you have no objection to co-operating with the police, and armed forces, Mr Watson?' Trist checked the time. A meeting of the Trust Board was scheduled to begin in half an hour and he wanted to clear the conference room, arrange refreshments, and ensure everything was spick and span before it commenced.

'I have no objection provided that either Dr Santer or myself are present at any interviews conducted by anyone other than internal hospital staff.'

'That will be in order, as long as you both sign the Official Secrets Act,' the lieutenant-colonel agreed.

'Shall we schedule your interview with the patient after lunch, gentlemen?' Dave left the table. 'That will give us time to carry out our normal ward rounds.'

'I think they know who he is; that's why the army has been called in so quickly,' Elizabeth declared as she sat opposite Dave in the staff canteen over the remains of a bacon sandwich.

'Or it's as the man said; they don't know, but they're not taking any chances. If they have checked all the military records and there's no one missing… '

'Overnight?' she questioned sceptically. 'Besides, even if he was in the army, he could have been discharged months or even years ago.'

'In which case there would be a record of his service.' Watson pushed aside the remnants of his late breakfast of omelette and sausages. 'What do you make of him?'

'Trauma-induced amnesia… '

'I didn't ask for a case history. Granted, you haven't spent much time with him, but it's more than I have. You must have **some** thoughts.'

She stared down at her plate. 'Even without the amnesia, I get the impression that he'd be a difficult person to get to know. The sort that keeps other people at arm's length.'

'Explain?'

'I don't think he's accustomed to talking about himself, so I can't imagine him being very different from the way he appears. Polite but aloof. Amnesia doesn't usually change basic personality, so I think what we're seeing, is what he is.'

'I bow to your superior diagnostic talent. You can assess all that in a trauma-induced amnesiac.'

She laughed. 'All right, sneer and call it female intuition if you must. I admit my diagnosis is not based on medical reasoning or logic.'

'With Anna for a wife, the last thing I can afford to sneer at is woman's intuition. More coffee?'

'Please.'

He glanced at her as he went to the counter. He'd worked with Elizabeth for three years, and was fonder of her than he was of his own sister. Fond enough to have chosen her to be godmother to his twins. But if Elizabeth had one fault, it was that her life was work and vice-versa, and had been since the death of her husband.

'What do you think Simmonds is planning on doing this afternoon?' she asked when he returned with two plastic beakers.

Dave handed her the coffee. 'He might be army and a major, but he's also a psychiatrist. Presumably that means he's received the same training as us, so I can't see him deviating from accepted practice.'

'I hope you're right.'

'You don't trust him?'

'I've a funny feeling about him – and that lieutenant-colonel.'

'More intuition?' Dave mocked gently.

'It's just that I'd prefer to tread softly with John West. You didn't see the blood and brain tissue plastered all over him.'

'You think we're dealing with a killer?'

'Or a witness?' She recalled the piercing blue eyes, the full, sensual lips. Hard, yes, forbidding, yes, but there was something more to "John West". Something she had difficulty squaring with what she knew of the psychological make-up of a killer.

CHAPTER TWO

After ward rounds, Elizabeth left Dave at the door to his office and took the lift to the seventh floor. Gaining admittance to the ward she proceeded down the corridor. A single policeman on duty nodded as she passed him and entered the patient's room. The man she now thought of as John West was standing, staring out of the window, an untouched plastic lunch tray abandoned on the table next to his bed. She glanced at the clean plastic fork and paper plate of congealing chilli, frosted with grease.

'I can't say I blame you.'

He turned and looked at her. 'For what?'

'Not wanting to eat that.' She indicated the tray.

'I hope I've eaten better.'

'Judging by your state of health, I think we can guarantee that. What are your favourite foods?'

'Smoked salmon on rye followed by T Bone steak with tossed green salad, onion rings and garlic bread.' He looked at her intently. 'It's crazy, I know what I like to eat, but I don't know my own name.'

'Your taste in food is a start.'

'Is that part of the technique?'

'What?' She picked up his chart from the foot of the bed.

'Sudden unexpected questions.'

'They can sometimes kick-start the memory.'

'I don't like the process.'

'That particular question was hardly earth-shatteringly personal.'

'But you'll follow it up with one that is.'

'We're trying to help you.'

He turned away from her and resumed his study of the grey November day.

'It's dismal out there.' She gazed at the gloomy vista of tower-blocks set in a sea of scabrous ground littered with the debris of fly tippers.

'That's the outskirts of London for you.'

'You know where we are?'

'I asked the nurse who brought my lunch.'

'Maybe you prefer the countryside to the city.'

He had a sudden vision of rolling, bracken-garbed hillside in autumn. Golden brown curling leaves interspersed with vast swathes of dry saffron-coloured grass sweeping upwards to high peaks, only just visible beneath crowns of low-hanging cloud. Up there the air would be cool; clean and pure enough to intoxicate a man more than a dozen whiskies ever could. And all around, as far as the eye could see, smooth weathered hills ribboned with frothing streams water-falling down the slopes. At this time of the year, everything would be veiled in a mist that sometimes, but not always, obscured the icing of snow in the deeper valleys and higher pinnacles.

Realizing he'd been silent long enough to raise the doctor's suspicions, he murmured. 'I suppose I do prefer the country.'

'What kind of country?'

'Woodland and lakes,' he lied, settling on a landscape divorced from his vision. He didn't know why he should hide what little he knew about himself but, until he discovered exactly who he was, and the cause of his memory loss, he decided it might be prudent to conceal the crumbs of knowledge he gained from her probing. 'When am I going to get out of here?'

'To go where?'

'How in hell should I know?' he showed signs of anger for the first time. 'Out is out. I'm not sick, and you can't keep healthy people in hospital.'

'I'll grant that you look fit enough. But illnesses of the mind are as real as illnesses of the body. Just because there aren't any obvious injuries, it doesn't mean they don't exist.'

'I feel well,' he countered stubbornly.

'You have no money, nowhere to go, and don't even know your name. You need help to put you back where you belong. And we'll keep you here until we find out where that is.' She joined him at the window. 'There are people waiting to interview you.'

'People?' His head ached with the stress of trying to remember who he was.

'Army officers. One's a psychiatrist.'

'I'm in the army?'

'We don't know.'

'But they think I am?'

'They are considering the possibility.'

'Have you tried looking for someone who really does know me, instead of hazarding wild guesses?'

She handed him a clipping she'd cut from the second edition of a tabloid. His photograph had been printed above the headline; DO YOU KNOW THIS MAN. She hadn't included the article beneath the photograph which had mentioned that he'd been covered with someone else's blood. 'No one has called in so far.'

'Perhaps I'm the black sheep of the family, and they're delighted I'm lost.'

'I can think of a more plausible reason why there's been no response.'

'You can?' He questioned sceptically. And she saw it again; that peculiar expression that sent a chill down her spine. She made a resolution to keep her imagination in check. She'd allowed the thought of murder to interfere with her professional detachment. "John West" was a patient and as such he was entitled to the best care she could give him. Besides, with a policeman standing guard outside his door he was less of a risk than some of her other patients. And – she touched the fake pen in the top pocket of her white coat – she carried the added security of a personal alarm connected to the switchboard that overrode all incoming calls. Standard issue for every member of staff who worked on Ward 7.

'Your family could be on holiday,' she suggested.

'And all my friends and colleagues?' he challenged.

'Where do you work?'

Just like the mountain scenario, a sudden vision of a room flooded his mind. A spartanly furnished, white-painted, clean and orderly office with computers, filing cabinets and desks – but the more he tried to focus on the details, the quicker the room faded. 'It didn't work that time, Dr – I know we've been introduced, but I can't recall your name.'

'Elizabeth Santer.'

The sound of footsteps in the corridor was followed by a sharp rap on the door. Dave walked in with the lieutenant-colonel and Major Simmonds. Although both officers were wearing civilian clothes, John rose to his feet, snapped to attention and saluted.

'That leaves little doubt.' Major Simmonds addressed the patient. 'It looks like you're one of ours, Mr West.'

'Or was one of yours,' Dave amended.

'I'm Major Simmonds.' Simmonds walked across the room and held out his hand. John West shook it. 'This is Lieutenant-Colonel Heddingham. And as you've already surmised, we're army.'

Elizabeth monitored the frown on John's forehead; a frown she already recognized signalled intense concentration – one that boded ill for the interview to come. The trivial advances she'd made in discovering John's taste in food and scenery had come from sudden surprise questions, tossed off when he'd been least expecting them.

'I'm in the army?' John asked.

'Judging by your professional salute, it looks as though you've had military training,' Simmonds replied cautiously. He looked around the small room.

'Five people in here are at least three too many,' Dave said. 'Perhaps we could leave the major and Elizabeth here and go and have a coffee, Lieutenant-Colonel?'

'If it will help discover my identity I'm happy to talk to all of you,' West offered.

'Is there another, larger room we can use?' Simmonds asked.

‘The day-room,’ Elizabeth proposed. ‘We encourage the patients to rest after lunch so it’s usually free.’

‘I’ll show you where it is.’ Dave opened the door. ‘Just to be sure, give us five minutes to clear any stragglers before you bring John along, Elizabeth.’

‘Ever get the feeling that you’re about to be discussed behind your back,’ John murmured.

‘At least we now have some idea what you do – or did – for a living.’

‘Who are those chaps?’

“Chaps” She made a mental note of the military expression. ‘Major Simmonds is an army psychiatrist.’

‘And the lieutenant-colonel?’

‘I know his rank, but not his function.’

‘Then he’s probably in intelligence. They’re always sticking their noses where they’re not wanted.’

‘You appear to know a great deal about the army.’

‘What are they going to do?’

‘I guess the same things that I have been doing. Try to kick start your memory by reference to familiar things. But as the five minutes is up, shall we find out?’

He tried to quantify his reluctance to leave the room. Possibly it was the result of the lieutenant-colonel’s abrupt manner. But there was no getting away from the fact that he had identified the army “civvie” uniform of blazer and grey slacks, not to mention the regimental ties. He had recognized both men as officers the moment they’d walked through the door. Did that mean that he, too, was an army officer?

The ring-marked coffee table in the centre of a circle of scuffed, vinyl-upholstered, hospital chairs was littered with brochures of military equipment and vehicles.

'And this one?' Major Simmonds moved on from tanks, Land Rovers and assault vehicles, all of which "John" had correctly identified, to weapons.

'Enfield L85A1 SA-80.'

'What can you tell us about that gun?' The lieutenant-colonel questioned smoothly.

'Known as the bullpup SA-80. Assault rifle, calibre 5.56mm, weight 4.89kg, including full magazine and sight. Effective range 300m, rate of fire 650-800 rounds per minute, muzzle velocity 940 metres per second… '

Dave scribbled a note on the pad resting on his lap, and slid it towards Elizabeth.

HE SOUNDS AS THOUGH HE'S SWALLOWED A TEXT BOOK.

'Have you ever fired a bullpup SA-80, John?' The question came from Simmonds.

'If I have I can't remember.'

'Are there any problems with it?'

'There were in the early days.'

'Tell us about them.' The lieutenant-colonel leaned forward in his chair.

'The magazine catch was badly positioned on the prototype models, causing the magazines to fall off when soldiers ran with them slung across their chests but the advantages of this particular weapon have always outweighed the disadvantages, which was why the army stuck with the design.'

'Advantages?' Heddingham pressed.

Elizabeth realised that Simmonds and his superior had launched into a well-planned, rehearsed interrogation, and she wondered if Simmonds was the only one with qualifications in psychiatric medicine.

'It's light. It has low recoil and excellent sights. It's versatile, capable of semi or full automatic fire… ' John spoke quietly yet his voice filled the room as everyone present gave him their full attention. 'It's easy to handle in the confines of urban situations and the limited space of air and ground troop-carriers, making it an ideal weapon for guerrilla and anti-terrorist warfare. The CRW… '

'What do those initials stand for?' Simmonds interrupted.

'Counter Revolutionary Warfare.'

Elizabeth glanced at Dave, wondering if he'd picked up on the lilt in John's voice, but Dave's attention was fixed on John.

'And this?' Simmonds pushed another illustration across the table.

'Franchi Spas 15, semi-automatic, 12 gauge, weight 3.90 kg without magazine. Range 50m, single shot. Can be loaded with various cartridges, capable of both pump action and semi-automatic fire. A grenade-launcher can be fitted to the muzzle, and there's an optional extra of a scattering device which produces an instantaneous spread of pellets. Useful in hostage-rescue situations… '

'Used by special forces?' Dave suggested.

John looked at him through cold, expressionless eyes. 'It's used by forces specializing in hostage-rescue situations. It's a good all-round multi-purpose weapon that can blow door hinges, and fire tear-gas and smoke rounds into buildings prior to storming, as in… '

'And this?' Simmonds interrupted, glaring at Dave for daring to interfere.

'SSG 69 Sniper rifle.'

'There's no need to discuss its uses. This?' he overlaid the illustration with another.

'Milan anti-tank gun.'

'This?'

'Stinger.' The frown had reappeared on West's forehead, and Elizabeth sensed he was struggling to put his comprehensive knowledge into a framework that would explain his situation.

'Are you tired, West?' The major softened his voice; it was quiet, suggestive, almost hypnotic.

'Yes.'

'Would you like to return to your room and rest? We can resume this later.'

To the major's irritation, John looked to Elizabeth.

'Would you like to return to your room, John?' she asked.

'Yes.'

'I'll ask a porter to bring a wheelchair.'

'There's no need.' He rose to his feet.

'Hospital regulations, I'm afraid.'

Elizabeth accompanied John to his room, steeling herself against the squeak of the wheels as they turned on the vinyl tiles of the corridor. A police officer opened the door to John's room for them.

She closed it as soon as the porter wheeled out the chair. John went to the window and resumed his study of the dismal urban scene spread out in front of them.

'Looks like you know a great deal about the army and its equipment,' she commented.

'With emphasis on the weapons used by the Special Forces.'

'Special forces as in SAS?'

'Contrary to public belief, they aren't the only special forces.'

'You think you're a member of one of the others?'

His eyes were dark, anguished when he turned to face her. 'I don't know. I don't fucking know!' He slammed his clenched fist on the wooden sill. 'I performed like a trained seal. I barked in the right places, but I still don't know my fucking name.'

'You will.'

'You guarantee it?' he enquired cynically.

'When you stop trying so hard to remember and when you least expect it, your memory will return.' She glanced at her watch, 'meanwhile, I suggest you try to rest. I'll ask the nurse to bring you tea. Not that tea is any more appetising than anything else that comes out of the canteen, but there's generally a cake or two hidden away in the fridge. What's your preference?'

'I don't like sweet things,' he replied automatically.

'Then you're more of a savoury man.'

'Apart from dark chocolate. Give me a bar and it's gone. Everyone complains they can never leave one in sight… '

'Who's everyone, John?'

His eyes clouded as he fought to remember.

'It's a thin veil,' she reassured. 'We'll soon tear it down.'

'I prefer your type of questions to the ones I got from those two monkeys.'

'If that was meant as a compliment, thank you.'

'But I won't be left to your tender loving care much longer. They'll lock me away in a military hospital.'

'If you prefer to stay here, we won't turn you over to them.'

'After my performance just now you won't have any say in the matter.'

'We'll see.' Elizabeth opened the door. 'I'll rustle up a bar of plain chocolate – and some tea. Rest, even if you can't sleep.' She glanced around the room. The newspaper clipping she'd shown John had disappeared. Someone had given orders to keep the room clear and empty. She wondered who.

Elizabeth heard the murmur of voices when she retraced her steps along the corridor. A notice had been pinned to the door of the day-room; PRIVATE MEETING IN PROGRESS. Dave looked up when she entered.

'You took your time, Dr Santer,' Heddingham reproved.

'John was distressed. I stayed with him until he calmed down.'

'You have a special interest in this case?'

'No more interest than I have in any other patient's welfare,' she replied defensively.

'Dr Santer,' Major Simmonds lectured as though he were giving a tutorial to slow-witted recruits, 'we didn't ask you and Mr Watson to sign the Official Secrets Act as a routine measure. This case has alarming aspects, which could threaten the security of this country.'

'At the moment we don't even know who John West is.'

'Precisely.'

Dave moved to the edge of his seat. 'The lieutenant-colonel and Major Simmonds want to take custody of our patient.'

She recalled the conversation she'd just had with John.

'If you'd prefer to stay here, we won't turn you over to them.'

'After my performance just now you won't have any say in the matter.'

'Custody?' she repeated. 'You're arresting John?'

'We can't do that until we find out who he is and what – if anything – he's done,' the lieutenant-colonel stated baldly.

'Given his knowledge of the equipment used by British forces, I would have assumed that your files would be an obvious place to start looking for clues to his identity,' Elizabeth suggested.

'After an exhaustive search through our files and computers, we have found no records of any missing servicemen, from our own forces or those of other nations stationed in the UK,' Heddingham asserted.

'But surely some men would be on leave.'

'We have contacted all of them.'

'All of them?' Elizabeth murmured incredulously. 'Aren't some of them mountaineering or caving or white water rafting in the wilds? I thought the army encouraged such activities.'

'We do, Dr Santer. But all our personnel follow the basic rules. They always inform our rescue services of their projected positions and estimated time of return. We've had over twelve hours and in this day and age that's more than we need to establish all of our personnel's whereabouts. Every private, NCO and officer in the British Army has been accounted for. Whoever "John West" is, he's definitely not a member of the British Armed Forces. I'd stake my reputation on it.'

'And his finger prints are not on police record,' Major Simmonds added. 'So he's not a common criminal either.'

'But he could be a past member of the forces,' Dave persisted.

'We paid special attention to the records of all ex-servicemen in his age group who've left the army during the past ten years. We placed him somewhere in the twenty-six to forty age group.' Major Simmonds replied.

'I think forty might be pushing it,' Elizabeth sat back in her chair.

'As you said yourself he is superbly fit.'

'But you can't just take a man into custody without having the slightest idea who he is,' she protested.

'In this day and age we can't afford not to, particularly as the conference is imminent.'

'Conference?' Dave looked blank.

'The World Peace and Disarmament Conference. It was all over the news this morning,' Elizabeth reminded him.

'I must have missed it,' Dave said uninterestedly. 'Look, we've signed your Official Secrets Act, so we can hardly go running to the press. You wouldn't even be here if you didn't have some idea who he is. Can't you tell us?'

'We have no more idea than you, Mr Watson. But we cannot ignore the possibility that he might be a high ranking terrorist.'

'Would a terrorist exhibit the inside military knowledge our man just demonstrated?'

'The British Army has always been too open for its own good, Mr Watson. It wouldn't be difficult for a terrorist organisation to acquire a thorough knowledge of our weaponry and training methods. There are highly organised, well-staffed camps in Muslim territories as well as remote areas of Europe and the USA that specialize in training guerrillas – and not only Islamic fundamentalists. The IRA used to regularly fly their top-ranking operatives to those camps for training until the ceasefire. And terrorists these days embrace many creeds and races. The warfare they wage is devious, sophisticated and – as we have discovered to our cost – ' the Major raised his eyes, ' – deadly.'

'As you pointed out earlier, Dr Santer, John West has the speech and mannerisms of a public school-educated officer,' Heddingham shuffled the leaflets together and returned them to his briefcase, 'but both could have been acquired elsewhere. It's conceivable that his condition is the result of brainwashing – and, as we know, brainwashing techniques can go wrong.'

'You think he could be a terrorist who's been given an identity that's overlaid his own personality?'

'You suggested that, Mr Watson – not me.' Simmonds picked up the copy of John West's medical notes that Elizabeth had given him. 'Dr Santer's initial diagnosis is undoubtedly correct. His condition is almost certainly due to trauma. In my opinion suffered shortly after he murdered at least one person.'

'If he murdered anyone, wouldn't the police have found a corpse by now?' Elizabeth said.

'Not necessarily.' Heddingham snapped his briefcase shut. 'I believe John West is a trained terrorist and killer and, until someone proves otherwise, he should be held in a secure military institution.'

'He has a police guard outside his door.'

'National security is a matter for the armed forces.' Heddingham rose to his feet, effectively ending the discussion.

'But we don't know for certain that this man does pose any threat to national security,' Dave demurred.

'We have contacted the Home Office and the Ministry of Defence. Neither we,' Heddingham glanced at Simmonds, 'nor the ministers concerned are prepared to take the risk that John West is innocent.'

'I thought every man was innocent until proven guilty in this country,' Elizabeth said flatly.

'It's a nice ideal, Dr Santer, but since 9-11 and the London bombings, one that could cost thousands if not tens of thousands of lives, if adhered to too strictly,' the lieutenant-colonel warned.

Dave left his chair. 'For the moment John West is our patient and in our care. And he will remain so until I have been instructed otherwise by my superiors. Until such time, he stays in this ward.'

'The police guards will shortly be replaced by military guards. The actual transfer will take a little longer to arrange. However, within the next few hours, he will be sent to a military establishment, after you, Mr Watson, have been furnished with all the necessary documents and assurances. It only remains for us to thank you for the care that you and your staff have taken of John West, Mr Watson.' The lieutenant-colonel opened the door. 'If you have an office that we can use until the transport and escort arrive we'd be grateful.'

'As I'm in clinic all afternoon, you can use mine. I'll show you where it is,' Dave offered.

Dismayed by the cavalier way the officers were treating her and Dave, Elizabeth left the dayroom before the others. She saw two soldiers in full uniform, armed with rifles and handguns walking down the corridor.

‘We have orders to report to Lieutenant-Colonel Heddingham, ma’am.’

‘You’ll find him inside there.’ She pointed to the door and walked away, wanting to get as far away from the officers as possible. Psychiatry to her meant humanity, and she doubted that either the lieutenant-colonel or the major possessed that characteristic.

‘You took John West his tea?’ she asked the sister.

‘And a bar of dark chocolate. He told me to thank you.’

‘Sister?’ Dave left the day-room with the soldiers. ‘This is Sergeant Packard, and Corporal Summers. They’re here to relieve the police guard.’

‘I see. I don’t like guns on my ward, Mr Watson.’ Tight-lipped, the sister looked them up and down.

‘Neither do I, sister.’ Dave headed for the lift with Simmonds and Heddingham.

‘Then John West is from the army?’ the sister asked Elizabeth, as soon as the others were out of earshot.

‘We don’t know, but it’s a possibility. He’s being transferred to a military hospital this afternoon.’ Elizabeth was angry at having a case she’d expended time and energy on being snatched out of her hands by two military automatons. A case, she suspected, she would now never discover the outcome of.

CHAPTER THREE

'Dr Santer seems to be taking a personal interest in this case,' Lieutenant-Colonel Heddingham commented as he followed Dave into his office.

'Dr Santer is a dedicated doctor, and as such takes an interest in all her patients,' Dave replied formally.

'Really?'

Dave recognized, but chose to ignore, the scepticism in the lieutenant-colonel's voice. 'Really,' he reiterated. If Heddingham had been more sympathetic he might have mentioned the tragedy that had led Elizabeth to concentrate on her professional life to the exclusion of all else.

The lieutenant-colonel moved behind Dave's desk. He picked up the telephone. 'Nine for an outside line?'

'Yes.'

He continued to hold the receiver in his right hand. 'You can't help me with anything else, Mr Watson.'

'I've a clinic to run.' Dave picked up a pile of files and left, resenting being dismissed from his own office. He took the lift to the psychiatric ward. The two soldiers were standing to attention outside John West's door, no chairs and mugs of tea for them. Dave couldn't see their rifles and he wondered if the ward sister or Simmonds had insisted they leave them somewhere secure. But their hand guns were in their holsters. Like the sister he bristled at the thought of loaded guns on his ward. The thought had never crossed his mind that the police might have been armed. In retrospect he realised they probably had been, but at least they'd had the decency to carry their arms discreetly.

'Mr Watson, I wasn't expecting you. Do you want to see any of the patients?' the sister wheeled a drug trolley into the corridor in preparation to dispense the afternoon medications.

'I'm on my way to clinic. Have you seen Dr Santer?'

'She told me to tell anyone who was looking for her that she'd be in the archives, Mr Watson.'

'Thank you.'

'Mr Watson?' she hesitated. 'I hope you don't think I'm exceeding my authority, but this is **my** ward.' The sister pursed her lips, and Dave steeled himself to receive criticism. The nursing officer wasn't the easiest of people to get on with, but she ran a difficult ward efficiently and had done so for a number of years, which had earned her his respect. 'I appreciate a case like John West's can present difficulties, but is it really necessary to station armed soldiers outside his room? I persuaded them to leave their rifles in the lock up in my office but they insisted they be allowed to carry their handguns. I told them the main ward door is kept locked at all times and can only be entered with a pass key but it made no difference. Their presence is unsettling the other patients, not to mention the nurses.'

'I find the sight of guns and soldiers rather unsettling myself, sister but you need to speak to Mr Trist. He gave the army permission to post guards outside John's door.'

'You're the consultant, Mr Watson.'

'My responsibility covers patients' welfare, not ward security, and John West isn't my patient any more. He's being transferred to a military hospital.'

'The sooner the better,' she declared.

'If anyone wants me I'll be in clinic after I've tracked down Dr Santer.'

The "archives" was a grand name bestowed on a walk-in cupboard that housed a collection of photographs of various towns, cities, and well known locations in Britain. The staff used the postcards and snapshots to stimulate the memories of patients suffering from dementia, Alzheimer's, or memory impairment due to brain injury. Dave walked up the stairs to the top floor where the cupboard was sandwiched between the canteen and administrators' office.

'What on earth are you doing?' he asked, when he saw Elizabeth balance an enormous box on her knee so she could lock the cupboard.

'Didn't you hear it?' She allowed him to take the box from her.

'What?'

'John's accent.'

'English, army officer, public school… '

'You didn't pick up on the Anthony Hopkins lilt?'

'You think he's Welsh?'

'I heard the dialect in one or two words.'

'If it was there, it escaped me.' Dave looked at the side of the box. On it was scrawled, *Welsh towns and scenes*, in the thick black felt pen the librarian used for marking.

'I thought it was worth trying to see if he recognizes something.'

'Liz, it's not our case any more.'

'They've taken him away?'

'Not yet, but it's only a matter of an hour or two.'

'In an hour or two we might know who he is.'

'But the man's no longer ours,' he protested.

'He's my patient until the moment he's escorted out through the ward door. He trusts me. You've worked with amnesiacs, Dave. You know how difficult it is to win that trust. I've built up a rapport with him. A change in his treatment now could set him back to where he was last night. Silent and withdrawn.'

'I'm on your side, but the men in brass buttons aren't. They're running the show, Liz, and much as I hate to say it, their ideas aren't that implausible.'

'You think John's a terrorist?'

'He could be.'

'Free Wales Army?' she joked.

'Any accent you picked up on could be the result of coaching by a Welsh or Asian tutor. You did say you only heard the inflection in one or two words.'

'It's worth a try,' she insisted obstinately.

'It's time for clinic.'

'Can't you do without me, just this once?' she pleaded.

'I'll give you half an hour.'

'An hour?'

'I'll start without you, but you're going to have to carry some of the load.' He shifted the box in his arms and glanced at his watch. 'We're twenty minutes behind with the appointments already,' he complained when she pressed the lift button.

'I told you the army would take over,' John said when Elizabeth carried the box into his room after one of the soldiers had rifled through it.

'You've seen your new escort.'

'Armed guard, you mean.'

'Forget them. They're outside the door. We don't have to think about them.' She dumped the box on to his bed. 'Photographs,' she explained. 'I heard a slight accent in your voice. It may be nothing, but I thought it might be worth looking through these. You might recognize something.' She lifted the lid from the box.

'*Welsh towns and scenes*,' he read. 'You think I'm Welsh?'

'Everyone has to come from somewhere.' She flicked through the box. Because the photographs were mainly used with dementia and Alzheimer's patients, most of them were of places as they had been thirty or more years ago. 'What about this?' She handed him a snapshot of a gleaming modern shopping mall.

'A shopping centre. Do I get a reward for guessing right?'

'The name of the town?'

'It could be anywhere in this or any other country.'

'Unfortunately you're right.' She tucked the view of the latest out of town shopping development on the Cardiff outskirts back into the box. 'This?'

'Would flummox nine out of ten people who can remember further back than last night. It could be any run down town centre in Britain.'

'Right again. Perhaps we should start a campaign to preserve the differences between towns. But we have discovered something,' she smiled. 'If you have lived in Wales, you're not an inveterate shopper.' She handed him yet another photograph.

'A horrendous city centre. What are those purple and green things?'

She peered at the photograph. 'I have absolutely no idea.' She closed the Swansea file and tried an older snap of Cardiff.

'Now this is more like it. It has character and atmosphere. An arcade, possibly built in the early part of the twentieth century?'

'So you know a little about architecture.' She flicked through the files. If only she had more time. She was already half way through the time allowance Dave had given her. Not that she wouldn't take more if she needed it. She deliberated which place to try next. North or south? She opted for south.

She tried the town hall in Bridgend, the market place in Pontypridd, the pretty main street in Cowbridge, which pleased John aesthetically although it failed to jog his memory; the beaches at Penarth, Barry Island, Porthcawl, and the rural, seaside beauty of Llantwit Major, all to no avail.

'You probably heard an accident of speech.' He dropped the last photograph she'd given him and turned to the window.

'Just a few more,' she begged, realizing that he was losing interest. She pulled out a print at random and handed it to him.

'The castle, or rather what little is left of it, in Brecon. It's part of a hotel now.'

'John… '

'Michael,' he interrupted.

'Your name is Michael?'

He continued to stare at the photograph. 'There's a promenade in Brecon along the river. It's a pretty spot, but it's crowded in summer… '

She pulled the Brecon file from the box and laid it on the bed. Opening it, she rummaged through the sheaf of photographs and passed him one of a stretch of surfaced walkway set alongside a river. In the background was a car park filled with old fashioned vehicles.

'This is ancient, but Brecon doesn't change much. Show me what else you have there.'

She pushed the file towards him.

'The statue of Wellington outside the Wellington pub, High Street. The Boar's Head, they serve a damn good pint there.' He continued to flick through the postcard sized photographs. 'The Watton, Ship Street, Llanfaes church, St Mary's. There's a hook on the side of the church, myth insists they used to hang people on… '

'You know the town inside out.'

'Better than my own name.'

'Michael.'

His eyes clouded as the frown furrowed his brow again. 'It doesn't sound right. I don't know why I said it.'

'Carry on looking. I'll get the consultant. We're so close… '

'I'm being moved soon, aren't I?'

'Not if I have a say in the matter. I'll be back as soon as I can.' She opened the door and stumbled over Corporal Summers' boots. She mumbled an apology and ran down the corridor, passing two porters wheeling a steel-sided canteen trolley. Turning the corner she pounded the lift button. Why wasn't it ever on the floor when she wanted it? Tapping her foot restlessly she considered taking the stairs, remembered the seven flights and thought better of the idea. But when the lift finally did come it took an age to reach the ground floor.

She found Dave discussing the treatment for schizophrenia with the family of a newly diagnosed patient. She stood unobtrusively against the door of his ground floor office and waited for him to finish.

They had a town, a starting point. Twenty-four hours, that's all she needed. Surely Dave could negotiate her that much.

The two porters continued to wheel their trolley along the corridor towards the sister's office. The corporal moved into the doorway of West's room to allow them to pass. They drew the high sided wagon alongside the soldiers and stopped. Both porters turned. Twin thuds resounded simultaneously. The first porter scanned the corridor. They had timed it well. Two of the staff were on tea break in the canteen and the others were busy in the four-bedded side wards. Opening the door to West's room he pushed the body of the soldier nearest to him inside.

John looked up from the photographs to see the sergeant, blood trickling from his mouth, heaved head first through the door. One glance was sufficient. The man was dead. He realized he had only seconds to act if he was going to save himself. Throwing himself to the floor he rolled close to the body, seizing the standard issue Browning that the sergeant, even in his death throes, had automatically pulled from his holster.

Still rolling, John looked up at the window. He used one of the Browning's thirteen rounds to shoot off the locking device that prevented the window from being opened more than a few inches. Diving towards it, he head butted it open and climbed out on to the outside sill as two men ran into the room behind him.

Cursing the pain in his ankle, he looked down. Toy town cars and people moved around the car park below him. He looked up. There was only one more floor between him and the roof. He reached up. A shot whistled past his ear. Releasing his hold, he fell down one floor and scrabbled for the next window ledge. He gripped it with the tips of his fingers and hauled himself to his feet. The sky light in the window was open. He prised it as far as it would go and wriggled inside. A second shot burned in his leg before he reached inside. He forced his fist into his mouth, stifling a cry of pain as he tumbled on to a sink. He heard footsteps running closer. Brandishing the gun, he opened the door of the sluice room he'd fallen into and grabbed a terrified nurse. Clamping his hand across her mouth to prevent her from screaming, he stepped forward and confronted her colleagues.

'Anyone make a move towards me and she gets it in the head.' He pressed the muzzle of the Browning to his hostage's forehead and looked beyond the half a dozen terrified people. He was in a corridor. Up ahead there had to be a stairwell. Keeping the gun to the nurse's head, he propelled himself forward using her body as a crutch to support his damaged leg and ankle. People screamed and fell back as he advanced. He tried to think clearly and coherently.

Logic told him his assailants would expect him to head for the nearest exit. But he couldn't afford to do what was expected of him. Not if he wanted to live. He had to hole up somewhere, formulate an escape plan . . if only his leg wasn't so painful…

Taking a chance he opened a door to the side of him. It was a miraculously empty office. Throwing the nurse in before him, he locked the door on the inside. He heard footsteps and yelled, 'Anyone come close and I'll kill her.'

He fired a warning shot to emphasize his threat. Pulling a length of electrical flex from a wall socket he tied her hands and feet behind her back and stuffed a wad of paper into her mouth. Finally he propped a chair beneath the door handle and opened the window. A minute later he was back outside the building battling against the wind and the rain.

'I gave you half an hour, it's been three-quarters,' Dave complained to Elizabeth after he'd shown the family out of the room.

'His name's Michael. He's from Brecon, Dave. I need just a little more time… '

A sister burst into the room. 'Mr Watson, security's rung down from Ward Seven. There's a problem.'

'John West?' Dave raised his eyebrows at Elizabeth.

'They didn't say, but I could hear someone screaming.'

'Oh my God, he's recognized something else. He could have remembered the trauma. I should never have left him… ' Elizabeth ran towards the lifts.

'Wait.' Dave charged after her. The corridor was blocked by patients being shepherded to the front door by nursing staff.

'Emergency on the upper floors,' one of the nurses explained to his hurried questioning. 'Security's up there.'

Elizabeth hit the lift button.

'It might not be John.' Dave didn't believe his own words.

'Those damned army officers can't move him now,' she said earnestly not listening to a word Dave was saying. 'Not when I'm on the brink of a breakthrough. He said "Michael" after seeing the first photograph of Brecon. Dave, you have to back me on this… '

'I'll do what I can, Liz. But you saw them. They've made up their mind. Where the hell is the bloody lift?'

'I'm taking the stairs.' She pushed open the fire door and ran up them, two at a time.

A security guard blocked her when she reached the fourth floor. 'Can't go any further, miss.'

'You can't stop me.' She tried to push past him.

'I'm Dave Watson, consultant for Ward Seven.' Dave was panting from the exertion of trying to keep up with Elizabeth. 'This is my registrar. Elizabeth Santer. We are needed on the ward.'

'My orders are not to let anyone through, sir.'

A scream echoed above them. Elizabeth sprinted past the guard. Ignoring his shouts she continued upwards. Ward Seven was open and the sister and two nurses were standing in the doorway. Behind them Elizabeth could see that the door to John's room was open. There was no sign of the soldiers. Without waiting for explanations she brushed past them and lurched headlong into the room.

The first thing she saw was the open window. Rain had lashed through the casement soaking the bed and chair. She looked down, stepped back and clamped her hand over her mouth.

The two soldiers lay face up, limbs sprawled, limp and relaxed. She fell to her knees, and automatically followed the routine that had been drummed into her during her training. But even before she laid her hand on them, she knew they were beyond any help that she could give them. Third eyes, seared by bullets into the centres of both foreheads had killed both men.

‘The mark of the professional assassin, Dr Santer.’

She looked up. Lieutenant-Colonel Heddingham was standing over her.

John lay face down on the roof desperately trying to make himself invisible. He could hear the screams of nurses and petrified patients, the whine of alarms, the pounding of security guards’ feet, and all the while the sounds of confusion and chaos resounded below him he had continued to lie doggo. Rain soaked through the thin tracksuit drenching his skin. His nostrils were filled with the stench of the creosote that covered the roofing felt. The air cloyed, heavy with smog, and foul, greasy smoke from a stack belching a few feet away from his head. The chimney rose higher than the roof by some twenty feet, but the wind had lost its battle against the force of the downpour.

He tried to move his leg. His ankle and thigh hurt abominably. He inched his hand downwards. There was a tear in his track suit trousers. When he pulled his fingers away they were covered with blood. He pressed down on the wound, grimacing when the pain escalated, but he couldn’t feel any lumps. Hopefully the bullet had simply grazed him. He’d had worse. He didn’t know how he knew, but he was sure that he’d been shot before.

The sound of sirens shrilled above the relentless pounding of the rain. He rolled to the edge of the roof and risked looking out. He saw the flashing blue lights of emergency vehicles turning through the hospital gates. Five minutes at most before the police, emergency services, and remembering the dead soldiers, the army hit the building. Time to find that bolt hole.

Slithering forward, commando-style, on knees and elbows, he gained the side of the roof that overlooked the back of the hospital. He leaned over. A skylight was open directly below him. Women's voices echoed from the room beyond it. Gripping the edge of the roof, he hung upside down like a bat and peered through the narrow gap. He saw mirrors, washbasins and the back of a nurse disappearing out through a door. He couldn't find a better hiding place than a Ladies' room. All he had to do was crawl inside, sit in a cubicle and wait until the search moved on.

He climbed back on to the roof. Tearing his trouser leg open to his thigh, he covered his wound, binding it tightly, so his blood wouldn't leave a trail, then, after listening for a few minutes to make sure the room was empty, he edged over and swung himself through the window. Crawling into a cubicle he thrust the bolt home, turned down the seat and crouched on it keeping his legs off the ground.

Somewhere on route he'd lost his paper slippers. His wound was still bleeding despite the improvised bandage, he was shivering with cold and soaked to the skin, but he had a breathing space. All he had to do was plan out his next move.

'Dr Santer showed him some photographs of Wales in an attempt to jog his memory.'

'Looks like she succeeded,' Heddingham remarked caustically. He and Dave walked further down the corridor away from the pathologist and technicians who were zipping the corpses of the soldiers into body bags and lifting them on to stretchers. 'By alerting him to his identity, she probably reminded him of his mission.'

'You can hardly blame Dr Santer… '

'No?' Heddingham watched the trolleys containing the shrouded remains being wheeled away. 'No, I suppose I can't. After all, most of the catastrophic disasters of this century have been caused by sheer ignorance.' He looked from Dave to Julian Trist who joined them. 'I suppose the next thing you'll tell me is that Dr Santer was only doing her job.' He went into the ward office where Elizabeth was sitting, shocked and bewildered. Major Simmonds was at the window, leaning out in an attempt to plot the escape route John had taken.

'He could have been a member of the armed forces,' Elizabeth left her chair and walked restlessly to the door. 'He knows Brecon… '

'The Brecon Beacons are first class training grounds,' Heddingham snapped. 'It's common knowledge that we exercise our special forces on that terrain. Your John West would probably have been given that information as part of his briefing.'

Major Simmonds left the window and looked down the corridor. Elizabeth turned to see what he was looking at. Sticky pools of congealing blood, marked by evidence tape blotted the shining white surface of the floor tiles; cold, hard evidence that reminded her just how wrong she'd been about her patient.

'You asked me earlier to tell you what I know about John West, Mr Watson,' the lieutenant-colonel said to Dave. 'I didn't know very much then, but this incident has confirmed my worst fears. It's my guess, and it will remain a guess until we receive corroborating evidence, but I am fairly confident that your "John West" was planted in this country by a terrorist organisation. It is absolutely vital we apprehend him. Because the one thing that I am certain of, is that while he remains at large we face a terrorist outrage that will no doubt result in the destruction of a target of strategic importance and the murder of innocent people.'

Simmonds turned back away from the bloodstains. 'He has proved himself an accomplished assassin, capable of attacking and eliminating men with their own weapons.'

'Who is now, courtesy of the army's decision to place armed guards in this ward, running free with a gun in this hospital,' Trist stated forcefully, determined to shift the blame for the entire episode on to anyone's shoulders but his own.

'We'll get him,' Heddingham assured. 'It's only a matter of time.'

'Time is in short supply, Lieutenant-Colonel. This hospital is run by a trust, and as such paid on results. Not that we're going to generate any income today, with the clinics, half our wards and casualty closed, and all emergency cases diverted to other units.'

'You'd prefer to put your patients' lives at risk by allowing them to enter a building with an armed madman roaming free?' Heddingham enquired.

'All I am saying is, if you want to avoid litigation, you'll find him, and quickly.'

'As soon as we have sufficient armed personnel we will conduct a floor to floor search.'

A security guard burst into the ward. 'Hostage situation on Ward 6, Mr Trist.'

'Got the bastard!' Heddingham exclaimed.

'No, Dr Santer, Mr Watson,' Trist looked from one to the other, as the lieutenant-colonel and the major ran down the corridor. 'On no account are either of you to go near Ward 6 until this man is apprehended and disarmed.'

Dave took Elizabeth to the canteen. The place was almost empty. All non-essential hospital personnel had been sent home, including the service and cleaning staff. The staff who had been kept on the wards were busy, allaying the fears of the patients who were too sick to be moved.

'Do you think it's possible to get used to this coffee?' Dave attempted to distract Elizabeth as he stirred sugar into his cup.

'I've heard it's possible to get used to anything given time.'

'You think so? What are you doing tonight?'

'If you weren't a happily married man, I'd wonder at your motives for asking me that question.'

'I'm serious.'

'So am I. There's a good film on television at ten.'

'You look beyond tired, absolutely drained. Why don't you join us for dinner? Anna would love to have you. She's hardly seen anyone since the twins arrived.'

'Seeing as how they only arrived five weeks ago, I think that's a pretty good reason for pulling up the drawbridge and curtailing your social life.'

'We're having Spaghetti a la Dave.'

'Thank you, but not tonight.'

'It's a while since you've seen your god-daughters.'

'And by the look of things it might be a while before we leave here.'

'The ward's empty, clinic's cancelled, there's no reason for us to stay,' he reminded her.

'I think one of us should hang around until he's caught.'

'That's us.' A porter turned up the sound on the television in the corner of the room.

'… Armed and dangerous in the vicinity of the local hospital… '

'Vicinity,' the porter exclaimed. He's loose in here.'

'Quiet,' Dave ordered abruptly.

'… if seen, should on no account be approached by a member of the public… '

The photograph of John West that had been shown on the news that morning flashed on the screen.

'Come on, Liz,' Dave coaxed after the newsflash ended. 'They can manage without us here.'

'My shift doesn't finish for another hour.'

'I suppose I could find some paperwork. As my registrar is so bloody pedantic about the hours she works, I can hardly swan off an hour early.'

'Have you telephoned Anna since this started?'

'Good point, if she's seen that broadcast she'll have me down as one of the corpses.' He left his chair. 'I'll phone her now. See you in the office in ten minutes? We could go through those case files, lessen the work load for the morning.'

'Just because I want to stay, doesn't mean you have to. You should go home, Anna needs you.'

'With the manpower those two chocolate soldiers have at their disposal they're bound to corner him in the next hour. And an hour isn't going to make much difference to me, or Anna.'

Elizabeth left Dave at the door to the lift and walked down the corridor to the Ladies. She gazed at her reflection in the mirror. Her long dark hair was straggling out of the chignon at the nape of her neck. She pulled out the pins, unhooked the net and rummaged in her handbag for a hairbrush.

'Hello, Dr Santer. I hope we have a quieter day tomorrow,' a staff nurse from Ward 7 commented as she entered.

'Don't we all? How are things on the ward?'

'Under control. But Sister must be in shock. She told me to take all the time I wanted when I left for my break.'

'Tell her I'll be in shortly to check on the patients who couldn't be moved.' As Elizabeth brushed her hair she noticed dark circles beneath her eyes. Dave was right, she did look tired, but then she couldn't remember a night she'd slept well since… an image flooded into her mind of her husband, Joseph, alive, vibrant and healthy. When they'd been together she'd thought he'd be there forever and she still couldn't get used to the fact that he wasn't, even after two years.

The sound of a closet flushing jerked her out of her reverie. She nodded as the nurse left. Tying her hair into a restraining band, she slipped on the net and pinned it into a knot. After washing her hands she reached into her handbag for her powder and lipstick.

'Dr Santer.'

She turned around, unsure whether she'd heard her name being called, or not.

'Dr Santer.'

It was a whisper but definitely there. A cold trickle of fear ran down her spine. 'John?'

'I'm in a cubicle.'

'John, the police, army and everyone in the hospital is looking for you. You're not going to get out, not without giving yourself up.' She turned to the only door that was closed in the row of cubicles.

'I didn't kill that sergeant and corporal.'

She took a deep breath, and forced herself to remain calm. She'd never lied to a patient and wasn't about to begin. 'Open the door, John, and we'll talk about it.'

'I didn't do it,' he reiterated forcefully.

'If you're innocent it can be sorted, but not while you remain hidden here.'

'If I leave here I'll be dead in five minutes.'

'You have my word, no one will harm you if you give up your gun and come out quietly with me.'

'You're going to guarantee my safety? Forgive my cynicism, Dr Santer, but you're promising to do more than two armed guards managed to accomplish.'

'You can't stay in there forever.'

'I know, that's why I need your help. Get a wheelchair and a blanket. Bring them here. You can take me to the front door.'

'The hospital is crawling with police and troops. The building is surrounded.'

'Just wheel me to the door. I can take it from there.'

'John… '

'I have a gun,' he reminded her harshly, 'and I'll use it on the hostage I'm holding in here. Do you want to take responsibility for the death of an innocent nurse?'

CHAPTER FOUR

Elizabeth stood in the corridor and leaned against the door of the Ladies' room. She had to prevent anyone from entering but she couldn't do that unless she stayed there and if she did, she wouldn't be able to fetch a wheelchair. How long would John wait before killing his hostage?

She wished she'd offered to take the nurse's place. It would have made sense. She was the trained psychiatrist. She didn't doubt that he'd kill again. Not after seeing the corpses of the two soldiers.

A door crashed back on its hinges further up the corridor and the porter who had turned up the television earlier, came whistling out of the canteen.

'Thank God,' she breathed in relief. 'Could you please bring me a wheelchair? One of the nurses has fainted in the Ladies.'

'No trouble, Dr Santer. Be back in a tick.'

Suppressing an impulse to call out and ask him to fetch the army officers along with the wheelchair, she tried to plan what she would do when he returned with the chair. She couldn't understand why the corridor wasn't crawling with police. Shouldn't they be searching every inch of the hospital and wouldn't it be logical to start at the top of the building and work down?

The porter returned with a chair. 'Here you are, doctor. Only had to go down to five to get it.'

She blocked his path as he reached past her to open the door.

'I'd be happy to give you a hand with her.'

'I can manage. She's in a bit of a state.'

'So what's new? I've seen it all before.'

'She'd be embarrassed. You being a colleague.' Elizabeth put her hands on the back of the chair and pulled it towards her, creating a barrier between them.

'If that's what you want,' he capitulated. 'Don't try to take her down in the lifts on the west side. They're out of commission.'

'Packed up again?'

'No, they've cornered him in a room near the lift-shaft on six.'

'John West?'

'If that's the name of the psycho who topped the two soldiers.'

'You sure they've got him?' She tried not to sound surprised.

'If they haven't, half the army is down there for nothing. Rumour has it he's locked himself into the sister's office with a nurse. But he won't be there long. They've assembled more hardware in that corridor than I've seen in the television footage of Iraq.'

'Shouldn't you be helping with the evacuation of the patients?' she suggested, willing him to leave.

'Our Mr Trist's got the army doing that. Here let me.' He leant over her shoulder to push open the door.

She backed in slowly, trying to think how John could be in a room on the sixth floor, when she'd just spoken to him here, on the eighth. Then it came to her. She'd taken so long to fetch a wheelchair he'd panicked and moved on through the window – but the nurse…

'You sure you don't need me?' the porter looked over her shoulder.

'She's in one of the cubicles. Thank you for your help, but I really can take it from here.'

'As you wish,' whistling again he went on his way.

'Anything new?' Major Simmonds negotiated a path through the squad of silent, grim-faced soldiers who'd trained their weapons over every inch of the corridor on Ward Six.

Ross Chaloner, the Special Forces captain in charge of the operation, shook his head. If he'd outranked the major he would have told him to bugger off. In his opinion all psychiatrists were pains, including the ones who worked for the army.

'Getting ready to storm the office?'

The commander looked to the stairwell, where Lieutenant-Colonel Heddingham stood, deep in conversation with a senior police officer.

'All we need is the command,' he whispered. 'Although it would be stupid to take any risks until we know the hostage's condition. But, as it looks as though this particular bastard is cool enough to keep his wits about him, he'll probably have too much sense to neutralise his hostage while he's holed up.'

'You think it's going to be a long stand off?'

'Maybe, maybe not,' Chaloner replied unhelpfully. 'Take over, Sergeant Price,' he ordered a short, stocky, grey-haired man. He moved away from the group of men who knelt, poised, their guns trained on the door of the office. Walking silently on rubber-soled shoes, he proceeded into the stairwell.

'Helicopters will be here in fifteen minutes, Captain,' Heddingham informed him briefly. He disliked Special Forces intensely, regarding them as the prima-donnas of the armed forces, but HQ had insisted they be brought in. What was infinitely worse, they had remained under the autonomous control of their own officers.

'Do we know if he's closed the blinds in the office, sir?' Chaloner asked.

'He has,' the police officer confirmed.

'If they're equipped with heat-seeking equipment, we'll be able to put an exact fix on where they're located in the room.'

'You'll be able to differentiate between West and the hostage?' Heddingham asked.

'Doubtful.'

'You intend to break in through the window?'

'It's been done successfully before,' Chaloner answered. 'But it's Command Cell's decision, not mine, as to whether we go in or not.'

The chair wheels squealed when Elizabeth pulled it inside the washroom. Nerves jangling, she damned the porter for picking that particular one. There had to be at least one in the hospital with silent, smooth running wheels.

'John?' she called out tentatively, hoping against hope that he wouldn't reply.

'You took your time, Dr Santer.'

'I had to send someone to fetch the chair.'

'Who?'

'A porter.'

'He's with you?'

'No, I sent him away.'

'Is anyone outside the door?'

'No.'

Logic told West she was speaking the truth. If she'd alerted the police or the army they wouldn't have allowed her to return. No commander in a hostage situation would allow a civilian to walk unarmed into a room with a gunman.

'You armed?' he demanded.

'Where would I get a gun?' She looked up as his head appeared above the cubicle door.

'Strip.'

'What?' she stared at him in disbelief.

'Strip. I need to see you're unarmed.'

Her hands trembled when she unfastened the buttons on her surgical coat.

'Drop it to the floor.'

She did as he asked, then pulled off her sweater.

'Now the skirt.'

'For pity's sake, you can see there are no bulges that shouldn't be there.'

'The skirt,' he repeated.

She unzipped it and allowed it to fall to her feet.

'Step away.'

She obeyed, and stood shivering in a black bikini brief and bra set, and a pair of transparent tights.

'I'm opening the door. Keep back. This gun is primed with eleven bullets.'

Inching away from him she crashed into a washbasin, and shuddered. There was nowhere left for her to retreat to. She watched, mesmerized as he hobbled towards her. The cubicle door swung back behind him to reveal a lavatory pedestal and nothing else.

'Where's your hostage?'

'Here.' He pressed the cold muzzle of the gun against her temple.

'What did you do to with last one?' her anger at her humiliation momentarily transcended her fear.

'I left her – unhurt – in an office on the floor below. Take off your tights?'

'No.'

'Take them off,' he repeated savagely.

Paralyzed by fear she hesitated.

'Get them off – now.'

She pulled them down.

'Get dressed.'

She stared at him numbly.

'Put on your sweater and skirt.'

She didn't need to be ordered a third time.

'Now get in the wheelchair.'

'It's you who's hurt not me.'

'Into the chair.' He prodded her temple with the barrel of the gun. She fell on to the seat.

'You won't be able to get out of the hospital.' She realized that empty as her life was, she desperately wanted to live.

She heard the discordant tearing of fabric. West lashed her wrists to the arms of the wheelchair and bound her ankles against the steel frame at an awkward angle. He concealed the bonds with a blanket that had been folded on the seat. The fibres bit cruelly into her flesh when she tried to move.

John slipped on her doctor's coat. Moving behind her, he rested the hand that held the gun on the back of the chair. She could feel the muzzle cold against her neck when he manoeuvred the chair to the door.

'One sound and you'll be dead, and whoever else is around. I can take eleven with me.'

His voice was soft, controlled and she believed every word. 'Just tell me one thing. Did you lose your memory?'

He didn't answer her. Reaching across with his free hand he opened the door, and pushed the wheelchair through it.

Despite her fear, she remembered something her husband had once said.

"If you have no control over a situation, the only thing to do is sit back and allow events to take their course. The outcome will be the same, whether you worry or not."

But then a fireman would say that. It took courage and blind faith in your strength and ability to survive, to walk into a burning building, and that same faith had killed Joseph. He must have known that the roof of the burning house was unstable, but he'd also known there were children inside. And Joseph would never ask one of his men to go anywhere he wouldn't go himself.

Joseph had suffered the worst that could happen, maybe now it was her turn. But would death be so terrible if Joseph were waiting for her? And if he wasn't, there'd only be nothingness. A nothingness that suddenly petrified her.

The corridor was deserted. She could hear the television droning in the canteen and wondered if there was an audience to hear it.

West hesitated and the pressure of the muzzle against her neck increased slightly.

'Lifts either end of the building with stairwells running alongside?' he asked.

'Yes, but the ones behind us are out of order.' She wished she could stop shaking.

He pushed her towards the stairwell ahead of them. One of the wheels on the chair continued to squeal like a kitten in pain. Elizabeth saw their reflection mirrored in the windowpanes. West was turning his head from side to side, constantly monitoring the corridor. She wished she could read his thoughts.

West knew that if Elizabeth had alerted the army or the police they would have set an ambush. He didn't know how the police would react, but he knew army methods. Doors would be slightly ajar in the corridor and behind them would be men armed with guns, gas canisters and stun mechanisms ready to move in on him the second the signal was given. The ambush would take place in an area which a lone man with a gun couldn't cover. Somewhere like a stairwell.

He reached the lift but walked past it. If he used it, he'd be trapped and immobilised the instant they cut off the electricity and dropped a gas canister down the shaft.

He reached the end of the corridor and noticed a shadow lurking in the stairwell. He hauled the chair back.

'They're covering the stairs,' he hissed.

'I warned you that you'd never get out of here. The hospital is being searched.'

He looked at the glass door, and realised he had no choice. If he was going to reach the ground floor, he'd have to face the army at some point. He put his back to the door, opened it and dragged Elizabeth and the wheelchair through behind him. There was no sign of the shadowy figure he'd spotted and he assumed the man was patrolling further down the staircase.

'If you intend to take me down the stairs, I'm going to have to get out of this wheelchair.' Elizabeth managed to keep her voice steady. Apart from the gun barrel caressing her neck, West ignored her. He stood with his back to the wall, his eyes ranging wide as they focused first on the stairwell, then on the corridor behind them.

Suddenly he lurched forward. Elizabeth braced herself against the sickening, bone-crunching jolts as he bumped the wheelchair downwards. A figure appeared below them, and West fired without hesitation. A gasp was followed by the crash of a door slamming back on its hinges.

'I have a hostage,' West shouted. He gripped a handful of Elizabeth's hair and yanked hard. If he'd hoped to elicit a scream, he was disappointed; all she could manage was a choking sob. 'The next shot goes into her head.'

A disembodied voice floated up the stairwell. 'How do we know the hostage is still alive?'

'Tell them you're all right,' West ordered.

'I'm all right.' Mechanically, Elizabeth repeated his exact words.

'Dr Santer? Is that you?'

Elizabeth recognized Major Simmond's voice. 'He has a gun… '

'Try to keep calm. We'll soon resolve this situation.'

'Only if you let me take her down to the ground floor,' West qualified. 'Back off. If as much as a shadow crosses my path I'll kill Dr Santer. You have thirty seconds to clear this stairwell.'

'We need more time… '

'You don't have it.' West twisted his thumb into the soft flesh at the base of Elizabeth's neck. A shaft of pain shot through her spine and she screamed.

'Everyone back! Clear the stairwell!' was repeatedly echoed below them. West knew that all the exits on the ground floor would be heavily guarded but all he could think about was negotiating his way down. He proceeded slowly one step at a time, studying every inch of ground he'd have to cross before he came to it.

Elizabeth gripped the wheelchair's arms with her fingers, barely aware of the pain in her wrists and ankles. Closing her eyes, she concentrated with all her might on an image of Joseph, alive, and smiling. If only he could be there, waiting for her when they reached the ground floor. She conjured an image of his mouth curved into a smile, remembered the laughter lines at the corners of his green eyes…

The steel muzzle knocked against her skull bringing her sharply back to the present.

She opened her eyes. They had reached the bottom. The grey afternoon light had been superseded by murky black night, transforming the windows into misty wavering mirrors. They faced a plaster wall. A red arrow pointed to the basement. Alongside were painted the words SERVICES and MORTUARY.

West nudged the wheelchair against the door, and yelled, 'Fall back.'

Muffled footsteps scuttled away.

He hit Elizabeth lightly with the gun. 'Which is the quickest way to the outside?'

'Straight ahead, then first right.'

'If you're lying… '

'You'll shoot me?' She hoped she sounded braver than she felt. 'I can only die once.'

'It's not death but the way you die that matters. I could leave you a brain damaged, dribbling, incontinent wreck.' He pushed the wheelchair out into the ground-floor corridor. 'Cross my path and she's dead.' He raised his hand so the Browning could be seen.

Someone ahead shouted, 'Fall back!'

They moved on and Elizabeth read the names on the doors and the signs on the wall, as though she were seeing them for the first time; PATHOLOGY, X-RAY, ORTHOPAEDIC CLINIC. She looked down and saw the lines on the floor; blue for X-ray, red for pathology, yellow for… What was yellow for?

Another sign, TREATMENT ROOM. West halted and kicked in the door without warning. 'Move out. Now!'

A soldier in fatigues emerged. He lifted his gun above his head.

'Drop it,' West ordered.

He complied and West shot him. The man crumpled to the floor, clutching his knee. West opened the door with his back, kicked the soldier's gun inside, and heaved the wheelchair in behind him. Elizabeth closed her eyes, and wished the nightmare would end.

She heard West breathing heavily behind her. Directly in front of them was a treatment cubicle containing a couch and a trolley set out with swabs, scissors and the familiar paraphernalia of casualty. She recognized the grating of bolts being thrust down into the floor when West secured the door. The pressure of the gun on her forehead eased as he leaned forward and picked up a scalpel from the tray.

'I'd rather you killed me with the gun.'

The razor-sharp metal slashed downwards. He freed her from the wheelchair. But when she tried to rise, he pushed her down before gathering up bandages and plaster from the tray.

'No! In God's name no!' It was the last sound she made. Her eyes widened in terror as he wound a bandage tightly around her head and between her lips. He forced her teeth apart and the material rasped against her tongue, its antiseptic taste fouling her mouth.

He fixed the bandage in place with a plaster, before covering her with a suffocating blanket that blotted everything from view. Wrenching her unceremoniously to her feet, he hauled her hands high behind her back and secured them with strips of plaster that cut into her flesh. The last thought to cross her mind, before a sudden painful pressure on her neck thrust her into unconsciousness, was that she had been left with no more dignity than a chicken trussed for market.

West switched off the light and moved to the window. He pushed Elizabeth ahead of him, using her limp body as a shield. He knew the darkness wouldn't affect his stalkers. The men outside would be wearing infra-red sights and lenses that would highlight him and Elizabeth. He pulled the bolts on the door and pushed her ahead of him into the corridor. With his back to the wall, still using Elizabeth as a shield, he inched forward, following the exit signs, until he came to an arrow pointing downwards marked BASEMENT.

Beyond it lay another stairwell – and possibly a door to the outside? Time to take a chance; there'd never be a better moment. He wrenched a fire extinguisher from the wall and hurled it against a window pane. The air was filled with the sound of splintering glass. Clutching Elizabeth's blanket swathed body in front of his own, he threw himself and his hostage through what remained of the window.

He landed on his back in a flower-bed, Elizabeth on top of him, his outstretched hand still closed firmly around the Browning. He took a deep breath. He'd done it. He'd managed to get outside the building, and he still had his hostage and a weapon.

A tinny voice, echoed from a loudspeaker. 'You are surrounded. I repeat, you are surrounded. You cannot escape. Release Dr Santer and surrender. I repeat, you are surrounded… '

West grabbed the blanket he'd wrapped around Elizabeth's head and hauled her upright. She sagged limply in his arms. He threw her over his shoulder and dived back into the shadows at the side of the hospital.

Knowing they expected him to strike out through the gardens West remained close to the building. He spotted a door set below ground level. A flight of steps led down to it. It proved pathetically easy to open. Its lock had obviously been forced at some time and ill-repaired. All he had to do was prise out the new wood that had been hammered into the frame using the scalpel he'd pushed into the pocket of his torn tracksuit. Replacing the piece of wood around the lock, he closed the door softly behind them. He stole down a flight of stairs, heading for what he hoped would be the mortuary. What better hiding place than amongst corpses.

He reached another locked door and pulled out the scalpel again. He discovered that he knew as much about picking locks as he did about firing guns. It wasn't difficult to turn the tumblers with a narrow, sharp instrument with a curved end. After opening each door, he relocked them from the inside, stooping low to push the bolts into the floor. For the first time since the corpse of the sergeant had been pushed into his hospital room, he began to relax.

He removed the blanket from Elizabeth's head, laid it on the floor then placed her on top of it. He was operating in pitch darkness, but didn't dare switch on a light. He hadn't noticed surveillance cameras in any of the rooms in the hospital, only in the corridors, but that didn't mean there weren't any.

Sliding to the floor he placed one hand on Elizabeth's neck to check her pulse. She was alive, but the rhythm of her breathing told him she remained unconscious. His eyes became accustomed to the darkness and he looked around for a gleam of glass that might indicate a window. Not that he expected to find any in a basement mortuary. Reassured that there was no way for anyone wearing infra-red glasses to see in, he tried to forget the pains in his ankle and head and plan his next move.

The hunt for him would have probably moved on by now, out of the hospital building and into the grounds. They'd keep up the search all night, but by morning people would be growing tired, shifts would change, and the passing of hours without a single sighting of him would bring a slackening of vigilance. If he were lucky they might assume that he'd slipped through the cordon. He doubted they'd expect him to return to the hospital, but if they checked all the doors again, they'd find the one he had broken through. Would they assume the damage was old damage as he wanted them to?

All he could do was sit it out. That was the hardest. It had always been the hardest; the sitting and waiting. Why did he recall that? Had he endured similar situations in the past life he could no longer remember?

He didn't allow himself to sleep. He discovered that was also something he could do without. Instead he slipped into a still, almost meditative state, listening to Elizabeth's low, steady breathing. When she tried to cough he finally loosened the gag around her mouth.

If only he had a torch. There were so many things he needed to do, like change his bloodstained clothes. Gradually, his eyes grew accustomed to the darkness and he began to get a "feel" for his surroundings. The ceiling was high. He couldn't see it, but he sensed it. He could also smell formaldehyde. Somewhere close by had to be changing rooms for the pathologist and staff, and a bathroom. He wondered how many hours were left before dawn broke.

No sounds reached him from outside. He could hear only the hum of the building itself; water pumping around heating pipes, the click of time switches operating some distance away, the whir of the lift shafts.

Cramp set into his ankle, and he moved. He limped forward, trailing his hand on the wall, pressing every door he encountered, only to find them all locked. Then he found one that wasn't. He opened it and the smell of bleach and lavatory cleaner wafted out to greet him. Closing the door behind him, he felt around for the light-switch, reasoning that no staff union would allow security cameras to be placed in a lavatory. The ceiling, walls and corners of the washroom were reassuringly bare. There wasn't a window, only a ventilation fan.

He stared at his face in the mirror, pale and bloodless, his dark hair falling forward over his eyes. He could clean himself up here, but it would be better if he could find something to clean himself up with. Would there be a locker room nearby? Careful to turn off the light before opening the door, he moved on a few paces.

The locker room was next door. It too was devoid of cameras, probably because it served as a changing room. The locks securing the metal cabinets used for personal possessions proved childishly simple to open. Inside one he found a green operating-theatre suit. It was thinner than the tracksuit, and he shivered as he pulled it on over the boxer shorts the sister had found for him. There was a green cap and a surgical mask – a perfect disguise provided no one looked too closely. He found soap, shampoo and a safety razor, and returned to the washroom and washed. When he'd finished, he pulled the mask over his face and fixed the cap down low.

There was still Elizabeth Santer. He debated whether to leave her. But she could still be useful. All he needed was a trolley and a blanket. Bodies were shipped out all the time from mortuaries, but were they taken away by undertaker or ambulance? There had to be a door that led to a parking bay. Even during an emergency some vehicles would be allowed in and out of the grounds – hearses and ambulances evacuating patients. But how many hours away was morning? And how many more hours could he function without sleep?

CHAPTER FIVE

The faint humming of heating pipes was interrupted by deafening staccato banging. When the clamour ceased, the humming resumed at increased intensity. The difference in sound would have probably been imperceptible to anyone who hadn't been listening intently for a deviation from the pattern of noise in the hospital basement. But John West realised that the main pump on the boiler had speeded up its output to warm the wards for the morning shift. The night was finally drawing to an end. Leaving the light on in the washroom and the door slightly ajar, he risked checking the corridor they had spent the night in. Once he was satisfied there were no security cameras in the area, he went to Elizabeth. She was still sleeping. He shook her awake. She stared up at him, wild-eyed, disorientated for a moment, then – as realization dawned and she recalled the events of the previous day, she began to tremble.

'I've found a washroom.' Hauling her to her feet he produced the scalpel, and cut through the bandages on her wrists. She tore the gag further away from her mouth, hesitating when she noticed the gun in his hand.

'I won't try anything,' she mumbled hoarsely through chapped lips.

Gripping her arm he hauled her to the washroom, pushed her in and closed the door. He remained outside, and considered the escape plans he had formulated during the long night. Each seemed more preposterous and risk-laden than the last. But then an idea came to him; a simple, ingenious idea that just might work – if he could find everything he needed to carry it out.

Elizabeth sank even further into despair when she looked around the washroom. There were no windows, only a six inch ventilation shaft and heating pipes. She toyed with the idea of tapping a message in Morse code on the pipes, but dismissed it. Quite apart from the fact that the code she'd learned as a Brownie was rusty, West would undoubtedly pick up on it before anyone else.

Filling the sink with water she pulled off the remainder of the clammy bandages and spat the last threads of antiseptic-tasting gauze from her mouth. She lowered her head and drank deeply from the cold tap. She only hoped it was drinking water.

'Hurry up,' West whispered through the closed door.

'I'll be out when I've washed,' she snapped, irritability over-riding caution.

The door opened an inch and she caught a glimpse of the gleaming gun barrel. It closed again and she continued peeling the residue of plaster from the skin around her lips. The sweater and skirt she had taken from her wardrobe yesterday morning looked as though they'd been retrieved from the bottom of a charity clothing skip. Had she really been wearing them for only twenty-four hours? It felt like a lifetime.

Depressing the soap dispenser, she washed her hands and face and dried herself with paper towels.

She didn't attempt to wash any more of herself. Not with John West standing outside the door. The humiliation of being forced to strip in front of him still rankled. Deliberately taking her time, she pulled the remaining pins from her hair, and disentangled it as best she could with her fingers before bunching it into a pony-tail. If West was going to tie her hands behind her back again, she didn't want the added irritation of pins sticking into her neck. Finally she went into a cubicle and sat on the lavatory seat for ten minutes, delaying as long as possible the moment when she'd have to walk out of the door and back into the clutches of a man who was exhibiting all the classic symptoms of psychopathic behaviour.

It was all very well for experts to advise that hostages should do everything in their power to establish a rapport with their kidnappers. Those people had probably never met a John West who had no qualms about shooting a soldier who had dropped his weapons. Eventually, she could delay no longer. Shivering as much from fear as cold, she returned to the corridor.

'Sit on the floor.'

She did as he instructed. 'What are you going to do with me?' she ventured.

'If you do exactly as I tell you, set you free – eventually.'

'You expect me to take the word of a murderer?'

'Quiet.'

'You don't like hearing the truth.'

'I ordered you to keep quiet,' he repeated softly without raising his voice.

Using a sheet of gauze and some linen strips he'd found in a cupboard in the corridor, he retied her wrists and ankles and taped her mouth. Then he proceeded to bandage the whole of her head, including her eyes. She tried to struggle, but it was futile. He was stronger than her and, remembering Joseph's adage about uncontrollable situations, she resigned herself to the inevitable.

After West had reduced Elizabeth to a blind, inanimate parcel, he pulled up the mask, switched on all the lights and returned to the locker-room.

There was a row of white rubber surgical boots behind the door. He flicked through them until he found a pair his size. A search of the lockers yielded a stethoscope and a white coat that was cleaner and larger than the one he'd taken from Elizabeth. He slipped it on over his suit and thrust the stethoscope into the pocket. It would add authenticity to his costume.

In one locker he discovered two packets of prawn-cocktail flavoured crisps and two cans of soft drink. He pocketed them and continued to search but found nothing else edible.

Finally he heaped the entire contents of all the lockers – clothes, magazines, cigarettes and matches – in the centre of the room. Striking a match he lit a corner of a magazine and allowed it to smoulder. Pocketing one box of matches he left the locker-room and picked the lock on the mortuary doors. Bringing out all the bottles of flammable chemicals he could find, he placed them around the conflagration.

He pulled the paper-towel dispenser from the wall of the washroom, threw its contents, and as many toilet rolls as he could find, on to his bonfire. Flames licked towards the bottles, smoke billowed out of the locker-room into the corridor. He picked up Elizabeth, checked his mask was high over his face and unlatched the doors to the outside. The last thing he did before running up the steps was smash the glass on the fire alarm.

Bells shrilled, so high-pitched they hurt his ears as he hurried around the side of the hospital building. He needed to find the main entrance before the emergency services were mustered.

An ambulance was parked in a nearby bay alongside an array of army vehicles. He quickened his step. Jerking open the back doors he laid Elizabeth on a gurney, covering her to the chin with a sheet, so only her bandaged face was visible.

'Hey, what do you think you're doing?' A man in the green and white uniform of a paramedic ran towards him.

'You the driver?'

'Yes.'

'The burns unit, right away.'

'What burns unit?'

'Don't waste time. Can't you hear the alarms? She was in the basement when the boiler blew. The burns unit is her only chance.'

West waited until the paramedic was inches away, before pulling the gun from his pocket.

'Oh shit… '

'In the cab and drive,' he ordered brusquely. 'Get us through the cordon at the gate, and I'll release you. If you alert anyone, I'll start a shooting match that will end in a massacre – and you'll be the first victim.'

The driver glanced helplessly around the bay. His partner was inside, drinking tea in the casualty office with the charge nurse. No one was in the foyer. The casualty unit hadn't reopened since the trust had closed it the day before. Staring at the gun he climbed into his cab. The gunman climbed in alongside him, before sliding over the seat into the back. Sirens rang out homing in on the hospital.

'Switch on your siren and start driving.' West poked the muzzle of the gun into the back of the driver's seat.

'They'll stop me at the gate?'

'Tell them you're carrying a severely burned patient and there's no time to lose. If they want to know more, I'll deal with them.'

The driver turned the ignition key.

West crouched low in the back, ostensibly tending to his bandaged patient, while carefully keeping his gun concealed from the military and civilian police who stopped them at the gate. The wail of sirens from fire engines and police cars drowned out the conversation, but the driver must have given the right answers, because a few minutes later they were out of the hospital and on the open road.

'Where to now?' the driver asked nervously.

'Switch off the siren, and take the Brighton road.'

'If you've a body back there… '

‘Just do it.’ Keeping the gun pressed into the back of the driving seat, John thought through his next move. The sky was beginning to lighten. Dawn would soon break. He needed to rest. He had a long journey ahead of him, one he would prefer to make under cover of darkness. And before then, he would need to find transport, a change of clothes, money and food.

The sky gradually turned a paler grey and the driver switched off his headlights.

‘The traffic’s light on Sunday. We’ll be in Brighton in less than an hour. Where do I go when we get there?’ The driver was acutely aware of the pressure in the small of his back.

‘The largest hospital you know, but steer clear of the casualty department. And don’t park in the main car park. Find somewhere at the back or the side of the building. A separate car park for staff or one of the clinics,’ John barked. So far so good. He was free, but he had two hostages; one too many. He would leave the paramedic in the car park with the ambulance. A hospital car park would be a good place to steal a car. Did he know about stealing cars? He’d soon find out.

He dismissed the niggling questions worming uncomfortably in his mind. Questions centred on the skills he possessed; skills of dubious morality. He concentrated on his next move. He knew exactly where he wanted to go. The only question was how to get there. He had recognized Brecon from the photographs Elizabeth had shown him. Once there, the familiar surroundings would surely prompt his memory, and he’d recover his identity.

In Brecon he would discover who he was and what exactly had driven him to run blindly down a motorway into the path of oncoming cars. He might even find out why he was being hounded and why someone wanted him dead. And even if, as Elizabeth had suggested, he was a terrorist, then he would simply have to face the truth. It had to be better than the crushing emptiness of knowing nothing about himself.

He recalled the dead, cold eyes of the soldiers outside his room and wondered what creed or cause could be worth men's lives. A sentence came to mind. A sentence spoken in a maddeningly familiar voice.

"Some people deserve to be assassinated."

Did they? And why had that come to mind if he wasn't an assassin?

'There's a hospital. But the only ambulances I can see are parked outside Casualty.'

West sat up on his heels and peered over the driver's shoulder. 'Drive through the gates, and turn left.' He chose the direction because the wall of the main building that overlooked that side had small windows – staircases or kitchens and bathrooms? Whatever lay beyond them, they offered less of a view than the full sized windows at the front.

'Pull up at the end of the row. Turn off the ignition and hand me the keys.'

When the driver bent forward to remove the keys, West placed two fingers at the side of his neck. It took a little pressure before the man slumped, unconscious, over the wheel.

Leaning forward West locked all the doors from the inside. Bracing himself, he hooked his hands under the driver's armpit, and dragged him into the back of the ambulance laying him on the floor alongside Elizabeth. He wished the man was taller. It would be no use exchanging clothes with him; his trousers would be a foot too wide and six inches too short.

Unwinding the strips of linen from Elizabeth's eyes, he watched them grow large as she focused on the paramedic slumped beside her.

'He'll be fine when he wakes.' West finished removing the linen strips from the rest of Elizabeth's head but left the plaster covering her mouth. Taking the paramedic's jacket he draped it over her shoulders, but left her hands tied beneath it. As an afterthought he removed the man's trousers. Cutting the bonds on Elizabeth's ankles he bundled the trousers over her bare legs, tucking her skirt into the waistband. They were too wide, but better that than freezing. The air temperature was low and he had seen hoarfrost icing the grass verges at the side of the road on the journey down.

He went through the equipment boxes, found a hypothermia blanket and wrapped it around the paramedic before going to the rear window and studying the security cameras panning the car park. Most of them faced the main area. Only one covered the side section where they were parked, and that moved on its stand, scanning three areas in turn. He watched it for ten minutes, assimilating its rhythm. When he had timed its movements, he looked around for a car. He settled on a modest saloon with an inbuilt security system that could be disabled within minutes by anyone who knew the location of the wires.

Pocketing his gun, he opened the back door of the ambulance. Keeping an eye on the arc of the security camera, he dived beneath the car he'd targeted the moment the lens turned. He had the alarm disabled in seconds, the lock open within minutes.

Still watching the camera, he returned to the ambulance. In his next journey he transferred three blankets and a pillow. Arranging the pillow and one blanket over the back seat, he went back for Elizabeth. Pulling the coat high enough to conceal the plaster covering her mouth, he helped her to the door. She glanced back at the paramedic.

'You see his chest moving? He'll come around in an hour or two,' he reassured. Gripping her upper arms he lowered her on to the road. Releasing her, he pushed her ahead of him. She would have fallen if he hadn't kept a tight grip on her shoulder. Closing the doors on the ambulance, he guided her over to the car. Bundling her into the back, he propped her head on the pillow and covered her to the chin with the other two blankets.

'Comfortable?'

It was an odd question for a kidnapper to ask a hostage. If Elizabeth's mouth hadn't been taped she might have laughed, but as it was, she nodded resignedly, curled her legs and lay back on the seat.

Slamming the rear door shut, West climbed into the driver's seat, hit the central locking device and sped off, back towards the motorway and London. If the police spent a day or two searching the south coast for him, it might give him the time he needed to reach Wales.

Chaloner's face was bland, expressionless when he faced the lieutenant-colonel. 'He must have slipped through the cordon, sir.'

'How could he have?' Heddingham raged. 'We had every inch of this place covered.'

'He thinks like us, he operates like us, and so far he's been one step ahead of us all the way, sir,' the captain replied. It had been a long night, and he'd spent the last hour checking the images recorded by the hospital's CCTV cameras, most of which were indecipherable due to the smoke from the fire that had been set in the basement outside the hospital mortuary. He'd talked to firemen, checked reports from the gates, checked and double checked with the men covering the grounds and the wards, and drawn an absolute blank. Like Heddingham, he didn't know how John West could have left the hospital, but he sensed that he had somehow done so.

'Sir.' Sergeant Price snapped to attention in the doorway of the improvised Command Cell.

'Sergeant?' Chaloner inquired.

'Privates Evans and Jenkins's bullet wounds are not serious, sir. Doctor says they'll both be fit for duty within six weeks.'

'Luck? Or our man's talent as a marksman?'

'Private Evans reported West took careful aim, sir.'

'Pity Evans didn't think to shoot back instead of standing idly by and watching our man escape.'

'And the psychiatric consultant, Mr David Watson, has been found in the basement, sir'

Chaloner had been concerned about Watson ever since he'd disappeared around the time of Elizabeth Santer's kidnapping.

'He's dead, sir,' the sergeant said flatly. 'A single bullet in the head. Just like the two soldiers in the ward.'

It began to rain when they left the outskirts of Brighton. A heavy, sleet-filled downpour that blurred the windscreen and chilled the car. West turned up the heating and wondered how much longer he could go on without food, drink or rest. Remembering the two cans in his pocket, he opened one and sipped a sickly sweet liquid that reminded him of rotting fruit. Looking in the rear-view mirror, he saw Elizabeth watching him.

'I have another can. I'll try to stop soon and give it to you.'

Traffic flowed around them, heavier than it had been on the journey down. He tried to think of somewhere that would be safe to stop. A place where he could acquire food, clothes and money. He turned on to the motorway and headed for central London. Londoners tended to keep themselves to themselves, so maybe he could turn off the ring road and find a day school. One with a canteen and a gym where they might find tracksuits. The problem would be hiding the car. Even if it hadn't already been reported stolen, a car seen outside an empty school on a weekend was going to attract attention.

He kept to the slow lane, only occasionally overtaking. He'd discarded the surgical cap and the mask as soon as he'd left Brighton in an attempt to look as unobtrusive as the car he was driving.

Midday brought dismal winter twilight. He hit a ring road and turned off it at random, driving along street after street lined with anonymous houses. Rain continued to teem down heavy and blinding. Then he glimpsed railings and the concrete of a playground. He checked in his mirror, the street was deserted. No sane person would venture out in this downpour unnecessarily.

Pinned to the twelve-foot high wire mesh that fenced in the school-yard was a notice.

THESE PREMISES ARE PATROLLED BY SECURITY FORCES WITH GUARD DOGS.

He pressed the accelerator and drove on, but every public building carried a similar warning notice. He had no idea crime in the suburbs had escalated to such proportions. It was like America. Had he lived in the States? Was that why no one had answered the appeal for information about him?

He continued to drive aimlessly, by mid-afternoon he hit the main artery that led west out of London. He recalled that he'd been picked up somewhere on this motorway. Would he recognize the spot?

Rubbing his eyes in exhaustion, he stared at the petrol tank. It was low. He had no choice but to turn off at the next service station. It had a sign offering petrol, WC, food and telephones.

He parked on the fringe of the car park, some distance from the fast-food restaurant. He couldn't risk staying long. The car might have been reported stolen by now but he had to close his eyes… just for just ten minutes.

He glanced into the back before winding his seat into the reclining position. Elizabeth's eyes were closed. He assumed she was asleep. Stretching out his legs, he hid the gun in the folds of his suit and followed her example, sliding effortlessly into a deep, dreamless sleep.

He woke with a start, cold and shivering and looked at the clock on the dashboard. He couldn't see the numbers. Dark, moonless night had fallen while he'd slept. When another car drove up, its headlights lightened the gloom and he read four-thirty on the digital clock. Four-thirty morning or afternoon? He had no idea how long he'd slept. Then he saw the illuminated sign over the snack-bar flashing OPEN. Afternoon.

Car doors slammed. A young couple left the estate car that had just driven in. They wore snug quilted jackets, thick trousers and boots. He envied them. The temperature was below freezing.

He checked Elizabeth. She looked as though she was still asleep. When he laid his hand against her cheek it was ice cold. He had to get her somewhere warm as soon as possible.

He studied the estate car. A plastic case was strapped to the roof-rack, and he could see suitcases, rucksacks and sleeping bags piled high on the back seat. Either going, or returning from holiday. A couple with no children who would be annoyed but not life-threateningly inconvenienced. He looked down at his surgical suit. Hardly an inconspicuous outfit to walk across the car park in, and risk being seen from the burger bar.

He gunned the engine and edged forward, pulling up within inches of the driver's door on the estate car. Winding down his window he was able to pick the lock under cover of the pounding rain. Climbing in, he slid across the seats and opened the passenger door. Dropping out on to the ground he slipped beneath the car. A few minutes later he had unscrewed both number plates. There was no alarm. He exchanged the plates with those on the saloon he had stolen in Brighton. It aged the estate car by three years, but it was the model not the year that the police would be looking for.

He transferred Elizabeth from one car to the other, and turned the estate car's ignition with the scalpel. The needle on the petrol gauge hovered at maximum. They must have filled up before turning into the service station. The case on the roof-rack was a giveaway, but he could take the next turning off the motorway and jettison it. A few more miles further on he'd find a secluded parking place where he could search the luggage for food and warm clothing.

The engine was still warm. He turned the heater full on so the fan belched hot air into the interior. When he saw a brown lettered signpost, he turned off into a wooded country park. Given the dark and the downpour he wasn't surprised to find it deserted.

Slowing his speed he bumped out of the car park and on to a rough track bordering a river. Under the inadequate shelter of skeletal trees he left the car and opened the box on the roof-rack. It was packed with bottles of French wine. Closing the box he heaved it down and slid it into the undergrowth. Then he unscrewed the roof-rack and threw it into the river.

He carried one of the suitcases from the back round to the front seat. It was filled with clean clothes; jeans, boxer shorts, socks, and a black turtle neck sweater. There was even a pair of trainers, shabby and worn, but comfortable. Stripping to the skin, he threw everything he had been wearing into the river before hurriedly dressing. He found a jacket, not as thick or as warm as the one the man had been wearing, but waterproof and serviceable.

Elizabeth was still asleep, her face flushed in the pale glow of the interior lamp. She felt warmer. He hoped it wasn't the result of fever.

He discovered more wine in the boot; boxes of the stuff. The couple had obviously been on a shopping trip to France to stock up on Christmas drink – and food. French cheeses, tins of escargots, whole pates, lengths of garlic sausage and cervelat, smoked turkey and duck breast, French bread and pumpernickel, as well as brandy and beer. His mouth watered at the prospect. He'd been hoping to strike lucky, but he'd struck gold.

One small suitcase was full of women's clothes. After checking there weren't any lights, or other signs of human habitation, he shook Elizabeth awake and cut through the bonds on her wrists. The first thing she did was pull the plaster from her mouth.

'There's a case of women's clothes here. You can change in the back of the car, afterwards we'll eat.'

He turned up the collar of his jacket against the rain and opened the estate's rear door. The vehicle was packed full enough to attract the attention of a passing police car. He lifted out half the cases of wine and dumped them alongside the plastic case in the bushes.

'Can I get out and stretch my legs?'

'It's wet and windy.'

'I need to breathe real air.' She clambered out and stood out in the rain, her head lifted towards the downpour. Even in the inadequate light he noticed the skin around her mouth was red from the plaster. The jeans, trainers and sweatshirt she was wearing looked too big for her but they were thicker than her skirt and thin sweater.

'Where did you get the clothes?'

'They came with the car. If you get back inside, I'll organise some food.'

She picked up a blanket and wrapped it around her shoulders. 'I have to go behind the bushes.'

As she walked away, he called out, 'That's far enough.'

When she returned she climbed into the back and pulled the second blanket over her lap. He lifted a box of food into the front passenger seat and pressed down the central locking device before switching on the ignition to keep the heater running.

'What do you want to eat?'

'I'm too thirsty to think of food,' she replied.

'There's wine if you don't mind smashing the top off the bottle, beer, brandy, and this.' He offered her the remaining can of soft drink he'd purloined from the hospital locker-room. She made a face.

'Try a beer.' He opened a can and handed it to her. She drank half of it in one thirsty swallow, only to regret her greed when the alcohol hit her empty stomach and her head began to swim.

'Do you have bread?'

'Pumpernickel or French baguette?'

'Baguette,' she saw the cheese and added, 'Brie.' Forgetting the gun, she reached over his shoulder into the box and lifted out a full silver moon of her favourite cheese. 'Have you a knife?'

'To cut the cheese or stab me?' he enquired dryly.

'Sorry, stupid question.' She unwrapped the Brie and broke off a segment.

Mouth full of garlic sausage and pumpernickel he leaned against the dashboard and watched her.

She finished a second lump of cheese, and snapped off a piece of sausage. 'Can I have another beer?' she asked after emptying her first can. He handed her one. 'We're going to Brecon.' It wasn't a question.

'It's the logical place to start.'

'And if you don't like what you find there?'

He looked at her through narrowed eyes. 'I need to find out who I am.'

'Then you really have lost your memory?'

'Did you ever doubt it?'

'Yes.' She took the remains of the French loaf from the box. 'What do you intend to do with me when you get there?'

He looked her in the eye. 'You'll find out – when we get there.'

CHAPTER SIX

Simmonds watched Lieutenant-Colonel Heddingham replace the telephone receiver. 'Have they set up a Cabinet Office briefing room?'

'An hour ago.' Heddingham snapped.

'That's routine in a case like this,' Simmonds sympathized.

'It means they believe we're incompetent,' Heddingham pronounced flatly.

'I defy anyone to have done more.' The police superintendent took Heddingham's comments as personal criticism. He'd allowed the army officers to take control of the Command Cell he'd set up in his police station to oversee "Operation West". He'd remained on duty in the hospital grounds all night, in the hope that West would be found. And now, when he was on the verge of collapsing from exhaustion, the colonel had the brass to tell him that "they" – whoever "they" were – believed that the situation was being handled badly.

'We could have done more,' Heddingham barked. 'We could have caught the man.'

'He's obviously a professional. Your men searched that building from top to bottom yesterday… '

'While he was inside, and we missed him,' Heddingham interrupted.

'You're being too hard on yourself, sir,' Major Simmonds consoled clumsily. 'No officer could have done more.'

'If we'd put in more effort, that paramedic might still be alive.'

'And so might Mr Watson,' the superintendent murmured. 'But if there's one thing I've learned in twenty years of policing, it's you can't afford to think in terms of what might have been.'

'Are you going to the Cabinet briefing, sir?' Simmonds asked.

'They want me there within the hour.' Heddingham rubbed his chin. He needed to shave and acquire a clean shirt. Thank God for Simmonds; he was good at organising domestic comforts – if nothing else.

'I'll order you a helicopter, sir?'

'Very good, Simmonds. The minister overseeing this incident wants a full report. I suggest we check the sequence of events, to ensure that we are in agreement about what happened, superintendent.'

'A joint police/army report sounds like a good idea,' the superintendent answered.

'I don't know about "a good idea",' Heddingham said acidly. 'In the army we call it covering our rear.'

Simmonds went to the bank of telephones that connected directly to the nearest Army HQ, leaving the superintendent and lieutenant-colonel staring glumly at a road map of Britain.

'He could be anywhere by now,' Heddingham declared in disgust.

'As he seems to think like your chaps, it might be a good idea to bring in someone who can analyze information as and when we get it. Someone able to determine whether a pattern's emerging that could help us forecast his next move.' He glanced sideways at Heddingham. 'How about that special forces officer who was in the hospital last night?'

'He's back with his unit.'

'Could you ask for him to be transferred to us?' the superintendent asked.

The lieutenant-colonel looked to Simmonds, who'd just replaced the receiver. 'Simmonds will arrange it.'

West opened his eyes and turned on the inside light of the car to read the clock. It was just after eleven. He checked Elizabeth, and saw her eyes were open above the gag he'd retied around her mouth. She made a noise when he opened the car door and stepped outside. His feet squelched into icy mud that oozed over the top of his trainers. It took him a moment to extricate himself from the mire and by the time he finished, both his socks were sodden and filthy as well as the trainers, but there were plenty of clean pairs in the case. He tiptoed through the puddles to the fringe of woodland and relieved himself.

On his return, he discovered Elizabeth sitting upright. He opened the back door and cut through her bonds. She pulled down her gag.

'It's all that beer,' she apologized. She stumbled out of the car door and he followed her.

'Can't I do anything in private?' she complained.

'I can't risk losing you.'

'Damn you, and damn you to hell, John West.' She stepped behind a tree, but to her chagrin he didn't return to the car until she did. 'If I promise not to make a sound will you leave off the gag,' she begged.

'Not a chance.'

He trussed her up exactly as he had done before, laid her head on the pillow, her feet on the seat and covered her to the chin with a blanket.

'Looks like you've had practice putting children to bed.'

It was the last thing she said before he pulled the bandage tight around her mouth.

Children! The thought hadn't occurred to him. Did he have a child? A wife waiting, wondering why he hadn't come home? If so, why hadn't she answered the press appeals?

He reversed down the path, into the car park and switched on the car radio. The first thing he had to do was find another car or van; a vehicle that wouldn't be missed until morning in case the local police had already put out the description of the estate.

He drove down a secondary road to the accompaniment of an unmelodic pop song, covering two miles before he reached a straggle of upmarket houses built around a pub, a church and, further along, a small school. He opened the side window slightly. The cold wind froze his ear, but he had a long drive ahead and didn't want to risk falling asleep at the wheel. He continued north, by-passing the signs for the motorway, not wanting to run the risk of being picked up on CCTV while still in the stolen estate car.

He found what he was looking for shortly after midnight. It was another estate car; newer, flashier. It was parked at the head of a long straight drive to a house set back from the road, with no other house in sight. He slowed his speed. Shutting down his engine, he parked a couple of hundred yards up the road. He climbed out of the driving seat, leaving the door slightly ajar. Moving in the shadows, he stole back along the road and up the drive. The only noise he could hear was the rain splashing into the gutters. His luck was holding, if there'd been a dog around it would have barked by now.

Any complacency he felt disappeared when he examined the vehicle's alarm. It was the most complicated he'd encountered so far. It took him ten minutes to disarm the system, and he was tempted to give up half-way when he nearly triggered the mechanism. Once he had rendered it harmless, he opened the door and climbed behind the wheel. Releasing the handbrake he allowed the car to roll down the drive and on to the road. He climbed out and pushed it twenty yards further before starting the engine, and parking it behind the other vehicle.

He exchanged number plates again; keeping the number he'd stolen in Brighton. He transferred the blankets and pillow, Elizabeth, the suitcases and finally a selection of food and drink. Closing the tailgate, he checked the discarded vehicle carefully, to ensure he'd left no evidence of his presence. It was then he spotted a lump beneath the rubber mat on the passenger side. He peeled it back and found a wallet stuffed with credit cards and a hundred and fifty pounds in cash. He left the credit cards, but pocketed the banknotes. Fortunately for him, some people were complete idiots.

An hour later he was driving west along the M4, trying to keep awake by singing along to a song from the soundtrack of a film he had a vague recollection of watching. He tried to recall details of the plot. There'd been a girl and a man… and there was a lot of quarrelling and shouting, but then that was most films these days. Wasn't it?

Just before he reached the motorway services at the Severn Bridge he looked down at the fuel gauge. In his eagerness to find another vehicle he'd forgotten to check the tank. The needle was pressing against empty. He debated whether to risk buying petrol, or exchange cars yet again. Stealing another car would take precious time. He wanted to reach Brecon before the morning rush-hour. Preferably when the streets were still dark, and he could walk around without risking being seen by someone who might recognize him and ask awkward questions.

Glancing into the rear-view mirror he saw that Elizabeth had fallen asleep again. He envied her. Perhaps there'd be a car parked in the services he could siphon petrol out of, but even if there was, he had no tube – but he did have money.

He filled the tank until the pump cut out, then covered Elizabeth with the blanket before driving to the cashier's booth. The middle-aged woman in the kiosk barely glanced at him as he handed over a third of his precious supply of cash. Without any prompting, she also gave him the coins he'd need for the bridge toll in his change.

He plotted a route when he rejoined the motorway. If he could remember street names in Brecon, then he should be able to remember the main roads leading into the town. The lights of the toll booths flashed ahead, and he opted for an automatic coin bin. Tossing his money into the wire basket he pressed the accelerator. Wind buffeted the car as he crossed the Severn Bridge. Wales lay ahead – and Brecon.

He was pinning all his hopes on discovering his identity there. What if nothing happened? What if he only recognized the streets he had already identified? He dismissed the thought. Something would be familiar; he had to believe that much. And, for now at least, no one was following him.

'Captain Chaloner. I've been told to report to Lieutenant-Colonel Heddingham.'

Simmonds heard the young officer announce himself and looked up at the door of the Command Cell. Chaloner appeared to be fit and hard, he also had that other attribute Simmonds had often seen in Special Forces personnel; an ability to blend inconspicuously into the background, exciting little interest or notice. Few others in the room, civilians or police, had turned to look at the young captain.

'I'm Simmonds, Peter Simmonds. We met yesterday.' He crossed the room and held out his hand. The captain shook it. 'Lieutenant-Colonel Heddingham has been called away.'

Ross Chaloner's eyes flickered as though he knew precisely where and why the lieutenant-colonel had been summoned.

‘You’ve been briefed.’ Simmonds asked.

‘An hour ago, I was hoping there’d been more developments since.’

‘Is this the man we’ve been waiting for, Major?’ Police Inspector Barnes, with Sergeant Pickett close behind, joined the officers.

‘Captain Ross Chaloner – Inspector Barnes, Sergeant Pickett.’

‘Shall we continue our conversation in the Superintendent’s office, gentlemen?’ Simmonds led the way into a small secondary office furnished with two desks, a battery of telephones and a wall-board covered with a large scale map of England and Wales. Red plastic pins had been fixed in the map to indicate the location of the local hospital and the hospital on the south coast where the ambulance West had hijacked had been found.

‘Have there been any sightings since Brighton?’ Chaloner asked.

‘None,’ Barnes answered.

‘But we know the make and model of the car stolen from the hospital grounds around the time West was there,’ Pickett chipped in.

‘Did West force the ambulance driver to take him to Brighton, or did he drive there himself?’ Chaloner looked inquiringly from Simmonds to the police officers.

‘The results of the post mortem have come in. Apparently the driver’s breakfast was fully digested, which suggests he was alive when they reached Brighton,’ Barnes informed him. ‘Forensic are certain he wasn’t moved after he was killed.’

'So, our man drove to Brighton with the paramedic, shot him in the back of his ambulance in the car park, stole another vehicle… '

'Probably,' Barnes concurred. 'There are no witnesses, and nothing on the security cameras to confirm that it was our man who took that car. Ten cars a week disappear from that hospital. It could have been a joyrider.'

'And it could have been him. There've been no sightings of that car since?'

'None.'

'Then we're down to what we know about him.' Chaloner sat behind the larger of the two desks and propped his feet up on the corner.

'West claimed to have been suffering from amnesia,' Simmonds reminded him.

'Do you have any reason to think he was faking?'

'Other than it's an easy condition to fake – no,' Simmonds conceded.

'We have no missing personnel, West's fingerprints aren't on record, and he evaded our search-and-detain parties in the hospital like a professional,' Chaloner picked up a pen and stared at it. 'Do we know if he still has a hostage?'

'There've been no sighting of Dr Santer and we haven't found a body,' Barnes answered.

'There's been no contact?' Chaloner glanced at the array of telephones. 'No ransom demands?'

'No.' Barnes agreed.

'He made no mention of a name – a place – when he was in the hospital?'

The superintendent walked into the office. 'Not that I'm aware of.' He turned to Major Simmonds. 'Didn't you interview him?'

'Briefly, he confirmed our suspicions regarding his military knowledge, nothing more.'

'In that case, gentlemen,' Chaloner tilted the leather chair to a more amenable angle and moved his feet to a more secure position on the desk, 'we have no option but to sit here and wait for a sighting. And, while we wait, we may as well make ourselves comfortable. Do you think we could send out for some food? I, for one, am starving.'

When the Severn Bridge was ten miles behind them, West reached back and pulled away the blanket covering Elizabeth's face. Flicking through the channels on the radio, he stopped when he heard a voice. He glanced at the clock. There would be a news broadcast on the hour.

He continued to drive steadily as if on auto-pilot, rarely allowing his speed to exceed sixty or drop below fifty. At four o'clock when the sky seemed at its darkest a short burst of discordant music prefaced the news. He dropped his speed to forty and listened intently.

'… Known as John West. Six feet four inches, well built, blue eyes, black hair, scar on right leg, right shoulder, left forearm… '

Given the description he wondered if they expected him to run around naked, or were inviting the public to apprehend and undress him. As the newscaster droned on, the short hairs prickled on the back of his neck. '... wanted for questioning in connection with four deaths.'

Four!

'... Believed to be travelling with a female hostage. Five feet eight inches tall with grey eyes, dark hair. Last seen in the Brighton area, possibly heading for one of the sea-ports.'

The newscaster switched to the next topic, details of the funerals of the security personnel killed in the plane crash in Scotland. The news was followed by a discussion between Roman Catholic and Anglican Bishops on whether or not Jesus Christ had advocated celibacy. Flicking through the channels again, West found one that was playing jazz. Turning the sound down low, he switched his headlights to full beam. The road ahead was clear. His lights illuminated an overhead bridge, but no signs. Had he taken a wrong turn? How could he? He'd had no route in mind.

Somehow he knew that one of the most scenic routes to Brecon was via Merthyr; skirting the reservoirs below the Beacons, on the narrow, winding road that went past the Storey Arms – old coaching inn no longer, but Youth Hostel. He also knew that the ancient coaching road, now reduced to a rough track, still struck out along the hillside to the side of the building.

Encouraged by the flash of memory, he turned off the radio and drove on in silence lest Elizabeth wake and hear further mention of the four dead. The last thing he needed was to feed her existing suspicions that he was a cold-blooded murderer.

He saw a turn signposted for Merthyr, and remembering the Storey Arms, took it. At five o'clock, with the wind howling mercilessly down the slopes of the Beacons battering against the car and pelting rain into his windscreen, he passed the old inn. It looked exactly as he'd recalled it in his mind's eye. He even took the risk of pulling into a lay-by beyond it and looking back.

Mist obscured the topmost shadows of the Beacons, yet he could have traced their outline on the back of his hand, so certain was he of their height and shape. To his left he saw the ghostly silver ribbons of a frozen waterfall. Not far now, six miles as the crow flies and a little longer by road through the village of Libanus… he sped on, and there, shining ahead, were the lights of the roundabout marking the entrance to Brecon town.

Disregarding the signs for the bypass, he pulled into a lane beside Brecon golf club. He checked his rear-view mirror and was startled by the sight of Elizabeth sitting upright.

'We're in Brecon,' he told her. 'But I've no intention of untying you, yet. Don't waste any effort trying to attract attention to yourself or the car. There won't be many people around at this time in the morning.'

She stared at him through round, imploring eyes. He turned away from her and reversed the car down the lane. Twin rows of grey-stone houses bordered the road leading into the town. On the right was the site of a centuries-old prison and the boundary wall of a churchyard littered with gravestones. A few gleamed dirty-white in the darkness, and in the centre of the litter of marble and granite stood the church itself, rebuilt by the Victorians – as so many others had been in the area. He knew its name without reading the board. St David's, Llanfaes. Ahead was the bridge that spanned the river Usk. On the far side was the town centre. He dropped his speed. His intention had been to cruise the streets in search of something familiar. But once over the bridge, he swung the steering-wheel sharply to the right, and turned up an alleyway barely wide enough to accommodate the estate car.

Elizabeth continued to sit upright in the back, wondering if he had any idea where he was going. Towering above them, on the left was a solid wall, to the right a lower one but it was still too high to see what was on the other side. A gap appeared in the left wall, she saw a curved wall built from red bricks and a sign, PRIVATE CAR PARK.

West brought the steering wheel down sharply, and drove up a slope into a small yard.

On their right stood the square outline of a building that resembled a Dickensian warehouse, with two wooden doors and a casement window set in the front. The headlights picked out frosted glass in the casement and the outline of a light behind a bell-push. Negotiating slowly and carefully West drove around the side of the building and down another short lane bordered by high walls. He halted in front of a pair of solid-looking wooden doors. After a few moments of hard work with the scalpel he opened them. Returning to the driving seat, he drove the estate car into a large garage.

Elizabeth breathed in slowly and deeply to ward off a panic attack. If he left her here, bound and helpless, without access to food or water, how long would it take her to die? She almost preferred the thought of a bullet.

West left the headlights on, and climbed out of the car. She watched his fingers move over the rough, uneven wall. Digging his fingers around one large stone, he eased it out and plunged his hand into the cavity behind. When he replaced the stone she could see the silver glint of keys in his hand. He slipped them into his pocket. Moving to the rear of the car he opened the tailgate and lifted out the cases.

She continued to sit bolt upright. He disappeared and returned to the car several times removing boxes and suitcases on each trip. Finally, when the car was empty he opened the passenger door and helped her out. Slicing the rope around her ankles, he guided her outside. After locking the garage he led her into the warehouse building. One of the two doors was open, although everything was in darkness.

'There's a steep flight of stairs ahead,' he informed her.

She mounted them slowly. She heard the grate of bolts ramming home, and the click of locks snapping shut as he closed and locked the doors behind them. Taking her arm, he propelled her down a long passage. A window set high on their left shone marginally brighter than the surrounding darkness. He opened a door.

‘Bathroom.’ He switched on the light and cut her bonds. Walking in ahead of her, he pulled a curtain across the window. She noticed that the curtains were thick, almost blackout quality.

He left and she pulled down the hated gag. The area around her mouth was raw. She washed her hands and face. When she came out, she saw that West was holding the gun again. He opened one of the doors set in the corridor behind the bathroom. It was furnished with twin beds, neither made up. He walked across the room and opened another door. A small room, barely larger than a cupboard, housed a single bed, chest of drawers and wardrobe. Opening the wardrobe doors he removed a couple of blankets and a pillow. He threw them to her and left the room. She heard the key turning, and looked around. Apart from a tiny window high above her there was no way out.

She stood on the chest and peered through the glass. An outside light illuminated the top of a wall opposite, but she could see no windows in its blank expanse. Taking the blankets and the pillow she curled up on one of the beds – and slept.

Elizabeth woke feeling dirty, stiff, aching and itching. The rough woollen blanket had irritated her skin. She stretched and shuddered when her naked leg touched the icy mattress. The room was bathed in a soft grey light and it seemed like a long time since she had seen daylight. She left the bed and tried the door handle. It was still locked. She tapped tentatively and waited but there was no answering sound.

A key turned a few minutes later and the door opened. West walked in. He smelled of soap and toothpaste and was wearing a clean pair of jeans and a blue and black check lumberjack shirt.

'Coffee?'

She took the mug he handed her and wrapped both hands around it in an attempt to siphon some of the warmth into her chilled body.

'I've left the suitcase of women's clothes in the bathroom for you.'

'I see you've regained your memory. Tell me, did you ever lose it?'

'I still don't know my name.'

'No?' she mocked sceptically. 'That's why you drove directly to this place and why you knew exactly where to get the key.'

'I have no idea how I knew those things.'

'I'm in desperate need of a bath. And before you say a word, I know you have a gun.' She finished the coffee, handed him the mug and walked towards him. He stepped back to allow her to pass. Entering the bathroom she pulled back the curtain from the window. It was set as high as the one in the room she'd slept in. And, all she could see was another solid wall. Recalling the steep flight of stairs she had climbed the night before, she decided against trying to open it. Later, when she was clean and warm again, she'd think about escaping.

Dressed in jeans that were too large for her, a white cotton shirt and thick Aran sweater, Elizabeth left the bathroom, and made her way past a row of cupboards that lined one side of the long corridor leading to the front of the flat. Two doors faced her at the end of the passageway, both were closed, and when she tried the handles they refused to open. However one door on her left was open. Blissful warmth belched out to greet her when she walked in. An electric heater had been turned full on to warm a large square kitchen, fitted with gleaming black and white units and an enormous black ash table. West was standing in front of an eye-level grill, turning slices of bacon with a fork. Toast popped from a toaster.

'Breakfast?'

She didn't answer, hating the thought of being indebted to him for anything.

'The news will be on in ten minutes. I thought we'd take this into the living room and eat in front of the television.'

On her right was a serving hatch, through its open doors she saw a room furnished in the same harsh masculine style as the kitchen. Grey carpet, black leather suite, black ash storage and display units, and French doors framing an exquisite view of a river wending its way through lush green countryside that somehow managed to look inviting even on a damp November afternoon.

'Aren't you afraid that if I go in there, I'll open those French doors and start shouting for help?'

'All I ask is that you eat this,' he heaped four pieces of bacon and two slices of toast on to a plate, 'and watch the news. If you want to leave afterwards, you can.'

'You mean I can go?' she asked in amazement.

'I mean it.' He pushed the plate into her hand. 'There's frozen butter if you want it. Cut it with the cheese slicer.' He picked up his own plate and went into the living room. She realized she'd been wrong about the door. It had been closed, but not locked. She wondered about the door next to it. The door she presumed led to the stairs and the outside.

The living room was as warm as the kitchen, an electric fan heater, jewelled with fake coals had been turned up to full heat. West laid his plate on a black-tiled coffee table, and flicked through the television channels until he found a twenty-four hour satellite news programme. She gazed around the room, and decided that her first impression had been right. It was definitely a masculine room; not a picture on the wall, not a single photograph, no ornaments, nothing remotely personal in sight. Plain cupboard fronts with small, minimalist handles. Bare shelves. A black-ash sideboard. Grey velvet curtains.

'Who owns this place?' She sat down and sandwiched the bacon between the slices of toast.

'I haven't the faintest idea.'

'You expect me to believe that?'

'Let's listen to the news.'

She sat back and watched the logo of the news channel fill the screen. It faded into the familiar photograph of "John West" a lingering shot of bewildered blue eyes and tousled black hair. A voice-over supplied further details of height and appearance. She looked across to where West was sitting, the food untouched on his lap. The picture dissolved to a studio shot of the newscaster.

'… John West now wanted in connection with four murders… '

She dropped the sandwich back on her plate. She hadn't made a sound but he held up his hand to silence her.

Their food grew cold, congealing in puddles of grease on their plates as photographs of Corporal Summers and Sergeant Manners filled the screen, the voice-over supplying brief outlines of their personal lives, their wives, their children…

Elizabeth's plate clattered to the floor. She stared, horror-struck when a photograph of Dave Watson filled the screen.

'Mr David Watson, consultant psychiatrist in charge of the John West case, was found murdered in the hospital basement yesterday morning. He had not been seen since his registrar, Dr Elizabeth Santer, was taken hostage.'

Dave's photograph was superseded by that of the paramedic West had hijacked to take them to Brighton.

'Matthew Benedict was found dead of a gunshot wound in the back of his own ambulance… '

The final item was a filmed interview at the bedside of the private West had shot in the leg as they'd descended the hospital stairs.

'I'm lucky to be alive… '

'Luck had nothing to do with it,' West said flatly. 'I shot to incapacitate, not kill.' He stooped to pick up Elizabeth's plate, tossed the sandwich back on to it and laid it on the coffee table.

'… but that paramedic was alive when you closed the ambulance doors, I saw his chest moving. And Dave was alive when I left the canteen. I've been with you ever since… '

'Now do you believe I didn't kill those guards?' He dropped his plate on to the table alongside hers, and hobbled over to the French doors. Mist was rising from the river, clouding its banks, and veiling the woods. He tried to imagine the scene as it would be on a fine day. He must have seen it. The river a deep sky-reflective blue, the trees clothed in their summer finery.

He heard her move behind him, sensed her standing close. The tension between them was palpable. He turned to face her. 'I swear I don't know who I am. I only know that someone wants me dead enough to kill everyone I come into contact with. And that means you could be the next victim. I'm sorry; I never intended to endanger your life.'

'You wouldn't have killed me?' she asked quietly.

'Maybe if I had to, in order to survive.'

'You're limping. Your ankle?' she asked remembering the sprain.

'And a bullet graze,' he murmured carelessly.

'I'll see to it.'

'It is just a graze.'

'Which could become infected if it's not cleaned properly. Sit down.' Shell-shocked by the news of Dave, she found it easier to cope with the practical and immediate.

'You should be running as fast and as far away from here and me as you can. But I warn you, after hearing that news it might not be enough to keep you alive.'

'I could stay and try to help you.'

'That could be even more dangerous.' He returned to the sofa, propped his leg on the coffee table and rolled up the bottom of his jeans.

She studied the angry open red scar that was still weeping. 'This needs cleaning and binding.' She opened the door to the kitchen.

He leaned back, pulled out the gun he'd jammed into the waistband of his jeans and set it on the cushion beside him. 'And afterwards?'

She glanced at the gun. 'As you constantly reminded me yesterday, you have a gun.'

'It only has nine bullets.'

'Let's hope no one comes after us with more.'

CHAPTER SEVEN

Ross Chaloner detected Heddingham's presence in the building minutes before the lieutenant-colonel reached the inner sanctum of the Command Cell. There was a sudden drop in the noise level outside the door. The stamp of feet and clicks that accompany a snapping to attention was audible, even above the ring of footsteps over vinyl floors.

Chaloner swung his feet down from the desk, rose and tugged at the bottom of his camouflage jacket. Standing to attention alongside Simmonds, who was mannequin-elegant in the army-civvies uniform of grey trousers, black blazer, white shirt and regimental tie, he felt like a dog-eared, action man.

'Sir.' He saluted in synchronism with Simmonds when Heddingham entered the room.

'At ease.' Heddingham eyed Chaloner as though he'd been expecting something better.

'Chaloner, sir. We met yesterday.'

'Your CO gave you a glowing report. Hope you live up to his judgment.'

'I'll try, sir.'

The colonel sat behind the desk.

'How did the meeting go, sir?' Simmonds asked with all the authority of the second-in-command.

Heddingham ignored the question. 'Have there been any sightings?' he enquired.

'None, sir,' Simmonds replied.

'What have you been doing to earn your keep, Chaloner?'

‘Waiting for information about West’s background and an actual sighting, sir.’

‘Our subject purported to have amnesia, Chaloner. So how do you suggest we acquire that background knowledge?’ Heddingham enquired caustically.

‘I have no idea, sir,’ Chaloner replied blithely.

‘Have you two have been sitting on your arses, the whole time I’ve been in London?’

Simmonds stepped back warily, eyeing the waste-basket that had been mercifully emptied of fast-food wrappings less than half an hour before.

‘Sir,’ Chaloner answered, feeling duty-bound to respond to a superior’s criticism.

Heddingham pursed his lips. ‘I’ve heard rumours about your regiment, Chaloner. Too many chiefs and not enough Indians. Well, you’ve been seconded to the real world now, and I expect the people under me to pull their weight at all times. Understood!’

‘Sir.’

‘I know your type. All action, gung-ho and maverick ideas. You know how to say “sir” and how to make your superiors believe you’re complying with orders, even when you’re not and have no intention of doing so.’

‘Sir,’ Chaloner repeated.

Inspector Barnes rapped on the door and entered accompanied by Pickett. ‘Any news?’

‘Unfortunately not, Barnes,’ Heddingham snapped.

The Inspector closed the door. ‘So our man has gone to ground.’

‘The question is where?’ Chaloner walked to the map.

'Wales.'

'Why Wales, sir?' Chaloner asked Barnes.

'I saw a box of photographs of Welsh towns and cities lying on his bed in the hospital. The ward sister said that Dr Santer was using them to prompt West's memory. It's possible she succeeded, and that's why he went berserk.'

'Pure conjecture,' Heddingham dismissed.

'With respect, we have nothing else to go on, sir,' Chaloner observed.

'Wales covers a lot of ground,' Simmonds chipped in.

'The file relating to Brecon was out of the box,' Barnes perched on the edge of a desk.

'That's interesting,' Chaloner rubbed his chin thoughtfully.

'That he could have connections to Wales?' Barnes asked Chaloner.

'That he might have connections with our home training ground.' Chaloner picked up a stick of blue chalk and drew a circle around the town of Brecon.

'Do you want to move the Command Cell to Brecon, Lieutenant-Colonel?' Barnes asked hopefully. The investigation was playing havoc with his budget and policing schedules.

'Not until we have a definite sighting,' Heddingham declared. 'If we up sticks and move on every whim, we could miss our man completely. It's bad enough to helicopter-hop between here and Whitehall without adding another couple of hundred miles to the journey.'

‘It might be worth alerting 22 SAS Training Wing, Stirling Lines, Hereford, sir.’

‘And no doubt you think you’re just the man to do it, Chaloner. Can’t wait to get home, can you?’ Heddingham sat back in his chair and eyed the captain disparagingly.

‘We have no other leads, sir. If something better should turn up I could be back here in a couple of hours.’

‘I suppose you may as well go,’ Heddingham conceded ungraciously. ‘Get your own regiment to do any donkey work that needs doing, and report to me the instant you discover anything.’

‘Shouldn’t someone go with him, sir?’ Simmonds suggested.

‘Fancy a trip, Simmonds?’

Simmonds found it difficult to ignore his superior’s sarcasm. ‘As a psychiatrist, I hope to be there when West is cornered, sir.’

‘Very well, and take an aide with you.’

‘No need, sir.’ Chaloner picked up his beret. ‘There’s plenty of willing bodies in Stirling Lines.’

‘And no doubt it would delight your CO to hear you making so free with his command. If you find nothing, I’ll expect you both back here by nightfall.’

West and Elizabeth decided to begin their search for clues to his identity in the basement. There was only one window, and as it let in a negligible amount of light, West risked switching on the light. A single, naked bulb hung from the ceiling. The cellar walls were the original stone, the floor paved with cracked and crumbling red quarry tiles.

Elizabeth looked around. 'I wonder what was stored here originally.'

'Nothing. It was a bake-house.'

'Are you sure?'

'Like the route to this place, the key behind the loose stone, and my knowledge of this town, I don't know how I know, but I am sure,' he answered.

The high ceiling was festooned with old Victorian kitchen racks, from which hung the paraphernalia of sporting and outdoor life. Wet and dry suits, motorbike leathers, wax jackets, oilskins, various types of helmets, rucksacks, coils of rope, grappling hooks, ice picks, as well as an enormous collection of odd-shaped tools that might be used for mountaineering or caving.

Below the racks were shelves that housed an array of boots, including motorbike, walking and climbing; tents, groundsheets, kerosene stoves, canoes, engines and inflatable boats.

'There's enough stuff here to equip an outward bound centre,' Elizabeth declared as she checked along the shelves.'

'And two motor-bikes.' West wheeled one out. 'Nothing but the best; a Harley Davison.'

'You know about bikes?'

'Enough to tell you these are scrambling models, built for riding over rough country. Look at the size of the tyres.' Leaving the bike he picked up a claw hammer and prised the front off a wooden case. 'Rifles.' He lifted one out. 'Someone shoots seriously.' He thumbed a box of ammunition in the bottom of the case. Lifting down the largest pair of walking boots, he kicked off a trainer and laced it on. 'It fits.'

'So it's likely some of this equipment is yours.'

'Possibly. But there are no invoices, bills or name tags that I can see.'

'Nor me,' Elizabeth concurred. 'But there might be upstairs.'

They left the cellar by a side door that opened into a small hallway. The stairs rose steeply to their right.

He followed her into the living room after locking all the downstairs doors. They began with the black-ash storage units. While he opened cupboard doors at one end, she searched a bank of drawers at the other. The top drawer contained receipts dating back over five years, all for items of sports equipment and climbing gear. All bore the names of suppliers in South Wales, but none the name of the purchaser. And there were no credit card details. Everything had been bought for cash. The drawer below the receipts held an assortment of felt tip pens and biros. The rest were empty.

West opened a cupboard full of china.

'Expensive.' She lifted out a simple black and white cup. 'Someone has good taste.'

A desk unit contained ordnance-survey maps of the Brecon Beacon area, with cross-country routes highlighted in luminous marker pen. Alongside the maps were a stapler, a stack of envelopes and writing paper and a book of postage stamps. Another cupboard was filled with DVD's, mainly comedy, and action. The cocktail cabinet was stocked with bottles of spirits, including extra-strength navy rum.

She stood back and studied the rest of the room. 'Short of lifting the carpet and looking beneath the floorboards we've checked everything.'

He walked to the window and glanced out at the narrow balcony. A green plastic table and four matching chairs were stacked against the wall. Nothing could possibly be concealed beneath their spindly legs.

'Kitchen?' Elizabeth suggested.

They trawled through cupboards and found saucepans, utensils, cutlery, Formica tablemats, tea towels, cleaning materials, a stock of tinned and dried food, and a freezer filled with convenience packs of ready meals, bread, bacon and butter.

'I wish my kitchen looked like this,' Elizabeth murmured.

'In what way?' he asked.

'Rubbish free. There's not a screwed-up supermarket receipt, no money-off coupons, not a chipped mug in sight. This is colour-supplement living. No one could live in it for long without messing it up.'

They continued their hunt in the floor-to-ceiling cupboards in the passage, searching through piles of pillows, bedding, duvets, blankets and towels, all of which were clean, laundered and neatly folded. They found enough toilet rolls, toothbrushes, toothpaste and soap to last an average family for six months, and supplies of Kendal Mint cake and slabs of hard bitter chocolate that West recognized as hill walkers'survival rations.

Elizabeth moved on to the first bedroom. There were four in all. The one she'd slept in was the smallest, and the only one without direct access to the corridor, opening as it did from the third bedroom. Two rooms had twin beds, one a double, hers a single. Apart from the beds they were all furnished in identical, white bedroom suites. The dressing tables, wardrobes and bedside cabinets were empty apart from anti-moth sachets, hangers and bedding. And in every room, the mattresses were stripped bare beneath the bedcovers. West lifted the covers and heaved the mattresses on to the floor, but still found nothing.

'Looks like a holiday let,' Elizabeth declared finally.

'Holiday let?' he queried.

'An apartment that's regularly rented out. Did you notice there's a separate access to the basement? Where did you find the key to that?'

'Behind the loose brick along with the other keys.'

'The bathroom,' she said suddenly. 'There could be a prescription with a name on.'

The only medicine they found was a chemist's bottle of aspirin. There was also a pack of plasters, a tube of antiseptic cream, a few disposable razors and a deodorant spray.

'Healthy lot,' Elizabeth closed the cabinet door.

'Evidently,' he concurred despondently.

'But we do have something,' she said, in an attempt to lift his spirits.

'What?'

'Remember when I showed you that first photograph of Brecon, you said "Michael". If I start using that name, you might remember more.'

'You didn't see the street sign when we turned in from the main road?'

'No.'

'We're in St Michael Street.'

'Is that it?' Peter Simmonds peered down through the helicopter's rain-speckled windows at a sprawl of low-built buildings set inside a large compound.

'That's it. SAS Regimental HQ, Stirling Lines, Hereford.' Chaloner planted his feet firmly on the floor, bracing himself for touch-down.

'And you're sure your CO will co-operate with us?'

'He will have had the directive by now.'

Simmonds gave him a hard look. 'Both you and I know there's several ways of obeying directives.'

'This is a training centre.' Chaloner gripped the sides of his seat as the helicopter gave a sickening lurch. 'An exercise with a real objective is always better than one without.' The helicopter landed on the pad, he slid back the door and dived out of the cockpit, keeping his head low until he'd cleared the rotor blades. A sergeant with grizzled grey hair showing beneath his beige beret stood outside the nearest building.

'Sir.' He snapped to attention as Chaloner approached.

'You remember Major Simmonds from the hospital?'

'Yes, sir. Welcome to Stirling Lines, sir.'

'How are things, Sergeant Price?' Chaloner asked.

'I dare say they'll be livelier than they have been, now you're here, sir.' The NCO grinned then jerked his head towards the door. 'They're waiting for you inside.'

'We have our manpower?'

'As many trainees as you want. Not that any of them are up to much.'

'You say that every selection training intake.'

'These are a particularly shoddy lot, but what they lack in quality they make up for in quantity. Their prime merit is their expendability. There are plenty more where they came from.' With a sly look at Simmonds, the sergeant glanced at a row of headstones set against the wall of a hut opposite.

Simmonds began reading.

BILLY MISE, HE DIDN'T PRACTISE, HERE HE LIES.

FRANK HOE, FOOLS MAY COME, FOOLS MAY GO, THIS ONE WENT HE WAS TOO SLOW.

'That's my favourite,' Chaloner pointed to one.

UNDER THIS SOD, LIES MORTIMER TODD,
HE PUT HIS TRUST IN A RUSTY ROD.

'I wouldn't have thought this is the best way to boost the morale of candidates,' Simmonds commented.

'They give would-be recruits to the Regiment an indication of the rigours that lie ahead,' Chaloner winked at the sergeant when Simmonds turned away.

Chaloner led the way into the building. Heading purposefully down a long central corridor, he opened a door at the far end. They entered a large conference room, spartanly furnished with standard army-issue grey furniture designed with economy and durability, not comfort, in mind. A dozen officers and senior NCOs were grouped around the table studying an ordnance survey map of Brecon.

'Chaloner.' A man in colonel's uniform nodded to the captain.

'Sir, this is Major Simmonds, psychiatrist.' Chaloner managed to make the last word sound like an insult.

'You think John West could be in our area, Major Simmonds?' The colonel asked.

'It's a long shot, sir, but the only one we have at the moment.'

'We've sent half our men out on hill patrols. We've shown them the man's photograph. If you have anything to add, we can contact them by radio.'

'There's nothing to add,' Chaloner answered. 'But there's a possibility our target might be in Brecon town.'

'We'll set up an urban undercover exercise. You have any more photographs that we can use in the briefings?'

'This is all we have, sir.' Chaloner laid a file on the table.

'We'll brief in five minutes. Send out in thirty.'

Simmonds stared in amazement. He'd never known decisions to be made so quickly.

'You were close to him?'

After their search had ended fruitlessly, and there was nothing to do except sit, think and remember, Elizabeth's tears had begun to fall for Dave Watson – for the shock and trauma of yesterday – even for the loss of her husband Joseph two years before.

She struggled to compose herself. 'I've worked for Dave for three years, long enough to value him as special, both as a man and a doctor. And I feel so desperately sorry for his wife. She's just had twin girls.'

'I'm sorry.'

'It's not your fault. You didn't kill him.' She went to the bathroom, pulled a length of tissue from the roll, wiped her eyes, and blew her nose. When she returned to the living room West was looking through the window.

'I thought I'd recognize something that would trigger total recall.'

'You recognized the road, this flat… '

'But it's not enough.' He turned and faced her. 'Like you said, I feel as though someone has pulled a thick veil over my mind. I can see the shapes, even recognize some of the things beneath the shroud, but I know there's more. A world and a life more, if only I could tear a hole through that veil.'

'I have some experience with cases like yours. Not as much as Dave Watson,' she faltered when she spoke Dave's name, 'But I'm here and prepared to do what I can to help you.'

'I'll make us some more food.' He picked up the plates of cold bacon and toast.

'I'm not hungry.'

'You have to eat. If you don't, you'll be ill, and then you'll be no help to anyone.'

'Appealing to my sense of duty?'

'Old army adage, useful when dealing with stubborn team members, I think,' he added.

'If we wrote down everything that we do know about you, perhaps something other than old army adages might come to mind.'

'You write, I'll grill. Let's go into the kitchen.' He defrosted more bacon in the microwave while she fetched pen and paper from the living room.

She sat at the table and reflected that here, in this high-tech kitchen, he looked normal, civilized, domesticated even – totally different from the wild-eyed, grim-mouthed man who'd abducted her at gunpoint from the hospital. But there was something else… she suddenly realised what it was. He was reaching for things around him as though he'd worked in the kitchen all his life. He was obviously completely at home here.

'On the skills I've exhibited so far, familiarity with weapons, stealing cars, money, food, clothes, would you say I'm a terrorist or a common criminal?'

'Let's begin with the first moment you do remember.' If they'd been in the hospital, she would have tackled his rehabilitation slowly, one step at a time, a few fresh questions every day. And, if those questions hadn't elicited a response, she might have resorted to hypnosis after a week or two. But the announcement of Dave and the paramedic's death had left her with a sense of time running out. Low-key, gentle therapy sessions, spread out over days or even weeks, were a luxury they couldn't afford. Not with four people dead. Who was going to be next? Her or John, or both of them.

'I remember running down the motorway.' The microwave shrilled and John removed the plate that held the pierced packet of bacon. Taking the kitchen scissors, he snipped through the plastic, and laid out the rashers on the grill pan.

'Do you remember being covered in blood?'

'I was cut. There was glass.'

'Most of the blood wasn't yours. You don't remember how it got there?'

'No.' He pushed the pan beneath the grill.

'I could try hypnosis,' she suggested gingerly, not wanting to think about the possible consequences of further trauma.

'Maybe, but after we've eaten.' He lifted two slices of toast from the toaster. 'Good thing about waiting is that the top of the butter is almost soft enough to spread. But I have to warn you, I'm not a good subject for hypnosis.'

'You can't be certain of that.'

'Like I couldn't know how to drive or steal cars?'

'It has to be worth a try.'

'Perhaps.'

'I've used hypnosis successfully with other patients.'

'And I need to prove my innocence, without resorting to weird methods.'

'Hypnosis isn't weird, and for what it's worth I know that you didn't kill Dave or the paramedic.'

'That doesn't mean I haven't killed someone else.'

She didn't dare tell him that three distinct and separate blood groups were found on him including a young child's. 'Have you any recollection of anyone being injured before you were picked up on that motorway?'

'None.'

'You found this place. You knew how to get in. Someone in the town must have seen you before.'

'You suggesting we should take to the streets and ask around with one of the country's biggest manhunts in progress, so whoever wants me dead can get a clear shot.'

'Of course not. But if we disguised ourselves we could walk around to see if you recognize anything else?'

He looked through the window; the sky was darkening again. 'Doesn't it do anything in this damned country except rain?'

'You live abroad?'

'This weather doesn't seem familiar.'

'I could say the same, and I haven't left the country in over two years.'

'I can't go out there with my photograph plastered all over the television, and the newspapers, but maybe you could get away with it.'

'I'm not the one who needs my memory jolted.'

'You could buy some things.'

'What kind of things?' she asked suspiciously.

He thought rapidly. 'Hair dye, tattoo transfers… I'll write a list.'

'And if someone recognizes me?'

'We'll have to make sure they don't.'

'I can hardly camouflage my face.'

'No, but,' he glanced at her bundled into the thick clothes that were several sizes too large. 'You could wear a hooded jacket and we could do something different with your hair.'

'I like my hair the way it is.' She laid a protective hand on her head.

'So do I. But that bun you tie it into is too distinctive.'

'And the hypnosis?' she persisted.

'Can we leave it as a last resort?'

'It might be as well,' she agreed resignedly. 'If I regress you into the trauma that induced you to attempt the four minute mile on that motorway, there's no saying what you'll do.'

'If I am a murderer, I could murder again.'

'Possibly,' she hedged evasively.

A selection of photographs of John West had been blown up on a photocopier, and pinned to a board. An officer standing before them was overlaying the features with sheets of clear perspex on which were sketched various disguises for the benefit of the assembled troops.

'Our man, bald.' John West's head of curly black hair was transformed to gleaming skin. 'With spectacles.' The officer flicked through a dozen pairs – black, horn-rimmed, wire-framed, overlaying them one after another on the bald, balding and full-haired photographs of West. 'Blond, red-head, brown. With beard and moustache, moustache only, beard only, scarred… '

‘He can’t possibly have the resources to alter his looks to that degree,’ Simmonds whispered to Chaloner.

‘Whether he has or he hasn’t, it’s worth covering.’

‘You all have your own photographs of our man. Use them as reference points. If you’re not sure about anyone,’ a major stepped in front of the board, ‘and I mean anyone, contact us immediately. Never forget our target may be a trained terrorist. If he is, he’ll be skilled at making himself invisible. Check out everyone in your frame of vision. Discount no one; not the road sweeper, the youth hosteller, the lager lout, the newspaper boy – no one. Work in pairs. If anyone spots him, make immediate contact giving time and location. If one of you has to leave the location for any reason, the other stays with the target, never taking his or her eyes off him for a moment. You have ten minutes to change into civvies. When you reach the town, disperse. I don’t want any calls complaining about gangs of squaddies cluttering the streets.’

‘You going with them?’ Simmonds asked Chaloner.

‘No. The best place to direct this operation is from here.’

Simmonds studied the stern-faced young men and women as they left the room. Since the day he’d joined the army, he’d been sure of himself and his authority. But these were no ordinary personnel. They were clearly more used to working on their own than obeying orders. And, although he would never have admitted it to Chaloner, he felt threatened by their independence.

West returned to the basement while Elizabeth checked the suitcase again, only to decide she was already wearing the most suitable clothes. West brought up the smallest waterproof jacket he could find on the racks, and also collected the smallest pair of walking boots, and a pair of thick socks. At this time of year, he doubted that anyone would look twice at a girl in a wax jacket and jeans.

'These trainers are like boats,' Elizabeth complained when he joined her in the living room. 'I'll lose them before I go more than three yards.'

'I've brought you the smallest boots and thickest socks I could find.' He placed them at her feet.

She laced the boots on over the socks. 'There's no danger of me losing these.'

'They're too small?'

'Could be I'm just not used to walking boots.'

He handed her the jacket and she slipped it on. The sleeves dangled inches below her hands, and the hem flapped around her thighs like a smock.

'Give me some tent pegs. I'll crouch down and make a marquee,' she joked.

'Pull up the hood.'

'Given public opinion on Hoodies the police might stop me.'

'You're the wrong age. Now all we have to do is cut your hair.'

'Can't I just tie it back? No one will see it under the hood.'

Stepping back he eyed her critically. 'I suppose you could pull it forward and plaster it over your face. I doubt anyone will recognize Dr Elizabeth Santer beneath that scruffy hill walker look.'

'I'll need some money.'

He put his hand in his back pocket, pulled out the wallet, and peeled off five ten-pound notes.

'Where did you get that?'

'Same place I got the clothes and the French food. Turn left when you leave the courtyard and left again when you reach the main road. Walk straight through the traffic lights, and you'll see the shops. There's a Boots and Woolworths. You should find everything on that list in one or the other.'

She hesitated as she took the paper from him. 'I'll be back.'

'I'm relying on it.' His mouth dried at the prospect of her going to the police.

She read the look on his face. 'I'm as interested in seeing an end to this as you are.'

'Let's hope when it comes, it will be an end we can both live through.' He took the keys from his pocket and he unlocked the door at the top of the stairs.

CHAPTER EIGHT

West closed the outside door behind Elizabeth, sat at the foot of the stairs and tried to analyze just why he trusted her. Did she really believe him innocent, not just of killing Dave Watson and the paramedic, but also the two soldiers? Would she return after he'd taken her hostage at gunpoint and carted her half-way across the country bound and gagged on the back seats of various cars?

Perhaps he should make plans now in case she did alert the police and half the army arrived to storm the flat. He looked at the keys in his hand and unlocked the door to the cellar. He lifted a couple of rucksacks from the racks and began to make up a survival kit. Remembering the disguise he had in mind which would enable him to tour the town, he also took down the largest and the smallest sets of motorcycle leathers, boots and helmets. He ferried everything up the stairs.

He carried the largest suit of leathers into the bedroom and tried them on. Both trousers and jacket might have been tailor made for him. Perhaps they had been. After tugging on the boots he pulled the helmet over his face. A perfect disguise for his projected trip around the town, but a biking suit would be no good out on the open mountainside, and he'd already decided that if Elizabeth didn't return, he'd take refuge on the Beacons. He couldn't forget the dead soldiers lying on the floor of his room in the hospital, and he'd prefer to pit his wits and strength against the winter elements on the hills than whoever was after him.

Trying not to think how he'd react if the trip around the town proved as fruitless as the combing of the flat, he returned downstairs and slung thermal blankets, ropes, and sleeping bags into one of the rucksacks. He also selected an ice pick with particularly lethal points. He considered packing a kerosene cooker, but decided it was too bulky to carry. He raided the cupboards in the hall and kitchen and packed tinned food and slabs of chocolate and Kendal cake. He found plastic bags, and matches already packed into a watertight container. He took rolls of plastic sheeting, a tin-opener, a can for heating water, a tin mug and a bowl.

When he tried to quantify what he was doing, he couldn't. But without a past history, instinct was all he had. He was learning to trust it. So far it had kept him alive when several people he had come into contact with were dead. And he hoped it would continue to keep him alive long enough for him to fathom the mystery of who he was.

He packed the food supplies into one rucksack, everything else into the other and left them at the top of the stairs. Then he changed out of the leathers and wandered from room to room. The flat was quiet, still, ominously silent, and he sensed that thick veil clouding his memory again. More strongly than ever he wanted to reach out and tear it down.

He stood in the doorway of the living room, closed his eyes and imagined time tumbling backwards. There had been voices in this room, women's as well as men's, laughter… friendship? Or an exercise in terrorist training?

Turning his back, he stepped over the rucksacks and walked to the two bedrooms at the end of the passage. There was a window in the right hand wall of the first one that looked out over the car park of an office next door. He examined the back wall. It was papered with wood-chip paper and painted with white emulsion. Somehow he knew the paper covered a partition.

Sure enough, when he tapped it with his knuckles it resounded hollowly. It was made of plasterboard he had seen being nailed on to a timber framework and he also knew that behind it lay a doorway that led into an adjoining house that faced the street behind St Michael Street. A house with high-ceilinged rooms and long passages. A house, where there had been a coal-fired range that had heated radiators, a house with green carpets and comfortable, old furniture…

The veil fell, denser and more impenetrable than ever. He went into the living room and opened the cupboard that held the DVD's. They were stored in labelled boxes but one might conceal a home-made disc, one that possibly held a clue… He piled them in front of the TV, turned down the sound and began to slot disc after disc in the machine.

The first batch were all comedy; Fawlty Towers, Blackadder, Monty Python. Then came an assortment of action films with muscle-bound Hollywood heroes doing ridiculous things that must have stretched the skills of their stunt doubles to breaking point.

He smiled, remembering convulsive laughter, then that maddeningly familiar masculine voice again.

"Someone should tell them what it's really like."

Someone should tell them? Who was the someone? He buried his face in his hands, wondering if he'd ever remember.

Head down, hood up against the elements, Elizabeth battled her way to the crossroads, where she waited for a green light. She'd followed John's directions, and found everything just as he'd described. Although it was the tail end of a dismal Monday afternoon, there were several people around. She avoided making eye contact. It wasn't difficult. Everyone seemed intent on their own business.

She found Boots. Picking up a basket she headed straight for the hair dyes and the peroxide John had asked for. She stopped at a rack of tights and knee high socks and bought two pairs of each in the thickest denier she could find. Then on impulse she bought herself face-cream, a skeleton make-up kit, and the smallest bottle of her favourite perfume that they had in stock. She didn't know why she bought them. Maybe something to do with clinging to a semblance of normality, and wanting to look her best even in this bizarre situation.

A young couple were hovering at the jewellery counter when she joined the queue at the checkout. They appeared to be taking a long time to choose an item from the limited range on offer. The man, in particular, appeared to be more interested in the other customers than the display. Resisting the temptation to pull her hood down even further over her head, she totalled the cost of the contents of her basket. John had given her fifty pounds, but he hadn't expected her to spend any of it on herself. Fortunately everything came to just under twenty. She handed two notes over, took the change and the carrier bag the assistant handed her and left the store.

Holding the bag in front of her, she went into Woolworths and bought the tattoo transfers and a darning needle. Wondering what John intended to do with the latter, she paused for a moment to breathe in fresh air. She felt like a paroled prisoner as she revelled in the cool sensation of rain streaming into her eyes and mouth.

She saw a butcher's sign further down the street and recollected John telling her about his favourite meal. Smoked salmon on rye, T bone steak, salad, onion rings and garlic bread. Putting her hand back in the pocket of the wax jacket she retrieved all the money she had left. It should be enough. She went not only to the butcher but also a baker, grocer and greengrocer. She bought one enormous T bone steak, salad, garlic, frozen smoked salmon, onion rings and French bread. But she had to make do with pumpernickel because she couldn't find rye.

Time to go back? She touched her mouth with her fingers. Her lips were still sore from the plaster and gags. At best John was an unstable amnesiac, at worst a psychopathic murderer. Now was her chance to escape. There was a policeman standing on the corner talking to a group of young men. All she had to do was walk up to him and say, "I'm Elizabeth Santer. I know where John West is hiding."

It would be so easy. The police would take John into custody and see that he got the help he needed from another doctor. She would be able to pick up the threads of her life again. Then she saw the board outside the newsagent's.

NATIONWIDE POLICE HUNT FOR KILLER.

There was a rack of newspapers. A tabloid carried a photograph of Dave on its front page. If she went to the police would she end up dead like Dave? It was so bloody unfair. Dave had done nothing – nothing to deserve being killed.

'You all right, Miss?'

She looked at the man standing in front of her.

'Fine. Just faint for a moment.' She clutched the folds of her wax jacket. 'It's the baby kicking.'

His eyes flickered briefly before he moved on. Pulling the newspaper from the rack, she went into the shop and paid for it, barely listening to the assistant's grumbling about thoughtless customers who took display stock instead of papers from the piles inside the door.

When she left the shop she retraced her steps along High Street and into Wheat Street, crossing the road by the Catholic Church. Two men sheltering in the doorway watched her as she rounded the corner into the lane. It was then she saw the name set high on a plaque on the wall, St Michael St. Damn John, even that hadn't led anywhere.

'Can I help you?'

A middle-aged man, wearing a raincoat over a business suit was climbing into a BMW parked alongside the flat.

'No thank you,' she pulled the hood down even further over her eyes.

'This **is** private property.'

She noticed the sign that said PRIVATE PARKING. 'I'm sorry. I didn't mean to walk through your car park.' She backed towards the door of the flat.

'Oh, you're renting the flat.' His tone was distinctly friendlier

'Yes,' she stammered, unable to think of another excuse as to why she should be there.

'Sorry, we're so out the way here I've become wary of strangers. Seeing burglars under the bed as it were. You a friend of Martin?'

'Friend of a friend,' she said quickly.

'I haven't seen him in months. But then that's Martin. Here, there and everywhere, and never anywhere for more than ten minutes. Nice meeting you.'

'And you, goodbye.' She looked at the sign screwed beneath the names at the side of the building. ACCOUNTANT. If only she'd had the courage to ask him a few questions.

She walked up to the door of the old bake-house. It didn't look much from the outside, but she could imagine the advertisement in a holiday brochure.

AN IDEAL WEEKEND AND HOLIDAY RETREAT FOR THE OUTWARD BOUND ENTHUSIAST. Or was it a training centre for terrorists who wanted to exercise on the same terrain as the army's Special Forces?

She rang the bell. For one panic-stricken moment she wondered if West had left, then it swung open. She stepped inside. He was standing behind the door.

'You were a long time.' His voice was harsh, condemnatory.

'I bought food as well the things on your list.'

'There's plenty of food in the freezer.'

'Not smoked salmon, T bone steak, salad, onion rings and garlic bread. Your favourite meal, remember?'

'You were talking to someone.'

'A man in the car park. He works next door.'

'You told him you were staying here.'

'I was standing outside the door. What was I supposed to say? That I'd lost my way?' When he didn't answer, she continued. 'He's an accountant and he drove off after we spoke.'

John would have been more suspicious if he hadn't heard a car pulling away just before he'd opened the door. He stepped back into the small hallway, allowing her to walk up the stairs ahead of him so he could stay behind and lock the doors.

'I don't suppose there's any point in our groping around in the dark, now someone knows that the flat is occupied. But wait until I've pulled the blinds before you switch on the lights.'

She did as he asked, almost falling over the two bulky rucksacks propped outside the kitchen door. She dumped her bags on the kitchen table. 'Why have you brought those packs upstairs?'

'Because we might need them later.'

She tried not to imagine why.

The minister who chaired the meeting in the Cabinet Office briefing room was short and overweight, with the fleshiness that comes from too much of everything – food, good living and sensual pleasures the women who worked for him would rather not imagine. He took his seat at the head of the table. On his right sat personnel from the armed forces – most of them lean, hard and fit, in sharp contrast to the civil servants, senior police officers and Home Office officials sitting opposite them.

The minister wasted no time on preliminaries. 'Anything to report, gentlemen?'

An embarrassed silence settled over the room.

'I take it you are still looking for him.'

'Every available man,' Lieutenant-Colonel Heddingham answered smoothly.

'What I fail to understand is how he escaped the cordon around that hospital.' The minister's brows beetled together and the civil servants squirmed nervously. When the minister was displeased, it made them uneasy – with good cause.

'The man appears to have the security forces in this country, army as well as civilian,' the minister emphasised, wishing to be considered nothing if not even-handed, 'running around in circles.'

'We're looking into the possibility that he might be a terrorist,' a brave Home Office official ventured.

'The possibility?' The minister lowered his voice. 'The man was apprehended forty hours ago, and you're telling me that we still don't know who he is. Have we made any progress at all with identification?'

'I think I can be of assistance on that point, sir.'

'Johnson, anti-terrorist squad,' the minister's PA whispered in his ear.

'You've identified him, Johnson?'

'Not exactly, but we've pin-pointed half-a dozen possible candidates.'

'And?' the minister pressed.

'From the evaluation made by the army psychiatrist who interviewed this John West, we know he speaks English with no discernible accent, that he appears well-educated, possibly public school. But then so do many of the operatives of the international fundamentalist and extremist groups.'

'Are you suggesting he's an Islamic fundamentalist?' the minister asked.

'He could be working for them. The fundamentalist groups do occasionally employ mercenaries. Major Baker is an expert on Middle Eastern terrorist groups, so his ideas on that subject would be more relevant than any speculation on my part.' Having neatly passed the buck, Johnson sat back and tried to make himself invisible.

'Major Baker?'

'The likelihood of a Middle East connection crossed our minds as soon as he was found, minister.'

'I'm glad to hear something did,' the minister interposed sarcastically.

'But the situation may not be as simple as it initially appears. The IRA had many highly trained operatives. The cease-fire created the same problems for them that the cessation of hostilities in World War II did for members of the Resistance. After being trained in espionage, sabotage, undercover work and assassination they found it difficult to adapt to the monotony of civilian life. They continued to crave the excitement, the boost of adrenalin… '

'Is this going anywhere, Major Baker?' the minister demanded coldly.

'We've received confirmation from a reliable source that some of the former operatives of the IRA are now working for other terrorist organisations who are prepared to pay handsomely for men with their skills.'

'So you think our man could be former IRA?'

'It's possible, sir.'

'Could he have been sent to this country to sabotage the conference?'

'Again, it's possible, sir. World peace and a scaling down of armaments wouldn't be in the interests of several arms producing and dealing nations. Including us and the French… '

'But you can't be certain of anything at this point in time and you won't be until we find our man. Can you imagine the lurid headlines if we don't? DELEGATES MURDERED IN LONDON BLOODBATH. BRITAIN UNABLE TO GUARANTEE SECURITY AT CONFERENCE. Gentlemen we look like bloody fools now, don't turn us into the world's laughing stock.'

'Sir,' Baker risked courageously, 'to date we have tracked down fifteen known IRA terrorists, all trained by Arab organisations, whom we suspect of switching allegiance to their former trainers. We're engaged in trying to get a fix on every one of them now.'

'And in the meantime our man has gone to ground.'

'We are following every lead, sir.'

'This is the first I've heard of a lead, Heddingham.'

'We are looking into one or two possibilities, sir. But we have nothing definite as yet. The moment we do, you'll be the first to know.'

When John disappeared into the bathroom with the hair dye and the transfer tattoos, Elizabeth washed and prepared the salad, chopped garlic, mixed it into the butter and filled the French loaf. She battered the steak with a lethal looking metal tenderizer she found in a drawer, and laid it on the grill pan. A search of the freezer yielded a turkey steak which she slid into a frying pan for herself. She laid the table, wrapped the salad in a tea towel and pushed it into the fridge. Placing the onion rings on an oven tray and the smoked salmon on a plate to defrost, she found herself with nothing better to do than watch television.

She switched on the set which was still tuned into the news channel they had watched earlier. The funerals of the plane crash victims and the build-up to the conference due to start in three days took precedence over the manhunt for John West. Speculative questions about her plight as West's hostage were put to the police by a female reporter with an irritatingly, over-sympathetic approach. She could have quite cheerfully kicked her when she thought of her parents and brother.

The interview was followed by photographs of Dave and the paramedic, and an interview with Dave's brother who pleaded with the media to leave his sister-in-law in peace. Tears fell, scalding and bitter from Elizabeth's eyes when recent photographs of Dave and Carol with the twins were flashed on to the screen. She wished she could be with Carol now, to put her arms around her… .

'You should give up watching the news if it upsets you that much.' John was in the doorway.

'My God!'

He had shaved his black curly hair to a skinhead stubble that he had bleached white-blond. He'd even lightened his eyebrows and lashes to match his hair. He was wearing black leather trousers and a black T shirt, torn at the sleeve and across the front to display the realistic looking tattoos she'd bought. And, as though they weren't enough, letters had been scored over his knuckles in black ink, HATE on his left hand, LOVE on his right. A serpent twined down his nose, its tail ending in a silver ring. A skull and crossbones dangled from his right ear, a coffin from the edge of his newly pierced eyebrow.

'Where did you get the jewellery?' she asked.

He fingered his ear. The holes he'd pierced with the darning needle were painful. 'They were in the pocket of one of the leather suits downstairs. Do you think I'll pass muster?'

'No-one,' she turned to his photograph in the newspaper she'd bought, 'is going to connect you, the way you look now, with John West'

'I brought a leather suit up from the cellar for you. It should fit.'

'Is there any hair dye left?'

'Yes,' he crossed the room and touched her long black hair, 'but you're right, it would be a crying shame to do anything to this.'

'It will grow again.'

'It would still be a shame.'

'I'll see what I can do.' She left her chair. 'John, you're taking a risk in going out, you do know that, don't you?'

'I take it you mean a risk aside from the obvious?' he said seriously.

'If your memory returns suddenly there's no predicting how you'll react.'

'But you're prepared to take that risk?'

'I don't see how we have any other option but to run it.'

'Thank you,' he said quietly.

'For what?'

'The "we" and for believing in me.'

'I'm not sure I do, Martin.' She flung the name out casually, watching as he blinked, his eyes irritated by the hair dye. 'Martin?' she repeated. 'You know the name?'

'I do. It's… it's… '

'Yours?' she asked hopefully.

'No, but it's familiar it's… ' Anger and frustration welled to the surface, and he slammed his fist into the door frame. 'Fuck it! I thought I had it, but it's gone. Was Martin a lucky guess?'

'When the man stopped me in the car park he asked if I'd rented the flat from Martin.'

'Did he mention a surname?' he asked hopefully.

'Only Martin.'

West sat on the sofa after she left and continued to watch the news. An interview with America's foreign secretary on what they hoped to achieve in the disarmament summit. A similar interview with the Russian foreign minister and two Arab statesman. The arms summit faded to a news report on the privations being experienced by refugees in various camps in Africa. Then, as a special uplifting seasonal treat, there was a report on the dismal Christmas the London homeless could expect presented by a journalist who was accompanying a Salvation Army worker on a soup run. Having had as much misery as he could take for one day, West turned off the television.

'Am I a suitable partner for a Hell's Angel?'

Elizabeth hadn't dyed her hair, but she'd hacked it just short of shoulder length and spiked it. The leather biking clothes hung loose on her slender frame.

'You'll do. But gold stud earrings don't complement that outfit.'

'You want me to take them out?' She touched the studs superstitiously. They had been the last present Joseph had given her.

'Not yet. I'll see if I can find something more suitable downstairs.'

'Like a lavatory chain?'

'Now that's an idea. And I could paint a tattoo on you.'

'It wouldn't be seen.' She'd zipped her jacket over her shirt.

'It would be, if I drew it on your face.' He traced an imaginary line from her hairline to her chin. She trembled at his touch, hating herself for behaving like a fool. She'd broken every rule of self-preservation and safety that had been drummed into her during her training. Of course John seemed rational and sane at times. All patients had flashes of reasonable, charming behaviour, even sociopaths. But it didn't prevent them from killing when the mood possessed them. She should have run this afternoon when she'd had the chance. Why had she returned only to put herself completely at his mercy, yet again?

'As there have been no other leads or sightings, we've been given another twenty four hours.' Simmonds handed the telephone back to the clerk, and looked at Chaloner who was sitting with his feet up, eating fish and chips with his fingers.

'Very generous of them.'

'Do you think we'll come up with something by then?'

'Impossible to predict.'

The clerk had retreated to the other side of the operations room. Taking advantage of the privacy, Simmonds confronted Chaloner. 'You don't seem to give a damn about anything, Chaloner.'

Chaloner smiled. 'You're wrong, I could give a damn, but,' he broke off a huge piece of battered cod and looked at it, 'I see no sense in expending energy to no good effect. If and when we get a definite sighting, I'll get excited. Not before.' He pushed the fish into his mouth.

'And if we don't?' Simmonds demanded.

'We'll be rested for our next job,' Chaloner answered when his mouth was empty.

John reappeared from the cellar with a selection of gruesome silver ear and nose rings. Elizabeth balked at the idea of him making a hole in her nose with the darning needle, but she removed the gold studs from her ears and replaced them with twin silver coffins.

'They're heavy,' she complained.

'But they add just the right touch. You'll pass, providing no one comes too close.'

'Given the way we look, I can't imagine anyone wanting to.'

'This is a small town.'

'It didn't look that small to me.'

'It's small enough for everyone to know everyone else, and that means they stare at strangers.'

'You might not be a stranger, but then, I doubt anyone will recognize John West in your biker image.'

'But it's not John West we're looking for. It's… '

She watched the frown reappear on his forehead. 'Shall we eat?' She wasn't hungry, but she couldn't bear to see the pain of him trying to remember.

'Later. It may be only half past six, but it's as dark as it's going to get, and too early for the pubs to be crowded.'

'You want to go now?'

'The shops will be closed, the pubs open, and they'll be quiet. I can't think of a better time. Can you?'

'We might be less noticeable if we wait until the pubs get crowded,' she suggested.

'On the other hand if we go now, there'll be less people to notice us.' He picked up the leather jacket and pulled it over his torn T shirt. Taking the keys from his pocket he handed her one of the helmets.

'We're taking the bike?'

'It's one way to see the town, without them seeing us. One head covered with a helmet looks very like another.'

'I hate motor bikes.'

'You ever been on one?' he asked.

'No. Have you? That you can remember?' she challenged.

'Not that I can remember.' He smiled grimly.

'If you think I'm riding pillion on a motorbike with a man who only thinks he might have ridden one before… '

'And to think I had you down as courageous.'

'Where did you get that stupid idea from?'

'From your reaction when I kidnapped you.'

'What happens if we're stopped by the traffic police?' she demanded, mustering every objection she could think of.

'You get three days to produce your papers. A lot can happen in three days.'

'Like you remembering your name?'

'I might strike lucky.' He went into the passage and opened the door to the staircase. 'Ladies first.' Switching off the lights, he locked the door and followed her downstairs. She scrutinised him. She hadn't seen the gun since they'd watched the first news broadcast together, but the jacket he was wearing was loosely cut around the shoulders and across the chest. There was room under his arm for the Browning, and she didn't doubt he was carrying it.

He opened the cellar door and wheeled the bike out into the yard. Leaving the door ajar, he checked there were no lights on in the adjoining offices before sitting astride the saddle and starting the engine. It roared into life at the first touch. He checked the headlight and brake lights before cutting the engine and locking the front door.

'You seriously expect me to get on that thing?' The helmet muffled her voice. He nodded and zipped the apartment keys into one of his pockets. Adjusting his own helmet, he climbed on the bike again and patted the pillion saddle. 'Think of it as a new experience. You may even enjoy it. I'm a careful driver.'

Reluctantly she climbed on the back, locked her hands around his waist and tensed herself. 'Do you want me to sway when you go around corners?' she asked alarmed by the noise when he started the engine again.

'Just sit and hold tight,' he shouted back.

He took the first corner out of the yard into the lane slowly. Increasing his speed he raced up the lane barely pausing at the junction of the main street. Accelerating hard, they roared up Wheat Street in a deafening blast of exhaust noise.

Elizabeth was paralyzed with fear. She hated situations where she wasn't in total and absolute control, and plunging headlong through darkened streets, with only West's body between her, the elements and disaster, embodied all her worst nightmares.

The bike screamed and throbbed beneath them as John raced through green traffic lights and although commonsense told her that the cars alongside them couldn't be travelling at any great speed, she felt as though they were hurtling at hundreds of miles an hour. Raindrops obscured her visor as they tore up High Street, past the shops she had visited earlier. She closed her eyes and clung on as West negotiated corner after corner, turning into street after street. She doubted that he'd be able to recognize anything when he was travelling so fast.

But perhaps he no longer wanted to know who he was? Perhaps he had forgotten everything except the bike and the sensation of speed? And then again perhaps neither of them would be recognized after he'd crashed.

CHAPTER NINE

John didn't need to slow the bike to read the names on the plaques fixed to the walls. He only had to glance at the houses for the name of the street to come to mind, and he found himself navigating the roads by a map that had somehow managed to ingrain itself on to his consciousness. He drove out of High Street, knowing to a split second when the road ceased to be High Street and became The Struet. He glanced up Priory Hill and knew the Cathedral was just up on the right. He could have described the high vaulted ceilings inside the building, the old tombs with their effigies of seventeenth century notables, their faces crumbling, as they lay attired for eternity in stiff folds of marble and stone period dress.

He could have directed a tourist to King Charles' steps. He remembered the good draught beer in the Boars Head; the comfortable surroundings in the Castle, the George and the Wellington; the old world quaintness that still hung over the Sarah Siddons, the pub named after the actress who had been born there.

Then he recalled a pub that had been disparagingly described as the "squaddies haunt" the only one in town that welcomed military personnel. It wasn't a place to take a woman, especially a woman like Elizabeth, but as neither of them was dressed for the George or the Wellington, they may as well go there and see if anything prompted his memory.

Although he'd decided his next move, he was reluctant to relinquish the pleasure of the bike ride.

After being incarcerated first in the hospital, then in cars and the flat, it was good to feel the wind and the rain in his face, and the power of the engine roaring beneath him. For the first time in his short memory he was the one in charge. He'd known he could ride, what he hadn't known was how much he would enjoy the twin sensations of speed and freedom. Savouring every second, he turned up the Watton. Leaving the streets and houses behind, he drove out on to the bypass.

He wanted to see just how fast the bike could go. Elizabeth's hands tightened around his waist, and although he knew she was terrified, the touch of her body behind his felt oddly familiar. The thought of marriage crossed his mind again. Was there a woman waiting for him? A woman who had somehow missed the media coverage of the nationwide search.

She'd have to be brain dead, in captivity, or out of the country not to have seen or heard anything. Surely someone, somewhere had to know who he was? Someone… somewhere…

He circled the roundabout and re-entered the town through Llanfaes. Speeding to the bridge he turned into St Michael Street, finally slowing the bike to a halt outside the old bake-house.

Shaking, grateful that the appalling noise of the engine had finally been silenced, Elizabeth stepped on to the yard.

'That wasn't so terrible, was it?' he teased.

'It was dreadful.' She leaned against the wall and watched him unlock the door to the cellar. 'Did you remember anything?'

'The streets. I could draw you a map of the town.'

'Fine, as long as you sit at a nice quiet, table to do it.'

He wheeled the bike into the cellar, and locked the door.

'We're not going in?'

'Not yet, there's a pub I want to visit.'

'We could have stopped there.'

'I go even faster when I drink and drive.'

'Strange sense of humour you have. Dark, sarcastic.' She took his arm. 'Is it far?'

'Up the lane and across the road. It's the pub servicemen use.'

'And you've been in there?'

'I've been in there,' he echoed.

'Describe it?'

'The building's old. All the downstairs bars have been knocked into one, although at one time it had at least two separate rooms. The door's more or less in the centre of the bar, and there's no passageway, only a small porch. The tables and chairs are dark wood, the cushions covered with faded tapestry. There's a dart board, a pool table, a juke box on the wall and a blackboard on the right hand side with a menu chalked up. There are benches next to some of the tables; the carpet's old and burgundy. If it had a pattern you can't see it now. The door to the Ladies is in the top right hand corner of the bar, and you have to ask for a glass.'

'Ask for a glass?'

'You'll soon find out what I mean.' He crossed the road, pushed open the door and they walked in.

The place was empty apart from the barmaid and three men dressed in overalls covered with paint and plaster. They were sitting on stools at the bar drinking from bottles and Elizabeth realised what John had meant by "asking for a glass." He nodded to the right and she saw the blackboard.

'The window seat,' he muttered.

She walked over to a bench seat set below a window and heard John ask for two lagers in a credible Cockney accent. None of the men at the bar, or the barmaid who was engrossed in conversation with them, gave them a first, let alone a second glance. The place was exactly as John had described, even down to the Ladies door in the top right hand corner of the room, something he wouldn't have known unless he'd brought a woman here.

She wondered if he was married. Not many men of his age – thirty to thirty five – who were tall, dark and head-turning handsome had escaped a woman's clutches. Even if he wasn't with someone now, she was fairly certain from the casual way he treated her, that he had been in a relationship.

He sat beside her, opening the curtains slightly so he could look across the street.

'Someone following us?'

He shook his head and set his helmet next to hers on the table. 'But I've lived in that house.'

A short terrace of four storey Georgian houses bordered the pavement opposite. Further down the street towards the traffic lights and crossroads, was a cinema. Lights blazed above its door, illuminating a poster of a Hollywood hunk with a bare chest posed in kickboxing stance, but no lights illuminated the windows in the houses, and she saw the glint of brass plaques set next to the doors.

'They look like offices.'

'They weren't always. This place is just as I described it, isn't it?'

'Absolutely. But I would say from looking at this room, it hasn't changed in twenty years.' She noticed the juke box on the wall, exactly where he'd said it would be. 'What kind of music do you like?'

'Not the sort that was played on the radio last night.'

'Why don't you go over there and pick something?'

He rose, hesitating when half a dozen men walked in. They were younger than the men sitting at the bar, and their bearing and close cropped hair announced they were military personnel. Out to find him?

He waited until they'd been served before picking up his bottle and crossing the room to the illuminated box that held the list of song titles.

'You have money?' she followed him and fumbled in her pocket for the change from her shopping expedition.

'Yes.' He pulled a selection of coins from his pocket and picked out what he needed.

'Choose any you recognize.'

Slipping the coins through the slot he scanned the list, and punched a series of buttons before returning to the window seat.

'Sit back, close your eyes and allow your mind to go blank,' she instructed.

‘I feel a fool.’

‘Everyone has their back turned to us.’

‘Except the barmaid.’

‘She’s busy serving.’ The opening bars of Unchained Melody filled the air. ‘What can you see?’

‘A film, a pretty girl with dark, close cropped hair… ’

‘The film Ghost. It’s old and not much help, beyond telling me you’re a Demi Moore fan judging by the silly grin on your face.’ She looked around impatiently. ‘Do you think you spent much time here?’

He opened his eyes. ‘Possibly, it’s a useful place within easy staggering distance of the apartment, and they stock good beer.’

‘You come here when?’

He frowned, ‘presumably after I’ve ridden the bike, walked the mountains, wriggled through caves, canoed down the river… ’

‘You’re thinking of the equipment in the flat?’

‘That’s all I’ve bloody well got to go on. I’ve no fucking memory… ’Realising he’d raised his voice and one or two of the younger men were watching him, he finished his lager, pushed his helmet back on to his head and went outside. She followed.

‘John… ’ she placed a restraining hand on his shoulder.

‘Don’t touch me!’ he exclaimed angrily, shrugging off her hand. ‘My name’s not John. Hasn’t it occurred to you, that you could be keeping company with a killer, and that you might be next on my list of victims?’ He crossed the road to the Georgian terrace.

Concerned by his outburst she followed but was careful not to get too close.

'Something's wrong here.' He ran his fingers over the smoothly plastered concrete on the wall. 'There should be another door between these two.' He looked at the doors further along the street. Retracing his steps, he returned to the same window. 'Here. Definitely here.'

'But this window is exactly like the others, it looks as though it's always been here.'

'I'm telling you it should be a door,' he repeated pedantically. 'It opened into a small hall. A flight of stairs opposite led up to a long passage. Turn right and you were in the drawing room, walk straight ahead and you were in a kitchen. There were only two rooms on that first floor, but there were three bedrooms and a bathroom on the floor above. Damn it all, it **was** here.'

She looked carefully. There was a crack in the cement skim at the bottom of the house where the wall met the pavement. She followed the line with her finger. It was there, hair line but definite. She traced it to the top of the window and realised that the decorative coping above that particular window wasn't the same as the others.

'I believe you,' she said softly. She looked around the deserted street. 'Someone must know who lived here.'

'Who do you suggest we ask?' His voice was tinged with bitterness.

'Someone might know in the pub. An old man just went in.'

'You're prepared to risk going back in there?'

'You weren't recognized before, there's no reason to suppose you will be now. Besides, if anyone had any suspicions they'll hardly expect you to walk back in.' Making the decision for him, she crossed the street and opened the door of the pub. This time she went to the bar. Digging in her pocket for money she studied the other customers. The men dressed in working clothes were downing the dregs in their bottles and making bad jokes about nagging wives. The young men in jeans had commandeered the pool table. The barmaid was exchanging banter with them in between serving drinks, but Elizabeth dismissed her as too young to be of any help.

She spotted the old man she had seen in the street. He was sitting in a corner nursing a pint of Guinness, reading a copy of the *Brecon and Radnor Gazette* and soaking up the heat from an electric fire. Momentarily forgetting the coffin earrings, leathers and spiked hair, she walked over to him. He stared at her belligerently over the top of his glass.

'I wonder if you can help me?' she asked, wishing she had a plausible cockney accent like John.

'That depends on what you want?'

'I used to know someone who lived across the road.'

'There are offices across the road.'

'I think he lived in one of the houses before it was converted into offices.'

'How long ago would this be?' He peered up at her through bloodshot eyes.

'I would have been about ten or eleven,' she answered, neatly evading a definite year.

'That must have been before the accountants took over the buildings. They've been offices for the last ten years.'

'More like fifteen, Dai,' a voice chimed from the other end of the bar.

'Aye, aye, Winston, time has a habit of slipping by.'

'What was the name of this friend of yours?' The newcomer was small, wizened, with brown, leathery skin.

'Martin,' Elizabeth answered.

'I don't remember any Martin, but after the old lady died they had families in and out of there every whip stitch. Rented it out to all sorts. They weren't particular, but then what could you expect. They didn't have to live close to them.'

'When was this?' West joined them. He was careful to keep his cockney accent.

'About fifteen years ago, just after the old lady passed on. Her husband was Davies the builder. They lived on the top two floors of the house next door but one to the cinema. He rented the bottom floor even then to the accountants, and kept his building materials and van in the cellar. Not that he was a builder in a big way. More of a jobbing craftsman, if you know what I mean.'

'When did he die?' John tried to sound casual.

'You really are going back some time now. What would you say Winston?'

The old man pulled off his cap and scratched his bald head. 'Must be close on twenty years ago.'

'I'd say more like twenty two or three,' Dai contradicted contrarily.

'Whatever,' Winston dismissed. 'The old lady stayed on. The house was way too big for her but she wouldn't be moved and she wouldn't let anyone help her. None of that meals on wheels or home help. Her son, I think he lived Devon way, came up one day and found her dead on the kitchen floor. But then what do you expect. Old people shouldn't keep themselves to themselves.'

'We'll all know the minute anything happens to you Winston. There'll be more beer than usual in the pump,' Dai laughed.

'Aye, well, when she went, that was the end of people living in this street. The Davies's were the last. But they belonged to the days when business people lived above their shops in the centre of town. Nowadays it's different. People don't want to live in the town any more and see their places wrecked when the Jazz festival starts. Load of riff raff coming in if you ask me… '

'Who's asking you, Winston?' Dai said belligerently.

'I've as much right as the next man to say what I feel… ' Elizabeth had hardly touched her lager but she noticed John had finished his. She'd watched him the whole time the old men had been speaking, but hadn't seen a glimmer of recognition on his face. Only a frown that meant he was trying to remember. If the story of old Mrs Davies who'd lived and died alone in the house across the road, was relevant to him or his family he appeared to be unaware of it.

'… course the old lady didn't have to live there. The old man bought the old bake-house at the back.'

'I didn't know there was a bake-house around here?' Elizabeth didn't dare look at John lest her excitement show.

The two old men stared down at their empty glasses.

'I'll get a round in.' John dug his hand into his pocket. 'Same again?'

'Two pints of Guinness, seeing as how you're offering.'

'And two bottles of lager, please,' John said to the barmaid when she took the empty glasses from the counter.

'Well as I was saying, old man Davies bought the bake-house and converted it into a nice little flat – or so I heard from those that saw it.'

'He moved in there?' Elizabeth asked.

'That was his plan. He got it all ready but up and died just as it was finished. The old lady wouldn't rent it out neither. Got all stubborn about it and insisted on staying on in the house.'

'And the flat?'

'It's a holiday place now. Like everything else around here. Look at the old stables. Beautiful building that was before they pulled it down and built those flats.'

'Go on, Winston, it was falling down,' the barmaid interrupted.

'Falling down maybe, but it could have been saved and there was a lot of history in those walls.'

‘I don’t doubt it,’ she said wryly, ‘but I’ve lived in the town all my life and never spoke to anyone who knew what it was.’

‘Well it should have been done up, kept for tourists… ’

‘The tourists stay in the flats, what more do you want?’ she smiled.

‘The old stables back. What’s the point of putting up flats that no local can afford to buy? The price they were asking was downright criminal,’ Dai retorted.

‘Who in their right senses wants to live in a flat when you can have a nice house with a garden,’ she argued.

‘The flat in the bake-house,’ Elizabeth turned the conversation back. ‘Who lives in it now?’

‘As we said it’s a bloody holiday let,’ Dai cursed.

‘It sounds an interesting place. Who owns it?’

‘One of old Davies’s grandsons.’

‘Nothing to do with old Davies’s family. It was put on the market years back,’ Winston corrected.

‘The estate agent never sold it.’

‘Evans was after it.’

‘Evans never got it.’

John caught Elizabeth’s eye and inclined his head towards the door.

‘Thank you for talking to us,’ Elizabeth abandoned her almost full bottle of lager on the bar. ‘Time we were off?’

‘If we want to make Crickhowell tonight,’ John glanced at his wrist, forgetting that he didn’t have a watch.

‘You staying in Crickhowell?’ Dai asked.

‘With my sister, she’s just moved there,’ Elizabeth added in case the old men knew everyone in the town.’

‘Nothing but bloody strangers and incomers everywhere,’ Winston muttered.

Elizabeth ignored him. She left the pub but couldn’t resist looking back into the bar through the window from the street. Dai had picked up her bottle of lager and was pouring the contents into his own glass. She could almost hear him say.

“Pity to waste it. Don’t know why people pay good money to buy beer they don’t want. No sense, no sense at all.’

‘Anything from the men on the ground?’ Simmonds asked Chaloner when he returned to the operations room after a shower that had done nothing to make him forget his lack of sleep.

‘No. The coffee pot’s full. Help yourself.’

‘Thank you,’ Simmonds replied stiffly. He filled one of the mugs set on a tray next to the pot. ‘Do you think there’s any point in keeping the men out as they’ve found nothing?’

‘Not on the hills,’ Chaloner concurred. ‘We could play hide and seek in the dark for hours and still pass him by. A couple of patrols are on overnights, but I don’t hold any hope of them picking him up. But we’ve left the teams in the town centre. We’ll start calling them in an hour after the pubs close.’

‘Do you really think he’s here?’ Simmonds asked seriously.

‘Your guess is as good as mine. If he’s gone to ground, the chances are we won’t find him, if he’s out and about and on the scrounge for food and shelter we might get lucky.’ The telephone shrilled at his elbow. He picked it up. ‘Chaloner.’

Simmonds sipped his coffee and wished he could listen in on all, not half the conversation. The expression on Chaloner’s face was deadpan, giving absolutely nothing away.

‘I’ll set everything in motion, sir, but shouldn’t we wait for absolute confirmation… No, sir, I am not questioning your authority… The last thing we want to do is upset civilians… I’ll wait, but I’d appreciate more information than you’ve just given me.’

‘A sighting?’ Simmonds asked when Chaloner replaced the receiver.

‘No.’ Chaloner rubbed his chin thoughtfully. ‘Someone in HQ has come up with an address for our man. In the centre of Brecon. They want us to storm the place.’

‘Us? You mean, Special Forces?’

‘I don’t think they were referring to the psychiatric squad.’

Simmonds only just managed to swallow his anger at the jibe. ‘They’ve identified him?’

‘Apparently not. The officer I just spoke to insists they still don’t know who John West is.’

‘Then how did they get the address?’

‘That’s the question I’ll be asking the CO when he arrives.’

* * *

'Where are you going?' Elizabeth asked John as he walked down the street towards the traffic lights.

'To the other entrance to St Michael Street. After asking all those questions about the flat in the pub, we can hardly walk past the Catholic Church.'

'I suppose not.' She wondered, yet again whether John was feigning amnesia. She couldn't imagine anyone, no matter how strong willed, overcoming the distress and disorientation he seemed to have suffered such a short while before, so quickly. He was thinking, planning and scheming – though she hated to admit it – like a terrorist.

He stepped into the shadows at the entrance to the lane and checked the alleyway and the street to make sure no one was watching them before leading the way back to the flat. It was dark below the high wall, the lamps shedding little light that went beyond the bounds of each narrow circle. The creak of his leather boots resounded into the silence as he walked ahead of her. A cat screeched in the back of a cottage garden as they turned left again, into the yard that fronted the flat.

She gazed at the stone facade of the bake-house trying to imagine what it had been like when the town's bread had been baked within its thick walls.

'Where are you going?' she whispered when he walked past the front door and down the side of the building towards the garage.

'To check something.'

'Why?' There was no one in sight yet she felt the need to whisper. He held his finger to his lips and looked up at the bake-house. It wasn't possible to walk around it, because it shared a communal wall with the back of the house built behind it.

He checked the lock on the garage before returning to the front of the flat and opening the cellar door. She walked in. He locked the door behind them before switching on the light and unlocking the door that led to the flat, but he didn't go up straight away. Instead he walked over to the array of protective clothing and equipment.

'Tired of your leather gear?'

'It's bloody tight and uncomfortable.'

'Those boots,' she indicated the walking boots, 'look heavier and even more uncomfortable.'

'Over long distances they'd be like feather beds in comparison to these. You've obviously never done any hill walking.'

'No, and before you say anything, I know you're going to tell me that you have.'

'On so short and acquaintance you know me well.' He switched off the light and followed her out.

Leaving John to secure the locks Elizabeth went into the kitchen. She closed the blinds before switching on the lights and turning on the grill and oven to cook the steak, onion rings and garlic bread. Taking the salad she'd mixed earlier out of the fridge she laid it on the table. She rummaged through the boxes of food and drink John had carried in from the car, found a bottle of red wine and put it on the table. The door opened and John walked in, no longer in leather trousers and jacket, but jeans and black shirt and the trainers he'd found in the suitcase.

'I don't know why anyone would want to pierce their bodies.' He rubbed the bloody spots on his ear lobes and nose.

'Masochism,' she suggested. 'The meal's almost ready. How do you like your steak?'

'Cremated.' He picked up the wine. 'I'm sure we can do better than this?' He went to the box and sifted through all the bottles, reading the labels and slotting them back before coming up with a Spanish Rioja. He opened a drawer and extracted a corkscrew.

'I take it that's better than my choice?' She flipped the turkey steak she'd put in the pan for herself.

'I prefer Spanish red to French, and French white to Spanish. Blast!' He thrust the screw into the cork. 'There I go again. Spouting trivia when I can't remember my own name.'

'We could try hypnosis after we've eaten.'

'You said that could be risky.'

'It could, but we're running out of options.'

He sat at the table and looked up at her. 'If I had murdered someone before I ran down that motorway, and relived that moment, could I lash out and hurt you?'

'We won't know what will happen until we try.' She opened the oven door and checked the garlic bread. 'Is there any salt in that cupboard?'

'Salt and sauce.' He placed both on the table.

'I cook a gourmet meal and you want to smother it in tomato sauce?'

'Not tomato, barbecue.'

'There's a difference?'

'Taste it and see.'

‘I’d rather taste the smoked salmon and pumpernickel. They didn’t have rye,’ she apologized, ferrying the bread and fish to the table.

They ate in silence. Taking the empty plates to the sink, she went to the grill and lifted out the steak. It overflowed the edge of John’s plate, when she set it in front of him. She took her turkey steak and sat facing him.

‘Does this meal remind you of anything?’

‘That I’m hungry. Do you mind if we forget this guessing game for five minutes.’ When she didn’t answer he looked at the table. ‘There are no chips.’

‘You didn’t ask for them.’

‘They’re always a given. I love them.’

‘If I’d known I would have bought some oven chips.’

‘Not frozen chips. They’re an anathema, like plastic cutlery, and paper plates.’

‘They’re the only chips you can cook without a chip pan, and if you’d eaten some of the meals I’ve had to endure in the hospital canteen you’d consider frozen chips a delicacy.’

‘Forget I mentioned chips, the steak is good,’ he complimented, cutting a chunk and forking it to his mouth. She handed him the salad and onion rings and he helped himself. ‘No dressing on the salad.’

‘What’s your favourite?’

‘Oil and vinegar.’

‘There’s a bottle of virgin olive oil in the cupboard.’

‘The question is will it be within date stamp? It never is in this place, because it’s not used often enough.’

She watched him walk to the cupboard, thinking how right he’d been earlier. He could recall so many trivial things. Why couldn’t he remember anything important?

He found the bottle of oil and checked the date. ‘Three weeks to go,’ he declared as he brought it and a bottle of vinegar to the table.

‘How long does virgin olive oil last?’

‘I have no idea. Don’t you cook?’

‘I live alone and working the hours I do I tend to live off take-aways. Do you live alone?’

He halted, a forkful of steak half way to his mouth. ‘I don’t think so. At least, not always.’

‘You have memories of this place with people in it?’

‘Memories or guesswork. It’s obvious from the gear downstairs that it’s used by more than one person.’

‘But it’s not obvious whether they come here as a group or alone.’

‘No, it isn’t.’

She was beginning to feel as frustrated as him, as though the veil they’d spoken about actually existed. That all she had to do was reach out and tear it down for the mystery of his identity to be solved. And, like him, she hoped the solution would be one they could both live with.

She’d worked with a psychopath soon after she’d qualified. An utterly charming, handsome and personable man. It appalled her when the realization finally dawned that he was totally ruthless, manipulative and utterly lacking in conscience. She could still hear her tutor's lecture when she had explained her feelings.

'Why the surprise, Liz? Do you think Jack the Ripper, the Boston Strangler or Peter Sutcliffe had signs around their necks saying "murderer"? With half the local population alerted by serial killings they were still able to persuade their victims to go along with them. They had the gift of charm, and everyone should beware of excessively charming people. They may be making the acquaintance of another Jack the Ripper. To their cost, and his delight.

CHAPTER TEN

John offered to clear up and make coffee after the meal. Sensing that he wanted to be alone, Elizabeth went into the living room. She turned the electric fire on high to combat the sudden drop in temperature and switched on the television. Flicking the buttons on the remote she saw a shot of a West End Cinema. Hoping it meant nothing more serious than a film premiere she sat on the sofa, pushed a cushion into the small of her back and waited to be entertained by glamour and glitz.

She wasn't disappointed. An anchorman in a tuxedo and bow tie was joined by a shivering starlet in a backless, sleeveless, green sequined dress that defied gravity. Both were shouting into the microphone in an attempt to make themselves heard above the noise of a penned in cheering crowd. A line of limousines drew up in front of the cinema entrance and disgorged their occupants.

Celebrities stepped out on to a narrow strip of red carpet, the men darkly handsome in long overcoats, suits and white scarves. The women blue and shivering like the starlet, in dresses that revealed more than they concealed. As the noise of the crowd became more raucous, the anchorman gave up, and the scene faded. It was replaced by a shot of a Norman Castle. A knight in a full suit of armour was striding along the ramparts, calling out to an unseen foe in an East Coast American accent.

John opened the door and brought in a tray of coffee. 'What are you watching?'

'News channel. It's focusing on a film premiere instead of you for a change.'

'Good. Look what I stole?' He produced one of the enormous, thick bars of chocolate they'd found in the cupboard in the corridor.

'I remember, you like dark chocolate.'

'Want a piece?'

'I've never seen that sort before.'

'It's good, try some.'

'Please.' She tried to smile, to pretend that this was just a normal evening, and he was just a friend, but she couldn't still her doubts. Malignant, suffocating, they poisoned her mind until she found herself questioning her own sanity.

He laid the chocolate bar, still in its wrapper over his knees and chopped it, karate style, with the side of his hand. Breaking off a section he handed it to her in the paper.

'I've never seen chocolate as thick as this before.'

'It's not so much chocolate as sustaining rations for mountaineering.' He pushed a piece into his mouth.

She unwrapped the segment he'd given her, and reeled at the high calorific content printed on the paper. It proved impossible to bite, so she pushed the whole square into her mouth. The castle had been superseded by the anchorman again as cheers greeted yet another limousine. The actor who'd been running around the castle in armour emerged from the interior with a willowy, dusky woman on his arm.

She continued to watch the screen, not really taking in anything that was being shown or said.

'Another piece?' he asked.

'No thanks, I haven't finished this one yet. It takes some eating.'

'You don't like it.'

'I think it's an acquired taste.'

The film premiere cut to a studio shot of a newscaster. She was about to change channels when the newscaster was replaced by an interior shot of a Bedouin tent. A group of Arabs were sitting on beautifully woven rugs and cushions in front of a television which looked ludicrous surrounded by the trappings of nomadic life.

'I wonder if they carry that around on a camel,' she murmured.

'More like a four by four these days.'

The Arabs, all men, were talking simultaneously, their words almost, but not quite, drowned out by the voice-over of an interpreter as they discussed the implications of the forthcoming peace and disarmament conference on the Arab nations and Islamic fundamentalist groups.

'Fundamentalists of every creed are the biggest threat to world peace since Hitler,' John declared authoritatively.

'You're interested in politics?'

'And distortion by the media. Look at that silly bugger,' he broke a second piece of chocolate from the bar for himself. 'He's only translating what he, or officialdom wants us to hear. That old Arab sitting in the corner has just said there are only two parties,

God's and the Devil's, and it's plain to see what side he thinks all Westerners are on. Bloody politically correct newsmongers, they lean so far over to give everyone equal opportunities, they make it look as though the fundamentalists are democratic. God help us all if the religious extremists take over any more countries. First thing the bastards do when they're in power is emasculate every other political party, put a stranglehold on freedom of speech and round up every liberal in sight.' He stared at her. 'What's the matter? You disagree… ' he looked back at the television set. Leaning forward he turned up the sound. There was no doubt about it. He could understand every word the Bedouin were saying.

'You're ordering me to storm this flat on the evidence of "information received" yet you won't divulge the source, sir,' Chaloner said evenly to Lieutenant-Colonel Heddingham.

'I am CO of this operation, Chaloner,' Heddingham barked.

'I don't need reminding, sir. Just checking. It will be my men who will carry out the operation.'

'Our information is accurate, Captain Chaloner. That is all you need to know. I am not at liberty to tell you any more than I already have.' The lieutenant-colonel placed a roll of plans and maps on the desk in front of him. 'Muster your men and we'll begin the briefing.' For a single anxious moment he wondered if Chaloner was going to obey him. In all his years in the army he had only heard of one case of insubordination, and he did not want to go down in regimental history as the officer at the receiving end of the next.

Chaloner obeyed because army discipline was ingrained in him, but force of habit and training didn't stop him from silently damning the CO when he rose to his feet, opened the door, and called to his sergeant.

'We know you speak Arabic, German, French, Italian and Spanish.' Elizabeth replaced her coffee cup on the tray. 'I wish I'd travelled more. You might speak Russian, Chinese and Serbo-Croat too.'

'We have no idea how well I speak any of those languages.'

'Only that your knowledge of all of them is a great deal better than mine, and I spent three summers working in Paris perfecting my French accent.'

He looked down at the remains of his coffee. It was cold. 'Do you want more coffee?'

'Yes.' She reined in her irritation with him for seeking refuge in domestic trivia. He picked up their cups and carried them into kitchen. She followed, watching as he poured the dregs down the sink and refilled the coffee pot.

'We've just added knowledge of languages to your list of skills… '

'I want you to promise you'll do something for me,' he interrupted.

'I've already told you that I'll do all I can to help you.'

'I'm leaving first thing in the morning. I want you to stay holed up here for a few days. There's plenty of food in the freezer. You have the television. You can keep up to date with developments. Stay out of sight until… '

'You turn up dead.'

'This is my show, not yours.'

She finally put her greatest fear into words. 'You can't believe you're a terrorist?'

'What do you expect me to believe?' he demanded savagely. 'I'm an expert on small arms, breaking, entering and stealing cars, a linguist, a man who can outwit the police and armed forces – just tell me, who beside a terrorist would need to acquire those particular skills?'

'Someone working for the Intelligence Services?'

'If that was the case, I'd have been hauled in by now.'

'I suggested that to Heddingham and Simmonds, but they insisted they'd checked all the records and no personnel were missing from any of the services.'

'You've proved my point.'

'Only as far as British services are concerned. You could be a member of some other service.'

'What country do you suggest I look at? America, Australia, France, Germany? I rather think the scope is limited by my accent, don't you?'

She recognized despair beneath the sarcasm. 'I think it's time we went into the bedroom.'

'You want to grant a doomed man a last roll in the hay?'

'I want to try hypnosis.'

'And if I try to kill you while I'm under the influence?'

'I can look after myself.' She hoped she sounded more confident than she felt.

'I'm not a good subject for hypnosis.'

'It's all we have left to try.'

'Aren't you being rather foolish to take the risk?'

'Not if you give me your gun.'

'Now that's an idea, if I come up with bad news you can shoot me.'

'I couldn't squash a worm much less kill a man.'

'You'd be surprised what you're capable of, if you're pushed into a tight corner.'

She took a deep breath and braced herself. 'Did someone push you into a tight corner?'

He lifted his shirt and produced the gun from his trouser waistband. 'I'll go into the bedroom. Put it somewhere where I can't get hold of it.'

He walked down the corridor and opened the door of the bedroom he'd slept in. Sometime, probably when he'd been changing, she'd made up one of the single beds with clean sheets, pillowcases and a duvet. He stepped back to the double bedroom. She'd made up the bed in there too.

'Which bedroom are you sleeping in?'

'The one with the single bed,' she replied.

'Good idea, it's further back, safer, more secure.' He sat on the double bed. 'What do I do now?'

'Lie down, relax.' She joined him.

'On the bed?'

'People do it every night.'

'I'd feel vulnerable.'

'You can't always be in control.'

'I warn you I'm not a good subject for hypnosis.'

'So you keep telling me.' She drew strength from her professionalism.

He took the keys from his jeans pocket and handed them to her before kicking his shoes off, and his legs up on to the bed. 'If I go crazy, lock me in here, run downstairs and bolt yourself into the cellar. Or even better, take the bike and get the hell out of here.'

She slotted the keys into the lock on the outside of the door. 'Now relax. Nothing is going to happen… '

'I hope something is.' He locked his hands behind his head.

'Place your hands by your sides.' For the first time she saw fear etched in his eyes. 'I'm not threatening you, just trying to create a safe, sheltered, secure environment.'

'I feel like I'm about to be caged.'

She looked at his shoes on the floor. 'Console yourself with the thought that you were brought up properly.'

He glanced at her quizzically.

'No shoes on the bed.' Having finally succeeded in diverting his attention, she began. 'Sink your head down deep into the pillows, push the palms of your hands against the mattress and relax.'

'I need half a bottle of brandy, not a couple of glasses of wine and a cup of coffee inside me before I do this.'

'You're doing just fine. Close your eyes. Relax… Relax… Relax… ' She didn't take her eyes off him for an instant as she slipped into the familiar routine. But no matter how slowly she spoke, or how soothing the tone, he persisted in lying rigid, every muscle in his face and body tensed. She debated whether to linger over the introduction before deciding to proceed in the hope that he would become more responsive with fewer interruptions. '… you're standing in front of a door… the front door to a house… ' Normally she suggested patients visualize their own front doors, but she made the reference to the door deliberately vague, forestalling any comment from him that would destroy what little progress she had made.

'… you're standing in front of the door… you're holding the key in your hand… you're moving towards the door with the key in your hand… slip the key into the lock… push it in gently… quietly… there is no noise… none at all… ' she continued to watch him. He was beginning to relax; the gain was slow but perceptible. '… the key glides smoothly into the lock… it fits… you are turning it slowly… feel the key turning… ' he was quiet, apparently restful but she sensed he was still fighting her.

'… now you are floating… floating gently upwards… ever upwards… the sky is light blue… there are a few clouds… soft white billowing clouds… you are floating among them… they are soft… downy and warm… you are floating through them now… rising above them… you are warm… warm and comfortable… totally relaxed… so relaxed… slipping gently down among the clouds… relax… '

She saw his muscles finally loosen. '… float… floating backwards… hours are floating past you… a day is floating past… let it go… let the hours pass…

float backwards… time is flowing gently past… and another day… release it… allow it to pass and float… float… floating… '

It took twenty minutes of soft, rhythmic chanting before Elizabeth felt confident enough to move on to the third stage. Shoulders tensed, fingers closed into fists she turned slightly to check the key was still in the outer lock of the door. If John became violent, all she had to do was dive out, slam the door and turn it.

But what would she do if he smashed the door down? It looked flimsy. Pushing the thought from her mind, she concentrated hard

'… the air is moving… flowing… and with the flow we are floating back in time… the clouds are getting heavier… you are drifting… drifting downwards… '

He thrashed uneasily on the bed.

'What are you doing?'

'Running.'

'To where?' She wished she had a name she could use. Something other than the anonymous John.

'Don't know. Have to run… faster… faster… ' his voice grew faint and he drew in great gulps of air.

'Who are you running from?' She asked quietly, at this crucial stage it would take very little to break the hypnosis. 'Who are you running from,' she repeated slowly.

'Don't know.' His body continued to thrash uncontrollably from side to side.

'We'll drift back up to the clouds… you are floating among them again… time is flowing past… just an hour further… the clouds are drifting… the hour has slipped past… you are floating downwards again… '

His movements became wilder, more agitated. Then he screamed hideously. The blood froze in her veins.

'In God's name no!' His screams turned to harsh rasping sobs, agonizing in their intensity.

'John?' she called out swiftly. Unable to bear his suffering she fought to bring him out of the trance.

He opened his eyes and stared at her.

'Where are you?'

He remained still.

'Where are you?' she repeated urgently.

'Lying on a bed in a flat in Brecon.'

She breathed out in relief. 'John…'

'That's not my name.'

'What can you remember?'

He sat up, his movements jerky, stiff like those of an arthritic old man. 'Pain,' he murmured. 'Excruciating pain. I never want to feel anything like that again. Did I say something?'

'Nothing new. You talked about running, but you didn't know to where, or who from. I think you returned to the time you were found on the motorway. When I tried to take you further back you became hysterical. I agree, you're not a good subject for hypnosis.'

He sat on the edge of the bed, swung his legs to the floor, bent his head forward and rubbed the back of his neck.

'We might have done better if I had your name.'

'Sorry, I can't supply it.' Rising to his feet he stretched his limbs. They ached as though he'd just raced a marathon. 'I didn't say anything else?'

'I only wish you had. You remember nothing?'

'A hand holding a gun, a Browning fitted with a silencer.'

'Was it your hand?'

'No. There was a scar on the thumb. A puckered scar with small red lines leading away from it, like a centipede. You're the psychiatrist, where do we go from here?'

She recalled his distress. How his torment had terrified her. 'I don't think we should try hypnosis again for a while.'

He sank down on the edge of the bed again. 'I honestly believed that once I reached here I'd find the answers. That I'd discover who I was, and what had happened. That I'd be able to do something… '

'Something?' she prompted when he fell silent.

'People are dead because of me.'

'That's ridiculous! You didn't kill Dave or that ambulance driver.'

He looked into her eyes. 'Did I kill the guards outside my room?'

She threw the question back at him. 'Did you?'

'If I did, I have no memory of it, but then I have precious few memories of anything, including how I became covered in blood before I was found on that motorway.' He lashed out, slamming his fist into the wall behind the bed. She watched an angry red stain spread beneath the skin across his knuckles. 'I don't know anything… '

She left her chair and crouched on the floor in front of him. 'You will remember. When you least expect it, everything will come back.'

'Unless the trauma of whatever caused me to lose my memory is so great, it permanently blocks my past.' He slipped his fingers beneath her chin, lifted her face and looked into her eyes. 'I am right, aren't I? It can happen that way.'

'You're only partially right. You might succeed in permanently blocking the trauma, whatever it is. But the chances are that sooner or later you'll recall who you are, and some aspects of your life before the incident that brought on the amnesia.'

'I want to believe you.' He was suddenly conscious of her not as a psychiatrist, but a woman. Since the moment he had been picked up on the motorway he had been obsessed with the burning question of his identity. There had been no time to think of anything other than who he was, and how he could stay one step ahead of whoever wanted him dead. But when he looked into Elizabeth's eyes he realized that there was more to life than mere survival.

Clasping her in his arms he pulled her towards him. She laid her head against his shoulder. He revelled in the feel of her skin beneath his fingertips, the warmth of her body against his. The clean, fresh smell of her hair. He touched her lightly, tenderly. His lips sought hers.

She closed her eyes. It had been such a long time since a man had held her in his arms. Over two years since Joseph had walked out through door one morning, never to return. She clung to John, wanting him as she had never thought she would want any man again, but when his hand travelled to the back of her neck and his kisses became more urgent, more demanding, a wave of cold, hard logic doused all emotion. Pushing him away she fell backwards and scrambled to her feet in the doorway.

'No!'

All pretence of tenderness died. His blue eyes turned to steel. 'Because I'm a murderer?'

'Because you're my patient. Can't you see what's happening here? We've been thrown together under impossible circumstances. We don't even know if we're going to be alive tomorrow. There's no one else around, so we're grasping at anything that makes us feel remotely human, simply because we need contact and compassion.'

'Hasn't it occurred to you, that this may be all the contact and compassion we'll ever get?'

'We're not going to die,' she insisted with more conviction than she felt.

'Elizabeth…'

'No.' She backed out. 'I can't help you, not this way. It would be wrong, especially as you don't even know who you are. You could be married. You could have children and a wife. A wife you love and adore. And in the next minute – the next hour – tomorrow – whenever your memory returns, you'll end up hating me if we do this.'

'I could never hate you.' He left the bed and walked towards her. She stepped back to the bathroom door and opened it.

‘I’m going to have a bath, and then I’m going to bed in that bedroom,’ she pointed to the room with the single bed. ‘I want you to leave the key in the inside of the door, and I suggest you get some rest in the other room.’ She retreated inside, slammed and locked the door.

He heard the key turning. Leaving the bedroom, he switched off the light and went into the living room. He cleared their coffee cups and straightened the cushions on the chairs. When the room was restored to its arid, soulless state, he switched off the light and opened the curtains. Resisting the temptation to look at the river he went into the kitchen, closed the serving hatch and washed their coffee cups, before putting them away in the cupboard. It took so little effort to keep the flat immaculate. There was no clutter – what kind of clutter?

He closed his eyes and saw suitcases overflowing with clothes, books, newspapers, bottles of whisky and glasses, plates filled with crumbs – toys – he thought he could see a giant pink hippopotamus soaked in blood. Was that the result of his imagination? Or hypnosis dragging some ghastly reality from the damaged recesses of his mind?

From the back of the apartment he heard the sound of water running. The bathroom door opened and closed. He heard footsteps cross the corridor and a key turn in a lock. Elizabeth had locked herself into the bedroom.

He walked through the flat turning off all the lights. Pausing for a moment in the bathroom he breathed in the warm, humid, soapy scent that lingered in the air. When his eyes became accustomed to the darkness he returned to the living room and walked to the window.

The lights on the promenade were shining, misty circles blurred by rain. A delicate, silent drizzle dropped isolated islands of water beads on the window pane, beads that melted into sudden, spasmodic streams when they became too heavy to cling to the glass. He remained there for a long time, watching the raindrops move with strange peculiar lives of their own – and thinking.

He'd known about the promenade before he'd driven into Brecon. He'd obviously spent time in this flat. He knew every piece of furniture, where everything was kept, which kitchen drawer to open for spoons, which cupboard the plates were kept in, which door to open for cleaning materials. Had he furnished the place or had someone else? Was this stark austere style and colour choice his? What was the purpose of this apartment? Had it ever been a home, or was it as Elizabeth had suggested and the old man in the pub had said, a holiday flat, or was there some other, more sinister purpose behind its existence?

Did it provide a cover for terrorists while they trained on the Beacons? That would explain the proliferation of no expense spared equipment in the cellar. Aids that would help operatives acquire and hone the same skills and survival techniques that had turned the British Special Forces into the finest assault troops in the world.

When the hands on the clock pointed to two he went into the double bedroom and threw himself down, fully dressed on the bed. But no matter how often or tightly he closed his eyes, sleep evaded him. He had a sudden craving for a cigarette. He could almost taste strong Turkish tobacco and that unnerved him even more than his knowledge of guns. No self-respecting soldier would smoke. Smoking was unhealthy. It slowed performance and clogged the lungs and arteries with filth.

Perhaps he should stop trying to think like a British officer, and concentrate on the thought patterns of a terrorist. What did he know about terrorists? They spoke Arabic, like him. They had a working knowledge of enough European languages to enable them to move easily around the globe. They had an exhaustive knowledge of small arms – they were trained to kill – he had been found covered in someone else's blood –

Once again he smelled the metallic odour, and felt the thick, sticky cloying gore on his chest. He was a terrorist. It was the most logical explanation. He could hardly be a member of the security forces when his face was plastered everywhere and no one had recognized him.

He should leave now. Slip away from Elizabeth. Steal another car – and then? He left the bed. It was useless trying to sleep while his mind was this active. He walked down the corridor, went into the kitchen and filled the kettle without bothering to switch on the light. He looked down at the empty car park below. A shadow moved. Then he heard it, the unmistakeable clink of metal grating over stone.

CHAPTER ELEVEN

John raced down the corridor to Elizabeth's bedroom. He tried the door only to recall she'd locked it. He put his shoulder against it and pushed. The wood holding the lock splintered and gave way.

She sat up in bed.

'There's no time. Dress, stay here and wait for me. Don't switch the lights on. Where's the gun?'

'In the oven… '

'Stay here.' He hurtled down the passage. Trust a woman to put a bloody gun in an oven. He hoped grease hadn't fouled the mechanism. Lifting out the baking tins he extracted it carefully, barrel foremost. He pushed it into the waistband of his jeans, picked up the rucksacks, walking boots and pickaxe from the corridor and dived into the back bedroom.

Was it his imagination, or was there noise on the balcony as well as the roof? Sliding his feet into the walking boots he swung the axe into the partition wall. It split beneath the weight of the head. One more blow and he was through.

'What's happened?' Elizabeth was at his side, dressed in a sweatshirt, jeans and the ridiculous biker's boots. He checked the size of the hole he'd made in the plasterboard. If he dragged the pickaxe downwards he would create a gap large enough for them to crawl through, but he'd have to be careful to keep noise to a minimum.

'Get the wax jacket you wore earlier and the walking boots.'

‘We’re leaving?’

‘Just do it,’ he hissed. He hit the wall again. He’d fought through to the other side by the time she reappeared with the jacket over her arm. He only hoped they’d find somewhere other than the mountains to hide. Dressed like this, they’d soon freeze to death.

John was helping Elizabeth through the wall when the sound of shattering glass echoed from the living room. He followed her in, leaned out, grabbed the empty wardrobe and pulled it over the hole he’d made. It wouldn’t fool anyone for long, but it might give them a few minutes grace. He stepped back alongside her into icy and absolute darkness.

‘Where are we?’ she whispered.

‘A back room in the house opposite the pub that we looked at earlier. Keep hold of my hand.’ He inched forward, sensing that they were in the old kitchen he’d remembered. He felt his way along the right hand wall, stumbling over a desk and chair before he reached the door. His hand closed over a door knob, pulling it inwards, he opened the door. ‘We’re about to go down a long passage,’ he whispered.

‘There’s a dim light at the end.’

‘Street light shining through a window.’ He stole forward, keeping her behind him. The light was coming through the open door of what he remembered as a drawing room. Keeping tight to the wall he went in and edged close to the glass. The street below was filled with army and police vehicles, their emergency lights flashing.

'You think all that is for us?' she whispered.

'I don't think they're having a quiet drink across the road. Keep hold of my hand and follow me.'

She did as he ordered, because it was easier to obey him than make any decisions of her own. They left the office and crept down the stairs into a small hallway. The upper part of the door that opened on to the street was panelled with etched glass, and the glare of headlights flooded through, illuminating the area. Ducking below the panels, John pulled Elizabeth down with him. Crouching on all fours he opened doors that led into offices on their right and left. Any thoughts he'd had of shooting his way out, died when he studied the strength of the force that surrounded them.

Troops armed with rifles and machine guns, Land Rovers, lorries, and jeeps completely blocked the narrow road. Searchlights had been set up, bathing the street and the inside of both offices in a bright, daylight glow.

He looked into the room on their right. There were two desks, their backs separated by a screen partition. Dragging Elizabeth behind him, he slithered over the floor beneath the desk on the opposite side of the screen to the door. Beside them was the reassuringly comforting bulk of a metal filling cabinet, just the thing to stop a bullet.

John listened to Elizabeth's breathing and sensed her fear. There was a pile of white, A3 sized paper on a computer trolley. He was tempted to pick up a sheet, smash the window and wave it. Then he remembered the consultant, Dave Watson, the two dead soldiers and the paramedic. How long would Elizabeth survive in that street with all that hardware pointed at her? Not long. Not long at all.

Chaloner had misgivings about the source of the intelligence that had prompted Heddingham to give the command to storm the flat, but he had no misgivings about his men. He would have, and frequently had, trusted them with his life. He stood out of sight of the bake-house windows, behind a wall, watching the shadowy figures of his squad crawl over the roof. Each man was dressed in flame retardant suits and respirators that made them look more like alien extras from a film set than special service operatives.

He waited until the two men detailed to break through the balcony doors were in position before moving to the front door. His partner followed. Every window and exit in the building was covered. He pressed the button to illuminate his watch. Uncertain whether or not there was a radio receiver inside the apartment, he'd insisted on maintaining radio silence until the operation was underway.

'Four – Three – Two – One – '

The crash of breaking glass rang through the rain-sodden night air as half a dozen windows were simultaneously sledge-hammered. He stood guard, gun primed when his own partner smashed down the cellar door.

Throwing a CS grenade in ahead of them, they negotiated the stoop into the cellar. Chaloner concentrated solely on his partner and the area designated to be searched by them. The plan had been discussed, approved and assigned. All that was left for him to do was carry out the task allotted to him to the best of his ability. His men were trained to work in pairs, and he was no exception.

They had all memorized the layout of the apartment. First they would carefully and methodically clear their apportioned areas. When the sweep and search was completed he trusted that West would be cornered, hopefully with his hostage still breathing. It was the plight of the hostage that had given rise to Chaloner's misgivings about the operation.

He'd tried to explain to Heddingham that sweep and search operations couldn't be rushed. That speed cost lives. That for their own and the hostage's sake, his men had to ensure each area was clear before moving on to the next, and that would alert their target, and give him ample opportunity to "neutralise" Elizabeth Santer. But Heddingham had refused to be swayed by his argument.

'Living room clear.' The message crackled over his receiver when radio silence was lifted.

'Bedroom one clear.'

'Kitchen clear.'

'Bathroom clear.'

'Corridor and cupboards clear.'

'Cellar and stairs clear,' he replied as he and his partner swept around the cellar and up the stairs.

'Bedroom three and four clear. Hole in back wall of three. Could be suspect escaped.'

'Bedroom two?' he demanded.

‘Clear, sir.’

He visualized the plan of the apartment as he walked up the stairs and down the corridor. Keeping his sights wide and his Heckler and Koch at the ready, he found everything just as his men had reported. The apartment was empty, a lethally sharp ice pick abandoned behind a hole in the end wall, evidence as to where their prey had bolted.

Chaloner hesitated. They had studied the plans of the apartment, no others. He hadn’t been aware that the wall between the apartment and the house that fronted it was a partition. He marshalled his thoughts, remembering the army maxim, “Any decision is better than no decision at all.”

‘Team one, follow CS gas grenades in. Sweep the first room. No further until you receive orders.’

Elizabeth cowered beside John scarcely daring to breathe lest the sound alert someone to their presence. His face, sallow-skinned and hollow-eyed in the glow of the street lights that shone through the office window, resembled a death’s head. Outside she could hear shouts, footsteps running, and from somewhere behind them, crashes as the men who had entered the flat tore down what remained of the panelling that separated the two houses.

She was terrified, yet somewhere deep within, a calm and ordered oasis remained providing a retreat that enabled her to divorce herself from both situation, and surroundings. Death was too big, too enormous a concept for her to consider while she remained hunched beneath a desk. Her mind turned to other problems.

John had to be more than just a casual visitor to the flat. No holidaymaker would have known about the flimsiness of the partition between the adjoining houses. He must have lived there at some time, possibly even during the conversion. She wished she'd asked the old men in the pub more questions. Perhaps she should have called John "Davies" when he'd been under hypnosis. He could be related to the old woman who had once owned the place or perhaps he'd bought it from her heirs and they'd told him about the plaster boarded doorway.

John was listening intently but he didn't hear the footstep on the stairs. Rubber soled boots don't make much noise. But he did hear the creak of wood when the advance party descended to the ground floor. He looked to the door knowing he'd see their shadows first, one covering, one entering. That was the drill, work in pairs, each watching out for the other – but first the stun and CS gas grenades.

As he and Elizabeth didn't have respirators, he had to prevent the grenades from being fired into the room. He slid out from beneath the desk and crawled to the open door. Taking the Browning in both hands he lay low, peering through a crack in the hinges. He could see the men's shadows in the hall. Two open doors posed a difficult choice for them; the wrong one might mean getting caught in an ambush.

The shadows moved and so did he. His plan gave him and Elizabeth no more than a slim chance, but a slim chance had to be better than no chance at all. He had time to register the Heckler and Koch sub-machine guns before thought failed and instinct prevailed.

Both men did what he'd expected them to. Stand back to back, each facing an office doorway. Thrusting their weight forward on their right legs, they were poised to fire in the stun and CS grenades, but he fired first. Not at the impenetrable body armour but their arms. There was a short lived scream as their guns fell to the floor but not before a grenade had been fired. Holding his breath, he lunged forward. Rolling over, he tore the respirator from the man nearest to him. Gas poured out of the grenade. Lungs bursting, John clamped his hand over the head of the soldier before dragging him back into the office. Slamming the door he pushed a desk against it. Pausing only to slip on the respirator he grabbed the man's radio and shouted.

'Critical hostage situation. Keep back until secured.' Stuffing his fist into the man's mouth he pressed on his neck until he slumped unconscious.

Footsteps pounded down the stairs. Taking the Heckler and Koch he laid it on the desk and stripped off the soldier's body armour, flame retardant suit and shoes. He dressed quickly. Elizabeth was already coughing from the gas seeping under the door.

He caught hold of her. 'Scream!'

She barely managed a whimper.

'Louder!' he urged. 'Keep back,' he shouted into the radio receiver. 'Going after female hostage.'

Elizabeth screamed again, more convincingly this time. John checked the Heckler and Koch and the spare ammunition in the leg pockets of the flame retardant suit. Adjusting the respirator, gloves and boots, he thrust the soldier's Browning into the holster on the suit, and fired the other at the wall, following the shot with a quick burst of gunfire from the sub machine gun.

A hole was blasted in the door, a gas grenade exploded at his feet. Picking up a chair he flung it through the window. His radio crackled, and he pressed the transmission button.

'Exiting into Wheat Street with hostage. Repeat exiting into Wheat Street with hostage. Suspect in possession of second hostage in right front office, proceed with caution.'

Snatching a metal disk box from the desk he pushed it and the spare Browning beneath Elizabeth's sweatshirt before swinging her high into his arms and stepping through the broken window out on to the street.

'Hold fire. Keep back. Booby trapped hostage.' He yelled. 'Bomb secured to hostage's body. Suspect armed in office.' He waited for an answering shout before walking towards an ambulance. Like an ebbing tide, troops flowed back into the side streets before him. He could scarcely believe it. The ploy was working. It was actually working.

A man ran towards him. 'Back!' he ordered brusquely, heading resolutely for the ambulance parked beyond the barrage of lights.

'Bomb squad.' A soldier shielded behind a full suit of body armour stepped forward.

'My hand's on the device. I move it, she blows.'

The officer shouted, 'clear area.'

Troops and police continued to fall back as John, carrying Elizabeth, and the bomb squad officer made their way steadily towards the ambulance. John heard shots echoing from the office behind them but maintained his pace. The bomb disposal officer reached the ambulance first and opened the doors.

John climbed into the back with Elizabeth.

'Have we time to get out of town?' the officer asked.

'As long as my hand stays where it is.' The driver started the engine and the siren. John glanced down at Elizabeth who was lying in his arms with her eyes screwed shut. 'Drive steady,' John ordered as the officer climbed in alongside him.

John assessed the arms the officer was carrying. He could see a handgun, nothing more, but the body armour might present a problem. The driver appeared to be unarmed but he wouldn't take that for granted.

He waited until the officer closed the doors and the ambulance was up to speed before seizing the officer's handgun and throwing it behind him.

'What do you think you're doing?' The man tried to look into John's eyes beneath the infra red lens on the respirator. The driver turned and looked at them.

'You want her to live, keep moving,' John ordered the driver, digging the Browning into Elizabeth's neck. 'And keep that siren on.'

The driver and the officer both stared at Elizabeth who kept her eyes closed. The driver turned back, pressed his foot down on the accelerator and roared through Llanfaes on to the open road.

‘Head for Prince Charles Hospital,’ John shouted to make himself heard above the siren.

‘You’ll never get away with this,’ the officer warned when they took the Merthyr Road.

John ignored him. Special Forces personnel were renowned for being proactive, but the paramount concern in a hostage situation was the safety of the person or persons being held. Keeping the gun pressed to Elizabeth’s neck he reached out with his free hand and unhooked the radio receiver from the dashboard.

‘Tell them you’re going to the Prince Charles hospital in Merthyr.’

‘Is there a bomb strapped to her?’ the driver asked.

‘If you don’t radio out, you may find out sooner than you’d like. Tell them in addition to the bomb, she’s seriously wounded. A bullet in the aorta and she’s clinging on by a thread.’ John didn’t wait for a return message. As soon as the driver finished speaking he jerked the receiver from its socket.

He looked through the porthole in the back door at the flashing amber and blue lights of the police and army vehicles trailing them at a safe distance. Keeping the gun trained on the driver and officer, he moved as far as could get from them taking Elizabeth with him. ‘I’m going to make a run for it’ he whispered in her ear. ‘I want you to stay here. You’ll be safe with them.’

‘As safe as the paramedic in Brighton?’ she whispered back without opening her eyes.

‘I’m going to hide out on the Beacons. It’s no picnic up there in summer. At this time of year it’s deadly without the right equipment,’ he muttered, regretting the loss of the rucksacks he'd been forced to abandon in the office.

'I'm not leaving you. You need me. I'm your doctor… '

'There's no time to argue.' He looked through the window again. There was a bend in the road just before the Storey Arms. A long sweeping curve carved into the hillside above a deep valley, part of a beautiful but desolate landscape. The drop to the valley floor fell steeply on the left about half a mile from the Youth Hostel on the Brecon side.

He checked the sky. Rain clouds had blotted out the moon and stars. It would be pitch black on the hillside. The ambulance would have to slow down to take the curve. He could open the door on the passenger side and jump. He primed the officer's Browning and pointed it in his and the driver's general direction, then dropped Elizabeth to the floor of the ambulance. 'Stay,' he ordered her abruptly.

'I'm coming with you.'

'You'll slow me down.'

'You're not getting rid of me that easily.'

The officer looked at John. 'You're John West,' he turned to Elizabeth, 'and you're no hostage.'

She took the gun from John and trained it on him.

West looked through the porthole again. The blue lights still hovered behind them. They were passing through Libanus; the road to Defynnog was on their right, ahead the great curve and the empty valley… a woman's voice echoed back at him from some almost, but not quite, forgotten time.

"Our own private Brigadoon, darling."

'Keep the gun trained on them, shoot if you have to.'

Elizabeth didn't remind John that she didn't know how.

John rummaged around the back of the ambulance. He picked up a couple of thick red blankets from the stretcher and opened a box. He took out thermal blankets, sterile dressings, plasters, plastic gloves, brandy, sheeting and bags and bundled them together in one of the blankets. Ripping off the driver's head protection he climbed into the passenger seat and pointed his own Browning at the man's temple.

'Slow down on the curve, but not enough to raise suspicions. Drive as close to the edge of the road as you can get.'

Keeping the gun she was holding trained on the bomb disposal officer, Elizabeth moved towards the front when they began to round the corner.

The driver saw her as John moved closer to the door. 'You're with him?'

'Yes,' she answered defiantly.

'A killer.'

'I'm a psychiatrist, he's my patient. I haven't left his side in two days. He hasn't killed anyone.'

'That's not what the news says,' the officer in the back protested.

'Someone is killing behind us.' She looked the officer coolly in the eye. 'That paramedic in Brighton was alive when we left him, so was my colleague Dave Watson. Do you think I'd stay with this man if I thought he was a killer? Please, tell the police what I said.' Her last words were blown away by the force of the wind and rain when John unlocked the door. It swung wide.

'I'm coming with you.'

'Don't.' He was gone.

A second later she threw herself out after him.

The soldiers either side of the office door nodded to one another. The coughing inside had stopped. Kicking the door in, they turned and fired. The body on the floor jerked convulsively.

'Oh Christ!' the exclamation was muffled by the respirator.

'Is he neutralised?'

'It's Alex.'

'Alex… in God's name how… '

'Get help. Now!'

It took time for the ambulance driver to slow to a halt after Elizabeth jumped. Sirens decelerated to cat-like wails as the escort drew up alongside him. The officer leaped from the back and ran out.

'The hostage?' The question came from an army captain, who left the leading armoured car.

'There was no bomb. The hostage wasn't even hurt. They've scarpered down the bank.'

The captain ran back to his vehicle, picked up the radio and started talking.

West remained curled on the ground for a few seconds after he landed. He explored his body, stretching limbs, fingers and toes, checking for pain. His elbows and knees hurt, but they'd taken most of the impact of landing. He'd heard Elizabeth crashing down the bank about fifty yards behind him. The sirens on the road above were winding down, but the loudest sound in the darkness was the patter of rain on his flame retardant suit.

It was time to move, and move swiftly.

'John?' Elizabeth sounded panic-stricken.

'I'll come to you,' he whispered, searching for a moving shade among the murky outlines of boulders and coarse, stunted bushes. He crawled in the direction of her voice. The ankle he had sprained two days ago hurt like hell, but he would just have to bear the discomfort. Five minutes, ten at the outside before they began hunting him in force. His hand touched her leg. 'Why did you come?'

'I want to be there when you remember,' she gasped.

'You're hurt?'

'Not badly.'

He took her hand. She was shivering. He pulled off his flame retardant suit and respirator, hooking the respirator on to his arm; he stuffed the 13 round magazines for the machine gun, the figure of eight descender and high power magazine into the bundle he'd made of the blankets and other things he'd taken from the ambulance. 'Here put this on.' He pushed the suit towards her.

'No.'

'You've slowed me down enough; they'll be bringing up floodlights any minute.'

She donned the suit. Gripping her hand, he set off. Elizabeth found it difficult to keep up with him as he scrambled down the hillside. Every part of her was in pain. Her elbows, knees, she had even grazed her face and the raw, bleeding flesh stung in the freezing wind and rain, but she forced herself on, concentrating on putting one foot in front of the other. Just as they reached the shelter of a few close growing bushes on the valley floor, the hill behind them was bathed in the blinding white glare of floodlights.

'Damn them, they were quick with the floodlights,' he muttered through clenched teeth. The ground was frozen solid and the cold had permeated through his feet and legs to his whole body. The air wasn't much warmer and the rain needled his face like shards of ice.

He looked up at the sky, heavy with dark grey snow clouds, and shivered in his jeans and thin sweatshirt. He still carried the blankets, but their colour was wrong, there was nothing worse than red for showing up in spotlights. Holding the bundle in front of him he followed the path of the stream on the valley floor. Hoping their pursuers would expect them to head down the valley towards Merthyr, he directed his steps back towards Libanus and Brecon.

He glanced up at the road, the outlines of soldiers, rifles and machine guns slung across their chests, stepped out of range of the floodlights and into the darkness. A single figure was silhouetted in the glow of one of the lamps. It was where he would have stationed himself if he'd been in charge of the operation.

He considered the terrain. If he was directing the men, he would fan them out from a central point, and it looked as though the CO was doing just that. He had to get as far from here as quickly as possible. Elizabeth stumbled behind him. A snowflake hit his sweatshirt. It turned to water as it touched the cloth, but he knew the country and this weather. Soon they'd be up to their neck in drifts. He glanced back. Elizabeth's face shone pale in the darkness. He didn't have to ask her how she felt. He recognized exhaustion when he saw it. If only she'd stayed in the ambulance. Another hour and they'd be leaving tracks.

He recalled the stone sheep pens that littered the hills. Ancient, rough circular walls the farmers used to corral their sheep during snowstorms. Had this storm been forecast?

What he needed right now was a pen full of sheep. Warm, smelly sheep that would mask the odour of the perfume and soap, he could smell on Elizabeth. The icy rain was becoming heavier, softer. Sleet or snow? At this rate they wouldn't even have an hour before their tracks became visible.

He continued down the frozen stream bed. Once, his foot broke through the thin layer of ice, and water splashed noisily over the top of his boot. He stood stock still, holding Elizabeth. Behind them torch lights continued to sweep the hillside. Gravel rattled downwards as the soldiers' feet slipped on the steep slopes. He continued to stand, Elizabeth's breath warm on his ear. Taking her hand, he set off again, setting a cruel pace, showing neither himself, nor her, mercy.

*   *   *

'Who shot this man?' Heddingham demanded of Chaloner.

'We don't know whether he was alive or dead before our men entered the room, sir.'

'Your men may be responsible for killing him?'

'We won't know who shot him until after the post mortem, and maybe not even then,' Chaloner divulged uneasily.

Heddingham walked over to where the body, wearing only army issue underclothes, lay slumped on the floor of the office. Blood had leaked out on to the wooden floor from a dozen bullet wounds sprayed over the chest. He noticed the single bullet wound in the arm. 'Issue a press release, Simmonds. John West has just killed his fifth victim.'

'Sir!' the major clipped smartly to attention, before leaving the room.

'Sir,' Chaloner stepped forward. 'We can't be sure West killed this man.' Chaloner tried not to think of the man Alex Hood had been. Friend – drinking partner – comrade – 'after the way our men burst into this room it is entirely feasible that he was felled by friendly fire.'

'Until a post mortem and inquest proves otherwise, I say this man was killed by John West.'

'Sir,' Chaloner murmured disconsolately.

'Don't forget that whoever John West is, he's a professional,' Heddingham advised. 'One crack SAS team, God knows how many squads of soldiers and policemen and he slipped through the net. Just as he's done every time we have him cornered. We need to find and neutralise him. Preferably as of yesterday, with this country playing host to an International Peace Conference. Surely I don't need to remind you of the importance of that?'

'No, sir'

'Any charge we can use to negate misplaced sympathy that some quarters of the public might be harbouring towards West, has to work in our favour. If he is innocent of this particular death, we'll apologize – after we have captured him.'

'Sir.'

'I've just spoken to Captain Perkins. West did a first class job of convincing the bomb disposal officer of his innocence. And, from the driver and officer's account, Dr Santer is no more West's hostage than you or I.'

'Are you saying she is with him voluntarily, sir?'

'Apparently he tried to leave her in the ambulance but she jumped down the hillside after him. There's a battalion running around the Beacons right now trying to find them.'

Chaloner walked to the window and looked at the snow falling over the vehicles that remained in the street. 'He won't last long on the Beacons in this.'

'I wouldn't take a bet on it. The man seems to have more lives than a cat, and more luck than a Cabinet Minister. And don't forget,' Heddingham looked down at the body on the floor. 'He's wearing one of our uniforms now.'

'Have the men been issued with red armbands, sir?'

'Not yet, arrange it, Chaloner. I just hope Dr Santer isn't wearing anything red so he can make his own and join our search from the rear.'

It was snowing thick and fast when West struck out and up the slope that led to the Beacons. His eyes panned wide, searching for a ring of dry stone walling. If he'd been alone, he might have been tempted to keep going. With luck he could have crossed the summit of Pen-y-Fan, the highest peak, before morning, and then he could have headed down the other side of the hillside to Tal y Bont. That's if he hadn't died of exposure en route. He could steal another car and then – then where? There was nowhere left for him to run.

Elizabeth was slowing up. What was the use in making plans? He'd saddled himself with a woman who wasn't used to exercise and was close to exhaustion. A woman who happened to be his only link with humanity; a woman, he reminded himself, who had risked her life for him.

'Just a few more yards.'

'I can't go another step.' She sank to her knees. 'You were right, I am slowing you down. Go on without me.'

He scooped her into his arms. Another fifty yards and he'd have to leave the stream and the cover of the trees. She slumped against his chest. He was still walking in the stream bed, but his feet were so wet and cold he couldn't tell whether he was stepping on ice or in water. He could hear voices but they were muffled by the steep sides of the hills and it was impossible to judge how close they were. He drew some comfort from the outline of the Beacons. He even knew the names of the peaks.

Corn Du was the one closest to him, Pen-y-Fan the highest and Cribyn the lowest of the three, but still a bastard to climb with its slippery, scree slopes. Hill walking! Had he ever regarded it as fun? A few more steps… he crept out of the shelter of the trees and then he saw it. A sheep pen filled with sheep. He looked at the ground searching for their tracks. He found them lightly covered by snow, but still lying darker than the surrounding blanket of white. Careful to tread only in their prints he headed for the pen. The sheep ran back as soon as they sensed his presence.

He had to be careful not to spook them. They were stupid, nervous animals and the slightest movement would alert the troops. He walked around the outside of the wall sticking close to the crumbling stones to avoid alarming them.

He laid a finger on Elizabeth's cheek. If he didn't raise her temperature soon, hypothermia would set in. He crept around the pen. When he reached the topmost part, he stumbled, hitting his knee painfully against something sharp that sliced through his jeans. Suppressing a cry, he fingered a sheet of corrugated metal. It must have been used to shore up the crumbling, centuries-old walls. Stooping, he felt where it was propped against the wall, bolstering a low section where most of the stones had fallen away. Still carrying Elizabeth he crept between it and what remained of the wall.

The ground was frozen solid, sheep were already moving away from that part of the pen. He felt in his pocket for his gun, screwed on the silencer and shot the three closest to them. The others bolted to the bottom of the pen.

Unrolling a thermal blanket he laid Elizabeth on it and covered her with the red woollen blankets. Creeping out cautiously, he dragged the carcasses of the dead sheep back to the sheet of corrugated metal. He plugged one entrance with a single carcase and blocked the other with the remaining two.

Scrambling down the centre of the pen he retrieved the bale of hay the farmer had left for the stock. He hauled it towards the top of the pen, scattering it about in an effort to entice the sheep to crowd around the corrugated metal. Throwing it liberally around his lair, he moved one of the dead sheep and crept inside pulling its body after him to plug the gap.

He crawled as close as he could get to Elizabeth and lay alongside her, wrapping the second hypothermia sheet and blankets around both of them. Gripping the machine gun he lay still and listened. Tomorrow, if the weather was fine the army would call out the heat seeking helicopters. If he and Elizabeth kept very quiet and still, the sheep might settle closer. It wasn't an ideal camouflage, but it was the best he could do – for now.

Rubbing Elizabeth's frozen fingers and face, he forced a trickle of brandy between her lips.

The last thing he did before he finally relaxed, was place his finger on the trigger of the Heckler and Koch. If he shot the first man to reach them, he might be able to barter enough time to ensure Elizabeth's safety. Suddenly that seemed the most important thing in the entire sorry mess that was his life.

CHAPTER TWELVE

The sound of a helicopter engine rent the stillness. West tensed his muscles and lay rigid. His face was so cold it was numb and he was grateful for the warmth of Elizabeth's body lying along the length of his. It was agonizing to move his arm up towards the cold, but he brushed aside a strand of her hair that had fallen across his eyes. He could barely feel his other hand; the only sensation registering in his chilled fingers was the even colder trigger mechanism of the Heckler and Koch.

He flexed his hand, only just remembering in time that the gun was primed. He peered at Elizabeth trying to establish whether her warmth was normal, or signified a feverish rise in temperature. It felt normal, but the air was so cold it was difficult to gauge. He lifted his head. The only light that trickled into their gloomy, makeshift shelter came from beneath the rough metal walls and around the heads of the dead sheep. The one above them appeared to be leering at him, its eyes wide open, glassy in death.

He glanced down at his feet and made out the outline of the heads of the other two animals that he'd shot. The helicopter moved away and he could hear the munching of the rest of the herd feeding on the hay he'd scattered around their rough hide. The combination of cold that had frozen the carcasses, stifling the smell of blood, stillness and silence had worked. The sheep had edged towards the side of the pen where they were hiding to get at the hay.

Then he heard it again. The harsh whirring of helicopter blades returning – coming closer – closer – he looked down again to reassure himself that the sheet of metal completely covered them.

Elizabeth opened her eyes. He moved his finger to his mouth and motioned her to silence. They continued to lie; bodies meshed together, their combined breathing resounding louder than any drum-roll in their ears, staring through the gloom into the depths of one another's eyes. The border around the sheet of iron was blindingly white. Snow! It wouldn't be so light if it was still falling and he couldn't hear the patter of rain. The day must have dawned clear, and they'd been left, sitting ducks on the hillside. Without the sheet of corrugated metal, they'd be visible for miles.

He imagined the heat seeking camera in the helicopter moving over the pen. Visualized the images it would generate on screen. If the operator looked down he'd see the back ends of the sheep sticking out of the cover of metal. Hopefully, he'd assume that the images outlined beneath the improvised shelter would also be sheep. But what if he didn't? What if he made out their human shapes and radioed the troops on the ground…

Heart thundering, West heard the crunch of feet compacting virgin snow. Slowly, inexorably, the footsteps drew closer. He gripped the machine gun tightly. The cold was seeping downwards from his face; his brain was a hyperactive frenzy. He prepared to spring into action the moment the corner of the sheet was lifted. The crunching stopped.

‘Nothing but bloody sheep.’ The voice was close.

‘He could be hiding among them?’

There was a short burst of laughter. ‘You don’t know bleeding sheep, mate. They run a mile if anyone goes near them. Come on, sooner we finish this patrol, sooner we get back into the warm.’

‘I reckon he headed for Merthyr last night. If he nicked a car there, he could be halfway to London by now.’

‘Who’d want to go to that God-forsaken hole?’ A broad Northern accent asked.

‘You want a fist in your mush?’

‘Nah, just a Welsh-free patrol.’

‘Why would any target head for these bloody hills?’

‘To get us out of our nice warm barracks and make us run around like blue-arsed flies in this fucking, freezing wilderness… ’

‘Call yourselves soldiers! You lot are worse than a load of bleeding fishwives. You’re here to do a fucking job not stand by gossiping.’

‘Stopped for a piss, sergeant.’

‘Then bloody well get on with it.’

‘Quick as it will come, sergeant. It doesn’t like the cold.’

‘Bloody Cockneys. You’re all comedians.’

The sound of water trickling against stone came from somewhere above them, followed by the stampeding of hooves as sheep charged down the pen.

West waited for one of the soldiers to notice that the sheep beneath the make-shift repair to the wall hadn't bolted with the rest, but the crunch of boots on snow resumed and the voices grew fainter.

Elizabeth's eyes, wide, fearful, focused on his.

'You all right?' he mouthed, barely articulating the words.

She nodded.

'Keep the blankets around you.' Digging the toes of his boots into the ground he pushed himself upwards, towards the point where the tin ended and the crumbling walls began. He peered out of a crack alongside the carcase of the sheep. The world had been overlaid by a thick, white quilt, but he'd been wrong about the weather. The sky was full of snow, and small flurries were still falling, specks he knew would soon turn to full-bodied flakes. But the soldiers had moved on. He could see the outlines of their grey boots and gloves and white snow suits trudging up towards the summit of Corn Du. He moved back down alongside Elizabeth.

'You cold?'

'Since you moved,' she admitted, through blue and chattering lips.

He slid back into the position he'd occupied all night and wrapped his arms around her.

'How come you're not freezing?'

'Trained to cope. At least I think so,' he qualified.

'After last night, one thing's certain. You have to be an army officer. No one but an officer could have barked commands the way you did.'

'And, which army do you think I'm likely to be an officer in?' he asked softly, suspecting that no officer worthy of the name, would manoeuvre himself, much less an innocent woman, into the position he had engineered them into; hiding out on a freezing snow-clad mountainside with only a sheet of tin and three dead sheep to protect them from the elements and their pursuers. It was bad enough he was here, but Elizabeth – he'd only met her for the first time three days ago, and in that time he'd taken her captive at gunpoint, gagged and tied her – yet here she was, prepared to believe in him to the extent of endangering her own life.

'The military angle gives us something to work on the next time I hypnotise you.' Her teeth were chattering. Her body was only warm where it touched his; the rest of her was chilled to the marrow. When she tried to uncurl her fingers, they moved infinitely slowly and stiffly, like plants turning towards the light.

'What I can't understand is how they knew we were in Brecon?' he murmured.

'The photographs,' she reminded him. 'We left them on the bed.'

'They covered all of Wales.'

'I removed the Brecon file from the box.'

'The photographs you showed me were of the town. They surrounded one particular flat.'

'Perhaps someone saw us there, someone who knew we'd been asking questions about the place in the pub.'

'We kept the curtains drawn when we were there.'

'I was seen walking into the place. Our faces were on every news broadcast, and in every newspaper.'

‘I looked into every face in that pub and I would have sworn that none of them identified us.’

‘Perhaps one of them was as good as keeping his reactions to himself as you are, and followed us.’

‘It’s academic now we’re in this bloody awful position, with no supplies, the wrong clothes and no survival gear.’ He pinched a finger of snow from beneath the sheet of iron with his thumb and forefinger and rubbed the tip of her frozen nose with it. ‘You should have another sip of brandy.’

‘I’d prefer to crawl outside and visit the Ladies’ room.’

‘With what’s outside, the Ladies’ room has to be in here.’

‘With you lying here. You have to be joking?’

‘You move out and we’ll be picked up in minutes. This spot can be seen for miles, especially from the road. Here,’ he handed her a couple of plastic bags. ‘Don’t mix one product with another,’ he warned. ‘If you do the bag will explode, and they’ll sniff us out.’

‘How in hell do you know that?’

‘I just know it. In order to spare your blushes, I’ll retreat to the drawing room.’ He wriggled out of the blankets wincing as his jean clad knees hit the frozen ground. He continued to push himself upwards on his elbows towards the dead sheep. Its body was as cold and hard as the ground it was lying on.

Crawling past the woolly face with its frosting of iced blood, he peered outside. There were a few stunted, misshapen trees in the centre of the pen. They didn’t afford much cover, but they were better than nothing, and as such, worth remembering. The night had been unpleasant, a day spent in these conditions without food, and only snow to serve as drinking water, wouldn't be much better. As soon as darkness fell he would move on for Elizabeth's sake. He doubted she could take much more.

He scanned the hillsides and the horizon as far as he could see. In the distance tiny, matchbox cars rolled along the Libanus road, but for how much longer? The snow was falling thicker and heavier. But no matter how heavily it fell, he doubted it would slow the army's four wheeled drive vehicles.

'I'm through.'

He turned, her face seemed bluer than before and damp.

'What have you been doing?'

'Washing in snow.'

'Here,' he wriggled back down on to the blankets, and held out his arms. 'Get as close to me as you can.'

'Intimate strangers.'

'I'm the only radiator in this mansion.'

'And I'm very grateful for the use of your body, believe me.' She stole close to him, while he re-arranged the blankets, tucking their edges around both of them. For the first time she noticed his eyes, dark, hollowed, ringed by shadows. 'You've been awake all night.' It was a statement not a question.

'Someone had to stand guard.'

'Let me take over for a couple of hours.'

'I'll be fine.'

'You've had about one night's sleep in the last three. I doubt even superman could survive on that for long.'

‘I’ll sleep tonight’

‘If we stay here we’ll freeze and starve to death.’

‘I know, that’s why I intend to move out as soon as it gets dark. If you’re the praying sort, I suggest you put in a word for another cloudy night.’

‘If you stay awake you’re not going to be in fit condition to move out.’ She glanced at her watch. ‘It’s midday now. I’ll wake you when it gets dark.’

‘Or the second you hear a noise?’

‘I promise.’

‘You have the gun I gave you?’

‘I can’t reach it, I don’t know how to use it, and I’m not sure I would, if I did.’ She looked at the machine gun tucked alongside them. ‘I’ll wake you if I think trouble’s coming.’

‘And when it gets dark.’ His eyes were already closing at the suggestion of sleep. Grabbing a handful of hay from the edge of the shelter he pushed it beneath the blanket at his head, and retrieved the bottle of brandy. ‘Take a drink, but go easy,’ he handed it to her. ‘I almost forgot this.’ He pulled half a bar of the thick dark chocolate from inside his vest where he’d stowed it when he’d changed in the office. ‘Breakfast.’ He snapped a piece off, pushing the rest back inside his shirt he handed her the square.

‘You’re not breakfasting?’

‘I haven’t slept yet. Be careful when you touch the guns. There’s a silencer on the Browning, but it’s a semi-automatic, all you have to do is squeeze the trigger mechanism for it to fire.’

‘I told you I’ll wake you if anyone comes.’

'Take it just in case I jerk the mechanism in my sleep.' He thrust it at her. Wrapping himself and the machine gun in the blanket they shared, he pulled her close. She lay quietly on her stomach, her side pressed against his chest, listening to his slow measured breathing, feeling the pounding of his heart against her rib-cage as she concentrated on the tiny slit of light that gave a door jamb view of the outside world. Within seconds he relaxed against her, and she knew he slept.

'No sightings, sir.'

'This is preposterous. The man has to be somewhere; he couldn't have disappeared off the face of the earth.' Simmonds carried a mug of tea into the room they had requisitioned as a Command Cell in the Storey Arms Youth Hostel.

'I thought your regiment trained for operations over this sort of terrain?' Needing a scapegoat, Lieutenant-Colonel Heddingham looked at Chaloner.

'We do, sir,' Chaloner answered.

'You knew within minutes that he'd jumped. Your officers and men were escorting that ambulance… '

'Our target obviously knows these hills. Apparently better than we do.' Chaloner moved to the window and looked out at the falling snow that had covered the slushy tyre tracks in the car park. 'He's obviously gone to ground. Built himself a hide, perhaps even an igloo. We know he has brandy and blankets. He's holing up somewhere.'

'In this? Rubbish,' Heddingham dismissed.

'He must have slipped through your cordon last night,' Simmonds added.

'A rabbit couldn't have slipped through that cordon.' Chaloner remained calm, controlled, all the more authoritative for his lack of emotion.

'It's a vast area... '

'Which he has to travel the same as us, and he doesn't have the advantage of our equipment, helicopters and four wheeled drive vehicles.'

'While you two stand here arguing. I have to return to London and face the committee and the minister. What do I tell them?' Heddingham demanded.

'That we have him cornered in a hide and it's simply a matter of time before we put our hands on him. That's if you are prepared to allow me to run this search without interference, sir,' Chaloner replied.

'Or,' the colonel looked to Simmonds, 'he's out of the area and on his way to God knows where?'

'No cars were reported stolen within twenty miles of this area last night,' Chaloner pointed out.

'That we know about,' Simmonds broke in. 'He could have flagged one down, killed the driver... '

'Where are you suggesting he flagged down this car? We had road blocks set up within ten minutes of him and Dr Santer jumping from that ambulance. We monitored the journey and destination of every car that travelled the Brecon-Merthyr road last night.'

'He could have done it in the first ten minutes.'

'Not without us seeing him.' Chaloner crossed to the map and studied it.

'Every road, every hill, every empty building for miles checked out, and we still come up with precisely nothing!' Heddingham hit the table with his fist, rattling the tea mugs and splashing their contents over the maps and plans spread out over the surface.

'Lieutenant-Colonel, sir,' a private marched into the room. 'Your helicopter is ready.'

Heddingham looked from Simmonds to Chaloner. 'I'm in charge of this operation, and I'm the one getting the flak because we haven't caught our quarry. You,' he pointed to Chaloner, 'pull your men out of this area and concentrate on covering a wider circle. Twenty to fifty miles from the central point at which he jumped.'

'But, sir… '

'We've played it your way long enough, Chaloner, and come up with precisely nothing. Simmonds, set up liaison meetings with all the police forces in Wales, and contact the ones in England. Let's extend the net.'

'Sir,' Simmonds smiled triumphantly. 'Just one more thing before you go, sir.'

'Make it brief, Major.' Heddingham lifted his overcoat from the rack and removed the gloves from its pocket.

'Should we be unable to contact you, sir, who is in charge of this operation in your absence?'

'You make every effort to contact me.'

'That is understood, sir.'

'In the unlikely eventuality I am unavailable; we'll have to trust to your judgement, Major Simmonds. Chaloner.' Heddingham acknowledged the captain before walking out through the door.

Simmonds turned to the map after Heddingham left the building. 'Shouldn't you be redeploying the search parties, Chaloner?'

The afternoon wore on, endless, tedious, cold and silent. The hush that had descended over the hills was so absolute, Elizabeth almost panicked over a buzzing she eventually recognized as originating in her mind. She stared at the slender margin of light beneath the tin and reflected the only differences between this shrouded silence and the grave was her degree of consciousness, the glimmer of light, and West's warm presence.

She could just make out a distant corner of road. A thin black ribbon in a world of blinding marshmallow white, where, from time to time, wheels turned, churning up a filthy spray. The gap wasn't large enough for her to make out the vehicles, only their wheels. Occasionally she heard the whirr of helicopter blades, but none hovered directly overheard and although West opened his eyes at the rumbles, he closed them as soon as the sounds grew fainter.

He slept uneasily, occasionally mumbling in his sleep. She tried to decipher his words and failed. Was he speaking in another language? Arabic perhaps? The seeds of doubt grew as the day wore on. In an effort to quell her suspicions she listed all of West's positive attributes.

Despite all his threats, he'd never shown any signs of undue violence. He was an expert at disarming people and rendering them unconscious, but she hadn't seen him kill, or hurt anyone needlessly. He hadn't exhibited any sign of enjoying the power he'd wielded over her, and even last night when he had tried to make love to her, he could have easily overpowered her, but one protest had been enough to stop him.

He wasn't a rapist – but apart from his personality which she sensed to be inherently and morally good, there was something else – something that went deeper than their doctor/patient relationship. An affinity? Like-minded friendship? She tried not to analyze it too closely.

Joseph wouldn't have wanted her to shut herself away and mourn him the way she had done for the past two years, but then after he'd died, she'd envied him, believing him to be the lucky one. She'd loved him completely and utterly with a passion that left little energy or time for other relationships. Her only fear after she'd met him had been that he'd die and leave her. But whenever she imagined that happening in those early days, she had pictured herself an old, bent, grey-haired woman living in sheltered accommodation or a small house in the country with live-in help, and her grandchildren's visits to look forward to, not when she was twenty-seven and still engrossed in carving out a career for herself, and never – never before they'd had children.

Joseph had wanted children as soon as they'd married, but she'd insisted on waiting until she'd gained enough experience to return to her career after a break to bring them up. With the result that after three years of marriage to Joseph, all she'd been left with were memories, a wardrobe full of men's clothes, and a newly bought house that needed gutting and rebuilding. Not much to show for a life she missed so much.

Darkness came and fell swiftly, bringing with it a thick, grey mist that blotted out the road and surrounding hills. She watched the mist fade from mid to dark grey. The only colour in the landscape was the snow falling through the air and carpeting the ground.

When she decided it was dark enough she prodded West. Her hand and arm were so numb with cold they barely obeyed her. But even before she touched West she could see the whites of his eyes shining in the darkness. She put her finger to her lips but she could have saved herself the trouble. He didn't wake like other people, half asleep and dozy, but completely and suddenly. One moment unconscious, the next roused, coiled, ready for action.

'What's the time?' he whispered.

'Almost five when I last looked at my watch. I can't see the face any more.'

'Anyone around?'

'There's a mist, you can barely see your hand in front of your face.'

'You did pray then.' His hand closed around the brandy bottle he'd put at her head. 'You didn't drink any?'

'No.'

'Have some now, and eat this.' He retrieved the chocolate and broke off another segment for her and one for himself.

When hunger pangs had struck earlier she'd felt as though she could have eaten the proverbial ox, now she couldn't even bite into the chocolate. She waited, hoping it would melt in her mouth. He slithered past her while she sipped at the brandy. Now he was awake and had taken over, her brain slowed, threatening to become as numb as her body. She didn't want to think about moving. The cold was paralyzing, but it didn't require any effort on her part to remain. And, after her attempts to move, she doubted she could walk any distance. And, even if she could, where would they go? Whichever route West took, sooner or later they'd have to face climbing a steep slope. What if he wanted to go over the hills he called the Beacons? She knew she'd never make it to the top let alone down the other side. And how long would they last on the bare hillside in the snow without protective clothing or food?

'You want to call some of the search parties in, sir?'

Chaloner studied the map as though the answer to Sergeant Price's question lay there. He'd widened the circle of operations, just as Heddingham had ordered. Simmonds had set up new, more distant road blocks to comply with their CO's orders, but he still couldn't dismiss his gut feeling that West had remained close to Libanus. Dug into a hide. And that soon, very soon he'd be moving on.

'There!' Simmonds brought his finger down hard on the map.

'Llanfrynach, sir?' The sergeant looked at Simmonds in surprise.

‘We would have seen him if he’d crossed Pen-y-Fan,’ Chaloner insisted. ‘We’ve had patrols out there all day.’

‘You were the one who said he knows this area. It’s the nearest point away from this road where he could steal a car.’

‘You spoke to the police. No thefts have been reported.’

‘So far,’ Simmonds said darkly. ‘Someone could be away and the vehicle might not be missed yet.’

Chaloner continued to look at the map. Sensing a power struggle, Sergeant Price looked tactfully at the window.

‘You have a theory, sergeant?’ Simmonds asked.

‘None, sir.’

‘None at all?’ Simmonds pressed.

‘If I were West, I’d head back over the road before attempting to scale the Beacons in these conditions, sir.’

‘We’ve had the road under surveillance all night and all day, sergeant.’

‘Even under surveillance it’s an easier route to take than scaling the Beacons.’

‘I’ll bear what you said in mind, sergeant.’ Simmonds turned to Chaloner. ‘Cover Llanfrynach and Tal-y-Bont.’

‘Sir?’ The sergeant looked to Chaloner.

‘You heard the order, Sergeant Price.’ Chaloner wondered how many men he could spirit away to continue watching the Libanus road without rousing Simmonds’ suspicions.

*   *   *

West tried to make out the trees he'd seen earlier in the sheep pen, but as Elizabeth had warned, the mist obscured everything more than a couple of feet from their hide.

'I'm going out,' he murmured. He crawled stiffly, rising slowly and agonizingly to his feet. As the blood rushed into his tingling and aching legs he stood stock still, conscious of his dark clothing against the white snow, listening intently for any sound. Over to his right he thought he could hear the faraway march of feet. Were they calling off the search? He turned full circle trying to get his bearings. They had entered the sheep pen from the East, which meant the road was now to their West and Pen-y-Fan to the East. If he was wrong, they had a bloody long climb ahead of them, one he'd be hard put to endure, and one Elizabeth probably wouldn't survive.

He listened again. The hillside was so still he thought he could detect the sound of falling snow. The officer commanding the search must have moved his men on in the assumption he'd long since gone. Whoever the clown was, he obviously hadn't been subjected to the same thorough training he had. He tried to stretch, but he couldn't feel his back or his legs. He knew his muscles were going to ache unbearably when he finally did start moving. And it wasn't just the snowdrifts they'd have to contend with, but the wind, keener and sharper than a hunter's blade. He stooped to the sheet of metal.

‘It’s dark enough to move out. Bring the blankets, and wrap the thermal one around your shoulders.’

‘The silver will be seen.’

‘Not in this.’

It took all her strength to push the bundle of blankets out ahead of her. ‘Where are we going?’ She fought an attack of nausea as she rose to her feet.

‘Back along the road we came.’ He’d toyed with the idea of heading down the valley, towards Merthyr and Cardiff in the hope of losing himself in a heavily populated area, knowing full well that the longer they remained in this wasteland the greater the risk of being caught. But one glimpse of Elizabeth swaying precariously had been enough. He doubted she had enough strength to get back up on to the road. ‘There’s a few isolated buildings on the outskirts of Libanus, farms, barns and suchlike, we’ll find somewhere warm where we can light a fire, and perhaps even cook some food.’

‘I’m not hungry.’

‘The first sign of starvation.’ “And hypothermia” he thought privately.

‘Will we be safe so close to a village?’

‘I’ve kept you safe so far haven’t I?’ He wrapped one blanket around her, and knotted their few possessions into a bundle with the others.

‘John…’

‘Don’t talk. Conserve your energy. If we stay here any longer the farmer will find us in the spring. Two atrophied, freeze dried corpses, minus whatever tasty bits the foxes and crows have picked.’ He held out his hand, she took it. Together they walked down the outside wall of the sheep pen. He was fairly certain there was no one to hear the sheep moving should they stampede, but there was no point in taking any risk, no matter how small, unless they had to.

Snow continued to fall, wetter than it had been the night before. Pulling Elizabeth behind him, he began the precarious descent to the valley floor. He checked every step, testing the ground with his weight before moving on. Glancing behind, he was gratified to see the snow filling in their footprints, obscuring them within seconds.

Reaching the valley floor proved relatively simple. The worst that happened was Elizabeth ploughed forward with so much momentum she crashed into him, but he managed to stand firm, until he took a final step forward and plunged up to one knee in freezing icy water.

'Stay back, it's flooded here.' He peered into the mist. Ahead of him the hill rose almost at right angles from the valley floor. Somewhere up ahead was the road, which meant negotiating cars, headlights, people – patrols…

'How much further?' She was standing just behind him her voice faint, as though it was travelling over a great distance.

'Just a short walk. Uphill I'm afraid.' He held out the bundle to her. 'Take this.'

She reached for it obediently, thinking how large and heavy it was. Placing his hands on her waist, he lifted her, and swung her over the stream bed.

'Tread in my footsteps.' He took the bundle from her, and gripped her hand. 'Keep that blanket around your shoulders.'

The climb was almost impossible. The ground beneath the snow was sheathed in ice that afforded no foot or hand hold. Whenever West managed to gain a tenuous purchase he turned and hauled Elizabeth up beside him, gripping her wrists firmly in his hands, but after an hour, even his strength began to fail. When he eventually peered over the ridge above him to see a mist shrouded expanse of churned grey and black slushy road he could have kissed it.

'We've reached the road,' he whispered.

She stared at him uncomprehendingly, too exhausted to smile let alone answer. He dragged her behind him, and swiftly crossed the road. The hill continued to rise steeply before them, but as he stepped forward his foot plunged into a snow filled ditch. Brecon and Libanus were along this road, they had to keep going and find somewhere where they could hide out.

'Just a little further,' he pleaded when she fell.

She continued to stumble behind him. Once headlights pierced the gloom. He threw her into the ditch and lay on top of her until the car had passed, but when he tried to rouse her afterwards, he found her in a white, dead faint. Picking her and the blankets up he stumbled on, driving his stiff aching limbs onwards.

Ahead were lights. He resolved to knock the door of the first inhabited house and beg for help. Nothing was more important than Elizabeth's life and health.

And, if he surrendered to the police they wouldn't kill him. Or would they hand him over to the army who would? He was no longer capable of coherent thought. It was as though the whirling, drifting snowflakes had blown into his mind, clogging his thinking.
'Not much further, there are houses.' He was talking to himself. 'Not much further and you'll be safe,' he promised rashly.

CHAPTER THIRTEEN

West kept well away from the road until he reached Libanus. Once there, he made his way stealthily around the back of the terrace that fronted the main road. He trod slowly and carefully, peering into the thick milky white fog that transformed the most commonplace objects into ghouls.

Lights shone from the backs of houses, blurred yellow jewels in a haze of tarnished mist. His hand tightened on the trigger mechanism of the Heckler and Koch slung across his chest. They were in farming country and that coupled with the high profile hunt for him made him reluctant to seek help for Elizabeth. He had been in houses like these, had seen the guns the occupants used to shoot crows and rabbits. He imagined the weapons being kept ready primed and loaded by front doors after all the recent police and army activity.

Stumbling over a pile of stones knocked from a back wall, he paused to rest. The only light that illuminated the area came from a kitchen window. He caught a glimpse of tiled worktop, split-level oven, and a spice rack on a wall. He could almost smell the warmth that came from the house; it would be redolent with the scents of winter food, beef stew, apple pies…

Suppressing the thoughts, he concentrated on his immediate plight. He had to get Elizabeth out of this snowstorm and into somewhere warm. There was a wooden shed next to the half demolished wall, the door broken and unlocked. He pushed the rickety slab of wood. Aside from a stack of firewood, the shed was empty. He laid Elizabeth, still wrapped in the blanket, behind the crumbling door.

'I'll be back.'

She opened her eyes. 'Don't leave me,' she whispered weakly, holding her arms out to him.

'I have to find shelter.'

'You'll be seen… '

'Some of the houses are holiday homes. One or two are bound to be empty.' He hesitated. 'If I'm not back in an hour go to a house with lights on and ask whoever's there to call the police. Insist on as much publicity as you can get. The press may be able to guarantee your safety.'

'John… '

She was calling to the mist. He was gone, no more than a shadow in the snow filled darkness.

He continued to creep along the back of the houses checking windows for lights when he saw a place he remembered as a guesthouse in darkness. Did it only open in summer? He climbed over the wall into the garden and crept to the back door. There was a burglar alarm. He knew too much about burglar alarms to attempt to pull the wires from the box.

He stole forward and looked through the glass panel at the corners of the ceiling in the room, noting the small white boxes that housed the infra-red detectors of the alarm system. It was electrically operated. If he shut off the incoming supply – and there was no battery, secondary or emergency back-up he could break in. That was a big "if" and for all he knew the alarm could be connected to the local police station.

To his left was a flat roofed extension, probably a kitchen. An idea occurred to him. He summoned his strength, braced his foot in the corner where two walls met, climbed on to the roof and looked through the upstairs window. Some people cut corners by not extending their alarm systems to the upstairs of their houses on the premise that any burglars, even if they broke in through an upper window, would have to carry their booty out via the ground floor. And he couldn't see any infra detectors.

He prised open the window. The wood was rotten and he dug a hole around the catch with the scalpel he still carried. Stepping over the sill he found himself in a darkened bedroom. He could make out very little beyond a white painted door opposite. Standing behind it, he opened it cautiously. He looked out. A street lamp shone through a window at the far end of a long passage, providing enough of a glow for him to see that there were no infra red detectors in the corridor either. He could carry Elizabeth up here. Provided they remained on the top floor they wouldn't run the risk of setting off the alarms, but would they gain anything? It was as cold in here as it was outside.

He stole along the corridor, opening other doors along the back wall. He found a bathroom with dry taps and an airing cupboard with a tank and an immersion heater. He dropped the switch and a red light glowed. Suspecting the water had been switched off and the tank drained, he switched it off immediately. There was electricity – and that might mean warmth.

Further along the corridor he discovered a bedroom with a double bed, the mattress swathed in plastic sheeting, and an electric fire. He turned the fire on high. The only window in the room faced the back so there was no danger of the glow being seen from the road. The curtains were already drawn. He dragged the mattress from the bed and laid it on the floor in front of the fire.

If he brought Elizabeth here, she would be warm and safe for tonight and possibly even tomorrow. All he had to do was find the stop cock, turn on the water and steal some food. Where could he get food? Not this village. The last thing he could afford to do was alert the army to their presence.

He left the room and climbed back out on to the roof. The wind had whipped up, and he had to fight his way down through a snow blizzard. He returned to the shed where Elizabeth was beyond shivering, her body rigid, soaked and frozen. He picked her up and carried her and the blankets to the flat roof. Hoping no one was watching from a darkened window he propped Elizabeth against the wall and flung up the bundle of blankets. He climbed after them, lay on his stomach and offered Elizabeth his hands. Grasping her wrists he pulled her up beside him and opened the window. Throwing in the blankets, he helped her inside.

'Don't go downstairs or you'll set off every bloody alarm in the place.' He led her into the bedroom. The electric fire had already warmed the air. He dropped the machine gun beside the mattress. 'Strip off your wet clothes, wrap yourself in the driest blanket and stay there until I get back.'

'Where are you going?' she mumbled through frozen lips.

'Shopping, we're right out of groceries.'

'But… '

'I'll be back.' He left the room, closed the door softly behind him and walked along to the broken window.' He climbed out on to the roof, pushed the broken wood back into the hole and pushed the window shut before sliding down to the ground. He found the stopcock and turned on the water, hoping none of the pipes inside the building were frozen.

He backtracked to the edge of the village as swiftly as he could, given the wind and the depth of the snow, that sucked him down deeper with every step he took. Suddenly very conscious of the cold, he looked down at himself. He'd been a fool. He should have taken the flame retardant suit from Elizabeth, but then how could he have explained why he was wearing a flame retardant suit to a patrol, when everyone else would be in cold weather gear and snow suits?

He stopped when he reached the edge of the village. The mountain centre was within walking distance, no more than a mile or two, but although there was a cafeteria there it was also alarmed, and probably better alarmed than the guest house. What did that leave?

Back to Brecon? Too risky, the whole town would be alerted to him by now. He pictured a map, Defynnog and Sennybridge lay to the west,

Llansbyddydd to the north, various isolated farmhouses to the south. What he needed was somewhere where he'd be least expected, preferably somewhere that would lay a false trail. He flexed his fingers. He also needed weatherproof clothes and gloves, preferably an army uniform with a ski mask to hide his face. Somewhere up ahead there'd be a road block.

But what he needed most of all was luck.

Privates Moore and Jones were not the army's finest. They'd been released early from Shepton Mallet military prison, not because of any effort they'd made to atone for their misdemeanours, but because of a shortage of manpower that had led to the drafting in of every available man to help with the search for West. Their reputation as slapdash, slovenly soldiers had preceded them.

No platoon wanted to work with them so Chaloner had used them to man a roadblock on the back road that led from Libanus to Defynnog. He had been able to sideline two dozen men from the search for West, most of them poorly motivated, sloppy soldiers like Moore and Jones, and had used them to ring the area around the Storey Arms with roadblocks that covered every minor road and lane as well as the main A and B class routes.

Using the excuse that he was checking on the progress of the search on the Beacons, Chaloner travelled from roadblock to roadblock on the roads Heddingham hadn't considered worth searching, but he felt uneasy. From what little he knew of West from the storming of the flat, he knew he wasn't the type to go marching down a main road. He was more likely to creep up behind the troops manning the roadblocks and slit their windpipes, and with the quality of troops he had stationed at some of the roadblocks, he didn't doubt that West would succeed in immobilising them before they noticed anything was amiss.

When he stopped at the block that had been set up on the Libanus to Defynnog road, he found Privates Moore and Jones cigarettes in mouth, rifles slung carelessly over their shoulders, sitting, hunched and shivering on boulders at the side of the road. He debated whether to lecture them, but decided to save his breath. Better officers than him had undoubtedly tried – and failed – to lick them into shape in Shepton Mallet and he wasn't egotistical enough to think he could succeed where they hadn't. The best he could hope to do was galvanise them into tightening the security on the road block. Otherwise they may as well pack up and go back to barracks.

Shouting the password, 'White alert,' he climbed out of his Land Rover and prepared to deliver a morale-boosting speech.

West had trekked a mile out of Libanus on the back road that led past the mountain centre when he spotted a road block through the soup of swirling snow. A Land Rover pulled up almost alongside him. He heard the exchange of passwords, and saw a captain leave the vehicle and walk towards two privates manning the barricade.

He slipped behind a stunted tree. The roadblock didn't pose a problem, on foot it was easy to circumnavigate, but it did make him wonder just how many other roadblocks and patrols were in the area.

The captain's Land Rover was parked in front of the temporary barrier the men had erected. It had a canvas cover over the back, and he hoped there'd be spare sets of clothing and boots stowed there in case of emergency. Even if there weren't, it offered an opportunity to cut his journey time to the next village.

He crept forward on his hands and toes. The captain was berating the privates, but the snow veiled their figures, just as he hoped it would conceal his. Darting to the back of the Land Rover he clambered in beneath the canvas.

The vehicle was loaded with survival gear, boots, suits, hypothermia blankets, emergency rations, torches and sleeping bags. In less than thirty seconds he was crouched beneath them, his head just below the driver's seat, his Browning in one hand, a thin nylon rope he'd filched from a sleeping bag in the other. He tested its strength between his hands. It made a perfect garrotte.

Cursing the stupidity of Jones and Moore, Chaloner returned to his vehicle, switched on the ignition and windscreen wipers, turned up the heater and waited for the privates to lift the barrier. He wondered if there was any point in risking incurring Simmonds' and Heddingham's wrath by continuing with this pointless exercise. He had erected three more road blocks in this area, one on the main road between Defynnog and

Libanus, one on the Sennybridge to Brecon road, and the other on the Llandovery to Sennybridge road.

He decided he may as well check them out before returning to Tal-y-Bont and enough army presence and hullabaloo to alert a regiment of drunken lager louts, let alone the skilled professional West had proved himself to be.

He slowed down when he saw the road sign for the crossroads that opened on to the A road ahead. The snow was so thick both in the air and on the ground; he could no longer make out the actual road. If it hadn't been for the signpost he might have believed he was driving over the hill. His headlights bounced back at him, from the snow-spotted, impenetrable mist. No rational man would be out on a night like this, but he still knocked the indicator down to the right from force of habit.

A hand pulled back his hood; fingers clawed into his hair, and jerked his head back. A thin rope slipped around his neck biting into his flesh, almost – but not quite – cutting his air supply.

'Hit the brake and pull on the hand brake.'

The instinct for survival kicked in and Chaloner did as he had been commanded. The last thing he saw before the world turned black was his windscreen coated in thick snow.

The moment West was certain the captain was unconscious he unwrapped a bandage from the first aid kit, stuffed it into the officer's mouth and secured it with the nylon rope. Taking a length of climbing rope and a hunting knife, he climbed into the front of the Land Rover. He secured the captain's hands behind his back, and tied his ankles together. Heaving the inert body into the back of the vehicle, he looped a rope between the bonds that secured the ankles and wrists and fastened the officer's legs high behind his back. It was then he noticed the captain was wearing a winged dagger badge. His captive was a fully fledged member of the SAS.

He switched on one of the torches and rummaged through the gear. He found a white camouflage suit and boots that fitted him. Donning a white ski mask, he filched the captain's insignia and badge, and noting the red ribbon tied high on the officer's arm, purloined it and tied it on to his own before covering the officer with sleeping bags. Jumping into the driving seat he continued on the route that unbeknown to him, the captain had intended to take, towards Defynnog and Sennybridge.

He hadn't travelled half a mile before he hit another road block. He stopped, kept his hand on the Browning, wound down the window and shouted, 'White alert,' as the captain had done.

Two soldiers snapped to attention.

'Anything to report?' he barked.

'No, sir.'

'Carry on, corporal.'

'Sir!' both men snapped.

He pushed the gear stick home, revved the engine and set off again when they raised the barrier. He'd succeeded in fooling them, but that was hardly surprising when every officer and man was wearing a ski-mask. The foul weather was working in his favour, and he'd had the good fortune to acquire an officer's insignia. Thanks to the ingrained army discipline that didn't encourage men to question officers' commands, and the size of an operation that had apparently led to troops being drafted in from any, and every unit that had men to spare, his confidence increased as he drove slowly but steadily towards Defynnog.

The tyres slipped twice, losing their grip on the compacted ice beneath the snow, but by dropping into low gear and slowing his speed he managed to inch forward. He tried not to consider what might happen if he was forced to abandon the Land Rover. He could hardly leave the captain to freeze in the back. He didn't dare risk setting him free, and the survival gear and emergency rations would be useless if the officer was immobilised and couldn't reach them. With the roads snowed up the vehicle might well not be found for days.

He concentrated on what little he could see of the road ahead and planned his return journey. He couldn't drive to Libanus, the vehicle would be an absolute giveaway parked in the village and, as he'd encountered two roadblocks in less than five miles, there was no reason to suppose there'd be fewer further on. He'd have to find somewhere safe to leave the captain, a place where both he and the Land Rover would be easily found, and preferably one where it might be assumed that he'd travelled on in the opposite direction to Libanus. But that would mean finding a different form of transport for his return.

One that wouldn't be easily tracked, not that anyone would be able to track anything for long in this storm.

He found what he was looking for outside Defynnog, a pub with a sign advertising lunches. He drove past it before cutting his lights and engine. After checking the captain was still breathing, he emptied two sleeping bags from their nylon covers. Taking the covers he walked back, sinking knee deep in the snow. A dog barked when he approached the back door. He inched his way along the wall of the house until he found the bins. He had little problem locating the pigswill, even in the cold, the smell told him which lid to open. Tipping it on to its side he trailed the mess it contained to the back door. He sprang the lock with the scalpel and stepped back as a Doberman leapt out. The dog rushed straight past him to fall on the slops.

He found everything he needed in the kitchen. He opened the fridge and tossed bread, butter, cheese, cartons of milk, and wine, packets of ham; an enormous veal and ham pie, and pasties into one bag. Opening another bag he packed an electric kettle, bread, coffee, tea, sugar, tins of corned beef and beans and soap. He enticed the dog back into the house with a lump of raw steak. Locking it in the pantry, he returned to the Land Rover. Dumping his bags in the back, he picked up the captain, slung him over his shoulder and returned to the pub. He left him, cushioned by a sleeping bag on the floor of the kitchen in front of the range. The officer would be warm and discovered first thing in the morning. It was the best he could do.

He drove the vehicle to Sennybridge and abandoned it outside the first house he came to. Delving into the back he filled a rucksack with a smaller camouflage suit and boots for Elizabeth, a torch, two sleeping bags, first aid kit and emergency rations. He only hoped the weather would ease enough for him to get back. He didn't relish the idea of digging in, even with all the gear he'd commandeered.

Piling the rucksacks and bags at the back of the Land Rover he shone a torch over the inside to check if he'd missed anything that might prove useful. At the side, half hidden by a mound of emergency rations and first aid kits was a rack of skis and poles. He had a pair fitted to his boots in minutes. Slinging the rucksack on his back and the two bags over his shoulders, he slipped on a pair of thermal gloves, took a pole in each hand and set off, back up the road to Libanus, careful to follow in the tracks of the Land Rover.

Although the wind had dropped, it was still snowing, less vigorously than before, but enough to cover the groove the skis cut in the tyre tracks. It was hard going, but he soon became accustomed to the darkness. He avoided the road blocks by leaving the road and skiing across country. Occasionally he hit a patch of ice and moved too fast for comfort but it was proving quicker and easier to ski over the drifts than trudge through them.

The ropes of the bags burned his shoulders and his arms and back were aching when the first houses on the outskirts of Libanus came into view. He had no idea of the time, but it was still dark and everything seemed quiet.

He halted at the beginning of the lane. The snow ahead of him was pristine, virgin white, crisp and untouched. He made his way forward as close to the garden walls as he could. Brushing great clumps of snow from the walls, he sprinkled them behind him in an attempt to cover his tracks. He stuck close to the wall when he entered the yard of the guest house. Lobbing the two bags and the rucksack on to the extension roof, he removed his skis and poles and pushed them up to the window. Dislodging as little snow as possible he climbed on the roof. Wrenching open the casement, he threw in the rucksack, bags and finally the skis and poles. The last thing he did before climbing in was stretch up to the roof and brush down a clump of overhanging snow, hoping, as he looked up at the sky, that just enough snow would fall before daylight to cover the worst of the marks he'd made.

Pushing the splintered wood back into the hole he closed the window and, leaving the skis behind, walked down the corridor with his rucksacks and bags. Heat blasted out, warm and enervating when he entered the bedroom. Elizabeth was lying on the mattress he'd dragged next to the fire, a blanket wrapped around her, basking in the glow from the fire. Her clothes and shoes had been laid out to dry on the bed springs. Following her example he stripped off. Laying his gun on the mattress, he took out the sleeping bags and unzipped them. He shook one out over Elizabeth and wrapped the other around himself.

The plastic that covered the mattress felt damp to the touch, but he was too tired to care. He stretched out next to Elizabeth, closed his eyes, and seconds later he too slept.

'We've received a report from one of our undercover intelligence operatives.' The minister looked down the conference table in the Cabinet Office briefing room. 'He has confirmed that an organisation affiliated to an Islamic fundamentalist group has plans to sabotage the peace conference. Captain Cartwright, an expert in Middle Eastern terrorist organisations, has the details.'

An officer rose to his feet. He looked ridiculously youthful in the company of so many middle-aged and elderly men. He opened a file, looked up and addressed the room in general. 'An experienced mercenary and assassin flew into London via an internal European flight that landed in Gatwick five days ago. He was met on arrival by operatives working for the fundamentalists.'

'Do you know the identity of everyone within the fundamentalist group?' a thin, anxious looking brigadier enquired.

'Not at present. We have all known members under surveillance but there may be others,' Cartwright conceded.

'Could these "others" be in positions of trust, possibly even within the security forces?' Lieutenant-Colonel Heddingham asked.

'Possible, but improbable. All members of the security forces are subject to rigorous background checks. However we are studying the files and backgrounds of all personnel assigned to the conference.' The captain continued to deliver his prepared statement. 'We believe the assassin's brief is to infiltrate the conference and kill delegates.'

'Is John West the assassin?' Heddingham asked the captain. Due to delays caused by the weather, both in the air and on the road, he hadn't reached London until two in the morning, and urgent messages, paperwork and a debriefing session had kept him awake until five. Which had given him exactly one and a half hours sleep before he'd had to rise at seven to attend the breakfast conference.

'We were hoping you would be able to answer that question for us by now, Lieutenant-Colonel,' the minister interceded. 'Is West in custody?'

'Unfortunately not, sir,' Heddingham answered.

'This will be the fourth day of the search since John West escaped from the hospital, will it not?'

'It will.' Heddingham wished himself anywhere but the conference room.

'Are you any closer to capturing him?'

'We believe so, minister,' Heddingham answered.

'A media conference is scheduled after this meeting. Can I intimate that you are close to capturing this man, without incurring the risk of looking extremely foolish in today's news bulletins and tomorrow's press?'

'When I left the Brecon area last night we had thrown a fifty mile cordon around the area he was last seen in.'

'Am I to assume that he's within that cordon?' the minister enquired.

'Not even our special forces operatives can cover fifty miles over that terrain within the allotted time span, particularly given the present weather conditions on the Brecon Beacons,' Heddingham replied confidently.

'Are you suggesting that this man's training is on a par with that given to our Special Forces, sir?' Captain Cartwright asked.

'I think Brigadier Cullen-Heames can answer that question better than I.' Heddingham looked to the brigadier, who cleared his throat before speaking.

'Bearing in mind the projected age of this John West, we have searched through all our records covering the last fifteen years, and we have accounted for all of our present and ex-personnel, so whoever this man is, I can confidently say that he wasn't trained at British taxpayer's expense.' The brigadier looked to Captain Cartwright. 'If you have any information that might help us pinpoint his identity we would be most grateful.'

'You know as much as the rest of us, Brigadier,' the minister said flatly. 'You have his photograph, description and psychological profile and an account of all the moves he has made since he was picked up on the motorway.' He gazed at Heddingham. 'Hopefully we'll find out more when you have him in custody.'

'I hope to have him before the end of the day, sir.'

'Before he kills anyone else, I trust.'

'Yes, sir.'

The minister rose from his chair, and the entire company stood to attention. 'See to it that I am informed the minute he is in custody, Lieutenant-Colonel.'

'Yes, sir.' Heddingham watched the minister leave the room.

His aide was at his shoulder. 'Back to Brecon, sir?'

'To Stirling Lines, and get them and the Storey Arms on the telephone before we leave.'

West woke to a blinding headache. The room was hot and airless with a stuffy, dry heat that had parched his throat and seared his lips. Elizabeth slept soundly next to him. He touched her forehead lightly with the back of his hand. It was no warmer than his. He looked around. Grey light filtered through the grimy cream and blue flowered curtains, casting grubby rays on the dust balls that littered the floor. The carpet beneath the mattress they were lying on smelt damp and fusty, its green pile heavily worn and stained around the bedstead, where too many feet had trodden and too many cups of tea and coffee had been spilled.

He moved, the soft, padded sleeping bag he had wrapped himself in felt warm, light and comfortable against his bare skin. He reached out to the springs of the bed where he had abandoned his clothes next to Elizabeth's. They were dry. He stretched his arms above his head. He was aching, either from the exertions of last night, or the long, cold hours he had lain cramped and immobile beneath the tin sheeting on the freezing hillside.

He turned back to Elizabeth, watching her as she slept, her arm bent beneath her head, her lips slightly parted, her long dark lashes grazing her flushed cheeks, her hacked hair spread loosely over the mattress, her whole body passive, relaxed.

He read the watch on her wrist. It could still be called morning – just. Reluctant to move, he continued to lie there until Elizabeth opened her eyes. She smiled sleepily.

'Good morning, Dr Santer.'

She stretched out languidly and held her hands out to the fire. 'After yesterday I thought I'd never be warm again.'

'I'm sorry; I've put you through hell.' Unable to resist touching her he stroked her shoulder with his fingers. Without thinking, she cupped his face gently in her hands. Leaning on his elbow he bent his head to hers and kissed her, a long, drawn out caress that ultimately embraced their entire bodies.

Blankets and sleeping bags were tossed aside as they fused, breath to breath, lips to lips, skin to naked skin, with a sensuous, tantalizing fervour that left her wanting more – much – much more of him.

All thought fled. Passion heightened and held sway. Elizabeth was aware of the beating of his heart, the clean, sharp smell of his perspiration, the whisper of his breath, the texture of his fingertips as they travelled over her throat to her breasts. But when she crushed her body against his, tenderness waned, to be replaced by a fierce, all-consuming hunger that was only sated when he finally pierced her body with his own.

It had been so long since she had made love, or wanted to. She had never thought another man could touch her body or her emotions in the way Joseph had; but there was no shame, no sadness in what she did with John.

He was not a substitute for Joseph. His body did not even feel like Joseph's. His muscles were like steel beneath her hands, and his lovemaking was altogether harsher, more savage and passionate than Joseph's had ever been.

Afterwards, she curled against him, wrapped her arms around his chest and wished she could hold him, imprisoned against her forever.

Forgetting hunger, thirst, the danger they were in, she sank back into a dreamless sleep, happier than she had been in two long, lonely years.

CHAPTER FOURTEEN

'Are you really all right, sir?' Lieutenant Dawkins hovered irritatingly around Chaloner. The captain was sitting at a table in the pub dining room, a cafétiere of black coffee and a cup and saucer in front of him.

'Perfectly well.' Chaloner filled the cup with coffee. 'I enjoy spending the odd night trussed like a chicken on a kitchen floor.'

'They've found the Land Rover, sir.' Sergeant Price stamped the snow from his boots on the doormat. 'It was parked on the outskirts of Sennybridge.'

'Damage?' Chaloner asked.

'Initial reports indicate none. They've searched the back, and if you went out fully loaded… '

'Which I did,' Chaloner interrupted.

'Some items of survival kit and a pair of skis have been taken. There's nothing there that shouldn't be. Forensic are checking the vehicle for DNA and prints.'

'I don't know why they're bothering. They checked the flat in Brecon after we stormed it and found plenty of samples, but no matches on any data bank. Any clothes in it that belonged to our man?'

'None, but HQ are sending us dog handlers, although I doubt there's much of a trail for them to follow after the blizzard last night.'

'Let's go and meet them, sergeant.'

'Sir.'

Chaloner finished his coffee and left the table. The humiliation of being overcome by the target in his own Land Rover incensed him. It was an incident that had made him a laughing stock, amusing half the men in his regiment and infuriating the others who'd undoubtedly feel that he'd let them down. He knew the episode would be recounted time and again, attracting more embellishments with each retelling. He could still hear the biting sarcasm in Simmonds' voice when he'd telephoned him at Stirling Lines earlier that morning.

"And exactly what were you doing on the Libanus to Defynnog Road, Major Chaloner?"

Not a word about allowing himself to be overpowered by the man half the army was out searching for. No doubt that would be something to bring up later, when he faced Heddingham.

The woman who had found him in the kitchen that morning came in. 'You off now, captain?' she asked in a cheerful voice.

'I am. Thank you for rescuing me.' He tried to forget the screams that had roused her husband, and the ten embarrassing minutes of hard explaining he'd had to do after her husband had cut through the gag.

'If you catch him ask him if he enjoyed that veal and ham pie. It wasn't touched and we would have got eighteen lunches out of that.'

When West woke for the second time, he found himself curled around Elizabeth, his arm resting on her waist, his face buried in her hair, both of them naked beneath the down filled sleeping bag. The headache that had been caused by cold, stress and lack of sleep had gone. He felt warm, comfortable, and when he gazed at Elizabeth, dangerously relaxed considering the precariousness of their situation.

Sliding carefully away so as not to wake her, he eased himself out from beneath the sleeping bag, took the soap from the rucksack, grabbed one of the blankets he'd taken from the ambulance and sneaked to the door. A blast of damp, freezing air, hit him the moment he stepped into the passage. There was an electric oil filled radiator fitted in the bathroom. He turned it, the immersion heater in the airing cupboard, and the electric shower on. Putting the plug in the bottom of the bath lest the sound of water running in the outside drainpipes alert the neighbours to the presence of someone in the house, he washed quickly, rubbing his hand ruefully over the stubble on his chin, wishing that he'd thought to look for a razor in the back of the Land Rover.

He wrapped himself in the blanket because there were no towels and returned to the bedroom. Elizabeth was still asleep, curled on the mattress in front of the fire in an atmosphere that was too hot for comfort. Rummaging through the bags and rucksack he'd left in the corner of the room, he retrieved the electric kettle and went to the bathroom to fill it. She was awake when he returned.

'Hungry?' He plugged the kettle into a socket behind the door.

'I think so. I'm having difficulty remembering food.'

'I'll make breakfast while you shower. There's soap in the dish, but no towels, shower gel or shampoo and I'm sorry, but you'll have to stand in my dirty water. I've left the plug in lest the sound of water running into the drains gives us away.'

'I'll manage.' She recalled the happenings of the early morning, and blanched.

'Your dressing gown, Madam.' He picked up the other blanket from the bedsprings and handed it to her.

'We need to talk.' She turned her back to him and wrapped the blanket around her shoulders.

'Later.' He opened the rucksack and untied the bags. 'After we've eaten.'

Chaloner watched the handler send his dog into the back of the Land Rover. The animal pawed at the clothes and first aid boxes, sniffed around the plastic sheathed sleeping bags and emergency rations, and suddenly became very excited.

The handler pulled a piece of raw steak out from beneath a first aid chest. 'This chap really knows his business.'

'We know he took some survival gear. I was hoping he left his own clothes,' Chaloner looked around the back of the vehicle.

'Nothing here that's not army issue, sir.' The handler bagged the raw steak and ordered the dog from the back of the vehicle. 'I'll run the dog around the area to see if there's a scent worth picking up. But I doubt it on a main road like this.'

‘Thank you, I knew it was a long shot before we started.’ Chaloner took the coffee Sergeant Price handed him in a steel cup from the top of a flask. He was still angry – and exhausted. He had woken in the early hours of the morning, his legs and arms jerked half out of their sockets by nylon ropes that had burned the skin around his wrists and ankles. Not knowing where he was, or what to expect, he had lain awake until six o’clock, by which time the Doberman had eaten all it could reach in the pantry and begun whining to be freed.

He wanted to return to his quarters in Stirling Lines, take a shower, change his clothes and plot the downfall of the bastard who had outwitted him. Before it had been a job, now he had been made to look like a fool, it was personal.

‘Nothing, sir.’ The dog handler returned. ‘The blizzard has carried away whatever scent there was.’

‘At least we tried.’ Chaloner replied grudgingly. ‘All we have to decide now is which way our man went.’

‘He couldn’t have picked a better place to leave the vehicle, sir,’ Sergeant Price observed. ‘He could have gone in almost any direction from here. Llandovery, Brecon, Ystradgynlais, Merthyr, Hirwaun… ’

‘He wouldn’t have got far last night on skis,’ Lieutenant Dawkins joined them, fresh faced and eager as a puppy.

‘Unless he stole a car, in which case he could have moved on to Swansea, Cardiff, North Wales, or almost anywhere in the UK.’ Price screwed the top back on to his thermos.

'Or he could be sticking to the place he knows,' Chaloner said thoughtfully.

'You think he's gone back to Brecon, sir?' Price asked.

'I haven't a bloody clue, sergeant,' Chaloner swore with uncharacteristic exasperation. 'But one thing's certain, we're not going to find him by standing around here talking.'

'Stirling Lines, sir?'

'ASAP. We'll contact the patrols when we're there. Let's hope one of them fared better than me last night.'

West stood at the side of the window and peered through the narrow gap in the curtains on to the road. It had stopped snowing, but judging by the lack of tracks, it hadn't stopped long. He read the watch Elizabeth had left on the mattress. Half past three. Soon it would be dark again and he would have to decide his next move. For the moment he didn't want to think further than this room and the meal they were about to eat.

Moving away from the window, he carried the bags to the mattress, straightened the sleeping bag and laid the food on top. Bread, cheese, knives, no plates, foil wrapped butter, ham in a plastic bag that he tore open with the knife, the great slab of greaseproof paper wrapped veal and ham pie that was now crumbling at the edges, the cartons of wine and milk, and a box of ready washed salad. Too hungry to wait for Elizabeth, he hacked off a ragged slice of bread, wrapped it round a piece of ham and started to eat.

She walked into the room, wet hair dripping down her back, as he was biting into his second doorstep sized sandwich.

'Coffee?' He flicked down the switch to boil the kettle for the second time and produced two tin mugs he'd appropriated from the Land Rover.

'With milk and sugar?'

'Of course.' He pulled half a bag of sugar out of one of the sacks and pointed to the carton of milk.

'You're a genius.' Tucking the blanket high under her arms, hooking the loose end into the top to secure it, she sat on the mattress, picked up a knife and chopped at the pie.

'Sorry, there are no plates.'

'Hands were made before plates,' she mumbled through a full mouth.

He sawed off another hunk of bread and cut himself a piece of cheese.

'I'm afraid to ask where you found all this.'

'There was a Mercedes parked in the drive so they can afford to stand a loss in a good cause. That's if you consider us a good cause,' he added dryly.

'Of course we are. This is absolute bliss. Warmth and food. One day on that hill has taught me to appreciate the simple things in life.'

'Some people would call a full stomach and a warm room luxuries.'

'Like who?'

He knew she was testing him. 'People who rarely experience either and have to fight for survival. And that's just what I've reduced your life to – a fight for survival.'

'I'm doing nicely at the moment thanks to you.'

'We can't hole up here forever.'

'No, I suppose we can't.' Tearing a piece of the pie wrapping she dropped the chunk she'd been eating on to it. 'What do you intend to do?' she asked, dreading his answer.

'I don't know. But what I do know is it's inevitable that we're going to be captured.'

'You've managed to successfully avoid that happening so far.'

'We've been lucky. But with the manpower they've got searching for us, sooner or later we'll be caught like rats in a trap. And I don't want to be driven up a blind alley where… someone… ' he faltered, only just stopping himself from saying "you" 'could get hurt.'

'You can't be considering giving yourself up?'

'On my terms.' He cut two more pieces of ham and handed her one.

'What terms do you think you could negotiate with the armed hordes they've sent after us?'

'I won't know until I negotiate.'

'You wouldn't even be thinking of giving yourself up if it wasn't for me.'

'It's no use running when there's no place left to run to. I thought I'd find at least some of the answers in Brecon. I have to face facts. I don't know who I am, or what I've done to warrant having half the army and all of the police force after me. The temperature on the hills is below freezing. The weather's foul, with probably more blizzards and snowstorms on the way. The only reason I've stayed alive this long is because I've proved myself an expert thief and ruthless… '

'You did what you had to, in order to stay alive. There's no crime in that,' she interrupted.

'Is that your personal or professional opinion?'

'Both,' she asserted forcefully.

'Moralists and the law would say you're wrong. I should never have taken you hostage much less allowed you to jump from that ambulance.' He ran the knife blade over the lump of cheese tracing patterns on the smooth golden surface.

'You couldn't have stopped me from jumping after you. We're here, and now we have to decide where to go and what to do next,' she asserted practically.

'I'm not going to regain my memory, am I?'

'I honestly don't know.' She finished her coffee and leaned back on her hands. 'Don't look at me like that. That's the truth. As I said to you that first day in the hospital, you could remember in the next ten minutes, hour, day… '

'Or never?'

'Or never,' she agreed quietly.

'We could try hypnosis again.'

'You're afraid to pull the plug on the bath lest the sound of running water alerts the neighbours, yet you're prepared to risk the noise of hysteria?'

'Can't you order me to be quiet?'

'I could order you to do a great many things, Captain,' she answered, glancing at the insignia on the suit he'd laid out on the bedsprings, 'but I doubt you'd obey me.'

'Captain?' he mused.

'Did it sound familiar?'

'Vaguely.'

'Perhaps you hold – or held – that rank.'

'The question is in which army.'

She shook coffee powder into her cup and switched on the kettle. She didn't want another coffee, but she needed to do something – anything rather than face him and think through the consequences of what had happened between them.

He pushed his tin mug towards her. She shook powder into it and filled it from the boiling kettle, conscious of him watching her every move. Unable to stand the tension between them a moment longer, she finally looked into his eyes, and saw confusion – and pain mirrored in them.

'What happened between us... ' he began.

'Happened,' she interrupted, not wanting to add to his problems. 'It was one of those things, ships that pass in the night and all that.'

'Perhaps, but that doesn't make what I did right. Not even knowing my own name, I should never have touched you.'

'I'm not sorry,' she said defiantly.

'You might be if you knew more about me.'

She set the mugs on the floor and moved towards him. Linking her hands around his neck she stared into his eyes. 'I can tell you exactly who you are. You're a kind, gentle, decent man. You're incapable of doing anything underhanded, dirty, or as foul as murder.' She conveniently forgot Dave's warning that psychotics were among the most charming people in the world. 'Be honest, the only reason you want to give yourself up is that you care about me. In the middle of all this mess, with God alone knows who after you, you haven't knowingly hurt a single person… '

'I shot two soldiers in the hospital and one in the house in Brecon.'

'Only because they were firing at you, and even then you shot to wound not kill.'

'I wish I could believe you.'

'People's characters don't change just because they've lost their memory.' She kissed him lightly on the lips, before moving away.

He clenched his fists around the empty rucksack, squeezing it with all his strength. It would have been so easy to follow her and take her into his arms.

'You went to all the trouble of stealing this food, yet neither of us has eaten very much.' She scarcely knew what she was saying. Aware of his desire for her, she was fighting to suppress her own feelings.

'I want to try hypnosis one last time. If you're afraid of noise, I'll muffle my face in blankets,' he added.

'What if you become hysterical and throw them off? What if it doesn't work like last time?' she questioned seriously.

'I'll turn from prey to hunter. Find an army patrol, and ask if any of them knows who I am.'

'You really think you're an army officer?'

'If I'm not, why is everyone in a uniform in such a damned hurry to kill me?'

'Because they think you're a murderer.'

'Whoever killed those soldiers knows I'm not. But they say it takes one to catch one.'

Not wanting to get caught up again in the endless argument as to whether or not he was a killer, she said, 'all right, you win. Let's clear away this food so you can lie down. Then we'll try hypnosis one last time.'

'I heard you excelled yourself last night, Captain Chaloner.' Lieutenant-Colonel Heddingham was a model of self-control. The only sign of anger was in the grim set of his lips.

'I apologize, unreservedly, sir.'

'You apologize!' Heddingham spat out the words. 'You present West with a gift of your Land Rover and all it contained, and you apologize!'

'Sir,' Chaloner replied briefly, focusing on Simmonds' bald head.

'And now you've made your apology, what do you intend to do to capture the man?'

'Go out on patrol on the Beacons, sir.'

'We've had patrols out combing the Beacons for two days, what makes you think you'll be any more successful than they've been?'

'The suspicion that he's gone to ground somewhere in the hills. I've had experience of identifying and neutralising enemy observation posts, sir.' Chaloner wasn't boasting, he'd had plenty of experience in doing just that, in desert, arctic and jungle conditions, but he also had no more idea as to where West was hiding than any other man in the Command Cell. He had studied maps of the area until his eyes could no longer focus. He had imagined himself out on the Beacons with a rucksack of emergency rations, sleeping bags, and survival equipment, and plotted moves that made less and less sense as he thought the situation through.

If West was a terrorist working for one of the Islamic fundamentalist organisations, as everyone in authority seemed to think he was, then why hadn't he high tailed it to London as soon as he had escaped from the hospital? There were embassies who would be delighted to give sanctuary to a warrior fighting a Jehad. Going to Brecon made no sense, staying out on the Beacons even less. Yet if West had any intention of leaving the area, why steal survival equipment, with a Mercedes going begging outside the guesthouse? A car that would have presented no problems to the man who had stolen the estate-car they had found in the garage of the flat in Brecon.

'If you're hoping to avoid the flak that's going to be flying out of the Ministry in this direction at the end of the day by heading for the hills, you're being over-optimistic, Captain,' Heddingham warned.

'I don't think West would have taken the equipment if he hadn't intended to hide out in the hills,' Chaloner persisted.

'Equipment which you handed to him.' Simmonds felt obliged to contribute something to the conversation.

'Do I have your permission to go out on patrol, sir?' Chaloner pressed.

Heddingham was already phrasing his excuses to London, excuses that laid the blame squarely on the

Special Forces officers who had flagrantly and blatantly ignored his orders.

'Sir?' Chaloner prompted.

'Go to the devil if you so choose, Chaloner, as long as you're back here by six tomorrow morning for a briefing.'

'Sir.' Chaloner wondered why the briefing had been called so far in advance, but concerned only with going after the man who had humiliated him, he didn't ask.

Whether it was because their lovemaking had broken down some of the barriers between them, instilling trust as well as lust, and Elizabeth hoped – a little affection, or whether it was because West was more relaxed and secure in the haven he had found, Elizabeth didn't know, but it proved easier for her to hypnotize him a second time.

She worked at a slower pace; asking questions about the door he was visualizing. The dark wooden door with brass furniture and stained glass panels he described wasn't the door to the flat in Brecon. Resisting the temptation to ask him to open it, she took him slowly and methodically back through the drifting clouds to the first moment of his life he could actually remember – running down the motorway.

'I know you're running, but we want to go back further. Just a little further. Where are you?'

'Running, down a road. It's dark… '

'What can you see at the side of the road?'

'Houses.'

'What kind?'

‘Semis, curtains closed, lights shining… it’s dark, and raining. I’m wet.’ He tossed fitfully on the mattress. ‘Cold and wet.’

‘Go back… Float upwards… upwards in the clouds… and back. Half an hour, no further… You’ve floated back. What are you doing?’

‘Walking down the stairs.’

‘Where are the stairs?’

‘In the house,’ he answered impatiently. ‘I’m cold. I’ve just left the shower. My hair is wet.’

‘Is there someone downstairs?’

‘Visitors. They want to see me.’

‘Who are they?’

‘Oh Jesus Christ!’ His voice pitched high, ending in a chilling scream. ‘Oh no… ’ He flung himself face down on the mattress and covered his head with his hands.

‘Are they shooting at you?’

‘They’re dead,’ he mumbled thickly.

“They’re dead.” There was raw agony in the pronouncement that induced a tide of self-loathing. No one had the right to inflict the kind of pain she was subjecting John to. Dave had once told her that if a patient had blotted out something, they had done so for good reason. And, he’d believed that some experiences were better left buried, for all the modern confrontation theories and group therapy treatments.

‘They didn’t have to kill them. Not when they wanted me.’ The intense anger in his voice was tempered with an almost unbearable grief. ‘Come and get me you bastards!’ he taunted. ‘I’ll make you pay for this… ’ He rose and ran to the window.

'John!' she realized he was about to hurl himself through the glass. 'It's over. You're not there any more.' She blocked his path with her body. He bulldozed her to the floor. She gripped his ankles with both hands, straining to hold him. 'You're back in the house in Libanus. It's over. John it's over… ' She looked up. His eyes were open. He was staring down at her. 'John?'

'There was a gun pointing at me. I ran through a window, it shattered… ' he screamed again, a scream so piercing she was afraid it would be heard from one end of the village to the other.

'It's all right.' Rising to her feet she wrapped her arms around him and held him close. It didn't matter that the blankets were slipping away from both of them. Only that he was frightened and in pain, and needed what little comfort she was able to offer him.

'I saw that hand again. The one with the scar and the gun. There was blood… lots of blood… ' He looked down at his own hands as though he were checking them for the scar.

'You didn't have a gun.'

'I wasn't firing one.'

'Did you see the face of the man who held the gun?'

'He was middle-aged, fair skinned.'

'Do you remember your name?'

'No.'

'You were in a house. Walking down the stairs in a house. Can you remember where it was?'

He closed his eyes and covered his face with his hands.

'We have time… '

'No we don't,' he broke in bitterly. 'That is the one thing we don't have.' He dropped the blanket, rose to his feet and walked naked to the bed where he'd left his clothes and the camouflage suit. She watched him dress. Strange, she'd never thought of a man's body as beautiful before. Not even Joseph's. The desire to go to him was overwhelming, but he didn't need her. She'd done all she could, and it wasn't enough.

'You're leaving?'

'I was far gone, but I know I screamed loud enough to be heard in Brecon, let alone Libanus.'

'I'm coming with you.'

'No. Stay here, wait a couple of hours then go a house and telephone the police.'

'They know I stayed with you because I wanted to. No one made me jump after you from that ambulance.'

'I won't expose you to any more danger.'

'Will it be as dangerous where you're going, as it will be for me if I stay here?' She raised her eyes to his. 'Dave, the paramedic… '

'Put these on.' He handed her the small camouflage suit he'd scavenged from the Land Rover. Dropping her blanket she started to dress.

'I still think you should stay here. If you can't trust the police, call a newspaper, they'll give you protection.'

'And what story do you suggest I tell them?'

'The truth.'

'Do you know what that is?' she asked flatly. 'Because, I don't. Not any more.'

'Donovan O'Gallivan.' Captain Cartwright passed a photograph pinned to a file down the conference table in the Command Cell that had been set up in Stirling Lines. 'IRA terrorist, who offered his services to a Middle Eastern based group after the ceasefire. This is the only known photograph of him. The minister thought I should brief you with what we know about him.'

'We're expected to recognize him from this?' Major Simmonds held up the blurred photograph of a man wearing dark glasses and a beret, a black scarf tied, bandit fashion, over the lower part of his face.

'It was taken at an IRA funeral. His description is in the file. Six foot four inches, well built, black hair, blue eyes, no distinguishing features apart from various scars and healed bullet wounds, gifted linguist who has been known to successfully adopt various accents.'

'It has to be our man,' Heddingham affirmed. The operation was wearing him down. All he could think of after a day spent in fruitless conference, staring out of the windows at a bleak, white frosted landscape, was a month's leave. Preferably in Barbados with a woman prettier and more amenable than his wife had been of late.

'The description fits many men,' Captain Cartwright advised prudently.

'But it also happens to fit our man,' Heddingham commented. 'The photograph resembles him, and you chaps must have been fairly certain it was him before you went to the minister with this?' He tapped the file.

'He is a known Islamic fundamentalist operative whose movements cannot be accounted for at present. Our intelligence services believe he is on assignment in Europe.'

'Well, there you have it then, Cartwright. And the minister is satisfied with the identification?'

'Neither the minister, nor the cabinet will be satisfied until this man is caught,' the thin, runny nosed brigadier, Cullen-Heames, who had flown down to Stirling Lines with Cartwright, ventured.

Heddingham looked to Simmonds. 'I'm in charge of this operation, and I say it's time to stop pussyfooting around. West has killed four times already. Shoot on sight. You'll relay the order, Major?'

'Sir.' Simmonds left the room.

'Shoot on sight, sir?' the radio operative asked Simmonds as he approached.

'How did you guess?'

'With the disarmament conference starting tomorrow there's no way they can afford to take any chances.'

West left the guesthouse the moment it was dark. With the memory of his screams still echoing in his mind, he packed the rucksack with food and the sleeping bags, checked and primed the guns, slung one over his shoulder and thrust the other into a holster. He tied red bands cut from the blankets to both his and Elizabeth's upper right arms. He had covered everything he could think of, but decided he could forget the password. After last night they would have undoubtedly changed it.

Elizabeth switched off the fire. They hadn't even spent twenty four hours in the dilapidated room. It was little more than a squat, but she had lived more vividly within its walls than she had done at any time since Joseph's death. She had even experienced a fleeting, momentary happiness. Whatever the future brought, that at least would stay with her.

'Ready?'

She looked at John, already he seemed harder, more remote than the man she had made love to, and it wasn't simply the clothes and weapons.

'Yes.' She pulled the ski mask over her head.

He unzipped her suit and thrust the spare Browning into the inside of her waistband.

'I don't want it,' she protested.

'I know.' He led the way out of the room, switching off the immersion heater as he went. 'But I might.'

CHAPTER FIFTEEN

'You can oversee the search from here, sir,' Sergeant Price suggested as Chaloner pored over a map of the Beacon area in the room they'd requisitioned in the Storey Arms.

'I'm going out with one of the patrols, Sergeant,' Chaloner informed him abruptly without looking up from the map.

'You didn't get any sleep last night, and not much in the two nights before that,' the sergeant dropped tact in favour of common sense. 'The men are fresh…'

'I'll keep up, Sergeant.' Chaloner rammed his finger on the map. 'He's around here somewhere,' he declared decisively.

The sergeant looked down. 'You think he's in Libanus, sir?'

'Somewhere close by.'

'But the police conducted house to house searches the night he jumped from that ambulance and again the following morning. They found nothing in the village, or the surrounding farms. And neither did the dogs that picked up his scent from the clothes in the St Michael Street flat.'

'Let's look at what we do know, not at what we don't.' Chaloner took a pink marker pen and drew a triangle half way along the curving road between Libanus and the Storey Arms. 'He jumped here. We had two hundred men out looking for him within the hour, and they came up with absolutely nothing. That tells us he did one of two things… '

'You think he had someone waiting for him?' Sergeant Price interrupted.

'If there had been, they would have had to be in a helicopter. Within an hour of him jumping the police had road blocks set up in every direction for fifty miles. And if he had flown off, he hardly would have returned to ambush me.'

'So, he knows the terrain, and used the cover of the snow storm to dig himself in on the mountain.'

'Precisely. For my money he went to ground. And that's why he took brandy and hypothermia blankets from the ambulance. Men have dug themselves into a hide with less and survived.'

'And Dr Santer? You think she's still with him?'

'If she's alive. The driver told us that West didn't want her to stay with him. Yesterday, we mounted an intensive search of this entire area,' Chaloner drew a circle on the map that encompassed the three peaks of the Beacons, the Storey Arms, the areas both sides of the Libanus Road and the Mountain Centre, 'and we come up with precisely nothing. Then in the early hours of the morning our man turns up here.' He brought the pen down on the back road that led from Libanus to the Mountain Centre. 'He ambushes me, steals water and wind proof clothing, survival equipment, skis and food, all of which will enable him to continue living in a hide. A hide he could have left Dr Santer in, a hide which must be less than an hour's walk from the point at which he jumped. Any further and one of the patrols would have seen him going in.'

'And you think he's still there?'

'Wouldn't you be, if you were him? He's evaded us so far. Therefore it's logical to assume he knows our methods and thought patterns. And he's probably assumed, quite rightly so, that the brass will want the search moved on soon. All he has to do is sit tight for a few more days before making his next move.'

'So what do the patrols cover tonight, sir?'

'We have a dozen?'

'Forty men, eight NCO's, including me, and four officers including you, sir.'

'Form thirteen patrols. We concentrate on a five mile area from the point at which he jumped, and,' Chaloner smiled frostily, 'let's hope we find him before morning. If we don't, I have a feeling the CO isn't going to be slow in laying the blame for his escape at our door.'

'We'll need luck, sir,' the sergeant rolled up the map. 'And a bucket of morale. The lads are getting a little tired of all this arctic weather training.'

Elizabeth followed John to the window that overlooked the flat roofed extension. He checked all three guns for the last time. While Elizabeth had dressed he'd cleaned every last smear of grease from their mechanisms, lest they freeze and jam when they were taken into the cold. He pulled his white ski mask over his face before opening the casement. He studied the buildings and backyards that gleamed white in the twilight. Encouraged by the silence, he stepped into the thick snow on the roof. Putting his hand on his gun, he glanced back, watching Elizabeth climb out alongside him.

Despite the layers of clothing and the boots, she shivered as soon as her lungs drew in the freezing air. He moved his head, signalling for her to go down first. She sank to her knees on the edge of the roof. He gripped her wrists and lowered her down. Closing the window, he pushed in the splintered wood and smeared snow over the broken area around the catch. The village was eerily silent, almost like a ghost town.

They padded quietly down the lane. Half hearted attempts had been made to clear the snow from the backs of some of the houses, but the temperature hovered well below freezing and John sensed it was continuing to plunge. Layers of ice had formed over the paths that had been freed from snow, frosting them with a clear, crystalline ice. He walked unhurriedly to the end of the lane, then he remained in the shadows for what seemed like an eternity to Elizabeth. Finally he rounded the last house warily and beckoned her forward. Together they slipped across the road, heading away from Brecon towards the Beacons and the Storey Arms.

His pace quickened as they left the road for the hills, his senses on the alert for any flash of movement or unusual sound. He had all night to search for a patrol. And he was determined that when he finally met one, he'd greet it on his own terms. Perhaps then, he'd finally find the key to the corpse-strewn mystery of his past.

*   *   *

Elizabeth had always considered herself fit. No matter how long her shifts in the hospital, she had tried to find time to exercise, but when she followed John down the steep, slippery slopes to the valley floor, every muscle in her arms and legs began to burn, and her chest heaved sluggishly when she struggled to draw air into her beleaguered lungs.

Oblivious to her discomfort West continued to forge ahead, only occasionally turning to check on her progress, and although she was unable to see anything other than his brilliant blue eyes and the small hole that exposed two chapped lips, she sensed that he was growing restless with her inability to keep pace.

He crouched low and waved her down when they came within sight of the floodlit car park of the Storey Arms. Men were piling in and out of trucks and milling around the vehicles outside the Youth Hostel.

'Ten minute, break.' He led her towards a rocky outcrop that afforded some, but not much, shelter, hoping that by the time the mass of soldiers in the car park would have broken into separate patrols, he'd have isolated a likely quarry. Squatting beneath the largest of the stones he swung the rucksack from his back, opened it and handed her the bottle of brandy. She rested her back against one of the icy rocks, feeling almost too exhausted to grip the bottle, but when she sipped it she was glad she'd made the effort. A welcome albeit weakening warmth coursed through her veins. She returned the bottle to him. Her idea of bliss at that moment would have been to rest long enough to regain her breath, before retracing their steps to the bed and breakfast in Libanus. There, they could have turned on the fire and finished the brandy before wrapping themselves in the blankets and curling up together for the night.

'Where are we heading?' She felt that if she had a goal, no matter how remote, it might give her the encouragement she needed to make a greater effort.

'Wherever they are going. Look, but don't move more than absolutely necessary,' he warned as she strained her neck towards the car park. 'These camouflage suits are good, but any movement is a dead giveaway.'

'You're going to follow a patrol?' She blanched at the thought of trying to keep up with a squad of fit young men.

'Only until they're isolated. Then we capture an officer.' He made it sound ridiculously easy.

'You think an officer might know who you are?'

'I know the SAS headquarters are at Stirling Lines in Herefordshire, within easy driving distance of here. They're probably using the place as HQ to co-ordinate the search. If I get the officer to take me back there, I might reach the man in charge. If anyone will know my identity, he will.'

'Do you think they'll just let you just walk in there?'

'No.'

'They'll shoot you on sight,' she warned.

'Not if I'm unarmed.'

'How will they know you're unarmed?'

'The officer who will take me there will know I'm unarmed, because I will have surrendered to him.'

'He could kill you… '

'Officers in the British army don't generally shoot people if they're waving a white flag.'

'They wouldn't shoot you if you use me as a hostage.'

'It wouldn't work.'

'It did before,' she reminded.

'It wouldn't now.'

'Because you made love to me?' she challenged.

'Because they know you stayed with me willingly.' He rose to his feet. 'A patrol is moving up Corn Du. The back marker is slow. Half an hour and he'll be struggling to keep up. Keep low, and follow in my tracks.'

She rose, her limbs stiff with cold. Pulling down her ski mask, she lowered her head and followed in his footsteps, one grey-white shadow stumbling after another in the snowy wasteland. She considered the neat, sterile life she had organised for herself since Joseph had died. How she had become accustomed to a complete absence of emotion, never feeling much of anything until Dave's death, and how the last forty-eight hours had set her vapid little world on its head.

They concentrated on putting one foot in front of the other as they climbed for what seemed like hours until she looked at John's back and realized that a thick mist had descended. He took a step forward and sank to his thighs in a drift. Everything, the valley below, the road cut into the hillside, the Storey Arms, the vehicles in the car park, the patrols – all had been swallowed by fog.

‘Stay still. I’m going to tie a rope to your belt so we don’t lose one another.’

‘Surely the patrols won’t stay out in this?’ she demurred as he pulled at her belt.

‘They have compasses, they’ll carry on.’

‘Do you know where we are?’ She swayed, as a patch of mist swirled away, to expose a sheer cliff plunging giddily below them, only to be veiled moments later as a second cloud moved in.

‘Roughly, there’s a sheltered spot over here.’ Taking her hand he guided her over a ridge. He opened the rucksack, pulled out the hypothermia blankets and the sleeping bags and handed them to her. ‘Get some rest, while we wait for them to come to us.’

She didn’t argue. Emotionally and physically drained, she was too tired to eat the food he offered her. Wrapping herself in a blanket she crawled into a sleeping bag, lay beside him, closed her eyes and slept.

Chaloner had hand-picked his men. Three privates seconded from the paratroopers, who hadn’t finished their continuation training, so were not yet fully fledged members of the Special Air Services Regiment. His sergeant had remonstrated with him to no avail. He had ensured a mix of experienced and inexperienced men in all the four-man patrols except his own. But, as he followed his three men up the mountain side, he realized he hadn’t chosen badly. The men might be only half way through the fourteen week continuation training, but they had all passed the rigorous selection test, and, judging by the way they handled themselves, they were no strangers to physical hardships or route marches.

The man he had elected as leader was doing well with the compass. He knew because he took the time to double check their position every ten minutes. He had taken the post of "tail end Charlie" which entailed stopping, and looking around every few yards. After the fiasco of being overcome in his own Land Rover, he reasoned he'd be more vigilant than any other man – and he knew what their target was capable of.

West sat next to Elizabeth and peered into the mist, his mind awash with confused and menacing images. He didn't know whether some were real memories, or simply visions created by his overwrought imagination after Elizabeth's attempts at hypnosis.

He tried to recreate the events since he had been picked up on the motorway in an attempt to sift fact from fiction. He could remember running on the motorway, the feel of the skim of cold water beneath his bare feet, the warmth of the plastic the paramedics had shrouded around his body before putting him in the ambulance. The white suited figures in casualty who had taken swabs from his hands, face and chest. The "hoovering" of glass splinters from his hair and face. Being taken to a treatment room to be cleaned up, given a gown, having his ankle bandaged… from that point onwards he could clearly recall the sequence of events. So why couldn't he remember what had happened before he'd landed on that motorway?

Elizabeth had told him – or did he remember running down a street, across a school playing field, vaulting a gate? He closed his eyes and tried to recreate Elizabeth's hypnosis technique; playing the tape of memory backwards as he floated through the clouds, then downwards to the street of suburban houses, the playing field and back to a house. How did he leave the house? Through shattering glass. He had curled himself into a ball, head down, and thrown himself through a window, not a patio window, but a bay – the front panel of a large bay.

He could see the glass gleaming darkly in the lamplight, mirroring wavering images. Images of what? A leather sofa, himself… he'd looked at the glass, gauging the distance as he lay crouched on the floor, holding the broken, bloody body… whose body? Someone close to him? A relative? His wife? Had he killed her? Was that why no one had claimed him?

His eyes strained through the fog that blanketed him in then, as though it were hovering in the air before him, he saw the hand holding a gun, the scar running along the thumb – the scar resembling a many legged centipede. He saw it! It was there. That at least had to be real.

'Bloody pea soup, this… sir.' The recruit tagged on the 'sir,' for Chaloner's benefit as they reached the top of the ridge. He hadn't realised the captain was close until Chaloner was standing alongside him.

'Good Brecon weather isn't it, sir?' another private chipped in.

‘Move on in silence,’ Chaloner ordered to discourage small talk. He pressed the button on his watch. Midnight. He couldn’t remember the last time he’d lain in a bed. The recruit was right about one thing, this was good Brecon weather – good for survival exercises. If troops carrying full packs could negotiate their way through mist and weather as foul as this to a pre-arranged rendezvous, chances were they were half way towards picking up the endurance skills needed to operate behind enemy lines.

The other skills would be hard won later, he reflected ruefully, thinking of some of the men who hadn’t made it back to base after being out on the Beacons in conditions no worse than this. Men who’d frozen to death with equipment and rations that would have saved them from hypothermia and death, untouched in their packs.

Perhaps that was what had happened to John West. Perhaps he was lying beside Dr Santer right now, in a hide scraped into the snow somewhere in this desolate frozen wilderness. But somehow he knew John West wasn’t dead. The man had won through too much to die cornered in a hide like an animal. The man who had outwitted him and the highly trained force in the hospital, successfully by-passed police roadblocks, escaped from the flat in Brecon and hijacked him last night wouldn’t allow himself or his hostage to die needlessly. Not without getting what he wanted. The question was, what did this professional who was capable of anticipating and out-manoeuvring every move made against him, want?

* * *

John sat so still in the darkness that a sheep that had escaped the round-ups came and stood no more than three feet away. It dug its nose into the snow in search of grazing. John continued to sit and watch, resisting the temptation to open his bag and give the sheep bread lest the movement alert someone just outside the curtain of mist.

He listened hard but could hear only the wind as it blew down from the hill top. But they'd be here soon. He knew they'd be aiming for the ridge, just as he knew there'd be four of them. A pathfinder, two in the middle, and a tail end Charlie to deflect and minimise the risk of ambush.

How did he know? Because he had once been one of them, or because he'd studied them so he could outwit them in a fight? He glanced down at Elizabeth curled into her sleeping bag alongside him, her hair hidden beneath the hood, her face covered by the ski-mask. Whatever else happened in the next twenty-four hours he was determined to do all he could to ensure that she survived.

He crawled out of his blanket, crept to the edge of the hollow and listened. He thought he could hear ice cracking as the water trapped beneath the surface of the snow hardened and froze. Already the make-shift comfort of the warm bedroom and bathroom in the empty guest house seemed a lifetime away. He returned to the rucksack, drew out the flask of brandy, took a nip and checked his guns. Both were still dry. He slipped the ammunition from the Browning. The parts moved freely, the mechanism hadn't iced up. He reloaded the gun and slid it back into the holster, leaving the flap unbuttoned.

Noting his position he left Elizabeth and climbed higher. His senses told him he was half way up the slope of Corn Du but there was nothing for him to set a fix on. The mist shrouded everything. Perhaps if he climbed down just a few yards?

He had barely gone twenty steps when he heard the unmistakeable tread of footsteps biting deep into iced snow. He knew he'd find no better camouflage than the mist. Dropping to his knees he peered in the direction of the footsteps.

If Sergeant Price had been walking behind Ross Chaloner he would have crowed "I told you so." Chaloner's feet were dragging, a slight, but unmistakeable, sign to an experienced NCO accustomed to spotting the signs of fatigue in a rookie. Chaloner watched the men walk into the mist ahead of him, turned and looked around in a routine check. The only sounds he could hear were the men's footsteps.

He listened to his radio for a moment. It was silent in accordance with the order only to transmit if there was a definite sighting of West. He had chosen this route because he had a hunch that this was where West would be. In a hide that overlooked the sweep of the hillside, the road, the valley and the village of Libanus. He wanted the man so badly his fists ached.

Adjusting his goggles he carried on up the steep slope. Snow-laden air blasted into his eyes. He put his head down and crashed into the man in front. His curse died in his throat. A hand clamped over his mouth. He was lifted off his feet and dragged sideways, as helpless as a sacrificial lamb.

Elizabeth opened her eyes to see John hauling a figure dressed in the same military camouflage suit and ski mask that they were wearing, into the hollow.

'Your men have moved on.' West pulled the guns from Chaloner's back and holster and tossed them away. 'If you want to see them die, call out and I'll shoot them when they appear.'

'You bastard.'

'You know that for a fact?'

'It's not enough that you made me look a bloody fool last night… '

'That was you? Bad luck,' John commiserated. He aimed his machine gun at Chaloner's chest and kept it there.

'How many more men are you going to kill?' Chaloner watched John pull his hood back and strip off his mask.

'Do you recognize me?'

'Your face is plastered all over HQ.'

'I mean from before.'

Chaloner stared at West's face not knowing how to react. The wind wailed down the mountain. Bitter cold crept upwards from the frozen ground through his thick boots and socks. Was this it? The end of the line? The last sensations he would feel?

'Do you?' West reiterated.

Chaloner tried to look beyond the face he knew from the photographs he'd been studying for the past few days. The square jaw line, the deep blue eyes, the black tousled hair. The features looked vaguely familiar, but wrong, as though he had seen them in a different pattern, perhaps in the photograph?

'No.'

Someone climbed out of a sleeping bag on the ground and stood next to West. Dressed in camouflage and a ski mask it could have been anyone but he presumed it was the psychiatrist West had taken hostage. He wondered if she was armed and if she was, whether she would come down on his or West's side if there was a shoot-out.

'What do we do now?' Chaloner kept his voice as low as West's, playing for time in an attempt to establish a rapport.

'We go down the mountain,' West answered.

'And from there?'

'What's your name?' West ignored the question.

'Chaloner, Ross Chaloner.'

'Captain Chaloner, SAS, this is your lucky day.' To Chaloner's astonishment West dropped the machine gun at his feet but he kept his handgun. 'I surrender to you on two conditions.'

'What conditions?' Chaloner demanded suspiciously, eyeing the handgun.

'First, you give me your word as an officer, that you'll guarantee Dr Santer's safety.' He pointed to Elizabeth. 'That you'll take her to a police station, and once you're there, you'll call in the media for a photo call.'

'Why would you want me to do that?'

'To prove she's survived an encounter with me.'

Chaloner allowed the suggestion of conspiracy to pass. 'And the other conditions?'

'That you take me with you to Stirling Lines.'

'Unarmed?'

'Yes.'

'You would be taken back to Stirling Lines after capture anyway. Why would you give yourself up when you're the one with the weapons?' Chaloner stared at the machine gun, but was reluctant to reach out for it until he was certain there was no trick involved.

'Because I know that by surrendering to you, I'll live – at least until I get to Stirling Lines. Do you agree?'

Chaloner didn't hesitate. 'I agree.'

West pulled the handgun from his holster. Holding the barrel between his fingers he allowed it to fall on top of the machine gun.

'What makes you think I won't shoot you when I pick up those guns?' Chaloner gazed at the weapons.

'Because you're an officer and a gentlemen.' West managed to turn both adjectives into insults. 'There is no catch.'

'And you won't kill me when I pick them up?'

'I have no other arms. You can shoot me right here and now if you want to. As I said, all I want is Dr Santer's safety and entrance to Stirling Lines.'

'You really don't know who you are, do you?' Chaloner asked.

'No.'

'And you think someone will recognize you in Stirling Lines?'

'Or I'll recognize someone there.'

'You've obviously had military training, but we have no missing personnel.'

'You're sure?'

'One hundred percent. All the services have been checked and double checked, even down to MI5 and MI6.'

'He could have left the forces,' Elizabeth argued.

'Not in the last fifteen years.' Chaloner debated whether or not to mention the IRA identification, and decided against it. There was no saying what the man might do if he was a terrorist and suddenly remembered his orders. He looked from West to Elizabeth Santer. Although her face was masked there was a tension between them that was almost palpable. 'Is there anything else I need to know?'

'Only that you're the one in control.' West stared pointedly at the weapons that Chaloner had made no attempt to retrieve. 'Perhaps you should start behaving accordingly.'

'I don't trust you.'

'I've told you what I want and given you my terms. I won't go back on my word.'

'Forgive my scepticism but how do I know that you haven't a bomb strapped under that suit? That you won't blow us all to kingdom come once I get you into Stirling Lines?'

'Do you want me to strip?' West challenged.

'Yes.'

He unzipped his suit. Keeping his eyes focused on Chaloner, he removed all his clothes. He stood blue and shivering while Chaloner checked every garment.

'Turn around, slowly,' Chaloner ordered. 'Bend over.'

'You want me to spread myself?'

'You obviously know the drill, so I don't need to give the order.'

He shone his torch over every inch of West's body before kicking his clothes back to him. 'Dress.'

'You'll take Dr Santer to the police station in Brecon, and me to HQ?'

'It's a long walk.'

'Not to the Storey Arms, you can call for transport from there. But do yourself a favour; don't tell them that you have me until they actually arrive.'

'Why not?' Chaloner watched West fasten the buckles on his suit and pull on his gloves.

'Because you could end up dead before they get there.'

Chaloner laughed.

'He's not joking,' Elizabeth rejoined shortly.

'You're the doctor he took hostage?'

'I am.'

'And because he spared your life you've thrown your lot in with him.' Chaloner finally picked up the guns and checked their mechanisms.

'I degreased both of them before I brought them out,' West informed him.

'I'll do whatever I can to help this man because he's my patient,' Elizabeth interrupted. 'And he hasn't killed anyone.'

'There are four maybe five corpses that say otherwise.'

'I saw the dead soldiers in the hospital and like you I assumed that he had killed them. He took me hostage shortly afterwards, and since that moment he's only left me once, and that was last night to get food. He didn't kill the consultant Dave Watson. Dave was alive when I last saw him in the hospital and there's no way John could have reached him without me knowing about it. I checked that paramedic myself before we left the ambulance in Brighton. The man was fine, he was unconscious but breathing, he should have come round in an hour… '

'Possibly he would have if he hadn't been shot.'

'Not by John West.'

'And the captain in the house in Brecon?' Chaloner demanded. 'He was a friend of mine.'

'He came after us into the front office. He was Special Services working in a hostage situation, trained not to take chances. I shot him in the arm… '

'His chest had more holes than a sieve.'

'Then someone went into that office after we left. He was alive when we last saw him.'

'I can testify to that,' Elizabeth insisted.

'You expect me to believe that five people were killed after you left them?'

'It's the truth,' Elizabeth asserted.

West pulled the ski mask over his face. 'If I remember rightly,' he murmured, his lips moving oddly under the small round hole in the cloth. 'This hill always was more fun to go down than up.'

CHAPTER SIXTEEN

Chaloner kept his position of "tail end Charlie" – it was the best vantage point from which to watch West – and Dr Santer. He'd guessed right when he'd suspected West knew the Beacons. Although the hills remained shrouded in mist and snow the man unerringly picked the least hazardous route. He also paused frequently to help Dr Santer over the most difficult obstacles. Chaloner didn't believe their relationship was doctor/patient. The more he observed them, the more he was convinced they were far closer.

He wished they weren't wearing ski masks so he could read the expressions on their faces. But his major concern was West's identity and motives. He tried to imagine what one unarmed man could do in HQ and drew a blank. Surely West realised he would be kept under armed guard in Stirling Lines.

He fought off exhaustion. He couldn't afford to allow West out of his sight for an instant Two ambushes in two days were two too many for any officer, particularly one as ambitious as himself.

The more he considered the situation West had engineered, the more bizarre it seemed. He simply couldn't see what the man hoped to gain by going into Stirling Lines. Was he really naive enough to believe that a trained soldier could disappear from the army and not be missed?

Elizabeth realised John intended to leave her behind as soon as they reached safety, and she was equally determined not to be abandoned. She didn't trust the young officer swaggering behind them with a machine gun aimed at their backs. There was a callous tone in his voice, and what little she could see of his eyes and mouth beneath the mask, looked sadistic and vicious. She could imagine him shooting two unsuspecting guards in a hospital corridor… she remembered Dave and wondered if he had suffered before he'd died. The news reports had said he'd been shot. Had he been killed instantly? Or did he die later, screaming and in pain?

Engrossed in her thoughts, she slipped when they reached the foot of the mountain, plunging up to her elbows in a snowdrift. John braced his legs against a dry stone wall, leaned forward, locked his hands around her chest beneath her armpits, and hauled her out. All she could see of him was his eyes, gleaming in the snow-lightened darkness. She concentrated hard, willing him to read her mind and understand what she was about to do. As he lifted her, she pulled down the fastening on her camouflage suit and thrust herself against him. Just as she'd intended, he lost his balance. She fumbled, damning the thick padded mitten that prevented her fingers from closing over the gun he'd given her.

'Here, you're coming undone,' West said loudly. He zipped up her suit and heaved her to her feet. The weight of the gun was heavy against her. He'd understood what she'd tried to do, but had left the gun there. Why?

'You all right?' He brushed snow from her arms and legs.

‘Cold.’ She glanced at Chaloner who was aiming the barrel of West’s gun at them.

‘Aren’t we all,’ Chaloner muttered. ‘Sooner we get moving, sooner you can get into the warm, Dr Santer. They have fires and hot food in the Storey Arms.’

‘You promised a Police Station,’ West reminded.

‘I did, but as you said on Corn Du, I’m the one in charge now.’

‘You gave your word,’ John remonstrated.

‘Keep moving.’

‘I won’t be put somewhere safe so you can go off to this Stirling Lines to get your head blown off,’ Elizabeth warned when West helped down the final half a mile of hillside that separated them from the Youth Hostel.

‘You have no choice. You heard our keeper, he’s calling the shots.’ Picking her up again he lifted her over a ditch filled with snow.

‘How did you know that was there?’ Chaloner demanded.

‘Slight sinking of snow around the edges. How’s your snow craft?’ John replied.

‘I’m not leaving you,’ Elizabeth said emphatically.

‘After what he’s put you through, I’d assumed you’d want to run as far and as fast from him as possible.’ Chaloner was closer to them than she’d realised.

‘I’ve begun regression therapy. He’s unstable. The slightest trigger could cause a relapse or hysteria.’

‘This is a cure for hysteria.’ Chaloner waved the gun.

‘Regression therapy takes a patient back to the initial trauma that caused the problem. Should John lapse into that state, he may not even see your gun.’

‘For someone who’s lost his memory he remembers a great deal. The road out of London, the flat in Brecon, survival tactics on a snow covered mountain.’ Chaloner paused to stamp an accumulation of snow from his boots. ‘The psychiatrist assigned to advise the Command Cell is not even sure that Mr West here, has lost his memory at all.’

‘If he hasn’t, he deserves an Oscar for his performance,’ Elizabeth responded warmly.

‘If you don’t think I’ve lost my memory, then you must have some idea who I am?’ John stopped and turned to Chaloner.

‘A terrorist?’

‘What terrorist would leave London for the Beacons in weather like this? What possible target could there be out here?’

‘Enlighten me?’

‘How about SAS recruits engaged in the Fan dance. Or do they call it the Long Drag now?’

‘So you know about SAS training techniques and jargon. Given the number of books that have been written about the Regiment that’s hardly surprising.’ Chaloner followed West and Dr Santer on to the compacted snow of the car park.

‘John’s amnesia is trauma induced and specific to his identity,’ Elizabeth said swiftly.

‘Meaning, Dr Santer?’ Chaloner asked.

‘He has a recall of military training and survival techniques.’

'I noticed.'

'Places, place names… '

'Like that flat in Brecon?'

'Precisely. Who owns that flat?' Even at this late stage Elizabeth continued to gather any information that might prove useful.

'It's in the hands of a letting agency.'

'Someone owns it. John had memories of the place… '

'That's interesting.' Chaloner opened the door and waved them into the Youth Hostel ahead of him. 'Hands on heads.'

'Do it,' John said to Elizabeth. He lifted his own hands and locked his fingers together on top of his head.

Chaloner stepped in behind them and opened another door. Prodding them in at gunpoint, he acknowledged two clerks who sat, stunned by their sudden appearance.

'I need transport and a driver,' Chaloner pulled off his mask.

'Yes, Captain Chaloner. Right away, sir. Is that who I think it is?' the clerk stared at Elizabeth and John's masked faces.

'Radio out to the patrols and order them in. Tell them the search has been called off, there's no need to give them a reason.'

'Yes, sir.'

The second clerk went to the door. 'I'll get a driver, sir. They're in the dining room.'

'I need two, both armed. And not a word about this prisoner to anyone,' Chaloner warned.

'Not even advance warning to Stirling Lines, sir?' the clerk with the radio asked.

'Especially Stirling Lines. If word of this gets out before I'm ready to release the information, I'll see both of you court-martialled.'

'Yes, sir,' they chimed.

'Send the drivers to the car park. I'll wait for them there.' Chaloner jerked his head towards the door and West and Elizabeth walked outside.

Whether the mist was beginning to lift, or whether it was because they were lower down the mountain, they could see across the car park.

'You promised we'd drop Elizabeth in the police station in Brecon, and you'd wait there for the reporters to arrive after you telephoned the media.'

'I did.' Chaloner swung the pack from his back and extracted a knife and a rope.

'You're not going to tie him up,' Elizabeth protested.

'Less painfully that he did me last night.'

'It's all right, Elizabeth.' John held out his hands.

Propping the gun against his leg Chaloner fashioned a slip knot and pulled it over West's wrists. Drawing it tight he proceeded to lash them together. When he finished he looked at Elizabeth. She'd pulled down the hood of her suit and removed her ski mask. Her face was flushed, her hair tousled, her figure hidden beneath layers of clothing, yet she looked beautiful. He could understand why West, whoever he was, felt duty bound to protect her. He would have felt the same way himself if he'd been fortunate enough to have had her all to himself for three days – and nights.

'Clerk said you want drivers, sir?' Two men walked out of the Storey Arms and joined them.

'That's correct. I'll need your gun, corporal.'

'My gun, sir?' the corporal asked in surprise, looking at the machine gun Chaloner was holding and the Browning in his holster.

'These are the prisoner's weapons. He could have interfered with them. You,' he nodded to the relief driver. 'Keep your rifle primed and aimed at the prisoner. You and I will sit in the back either side of the prisoner. Dr Santer, you will sit alongside the driver.' Taking the driver's rifle, Chaloner pointed it at West who climbed into the back seat. 'Swing your legs out.' Chaloner lashed West's ankles together.

'Shouldn't you tie me too?' Elizabeth demanded caustically.

'Is it necessary?' Chaloner asked her coolly.

'I have no intention of trying to escape, if that's what you're implying.'

Chaloner stepped back so the relief driver could climb in alongside West. Elizabeth sat beside the driver, Chaloner waited until she had fastened her seat belt before entering the vehicle.

'HQ, sir?' the driver started the engine.

'Stirling Lines via Brecon,' West broke in forcefully.

'Sir?' The driver turned to Chaloner.

'Take the Brecon road, corporal.'

Chaloner sat back, the rifle he had appropriated from the corporal aimed at West's ribs. He'd captured his man. After the disaster of the night before, his reputation would be restored with the Regiment. Nothing could possibly go wrong – not now.

Elizabeth sat, watching the road as intently as if she, not the corporal was driving. She knew that if she or John made one wrong move Chaloner wouldn't hesitate to fire. She thought through every detail of the past few days, searching frantically for any scrap of information that would help prove John's innocence.

The radio crackled and the driver's call sign echoed over the airwaves.

'Stirling Lines?' Chaloner was instantly on the alert.

'Probably Captain Clutson, sir. I'm due to pick him up in Tal-y-bont in an hour. Storey Arms would have radioed to tell him to expect a replacement; he probably wants to find out why I'm not available.'

'Ignore him,' Chaloner ordered.

'You will leave Elizabeth in Brecon?' West checked.

'No!' Elizabeth countered. 'You can't take John anywhere without me. He could regress at any moment.'

'We can look after him,' Chaloner assured her wryly.

'It's not your safety that concerns me, captain, but my patient's. Besides I'm the only witness who can corroborate his story. There's no one else who can vouch that the paramedic and the captain in the office in Brecon were alive when he left them.'

Chaloner looked at West sitting detached and enigmatic, the ski mask still covering his face. 'She has a point.'

'It's too much of a risk to take her into Stirling Lines,' West said flatly.

'What do you think could possibly happen to her in HQ?' Chaloner asked.

'The same thing that happened to the guards outside my door in the hospital, the paramedic and the hospital consultant.'

'You think someone in HQ is a murderer?' Chaloner snorted derisively.

'Several people I have come into contact with have wound up dead shortly after I left them, and most of the people following me are army.' West looked Chaloner steadily in the eye. 'It could happen to you, captain.'

'No it couldn't, because you're disarmed and immobile.'

'I assure you I didn't kill them.'

Something in John's calm denial struck a chord. 'All right, supposing – just supposing for argument's sake you didn't kill them. You can't really believe those people were killed simply because they came into contact with you?'

'If they were, it's obvious that as Elizabeth has spent more time with me than anyone else, she is at risk.'

'If all those men are dead because you talked to them, you must have some idea why they were murdered?'

'None.'

'Amnesia or not… '

'I assure you John's condition is real,' Elizabeth interrupted.

Chaloner decided to feed West a few crumbs of information and monitor his reaction. 'HQ has connected your appearance with the disarmament conference.'

'You have proof that I'm a terrorist?'

'We know an experienced assassin has been given a brief to kill delegates in an attempt to sabotage the conference.'

'By which organisation?'

'Testing my knowledge, West? Chaloner asked. 'Let's just say certain Middle East interests.'

Elizabeth suddenly found it difficult to breathe. All she could think of was John's command of Arabic.

'So, are you working for Islamic fundamentalists?' Chaloner continued conversationally.

'The conference is in London, isn't it? Where exactly is it being held?'

'I have no idea,' Chaloner answered warily.

'Neither have I, and if I'd been given a brief to wreck it, I doubt that I would have left London to come haring up to this wilderness.'

'Unless the briefing evaporated along with your memory.'

'You can't have it both ways, either I have lost my memory or I haven't.' John looked through the window and saw that they were approaching the roundabout on the outskirts of Brecon. 'Order the driver to the police station.'

'Leave me behind and I'll tell the police and the press that it was the army who killed Dave and that paramedic.'

'They won't believe you,' Chaloner dismissed.

'Aside from John I'm the only witness, and unlike him I'm a professional with a reputation for honesty and integrity.'

Chaloner didn't need any more persuading. He knew the last thing Heddingham, HQ and the government wanted was adverse publicity. 'Stirling Lines,' he briefed the driver.

'No!' West shouted. 'You gave me your word… '

'She'll be safer in HQ,' Chaloner justified.

'The storming of the house and offices in Brecon was manned by army personnel, and you tell me your friend wound up dead.'

'I'll personally guarantee her safety.'

'Who's going to guarantee yours, Captain Chaloner?'

Chaloner didn't answer. He asked for the radio receiver. After checking with the command centre in the Storey Arms that the call signal for the patrols he'd sent out hadn't changed in the last few hours, he began transmitting, first to Stirling Lines then to his patrols.

'Captain Chaloner wants all the patrols to head back directly to Stirling Lines and not linger in the Storey Arms, sir.'

Sergeant Price turned to the radio operator in his group. 'Then he must be organizing a celebration party.'

'You think he's got him, sir.'

'Don't you?'

The radio operator smiled. 'Yes, sir.'

'We have our orders, private.'

'Sir.'

Price checked their position on the map. 'Radio back to command, tell them to arrange for transport to pick us up at the Mountain Centre and to check that the other groups RV at the nearest road points. If the captain wants us there as quickly as possible, I suggest we do all we can to accommodate his wishes.'

John looked past Elizabeth through the window, and watched the darkened countryside speed past. He could make out the blue-grey shadows of trees, hedgerows and farm buildings that he thought he recognized. Houses with gleaming windows that hinted at cosy, warm living rooms. Comfortable Victorian and Edwardian villas that he knew he'd once walked past. He was pinning not only his own, but Elizabeth's life on being recognized in Stirling Lines. But what if no one did? What if he and Elizabeth were taken on a long walk down a corridor that ended with a bullet in the back of both their heads?

As though she'd read his thoughts, Elizabeth turned and squeezed his roped hands.

'No touching the prisoner,' Chaloner warned.

'You've broken your word once, Chaloner,' West said fiercely when the Land Rover slowed to turn into the lane that led to Stirling Lines. 'Don't do it again. Promise me, whatever happens you won't leave

Elizabeth for an instant. Not until she's safely in the hands of the press or police?'

'There's no need... '

'Please, you owe me that much for breaking your word. Don't leave her for an instant?'

'I promise,' Chaloner reassured.

The driver slowed to a halt at a barrier set before the gates. He pressed the button that activated the window but the soldier on sentry duty went to the back of the vehicle.

'Captain Chaloner?'

John lifted his hands and wrenched back his hood and ski mask. It wasn't easy with his wrists lashed together, but now he was finally in Stirling Lines he intended to expose his face to as many people as possible. He knew they would have all seen his photographs, but he still hoped his physical presence would spark someone's memory.

'Your patrols have all radioed in, sir. They're on their way. I've had orders from Major Simmonds to check your transport and ensure that your prisoner is immobilized and disarmed. Once that's done, you're to progress directly to Command Cell, sir.'

Chaloner opened the door and climbed out of the vehicle, still keeping his gun trained on West. 'Out,' he commanded.

John swung his hobbled ankles through the door. Slipping his hand through the cords on West's wrists, Chaloner hauled him to his feet. 'The prisoner is immobilized and disarmed, sergeant. You may check the vehicle.'

The sergeant inspected the inside of the cab, patted West's camouflage suit and directed the captain to a waiting jeep. 'You're free to proceed to company offices, sir. There's an escort waiting at the door.'

Chaloner pushed John towards the jeep. Elizabeth followed. The driver waited until they climbed in before heading for the building and the escort squad.

'Remember, you gave your word, Chaloner,' West reminded when Chaloner heaved him out of the jeep.

'I remember.' Chaloner cut the bonds on John's ankles before pushing him ahead. Elizabeth walked alongside John. The escort closed ranks around them. John was aware, not only of Chaloner's gun but the weapons of the twenty men in the squad. He felt acutely vulnerable. One sweating finger slipping on a trigger could blow him and Elizabeth out of this life. A simple, but convenient "accident" that could be explained away as the nervous reaction of a soldier to an attempted escape.

The door in the single storey building in front of them opened. Chaloner prodded John forward with his machine gun. They walked down a central corridor. A door was open at the far end. John caught a glimpse of a room furnished with steel grey desks and filing cabinets. Apart from the furniture, everything was blinding white. The vinyl tiles on the floor, the walls, the ceiling with its powerful, recessed lighting.

A man moved into the doorway.

'Come in, John West. It is good to see you again. It looks as though we're going to have that interview after all.' Major Simmonds stepped back as West entered the room. 'Dr Santer,' the major greeted her politely.

'Major Simmonds.' She looked across the room and saw the lieutenant-colonel who had visited West in the hospital, standing next to a tall, painfully thin man at the head of a conference table.

'Please, come and sit down, West.' Heddingham could have been welcoming a VIP visitor rather than a prisoner. 'Dr Santer, it is good to see you. I'm afraid we feared the worst. Are you well?'

'Perfectly, thank you.' She fought off an attack of giddiness at the change in temperature. The room was claustrophobically, tropically hot.

'Captain Chaloner, perhaps you would be kind enough to escort Dr Santer to more comfortable quarters?'

'No!' Elizabeth's reply was unequivocal. 'I haven't travelled this far with John to abandon him now.'

'You must be exhausted, Dr Santer,' the major began patiently.

'No, I am not.' She tried to ignore the unnatural warmth that threatened to sap what little energy remained to her after the stiff climb up and down the mountain, and the cold ride back to HQ.

'Captain Chaloner, may I suggest you clean yourself up?' Simmonds prompted.

'Later.' Chaloner noticed that the escort had left the room at a nod from the brigadier.

'That's an order, Chaloner.' Major Simmonds tempered his command when Chaloner gave him a sharp look. 'We're all very grateful to you, but your job is done. It's time for the doctors to take over.' He emphasized his professional status.

'Major Simmonds, Brigadier Cullen-Heames and I will take it from here,' Heddingham interrupted smoothly.

'The prisoner surrendered on condition that I remain with him and Dr Santer during debriefing.'

'The prisoner surrendered?' Simmonds raised his eyebrows.

'Yes, Major Simmonds, he surrendered.'

'That doesn't alter the situation, Chaloner,' the lieutenant-colonel barked. 'Get cleaned up and report to your CO.'

'With all due respect, sir, not until the prisoner has been debriefed.'

'Am I to understand that you are disobeying a direct order… '

'Sir.' Chaloner looked from the lieutenant-colonel to the major. 'I have already questioned the prisoner, sir,' he lied, gambling on bluffing his way to the truth.

'That was an extremely foolish thing to do, Chaloner,' Major Simmonds criticized. 'The man is a psychiatric patient, mentally unstable with a history of violence… '

'He struck me as being neither unstable, nor violent, sir. And, as I said, he surrendered voluntarily.'

Heddingham eyed the gun Chaloner cradled in the crook of his elbow. 'Captain Chaloner, for the last time, will you leave this room.'

'Not until the prisoner has been debriefed, sir,' Chaloner repeated obstinately. 'Dr Santer stated that he could be subject to a bout of hysteria, or even violence should he relive the trauma that caused his amnesia.'

'Captain, for the last time… '

'Chaloner, this is for your own good,' the brigadier interposed nervously. 'The man is a murderer… '

'He is not.'

All the officers turned to Elizabeth.

'Dr Santer,' Major Simmonds addressed her slowly and patronizingly, as though she were a difficult patient. 'I have bad news… '

'That Dave Watson is dead?' she guessed.

'This man,' his glance flickered to John. 'Killed him?'

'He did not.'

'If he didn't kill him, then how do you know Dave Watson is dead?' Simmonds asked.

'I saw it on the news.'

'Your kidnapper allowed you to watch television?'

'There was no "allowed", major. I remained with John West of my own volition.' She knew she wasn't telling Simmonds anything he wasn't already aware of. 'I haven't left his side,' she stretched the truth, 'since we left the hospital, and all the time I've been with him, he hasn't killed anyone.'

'The ambulance driver?'

'Was unconscious but alive when we left him.'

'The captain who stormed in the office in Brecon?'

'Had a superficial wound in his arm.'

'That's impossible,' the major refuted.

'It's the truth which is why I refuse to leave John until I can be absolutely certain that he won't be murdered as those other men were.'

'Dr Santer, you're a psychiatrist,' Major Simmonds addressed her calmly. 'Can't you see what's happened here? You're exhibiting all the symptoms of transmitted persecution complex. This man believes himself innocent but persecuted and he has convinced you his delusions are real.' He looked to the brigadier and the lieutenant-colonel. 'An easily understood phenomenon when you consider the strain Dr Santer has been under since she was kidnapped by West.'

'I am suffering neither from delusions nor hysteria, Major Simmonds. John West is innocent.'

'This is the ambulance driver on the Libanus road all over again,' Simmonds said impatiently. 'You managed to convince him of West's innocence… '

'Only because he is,' Elizabeth swayed on her feet.

'Dr Santer should sit down, sir,' Chaloner pulled a chair out from under the table and helped Elizabeth on to it.

'I think we should call the guards back,' Simmonds said flatly. 'As a psychiatrist and officer I will not take responsibility for interviewing a violent man with only one armed man present, especially, when I suspect the prisoner is a manipulative psychopath capable of exerting considerable influence over others. He appears to have mesmerized both Captain Chaloner and Dr Santer.'

'The truth has mesmerized me,' Elizabeth muttered.

'You have conclusive proof of his innocence?' Simmonds questioned.

‘No guilty man would willingly surrender himself,’ Chaloner pointed out.

‘Not even if he was suffering from exposure, Chaloner?’

‘We had food, shelter and everything we needed,’ Elizabeth looked at John who was watching and listening but contributing nothing to the argument.

There was a rap at the door. Heddingham shouted ‘Enter!’

Sergeant Price marched into the room. ‘Sergeant Price reporting to Brigadier Cullen-Heames, as requested, sir!’

‘We’re in a briefing, sergeant!’ Major Simmonds barked.

The sergeant kicked the door shut. West turned pale.

Elizabeth looked at the sergeant’s gun and registered the scar on his thumb. It ran the whole length with small lines like centipede legs spreading out from the main injury. She unzipped her suit, threw herself to the floor and removed the gun John had given her in one swift movement. Pointing the barrel at the sergeant, she closed her eyes and fired. West hurtled forward, knocking the sergeant off balance. Someone hit the light switch and the room plunged into darkness.

Elizabeth had fallen behind a filing cabinet. Around her the air was filled with noise, disembodied shouts, screams, and the sharp crack of gunshots. She clenched the gun and murmured over and over again.

‘Please let him be all right. Please God let him be all right.’

CHAPTER SEVENTEEN

Even in the darkness John continued to see the scar. It seared a glowing brand in a velvet blackness that prevented him from seeing his own body, let alone those of others. He crouched on the floor, his bound hands protecting his head as shouts, screams and gunshots resounded around him – and – the soft plop of a gun fitted with a silencer being fired. It was that sound that took him out of the room, out of Stirling Lines and back to London in another time…

'Damn, blast and fuck British weather.'

'You've had it too soft for too long, Richard McKenna.'

'Not that soft.' He switched off the ignition and turned from the dismal, rain soaked scene framed in the windscreen to the woman sitting in the passenger seat beside him. Slim, silver blonde hair, pewter eyes that could turn an uncompromising, steel-grey, or like now, a warm, loving silver. His wife was more beautiful than he remembered, and the separation had been a long one even by Special Forces standards. Ten months, and the most difficult element of every parting was the embarrassment of getting to know her all over again. But while he and Bonnie both insisted on following their chosen professions, there was no other way they could live. Not for the foreseeable future.

'I can't wait to see her.'

‘I think her mother deserves your undivided attention first,’ Bonnie teased in the Vasser, Eastern seaboard accent that had attracted him the instant he’d heard her speak over an internal telephone system in NASA headquarters. It had taken two days of hard manoeuvring for him to contrive a meeting after that.

‘So,’ he took her into his arms and kissed her briefly on the lips. The house she had chosen to rent didn’t appear to be overlooked on first inspection, but she had mentioned a baby sitter, and he didn’t like the thought of his private moments being under scrutiny. A phobia that came from having every move he made analyzed in his working life. ‘What’s the world of space technology doing these days?’

‘It could have disintegrated since I’ve been on maternity leave for all I know.’

He reached out and fingered her hair. ‘Thank you for picking me up from the airport.’

A stupid, commonplace remark to make to your wife when you haven’t seen her for forty weeks three days and ten hours, but his voice was husky with suppressed emotion.

‘Don’t mention it, colonel, sir, but we can’t sit out here all night. I’ve a baby sitter to relieve, dinner to cook, and – ’ mischief glowed in the depths of her magnificent eyes, ‘a bed already warmed.’

He opened the door and walked around to open the passenger side. Lifting the hatch back he took out his bag which was only marginally larger than an overnight case and a preposterously massive, giant pink hippopotamus he had bought for his daughter,

Rachel. Eight weeks old already and he'd yet to see her.

The baby sitter was hovering in the hall when Bonnie opened the door.

'She was very good, Mrs McKenna. Not a peep out of her. I've laid the table, and finished the ironing.'

'Thank you very much, Joanne.'

'You're back earlier than I expected,' the teenager gave Richard a shy smile. 'I owe you some money.'

'Put it towards your college fund.'

'If you need me again just contact the agency.'

'I most certainly will, and thank you again, Joanne.'

'Trust an American to land in a strange country and have an entire life and all the trappings, including house, and babysitter sorted in next to no time.' He dropped his bag to the floor and closed the door. The house Bonnie had rented for the week, all the leave he had been able to wangle before taking up his next post, was smaller than the last one they had rented in the States. But then British houses were generally smaller than American.

It had been so long since he'd lived in his home country he'd almost forgotten how cramped some suburban houses could be. But it would do. He'd have to live on the job for his next two weeks of work. And after that they had promised him eight weeks leave. Not that he hadn't earned it. Eight weeks that he and Bonnie planned to spend on her father's farm in Virginia.

'She's upstairs' Bonnie smiled, knowing he wouldn't be interested in a tour of the house. Domestic details bored him once they progressed beyond the stage of affecting his comfort. 'Follow me, Daddy.' She began to climb the stairs. 'There are only two bedrooms and one bathroom, but the garden's walled. I know how you appreciate privacy, so I thought it would do for a week.'

'You're leaving at the end of the week too?'

'No, I know you won't have time to visit us, but I thought I'd stay on, do some shopping, see some shows, visit some galleries, that way we can fly back to the States together.'

'I wish I could stay here with you.'

'I knew what I was getting when I married a man who was married to his job, but did you know what you were getting yourself into when you took up with me, Buster?' She lifted her skirt and ran her fingers through her hair, eyeing him seductively from beneath half closed lids.

Unable to resist a moment longer, he took her into his arms, and kissed her the way he'd wanted to, when he had first caught a glimpse of her waiting outside the barriers in the airport. He breathed in her perfume, the clean smell of her hair, kissed her lips, her neck…

'You have a daughter to get acquainted with, remember.' Holding her finger to her lips she opened one of the three doors on the landing and tiptoed into a room illuminated by the gentle glow of an amber nursery light that shone down on a china hedgehog tea party. He left the hippopotamus in the corner of the room and joined Bonnie at the end of the cot. The baby was sleeping on her back; two tiny fists closed either side of a scrunched pink face, her mop of black, curly hair the only touch of strong colour in a muted, pastel-shaded world.

'Her eyes are still blue, and the doctor thinks they'll stay that way,' Bonnie whispered. Rachel moved, her dark eyelashes flickered, but to his dismay she curled back into sleep.

'Can I pick her up?'

'She'll wake in half an hour and I'd rather you picked me up until then. Can you wait?'

He smiled. 'I'll try.' He followed Bonnie across the landing into the second bedroom. Nightlights burned either side of a four poster double bed, bathing the room in a soft glow. Delving into the pocket of the blazer he was wearing, he pulled out a box and presented it to her. 'Something small for a gorgeous and clever wife on presenting me with a beautiful daughter. And an apology for not being around when she was born.'

'You were there for the most important part; afterwards I looked grotesque, like an elephant.' She opened the box and gasped. 'Richard, they are magnificent.' She gently removed a gold band fashioned in the shape of two hands clasping a single glittering diamond, and matching drop diamond and gold earrings. 'They must have cost a fortune.'

'Only a small one.' He picked her up and lifted her on to the bed. 'God I've missed you, you've no idea how much.' He couldn't get enough of her, her hair, her eyes, her smile and wondered why photographs can never convey a person's inner light. The vibrancy, the personality the core of being that he'd fallen so much in love with.

'Pretty important job you've got for yourself, colonel,' she said after he'd kissed her. 'Martin stopped by and told me you're in charge of the security for the peace conference.'

'Martin came here?'

'Yesterday. He was on his way out of the country.'

'That's Martin up for a court martial. Disseminating classified information is a serious offence.'

'Then it's just as well he's the other side of the world where you can't get at him.'

'Where?'

'Canada for two months.'

'Arctic training. Do him good to cool his tongue for a while.'

'I don't suppose you can tell me where you've been for the past ten months?'

'Same place I spent eight months last year.'

'An undisclosed Arab country?'

'You get a straight A for that one.' He kissed her again, his hand exploring beneath her sweater.

'As we only have half an hour let's get undressed and into bed so we can do this thing properly.'

It was always the same, a strained reticence that gave way to a bout of crazy, mind blowing passion, and afterwards – thank God – it was always all right. They'd never had any problems slipping back into the easy intimacy that left no room for reserve or shyness. Sometimes he wondered what their lives would have been like if he'd taken the job he'd been offered in NASA.

He'd talked it over with Bonnie at the time, but she'd never mentioned the post again after he'd turned it down. It would have been almost, but not quite, nine to five, living within an easy drive of a confining office. There would have been no undercover operations, no travelling, but there would have been weekly, if not daily leisure time that he and Bonnie could have spent together. Rachel could have had a settled life with friends and a regular school she wouldn't have had to leave until she graduated...

'What are you thinking about?'

He threw one shoe on to the floor and turned to look at his beautiful, desirable and naked wife. 'The job I was offered in NASA.'

Laughter, delicate, silvery that somehow matched and conveyed her personality filled the room.

'What's funny?' he asked as she folded back the sheets and sat in the bed.

'The thought of you trying to living a normal life. You're many things, Richard, but normal isn't one of them.'

He leaned over. Imprisoning her with his elbows he tickled her until she begged for mercy. 'I love you,' he murmured seriously, 'and I'll do anything for you and that little scrap sleeping next door.'

'Little scrap! I'll have you know that's a fine healthy baby who regained her birth weight in record time.'

'She looks very small to me.'

'Only because you're used to being around great, brawny men. She'll grow up all too soon, and then,' she wrapped her arms around his chest after he removed his shirt, 'she'll need a brother or sister.'

'While I do what I do, I can't guarantee I'll be there when they or you need me.'

'But we'll have each other, and… ' she admired the ring he'd slipped on top of her wedding band, '-Christmas every time Daddy comes home. I love you far too to much to let you sacrifice yourself for us, Richard.'

'Do you mean that?' he questioned earnestly.

'No, but it does wonders for your guilt complex, and guilty men work hard to make the most of the time they spend with their wives, and do everything in their power to please them.'

He began to tickle her again, but not for long. Ten months of pent up desire and passion erupted, carrying both of them into a sweet private world that was never far from his thoughts during every interminable separation. His secret and most terrifying fear was that one day he'd return from an assignment to find both Bonnie and that world gone, which was why he'd never been able to take her for granted in quite the same way some of his fellow officers' did their wives.

Afterwards they lay quietly, her head on his chest, his arm wrapped around her shoulders, until a barely audible mewing broke into the stillness, a sound he wouldn't have recognized if Bonnie hadn't shot out of bed.

'That, darling,' she kissed him before reaching for her robe, 'is the end of peace for the moment.'

'Can I feed her?'

'You lack the basic equipment.'

'You're breast feeding?'

'You didn't notice the extra four inches?' She thrust out her chest.

'You always look great to me.'

'That's good to know, but this,' she patted her taut stomach muscles, 'is the result of six solid weeks of rigorous and painful exercising. I was even glad that you weren't around to hear all the cursing.'

'One of the things I most love about you is your ability to find a bright side to every situation.'

'Better to have one or two honeymoons a year than fifty two weeks of fighting. Martin and Jenny are divorced.'

'Little brother?'

'Little brother,' she repeated.

'Shit! He's ten years younger than me.'

'And looking for wife number three. Aren't you glad you've found one you can put up with for more than a few weeks? Stay there,' she called as he swung his legs out of the bed. 'I'll bring her in here.'

He listened to her talking to Rachel as she went into the other bedroom. It was peculiar to think of another person living with them. Bonnie had always taken care to make the time they spent together private. Now there was someone who was going to be with them, if not forever, certainly for a very long time.

Five minutes later she carried Rachel into the bedroom.

'Here, it's safe to hold her. I've changed and washed her, she's beautifully clean for five minutes, but I warn you, she won't stay pleasant for long without her feed.'

He took Rachel from Bonnie, drew up his knees and propped his daughter against them, holding her stiffly at arm's length, both hands clamped firmly beneath her armpits. Rachel stared at his unfamiliar face through deep blue, wary eyes. He laughed when she made a face. Laying her against his shoulder, he rubbed her back, looking away from Bonnie lest she see the tears of pride hovering at the corners of his eyes.

'You're supposed to do that after she's been fed, not before. Here hand her over.'

He lay and watched while Bonnie fed Rachel, his heart absurdly full. It was crazy, a grown man like him, who did the job he did, and did it well, reduced to tears by the sight of his wife feeding his daughter.

'As you see she's a greedy little monkey.'

He knew Bonnie saw through the ruses he used to conceal the emotions he was afraid to express, but she understood him too well to say anything that would embarrass him.

'I've two T bone steaks under the grill. How does smoked salmon on rye, followed by steak, tossed green salad, onion rings and garlic bread sound to you?'

'Good,' he murmured.

She took the baby, milk bubbling from her mouth, head lolling sleepily, from her breast. 'Wind her while I sort myself out.'

'What's that?'

'What you did before. Put her on your shoulder and rub her back until she burps. I'm going to shower and find an outfit that will do justice to this jewellery.'

He smiled down at Rachel when he took her into his arms and laid her against his bare shoulder.

'She's a very good baby,' Bonnie smiled.

'I wouldn't expect anything else from my daughter.'

'I had something to do with her as well,' she laughed.

Bonnie disappeared through the door, her long tanned legs stepping free from her robe. After two large burps from Rachel which made him feel extremely proud of his fatherly prowess, he lay the baby on the pillows beside him, propped himself up on his elbow and watched her.

When Bonnie reappeared, her make-up was perfect and she was wearing a black silk trouser suit.

'You look gorgeous. Good enough to eat.'

'Not until after we've had that steak. I'm starving.'

'Have I two minutes to shower?'

'Five if you need them. I'll take Rachel downstairs and put her in the day cot.'

He reluctantly handed his daughter over, relishing the feel of her tiny, soft, talcum-scented body. It was then he noticed something about the set of her mouth that reminded him of Bonnie, although her eyes had been so like his. Already, she had a certain individuality. So small, yet so different from Bonnie and him. A part of both of them. A being he had brought into the world, to whom he owed everything, and who owed him nothing in return. It was a most peculiar, solemn feeling.

'Five minutes,' Bonnie swept the baby into her arms.

He took his toilet bag from his case and went into the shower. Resisting the temptation to linger under the warm relaxing jets of water, he left time for shaving. He was splashing cologne on to his chin when he heard the doorbell. Alarm bells rang in his mind. He almost reached for his gun, then he remembered, he was home, not undercover. He had no need of a gun. He was living the normal life of a happily married man in suburbia, and in normal life, newspaper boys and milkman rang doorbells to collect money and make deliveries and neighbours occasionally popped round for drinks.

His wife was under the same roof he was, cooking dinner. His daughter slept in her cot. The constant threat of being found out and dragged off to a torture chamber in the middle of the night didn't apply here, and wouldn't apply for at least another three months.

He had a cushy number to look forward to. Conference security. Standing around, making small talk, watching diplomats sip champagne while looking for non-existent bogey-men under the bed, or the conference table. But he pulled on a clean pair of jeans that he took from his bag, and went to the head of the stairs.

'Who is it Bonnie?'

There wasn't a sound. Not even a clatter of dishes in the kitchen. He stepped warily on the first step, automatically sticking to the side of the wall so he could throw himself down to minimise his target size.

It was then he saw Bonnie. She was cradling Rachel, the small body slumped like a broken doll against hers in the living room, the hippopotamus he had bought lying, splattered with their blood next to them on the carpet. Throwing caution to the wind he vaulted the banister. He didn't need to go any closer, or feel the pulses in their necks. Their eyes, cold, lifeless, staring blindly upwards told him what his mind refused to accept, but he still went to them, wanting- willing it – not to be true.

He heard a scream. A long drawn out bestial scream, then he realised it was his. A gun pointed at his face. The thumb of the hand that held it was scarred. He saw a vivid red mark shaped like a many legged centipede.

There were two shadows in the room. He had no weapons, but the survival instinct that had been drummed into him during long, arduous, training sessions when he had been driven almost past the point of endurance took over.

He sized up the situation within seconds. Ahead lay the centre panel of a bay window. He kicked the gun from the hand with the scar, curled himself into a ball, and threw himself through the glass.

Picking himself up from a stretch of damp lawn he broke into a run, and kept on running – and running – from the house – from the guns – from the broken bloodied bodies of Bonnie and Rachel.

But no matter how far or fast he ran – he could still see them. And he couldn't bear it – he simply couldn't bear it.

CHAPTER EIGHTEEN

Shrouded by unrelenting darkness Richard McKenna crouched low, heart pounding, hands shaking. A telephone began to ring insistently, its remorseless high pitched tones escalating the tension. His hand brushed against a body. He recognized the quick, panic-filled rhythm of Elizabeth's breath. He fumbled with his bound hands for the gun beneath her suit, taking it awkwardly between his palms.

'Sergeant!' He shouted with the intention of getting a fix on the man by drawing his fire.

A flash rent the darkness. Hot, scalding pain trickled down Richard's arm but he stood his ground and fired back.

'Get down man.'

Richard recognized Chaloner's voice, above the noise of the telephone. Light flooded the room. 'Hold your fire!' Chaloner commanded, bewildered by the sight of his sergeant's four man patrol lining their sights on John West, and Simmonds. The brigadier and Heddingham nodded in unison to Sergeant Price. The NCO turned, aimed his gun at Chaloner's head and fired. Chaloner threw himself over a steel desk and the bullet whistled harmlessly past his ear. He knelt and fired West's gun, felling two of the patrol in quick succession.

The diversion was all Richard needed. He pulled the trigger on the Browning, firing once and firing to kill, but when the sergeant slumped to the floor and the astringent smell of cordite filled the air, all he could see was Bonnie and Rachel. His pain was agonizing. As intense and insupportable as it had been when he had first seen their bodies. He depressed his trigger finger again – and again – and again – watching bullet after bullet pump into the sergeant's body, jerking it like a marionette in the hands of a clumsy puppeteer. And he didn't stop until the chamber clicked empty.

Paralyzed by fear Elizabeth remained hunched on the floor. She stared at John in disbelief as he proved himself the cold blooded killer everyone except her had believed him to be. He had killed a man without compunction or compassion. How could she have ever believed herself close to him?

Chaloner was shouting through the closed door, warning everyone outside it to stay back. The telephone finally stopped ringing. A hand touched Elizabeth's arm. She looked up. Major Simmonds was standing over her. He stooped down and helped her to her feet.

'Are you hurt, Dr Santer?'

She stared blankly at him.

'Sit down, you're in shock.' He lowered her on to a chair.

Someone was speaking in a calm, controlled voice. The only hint of sanity in a world gone mad. She turned and saw Chaloner explaining to whoever was at the other end of the line that his sergeant had activated a time lock on the door that would hold for another hour. While he talked he trained his gun on the solitary survivor of the sergeant's patrol. The man was standing, hands high, with his back to the wall.

Less than six feet away from her, the sergeant's body lay sprawled where he had fallen, his legs bent awkwardly beneath his torso, his arms flung wide. Next to him were the corpses of the two men Chaloner had shot. She would have preferred not to have looked at their broken bloodied bodies, but she couldn't help herself. She continued to sit and stare. She jerked her head back when Simmonds tried to force brandy between her lips.

'I'll shoot to kill, corporal,' Chaloner warned the last member of the patrol when he moved his hands down slightly. Chaloner carried on speaking into the receiver. Heddingham and the brigadier sat silently at the conference table, both of them eyeing Chaloner's gun.

It was then Elizabeth realised that John was standing at the foot of the table, his empty gun pointed at the brigadier and the lieutenant-colonel, blood streaming from a wound in his upper arm.

'You're hurt!' Momentarily forgetting her outrage, she left her chair and ran to him. 'John… '

'Not John.' His voice was detached, remote. 'McKenna. Richard McKenna.' He dropped the empty Browning and took a gun from the hand of a dead private.

Chaloner stopped talking and stared at him.

Simmonds examined John's arm. Misunderstanding Chaloner's questioning expression, he murmured. 'Whoever he is, this wound isn't serious, he'll live.'

‘Rank?’ Chaloner asked.

‘Colonel.’ John looked past Elizabeth. In that instant she knew that he had regained his memory – and in his remembering John West had been as irrevocably lost as though he had never existed. ‘I am – was – in charge of security at the disarmament conference.’

‘Then we’d better get you to the hospital and patch you up so you can be debriefed as soon as possible.’ Chaloner didn’t bother to disguise the scepticism in his voice.

‘You don’t understand, captain.’ Richard was peculiarly composed for a wounded man who’d just killed an NCO. ‘If all military personnel are accounted for and none are missing, someone has taken my place.’

‘There’ll be an investigation,’ Chaloner dropped the telephone back on to its cradle.

‘An investigation, sir!’ Richard admonished. ‘What kind of an officer are you? Your sergeant tried to kill you, me and Simmonds. In my book that puts us, temporarily at least, on the same side. We can trust one another,’ he looked at Simmonds, ‘but I don’t know about anyone outside that door.’

‘There are people… ’

‘You’re prepared to allow their henchmen in here?’ Richard waved the loaded gun he’d taken from the floor at Heddingham and the brigadier. ‘How long do you think we’d last once these two start shouting orders to idiots who’ll obey them because they outrank almost everyone else on this base?’

‘He’s right,’ Simmonds was clearly shaken by the sight of so many bodies.

Richard focused his attention on the two senior officers seated at the conference table. ‘The answer has to lie with them. I suggest we debrief them, captain.’

‘Now?’ Chaloner asked.

‘Given the urgency of the situation. I can’t think of a better time.’

‘You’re wounded – this room – the CO wants in.’

‘Hasn’t it occurred to you that if the disappearance of a senior officer in charge of an international conference’s security has been concealed, so could the disappearance of other senior personnel? And we still don’t know what this is all about.’

‘I’ve never heard of a Colonel Richard McKenna.’

‘But no doubt you’ve heard of a Captain Martin McKenna. You should have, he’s in this regiment.’

‘I’ve heard of him,’ Chaloner answered warily.

‘He’s my younger brother.’

It was then Chaloner realised why “John West” looked vaguely familiar. He had recognized some of the features but not the man.

‘Whether you trust me, or not is immaterial. We have no option but to work together after being used for target practice. But first we debrief these two. We need somewhere private.’ Richard looked around. ‘There is a bunker below this room.’

‘There is but the CO… ’

‘Ask him not to blast off the time lock and give us an hour. Tell him… ’ Richard hesitated. His head was filled with telephone numbers, and codes he could use to establish his credentials as a senior officer with top rated security clearance. But it had been his immediate boss who had arranged his posting as chief security advisor to the conference. Was he part of this conspiracy? Whatever it was?

If he gave the coding for priority clearance and emergency, would it be believed, or would it bring down the full strength of the army on this steel lined conference room? Not even the inner wall would stand up to a battering by the explosives and devices the SAS used, and he doubted that the area was as secure as it initially appeared. The army was a conservative and cautious institution. Someone would have considered the possibility of the building being infiltrated by terrorists and there'd be an attack plan devised, for just such an eventuality. What other alternative did he have but to use the code? Staring Chaloner straight in the eye, he rattled it off, adding, 'and tell them to change it.'

Chaloner passed the message down the line. There followed a tense five minutes during which Elizabeth allowed Major Simmonds to lead her back to her chair.

'Sir… yes, sir.' Chaloner looked at Richard. 'And confine all the patrols that were on the Beacons searching for John West to close quarters as they come in until they have been debriefed.' Chaloner held out the telephone to Simmonds. 'They want an assurance from you that we're not being held captive. You too,' he said to Elizabeth. 'I don't know what that code means, or whether to call you McKenna or West, but we have until the time lock expires, one hour.'

Chaloner walked over to what looked like a plain wall panel. He pressed a button next to the light switch and a door swung open.

McKenna held out his hands to Chaloner who cut through the ropes that bound his wrists.

'Brigadier, Lieutenant-Colonel,' McKenna held the door open. 'After you.'

'You're risking a court-martial, Chaloner,' Heddingham threatened when McKenna moved towards him.

Chaloner looked at Simmonds. 'You handle a gun?'

'I'm a soldier,' Simmonds replied.

'Take over here. Shoot to kill if that man makes a move.' Chaloner indicated the surviving member of the sergeant's patrol before throwing Simmonds the dead sergeant's gun. He followed McKenna and the two officers through the door and closed it behind him.

A short flight of concrete steps led down to a large square room with cream washed concrete walls and a floor covered by a coating of rubberised black vinyl. A dozen bunks, erected in tiers of three, lined one wall, a steel table and half a dozen chairs stood in the centre, and a bank of computers and telecommunication equipment was ranged on a series of black metal shelves on the wall opposite the bunks.

Richard sat on one of the chairs. He lifted his injured right arm on to the table with his left but didn't relinquish his hold on the gun. Chaloner moved two chairs between the bunks and the table, motioning the lieutenant-colonel and the brigadier to sit on them.

'Are you going to tell us what this is all about, or do we have to beat it out of you?' McKenna asked softly.

Heddingham sat tight-lipped, but sweat was pouring down the brigadier's cheeks despite the chill atmosphere.

'Strip!' McKenna ordered tersely.

'I object!' The lieutenant-colonel countermanded. 'I'll have you… '

'You have to be alive to give an order. Strip!' McKenna reiterated.

A blow from Chaloner's rifle butt to the small of Heddingham's back stilled further protest, and once he was stripped and lashed, legs and arms to each leg of the chair with the rope Chaloner had taken from one of the shelves, the brigadier meekly submitted himself to the same humiliating treatment.

'This bunker is soundproof?' McKenna checked.

Chaloner nodded.'

'How much time do we have left of that hour?'

Chaloner glanced at his watch. 'Forty-five minutes.'

'Forty minutes should be enough. Bring one of those camcorders over here. Point it at our captives and switch it on. I have a feeling they are going to tell us some very interesting things.'

Chaloner reflected that for someone who'd only just remembered his name and rank, McKenna was presuming a great deal of authority, but he carried out his orders.

'You're absolutely certain this room is soundproof?' McKenna repeated.

'Absolutely,' Chaloner concurred.

McKenna leaned forward and pushed the barrel of his gun into the brigadier's exposed testicles. 'You know who I am?'

'Colonel Richard McKenna,' the brigadier stumbled over the words in his haste to get them out.

'This isn't debriefing, this is torture. It violates all human rights!' Heddingham blustered.

McKenna rose and walked round to the back of Heddingham's chair. Kicking the legs he brought it crashing down on its back. Heddingham lay with his legs tied high to the front bar of the chair. McKenna stood above him. Taking the machine gun from Chaloner, he hammered it, butt side down into Heddingham's stomach. The lieutenant-colonel screamed long and loud. The brigadier sobbed and cried alongside him.

'Who has taken my place as chief security advisor to the conference?' McKenna pitched his voice below Heddingham's screams.

'Donovan O'Gallivan,' the brigadier gibbered fearfully. 'He's been briefed to sabotage the conference,' he revealed when McKenna returned the barrel of the gun to his testicles.

'Who's paying him?'

'We are.'

'Who are "we"?'

'Army officers and MOD contractors… ' he screamed louder than Heddingham when Richard slowly eased back the trigger on the gun he was holding.

‘How many delegates has O’Gallivan been briefed to assassinate?’

‘All of them.’

‘For what purpose?’

‘You fools, don’t you see what’s happening?’ Heddingham shouted, the mixture of pain and humiliation making him reckless. He launched into a well-rehearsed speech he had obviously delivered several times before.

‘This conference will put even more nails into the coffin of the armed forces. More regiments will be merged, traditions lost, manpower cut to a level where we’ll be hard pressed to find guards for Buckingham Palace. Over the last few years this country’s finest institution has been being disbanded and reduced to a joke by idiot politicians who can’t wait to pour our military assets into a trough they can dip their snouts into. They’re fooling themselves and the world. They tell civilians that terrorism is the only threat to our security. That future wars will be fought differently, and large armies are old-fashioned and surplus to requirements. They’re putting tens of thousands of our finest officers out to pasture to cut costs. Ever since the Communist threat crumbled and terrorism emerged they’ve fooled civilians into thinking that all that’s needed is a couple of Special Forces regiments, to fight the terrorists on their terms. So, not only do we allow the enemy to set the rules, we kow-tow and play by them.’

His contempt was blatant and Chaloner recalled Heddingham’s attitude to the SAS when he’d been called in after West had escaped from hospital.

'It's 1934 all over again. Appeasement – peace at any cost and hang the professionals. Let them join the ranks of the unemployed and in the meantime we open our doors to the extremists, the fundamentalists, the nuts, any terrorist group who only need half a dozen nuclear or neutron bombs picked up at bargain basement prices from the old Soviet block to rule the world. They don't give a damn for national security or for the millions in the armament industry who'll be out of a job and… '

McKenna had listened long enough. 'Who's involved, Heddingham?' he cut in.

Heddingham fell silent.

McKenna crashed his gun butt down on to the side of the lieutenant-colonel's face.

'You can't do this!' Heddingham screamed

McKenna turned and pointed his gun between the brigadier's legs again. He didn't have to do any more. Names poured from the man's lips. Chaloner checked the camcorder to make sure the tape was still running. It was.

'Masters?' McKenna demanded, when the brigadier finished.

'There are no more that I know of,' the brigadier muttered wretchedly. 'Please… move that gun… '

'Heddingham, can you name any more?' McKenna looked down at the man, no longer belligerent, but cowed, battered and bloodied. 'Masters?' he repeated.

Heddingham shook his head.

'Who's in control?'

‘The minister,’ the brigadier supplied, unable to stand another scream from Heddingham.

‘Who is Masters?’ Chaloner asked McKenna.

‘My controller. He posted me as security advisor to the conference.’

‘The minister said he couldn’t be trusted.’ Now the brigadier had started talking, he couldn’t stop. ‘But he ordered Masters to recall you to control security at the conference. He used the excuse that no one knew the Arabic world like you. Masters believed him.’ He looked nervously at McKenna, beads of perspiration dripping from his nose. ‘Well Masters would, wouldn’t he? You’ve worked undercover in the Middle East for the past two years. And you had other attributes.’

‘Other attributes?’ Richard echoed.

‘Your physical description matched O’Gallivan’s.’

‘We’re alike?’

‘Not face to face, but that didn’t matter. Hardly anyone’s seen you in years. Before you were sent to the Middle East you were stationed in the States. We arranged for your brother to be posted abroad for the duration of the conference, you had no other family to report you missing.’

‘Only my wife and daughter,’ McKenna couldn’t keep the bitterness from his voice. ‘How did it feel to kill an unarmed woman and an eight-week-old baby, Brigadier?’

‘Heddingham gave the order,’ the brigadier gibbered. ‘It wasn’t me. I didn’t want to kill them… ’

‘You sent amateurs,’ McKenna said coldly. ‘They botched it. They managed to kill the unarmed civilians but couldn't manage me.' McKenna stepped slowly, almost leisurely towards Heddingham. 'Where are my wife, and daughter's bodies?'

'Buried… with respect,' Heddingham added, staring at the gun in McKenna's hand.

'Where?'

'The walled garden of the house.'

McKenna walked blindly forward keeping his face turned to the wall so no one could see the emotion in his eyes.

Chaloner was first and foremost a professional soldier, but he even he found it difficult to maintain his composure in the face of Heddingham's confession.

'Have you anything to add?' Chaloner asked the brigadier

'Only that the plane crash in Scotland was part of it,' the brigadier confessed. 'There was a man on board the minister had approached. He wouldn't join us. He said he wouldn't give us away, he didn't know much but the minister was worried… '

'How many people have you murdered' Chaloner demanded.

Both men remained silent.

'My God I could chop the balls off both of you myself.' Chaloner took a long bladed hunting knife from a sheath attached to his belt.

'We're entitled… '

'You're entitled to absolutely nothing, Heddingham,' Chaloner corrected harshly.

'You have to formally arrest us.'

'We don't have to do anything,' McKenna's voice cut through the still cold air.

'The CO on this post… '

'Major Simmonds and Dr Santer saw the sergeant try to kill us, on your orders. Both of you could have been carrying concealed weapons. Captain Chaloner and I have every right to defend ourselves.'

'Are you sure you have nothing else to tell us?' Chaloner was concerned about McKenna who was far too calm and rational for a man who'd just recalled his wife and child's murder.

'I swear I know nothing else,' the brigadier pleaded.

'Heddingham?'

'Nothing,' he echoed sullenly.

'How many conspirators are stationed here?' McKenna asked.

Chaloner counted a series of strokes he'd made with his pen on his wrist. 'Fifteen, if the brigadier's right.'

'The CO?'

'Not on the list.'

Knife in hand Chaloner leaned forward. He cut through the bonds on the brigadier's and Heddingham's chairs, and threw them their clothes. He sat on the edge of the table, gun in hand and waited while they dressed. They had five minutes, just as McKenna had prophesied.

McKenna sat coldly eyeing the two men, who stood nervously in front of their chairs as soon as they were dressed. When Chaloner motioned them to the steps at gunpoint McKenna moved like lighting.

Dropping his gun he pounced on Heddingham, slamming his head one handed against the edge of the concrete step.

'That's for my wife, and my daughter. If ever you get out of wherever they send you, start looking over your shoulder. One day you'll walk around a corner and I'll be waiting. And you won't die quickly, I promise you.'

Chaloner hauled him off the lieutenant-colonel. The brigadier had opened the door and Simmonds was standing at the head of the steps.

'Lieutenant-Colonel Heddingham fell over, Colonel McKenna was helping him up,' Chaloner explained. 'Stay in here and keep your gun trained on these men until you are relieved, Major. I'll organise it as soon as I've seen the CO.'

CHAPTER NINETEEN

Chaloner clung to the side of the helicopter and gazed down at the country house that had been chosen to host the International Peace Conference. It appeared quiet and peaceful in the frosted dawn light. He wondered how many of the security and domestic staff still slept. After his fraught few days and nights, he'd had to fight hard for his place on the team his CO had sent out to detain the men Brigadier Cullen-Heames had listed as conspirators.

Seven NCO's and junior officers out of the hundred strong security force had been named as targets, as well as the false "McKenna", who, according to Cullen-Heames, had already planted a bomb in the oak panelling that lined the conference room.

If the brigadier's information was correct, it was timed to explode at three o'clock in the afternoon. Four hours after the delegates were due to arrive, one hour after the conference had convened after lunch and fifteen minutes after the minister had been called away by "McKenna" to take an important telephone call.

And, courtesy of intelligence received before leaving base, they knew that the false "McKenna" was already up, dressed and working in the office assigned to him, next to the conference room.

The CO had given in to the pressure he had exerted on him and assigned him and his partner to apprehend O'Gallivan – if indeed that was his target's real name.

He had asked for the privilege as much for the real McKenna's sake as his own.

The statement the brigadier had signed detailing the events in the house Richard McKenna's wife had rented, had sickened every member of the regiment. Army personnel knew what to expect if their application to join the elite corps was successful. The training was demanding, tough and uncompromising. No quarter was given to those too weak – mentally or physically – to stand the gruelling pace.

But their families were sacrosanct. And every time he thought – and imagined – McKenna's eight-week-old daughter being shot to death, he pictured his own son. Lewis was two years old but he could still remember how small and helpless he'd been at two months…

The helicopter lost height. Chaloner's radio crackled as silence was broken. The signal was given. He jumped alongside his men before the helicopter landed. They hit the ground running, a closed circle of armed officers from dozens of helicopters. Guns hoisted at the ready they moved in on the house, every inch of the building in their sights.

Two more helicopters hovered above the roof; dark figures abseiled down from them. The first men to reach the building moved to the doors and windows. They raised weapons designed to shatter bullet proof glass and steel doors and blasted in smoke bombs.

Chaloner adjusted his respirator. The moment –

'Foyer clear,'

- echoed from his radio, he and his partner ran inside. Referring to the ground floor plan he had memorized, he headed directly for McKenna's office – into the main entrance – turn right – run twenty five yards – turn left – second door on the right –

He stood to the side of it and nodded to his partner. They knew that a smoke bomb had already gone through the window but they blasted the door and tossed in another.

One minute later they burst in. The empty room yawned back at them as the smoke cleared. Chaloner ran to the shattered window. One of his fellow officers was lying outside on the grass. He had been stripped of his uniform, but his weapon was still in his hand. His throat had been cut from ear to ear.

Six hours later, still dressed in his combat suit, Chaloner sat in his CO's office facing his superior and a bland-faced individual who had been introduced simply as "Mr Masters."

'Your men let him get away,' Masters said unemotionally, directing the statement at Chaloner as well as his CO.

'We're looking for him.' The CO glared at Chaloner.

'Given O'Gallivan's resourcefulness and chameleon qualities, he will be long out of the country by now.' Masters took a cigar from a pack in his pocket and lit it.

'All the other conspirators have been rounded up,' the CO pointed out defensively.

‘It’s just as well we prepared more than one venue for the conference given the mess your men made this morning. I trust the new man in charge of security is up to the job,’ Masters drew on his cigar.

‘He is,’ the CO confirmed briefly.

‘Ingenious plot,’ Masters mused. ‘We must never forget that McKenna was perfect for their purpose. Deceased parents, married to an American wife. Not stationed in this country for ten years, leave breaks taken in the States, worked as an independent undercover operative in the Middle East for the past two years, and his only living relative – apart from his wife and daughter, his brother, who was easily disposed of on a training mission.’

‘It’s strange that McKenna remembered the flat he and his brother had inherited, when he couldn’t even remember his own name.’ The colonel shuffled the papers on his desk.

‘Did Lieutenant-Colonel Heddingham have definite information that McKenna was holed up in that flat, sir?’ Chaloner asked.

‘Cullen-Heames said Heddingham made a lucky guess,’ Masters answered.

‘But thanks to your efforts, Chaloner, the conference will go ahead as planned without interruption.’

Chaloner knew the statement was as close as he was going to get to a “well done” from his CO.

‘But the situation remains unresolved,’ Masters qualified. ‘And it will continue to remain unresolved until we have O’Gallivan in custody. What we need now is your assurance, Captain Chaloner, that what has been said within these walls will go no further.'

'I've signed the Official Secrets Act,' Chaloner concurred.

'Look at these press releases. If you have any questions, now is the time to ask them.' His CO pushed two sheets of paper across the table. The headlines loomed black and large.

JOHN WEST – MY STORY BY THE MAN WHO SHOT HIM.

and further down the page.

MINISTER RESIGNS. ADMITTED TO REST HOME. RUMOURS OF DRUG AND DRINK-INDUCED MENTAL BREAKDOWN.

'Other resignations will be announced over the next few days,' Masters flicked his ash into the tray on the desk. 'There will be vacancies in the upper echelons, some of which will undoubtedly suit a man of your capabilities, captain.'

'What steps are being taken to ensure that nothing like this ever happens again, sir?'

'It's in hand, captain.' Masters firmly closed the subject.

'Any questions, Chaloner?' His CO reiterated.

'No, sir.'

'Twenty four hour rest period.'

'Thank you, sir.' Chaloner left the table. He thought of McKenna as he walked out of the door. 'Poor bugger,' he muttered to himself as he headed to his quarters. 'The poor, poor bugger.'

*   *   *

Elizabeth sat alone in the suite she'd been given when she'd been escorted from the conference room in Stirling Lines thirty-six hours before. There was a large double bedroom, a luxurious en suite bathroom and a comfortable, if unimaginative, sitting room. She'd been given everything she'd asked for and some things that she hadn't. Clothes, make-up, a television connected to a DVD with a selection of pre-recorded discs, even a hairdresser and a telephone to contact her family. The calls had been monitored and she'd been warned to restrict the conversation to personal matters or risk disconnection. The warning had been unnecessary, the conversation with her mother had been emotional, and personal enough, even for the senior officer who'd remained in the room, but she'd taken the telephone with her when she'd left, telling her that if she needed it again, she had only to ask the guard outside the door.

The things the army hadn't seen fit to give her, were what she wanted most; newspapers, access to news bulletins, and answers to her questions. But she wouldn't have minded the absence of news so much if she'd been allowed to see John.

As it was, she didn't know whether he was alive or dead and the silence that was generated whenever she mentioned his name, only served to confirm her worst suspicions.

She continued to sit and stare out of the window, watching the compound fill with men and vehicles. She was interrupted by a knock on the door. Expecting lunch she called out,

'Come in.'

An officer entered.

'Dr Santer, I'm Captain Wentworth.'

'How is "John West"?' She expected him to ignore her question as all the others she had asked had done.

'Colonel McKenna is physically well and in good hands. Captain Simmonds, whom I believe you're acquainted with, is caring for him.'

'Can I see him?' she pressed.

'That wouldn't be advisable.'

'I have to see him, he saved my life. I owe him that much.'

'Owe him?' he enquired quizzically.

'He believed that once he was in custody he would be killed.'

'I assure you, Colonel McKenna is not in custody.'

'He was wanted for murder… '

'The only person he killed was Sergeant Price, but, as Captain Chaloner and Major Simmonds testified, the sergeant was trying to kill them as well as Colonel McKenna and you, it was self-defence. Colonel McKenna will not be charged with any crime.'

'If he's not in custody why can't I see him?' she persisted.

'He's traumatised… '

'It was me who diagnosed trauma-induced amnesia.'

'Did you know that he witnessed the murder of his wife and his eight-week-old daughter?'

She knew he was evaluating her reaction. 'No.' She bit her lip and turned away.

'I can't tell you what all this has been about. But I promise you Colonel McKenna is a valued and valuable member of the armed forces.' He changed the subject and lightened the tone of his voice. 'We can offer you counselling, but we won't be able to release you until you sign the Official Secrets Act. After you've been fully debriefed – a painless procedure,' he added, concerned lest she'd witnessed the "debriefing" Lieutenant-Colonel Heddingham and the brigadier had been subjected to at McKenna's and Chaloner's hands.

'And Richard McKenna?'

'Will be rehabilitated.'

'How can he be after the manhunt and nationwide search?'

'It's been announced that John West was killed while resisting capture.' He took a newspaper clipping from his pocket and handed it to her. 'People soon forget. Any resemblance between Colonel McKenna and John West will be assumed to be coincidental.'

'How do I know that this,' she looked down at the newspaper headline, 'isn't true, and the man I knew is dead?'

'You have my word.'

'Not good enough. I won't sign any act until I see him for myself.' She hoped that he didn't know she'd already signed the act in the hospital at Major Simmonds' insistence.

'The army is not in the habit of murdering its own colonels.'

'I won't be convinced until I see for myself.'

'Very well, you can see Colonel McKenna,' Wentworth capitulated irritably. 'From a viewing room.'

'I want to talk to him?'

'Absolutely not. Apart from the question of national security there's his condition to consider. Seeing you, could set back what little progress he's made.'

'I **was** his psychiatrist.'

'I'm exceeding my authority in allowing you to see him. I can offer you no more.'

She swallowed her pride. 'Thank you.'

'You'll have to come with me now. He's about to be moved.'

'Where?'

'That's classified.'

He led the way out of the room. The guard jumped to attention outside her door. They walked along a corridor, and turned a corner. Wentworth unlocked a door flanked by yet more guards and ushered her into an office. He pressed a button set below a dark glass panel in the wall. The glass cleared.

'It's one way,' Wentworth informed her.

She stepped forward. "John" was sitting up in a bed, paler than she had last seen him, a drip in his arm. Simmonds was sitting beside the bed.

'He's hurt?'

'He was shot.'

'Major Simmonds said it was minor.'

'The wound was more severe than he appreciated at the time.'

'What will happen to John now?'

'No effort will be spared to rehabilitate him. I can only offer my apologies that you were dragged into this affair. You will receive compensation for the distress you've suffered. Now, if you'll come this way, Dr Santer, we can debrief you.'

She took one last look at John, and followed Captain Wentworth out of the office. There wasn't anything else she could do.

EPILOGUE

'And then there's Mr Hyde… '

'Is he the last one?' Elizabeth interrupted wearily.

'He is,' her registrar answered sympathetically. Dr Santer was the most efficient and considerate consultant she'd worked for, and she looked completely drained.

'Thank goodness. I'm whacked. Up all last night.'

'Poor you,' the registrar commiserated.

'I actually enjoyed it.' Elizabeth flicked through the patient's notes. 'Clinical depression… not responding… switch his medication to these and keep a careful eye to see how he goes.' She scribbled a new prescription. 'I'll examine him on Monday.'

'Hope you get a night's sleep before then.'

'Thank you. You on this weekend?'

'Philip is, first time.'

'See he gets my sympathy along with my home number.' Elizabeth picked up a bundle of files from her desk and dropped them into her briefcase. She looked out of the window. Perhaps it was the foul weather that reminded her of the events of fifteen months ago. But hardly a day went by without her remembering "John West" and the few frantic days they'd shared. She frequently wondered where he was, and if the army had succeeded in "rehabilitating" him as Captain Wentworth had phrased it. It would have been so easy to kill him after she'd left Stirling Lines. No one would be any the wiser. It was a terrifying thought.

It was hardly surprising she often thought of John when there were so many reminders. And not only in the hospital. On the weekly visits she made to Dave's wife who was still broken-hearted and consumed by grief. In seeing the twins growing up without a father.

She by-passed the lift and took the stairs, recalling how "John" had dragged her down them with a gun pressed to her head. Sometimes she wondered if it had really happened or if it had all been a crazy nightmare. Perhaps it seemed unreal because the statement she had signed prohibited her from talking about it, to anyone. She wished it had prevented the press from hounding her. One of the tabloids had offered her enough money to retire in style, not that she would have taken them up on the offer even if she'd been in a position to take it.

She raised her umbrella as she left the building. Hailstones pounded down, bouncing off the nylon cover and the tarmac, stinging her legs. Her car, a small – very small, new run-about was parked in one of the vast bays reserved for senior consultants. If it hadn't been for Dave's death she might have been pleased with her promotion. The hospital authorities had never replaced him. When she'd returned to work a week after being released from Stirling Lines, she'd assumed the responsibility for both jobs until they had appointed a new registrar and officially given her Dave's post and title. But she couldn't help feeling that she had achieved her promotion not by merit, but by stepping into a dead man's shoes.

Unlocking the car, she flung her briefcase into the back, closed her umbrella and took off her coat, because she couldn't stand driving with it on.

'Isn't it somewhat cold and wet to be undressing in the open?'

She whirled around. 'John.'

'Richard.'

'I know. Richard McKenna.'

'You'd better get in the car before you get soaked.'

'And you?'

'I'm fine here. Unlike you, my umbrella is still up.'

She sat in the driver's seat. Closing the door she wound down the window. 'You really are all right?'

'As you see.'

'They told me you would be, but… '

'Wentworth said he had trouble convincing you that I wasn't going to be shot at dawn.'

'Peculiar lot you work for.'

He smiled briefly, but his eyes remained cold.

'He told me that your wife and daughter had been murdered. I'm so dreadfully sorry.'

'Thank you.' Hailstones rattled over the roof of her car accentuating the silence. 'But,' he grimaced, 'contrary to the nursery rhyme, the king's or rather the queen's men managed to put this Humpty Dumpty together again.'

'Did they – really?' she asked earnestly.

'There are some cracks but they don't show – most of the time,' he qualified.

'Do they know you've come to see me?'

'Even soldiers are allowed private lives.'

'You're still a soldier?'

'I wouldn't know how to do anything else.' He looked down at her. 'I've managed to relegate most of what happened, to the past. You're the exception. I wanted to thank you for believing in me when no-one else did.'

'Anyone in my position would have done the same.'

'I doubt anyone else would have lasted the pace.' He turned his collar up making it difficult for her to see his face in the gloom. 'I thought that perhaps we could have dinner somewhere and say goodbye properly.'

'I could cook you dinner at my place.'

'I'd rather take you out.'

'I'd still have to go home and change. Would you mind giving me a lift?'

'You have your car,' he reminded warily.

'It's only a short drive. I'll get a taxi and pick it up later.' She didn't want to lose him all over again. Without giving him time to reply she lifted her coat and briefcase from the back and locked the door. He opened the passenger door of his Mercedes.

'There is one thing I want to make clear.' He turned the ignition. 'This is only thank you and goodbye.'

'You're going somewhere?'

'A short leave.'

'And afterwards?' she pressed.

'An assignment.'

'Filling your days with work.'

'Like you after your husband died.'

‘I don’t think anyone ever really recovers from losing someone they love. Not entirely.’

‘Love isn’t enough, is it? I love – loved Bonnie and Rachel as much as it is possible for me to love anyone. But I couldn’t keep them safe.’

‘You can’t blame yourself for their murder.’

‘They would be alive if I baked bread for a living.’

‘That doesn’t make their deaths your fault.’

‘You sound like a shrink.’

‘I am one, remember. Turn left at the gates,’ she directed as they left the hospital grounds. ‘Tell me about Bonnie… ’ she glanced at him in the darkness. ‘I’m sorry; I keep wanting to call you, John. Richard will take some getting used to.’

He recalled the things she had told him about her life with Joseph. ‘I don’t know where to begin.’

‘Where did you meet?’

‘America, she was American we both worked for NASA.’

‘Love at first sight?’

‘For me. I was never too sure about her.’

‘You’ve seen Bonnie’s family since?’

‘We buried her and Rachel on her father’s farm in Virginia. I spent some time with her parents and sister. They took it hard.’

‘But not as hard as you.’ She pushed her hands deep into her pockets. She longed to reach out and comfort him, but she sensed that he didn’t want her sympathy. Not yet. And perhaps not ever.

‘I remember you telling me how difficult it was for you to face your husband’s family after his death. How they blamed you for his accident, simply because he'd changed forces and followed you across the country when you were appointed registrar.'

'And Bonnie's family blame you, because you were the reason she was in England?'

'They didn't say so, not in so many words, but I think they do.'

'You can't go through life carrying so much guilt, Richard. It's destructive, take it from someone who's tried, and knows what she's talking about. And that's not the shrink but the widow talking.'

'It's not the same for you, as it is for me. Bonnie and Rachel were murdered because of the job I do. I still do it. Nothing's changed. If I allow anyone to get close to me again, they could be killed for the same reason. Which is why I'd rather be alone.'

'I'm still not sure what all that business in Brecon was about.'

'Better you don't find out.'

'And your Arabic?'

'As you've signed the Official Secrets Act I can tell you that I've spent a great deal of time working in the Middle East.'

'Next right. It's the house at the end; you'll see it when you turn into the drive.'

'Very nice,' he complimented. He drew up outside a Victorian rectory set back from the road in a large garden.

'Joseph thought so. He fell in love with the place, although it didn't look anything like this when he first saw it. But he recognized its potential and wanted to renovate it. After he died I moved in and used his insurance money to do what he would have done if he'd lived.'

'Bonnie and I used to dream of a place like this, but all we ever lived in was other people's houses.'

'You have the flat in Brecon. It is yours?' she asked.

'Mine and my brother's.' He gave her a small smile. 'His name is Martin. Bonnie only went there once.'

'You mentioned you're on leave. Is that where you're going?'

'I thought I'd do some hill walking.'

'When you introduced me to the sport I didn't think much of it.'

'It can be fun when you're not being hunted,' he protested. 'Believe me there's nothing like going back to the flat after a day spent walking on the hills. It's marvellous to soak in a hot bath, eat a good meal, down a few drinks… '

'I like the sound of the after activities.'

'We never got round to too many of those, did we.'

'Except in the house in Libanus.'

'Compensation was paid for the food and the use of the guest house.'

'I'm glad to hear it.' Elizabeth opened the car door and dashed through the rain into the porch. The door was opened by a plump, middle-aged smiling woman.

'Sorry I'm late, Betty,' Elizabeth apologized.

'That's all right, Dr Santer, I'm not doing anything tonight – or most nights come to that.'

'Everything all right?'

‘Perfect. The little darling’s been no trouble today, not like yesterday. I’ve made a nice chicken casserole for your tea, you never take the time to eat properly, you’re way too thin – Ooh sorry, I didn’t know you had company.’ She looked Richard up and down when he joined them in the hall and gave Elizabeth a sly wink.

‘Betty, this is Richard McKenna,’ Elizabeth introduced them. ‘Betty’s my housekeeper,’ she explained.

‘I was going to say the casserole would stretch to two nights, but seeing as you have company, enjoy it while it’s fresh.’

‘Thanks, Betty, I don’t know what I’d do without you.’

‘Starve and live in squalor,’ Betty replied cheerfully. ‘Have a good evening.’ She picked up her hat and coat from the stand and left.

‘Who’s the “little darling who’s been no trouble”?’ Richard asked. ‘You told me you didn’t have any children.’

Elizabeth opened the door and went into a cosy, brightly furnished living room, resplendent with Turkish tapestries and carpets. There was a playpen in the middle of the floor. ‘Richard McKenna meet John Santer.’ She didn’t dare look at Richard’s face. ‘I would say I’m sorry, but I’m not,’ she continued defiantly, taking the wooden bricks the child was playing with and setting them down before picking him up.

The baby gurgled, smiled and clasped his hands over her face. She was glad, it gave her further excuse not to look at Richard. 'I wasn't prepared for what happened in that guesthouse. I didn't even realise I was pregnant until two months afterwards and when I did, I considered abortion and rejected the idea. It was nothing to do with you,' she added hastily. 'More to do with losing Joseph, and not only Joseph but the children we'd intended to have when the time was right. So, to cut a long story short, I decided to keep John. I hope you don't mind the idea of him being here.' She hugged the baby. 'It's not as though either of us want anything from you. I'm managing very well financially, and in every other way. Betty is marvellous… we really are fine… '

Unable to bear the silence a moment longer she forced herself to look at him.

His eyes were damp and there was a strange expression on his face that she couldn't decipher. He turned away from her and walked to the door.

She clung to the baby and whispered. 'I'm sorry.'

Instead of opening the door as she'd expected him to, he whirled around. They looked at one another for what seemed like an eternity before he opened his arms – to both of them.

THE END

Katherine John

Katherine John is the daughter of a Prussian refugee and a Welsh father. Born in Pontypridd, she studied English and Sociology at Swansea College, then lived in America and Europe before returning to Wales and a variety of jobs, while indulging her love of writing.

She lives with her family on the Gower Peninsula, near Swansea.

Also By Katherine John

WITHOUT TRACE

In the chilly half-light of dawn a bizarre Pierrot figure waits in the shadows of a deserted stretch of motorway. The costumed hitchhiker's victim is a passing motorist. The murder, cold-blooded, brutal. Without motive.

Doctors at the local hospital Tim and Daisy Sherringham are blissfully happy. The perfect couple. When an emergency call rouses Tim early one morning, he vanishes on the way from their flat to the hospital.

And Daisy is plunged into a nightmare of terror and doubt . . .

ISBN 1905170262
Price £6.99

MIDNIGHT MURDERS

Compton Castle is a Victorian psychiatric hospital long overdue for demolition. Its warrens of rooms and acres of grounds, originally designed as a sanctuary for the mentally ill, now provide the ideal stalking ground for a serial killer.

Physically and mentally battered after his last case, Sergeant Trevor Joseph is a temporary inmate – but the hospital loses all therapeutic benefit when a corpse is dug out of a flowerbed. Then more bodies are found; young, female and both linked to the hospital.

Everyone within the mouldering walls is in danger while a highly unpredictable malevolence remains at large. And, as patients and staff are interrogated by the police, the apparently motiveless killer watches and waits for the opportunity to strike again . . .

ISBN 1905170270
Price £6.99

MURDER OF A DEAD MAN

Jubilee Street – the haunt of addicts and vagrants is a part of town to avoid at all costs, especially when it becomes the stalking ground of a brutal and ruthless murderer.

A drunken down and out is the first casualty, mutilated and burned alive but his grisly death raises even more problems for the investigating officers, Sergeants Trevor Joseph and Peter Collins. They discover that their victim died two years earlier. So who is the dead man? And what was the motive for the bizarre crime?

While they seek a killer in the dark urban underworld, the tally of corpses grows and the only certainty is that they can trust no man's face as his own.

ISBN 1905170289
Price £6.99